More Praise For Ava

The Chocolate Garden
"On par with Nicholas Sparks' love stories."
—Jennifer's Corner Blog

"A must-read...a bit of fairy magic...a shelf full of happiness." —Fab Fantasy Fiction

The Promise of Rainbows
"This is a story about grace, faith and the power of both..."
—The Book Nympho

French Roast
"Ms. Miles draws from her experience as an apprentice chef...and it shows...I loved {the} authenticity of the food references, and the recipes...looked divine." —BlogCritics

The Holiday Serenade
"This story is all romance, steam, and humor with a touch of the holiday spirit..." —The Book Nympho

The Town Square
"Ms. Miles' words melted into each page until the world receded around me..." —Tome Tender

The Park of Sunset Dreams
"Ava has done it again. I love the whole community of Dare Valley..." —Travel Through The Pages Blog

ALSO BY AVA MILES

Fiction

The Merriams Series

Wild Irish Rose

Love Among Lavender

Valley of Stars

Sunflower Alley

A Forever of Orange Blossoms

The Love Letter Series

Letters Across An Open Sea

Along Waters of Sunshine and Shadow

The Dare Valley Series

Nora Roberts Land

French Roast

The Grand Opening

The Holiday Serenade

The Town Square

The Park of Sunset Dreams

The Perfect Ingredient

The Bridge to a Better Life

The Calendar of New Beginnings

Home Sweet Love

The Moonlight Serenade

The Sky of Endless Blue

Daring Brides

The Dare River Series

Country Heaven

Country Heaven Cookbook

The Chocolate Garden

The Chocolate Garden:
A Magical Tale (Children's Book)

Fireflies and Magnolias

The Promise of Rainbows

The Fountain of Infinite Wishes

The Patchwork Quilt of Happiness

Dare Valley Meets Paris Billionaire Mini-Series

The Billionaire's Gamble

The Billionaire's Courtship

The Billionaire's Secret

The Billionaire's Return

Non-Fiction

The Happiness Corner: Reflections So Far

Home Baked Happiness

Country Heaven Cookbook

Reclaim Your Superpowers

A Breath of Jasmine

THE MERRIAMS

AVA MILES

ISBN-13: 978-1-949092-17-2
www.avamiles.com
Ava Miles

For everyone on the planet,
and for more moments of connection,
love, and hope.

Second chance love is sweet.
I know.
I am now married to a
woman I loved fifty some years ago.

Quinn Merriam, my nephew, was
parted from the love of his life fifteen years ago.
Frankly, while he might worry it's
too late for take two, I don't.
True love always wins.

But dark forces are gathering.
The company Quinn now runs is in trouble.
My dear wife Clara and I are prepared to
help her family's business at all costs.

However, there is a more dire threat on the
horizon, one that might endanger the whole
world—or so Hargreaves says.

As a Pulitzer Prize-winning journalist, I've seen
my fair share of events that reshape the world.
I hope Hargreaves is wrong.

Whatever comes, this family will stick together.
And somehow, we will join the last
Merriam standing with his soulmate.

Because what the hell else is this good life for if we don't live it with those we love?

Diary Entry of Arthur Hale

Chapter 1

Quinn Merriam hated groveling.

As the chief executive officer of Merriam Enterprises, the very notion made his stomach seize up like he'd eaten bad clams. He didn't grovel to anyone. Never had. Never would.

But Francesca Maroun was the kind of woman a man sank down on one knee in front of. He should know—he'd done it before, although last time he'd asked her to marry him. This time he was hoping to enlist her help for his family company.

He straightened his tie, an Italian blue silk one she'd favor, as he walked up the drive to the historic Frank House she'd rented on Cavallo Point Lodge's property outside of San Francisco proper.

Back then, unprecedented world events had split them up, and her perceived duty to her family had kept them apart. Those circumstances had been one in a million, though, and there was no way he was letting her refuse him today. He needed her genius Fortune 500 consulting skills to help turn Merriam Enterprises around.

He hoped like hell he could keep his mind strictly on business during this first meeting. The python-like constriction around his rib cage suggested otherwise.

Back then, Francesca's body had driven him to a depth of desire he hadn't thought possible. But her brain had been equally arousing. They'd come together at a party in London, both pursuing master's degrees, and ignited like a bonfire.

Their relationship had been short, in the scheme of things, but he'd never loved like that again.

He hoped she would remember it.

Because *he* had never forgotten.

His heart still hurt. He hoped to hell hers did too, because he had a second objective: winning her back. It was a lofty goal for a man who'd waited fifteen years, but his brother Connor had inspired him to try. Connor thought it meant something that he still yearned for Francesca after so many years apart, and Quinn was starting to think he was right. The Merriams had always known their soulmates, and he was no different.

Knocking on the door, he fortified himself. The bottle of Dom Perignon champagne casually tucked against his side had been meticulously chosen—a memorable vintage from one of her favorite vintners. In his other hand was a bouquet of jasmine flowers. They grew on her family's estate in Lebanon, or so she said—he had never gone, although they'd talked about him visiting—and she'd explained the symbolism: jasmine flowers were for welcoming family and friends alike. He hoped she'd understand the subtext.

He wanted to welcome her back into his life and make her feel at home there.

When she opened the door after his discreet knock, a whip of fire seemed to lash his skin. She was even more stunning than she'd been the day they met. The black hair he'd tangled his fingers in still reached her shoulder blades, thick and lustrous, and the radiance of her olive skin made him want to reach out and caress her. As he gazed into her almond-shaped violet eyes, he felt his heart rattle in the glass prison he'd put it in all those years ago. If her gaze hadn't been as direct and assessing as ever, he would have dropped the bottle of bubbly.

"You brought champagne," she said, her sultry accent redolent of her homeland and her European schooling. "I traveled from Paris for a *business* meeting, Quinn."

A reprimand was in her tone, but in her eyes was something altogether different. They were meeting on her turf and not Merriam headquarters at her suggestion, likely because she'd known any meeting between them would be emotionally charged enough to power a rocket ship. And while she'd always been good at shuttering her emotions, he could see what she was trying so hard not to show. He could see the same longing he felt for her.

Yeah, she still remembered everything they'd shared. God, the relief made his head spin.

"It is a business meeting, Francesca, but I brought you a bit of home as well," he said, resting his weight on his left foot, adjusting to her powerful presence. He'd once told her she could ruffle the velvet curtains in any storied London building by merely walking through the room. The air around her seemed to shift in response to the sheer force of her personality.

"You figured it wouldn't hurt, eh? Or were you hoping I'd treat you like an old...*friend*?" She arched a dramatic brow lushly enhanced with a kohl pencil.

"I figured we both knew this was more than a business meeting, and I thank you for coming to San Francisco," he said with equal honesty. "*Friends* is a bland word, and you know it. We loved each other. I asked you to marry me. No point in dancing around the past. Besides, this is your favorite champagne, and you know I had to search high and low for *jasminun sambac*. You always appreciated extra effort, whether in love or business."

She gave a Gallic shrug, which only brought his attention to the textured winter white suit she wore. He'd bet it was Valentino. She loved Italian fashion.

Extending the bottle and bouquet, he said, "So take the bubbly and the flowers and let me come inside and share my business proposal with you."

He met her stare and locked himself in place. All he wanted to do was yank her into his arms and kiss away fifteen years of senseless separation. But she'd rebuff that. In fact, she might break the bottle of champagne over his head.

"You know how I dislike being ordered around, Quinn. While the champagne and flowers are a gallant gesture, they're nothing if you don't mind your manners."

He fought a smile. This was the dance he remembered—and had missed. "I'll mind my manners like my mother raised me to do. I'll even carry in the champagne and flowers since you seem reluctant to take them."

"Well, of course you will, darling." She stepped back to allow him inside.

"The house surprised me," he admitted, noting the pleasant contrast between the high white-textured ceilings and light, airy interior.

"When you're on the road most of the time, you try to make home wherever you are," she said, closing the door.

He found himself remembering her flat in London. It had been small but neat, and full of touches that rendered it both comfortable and classy. A home. And although this wide-open house was much larger and grander, with a breathtaking view of the ocean and Golden Gate Bridge, it exuded the same feeling. The sage green walls in the main room were decorated with bold landscapes. A gas fireplace was nestled in the corner. He caught sight of an open dining area in a buttery yellow, white orchids gracing the table.

She'd always surrounded herself with the richness of life, a lesson learned from her parents, who'd weathered the Lebanese civil war. The Francesca he knew had always been ready to toast to life.

She'd taught him how to live in the moment.

Unfortunately, he'd long since forgotten how.

No, that wasn't entirely true. Her way of living had reminded him of her, and the memories were too painful. He hadn't only thrown himself into work to forget. He'd buried himself in it.

He set the flowers on the side table and walked to the silver bar stand against the wall, popping the champagne open. Two crystal flutes were within reach, and he filled them to the brim, noting the private glass-enclosed sunroom adjacent to this room. Man, she'd chosen a hell of a place. Then again, she'd always had style.

When he turned with the glasses, she was sitting on the arm of the caramel leather couch, an amused expression on her face. "So we are to drink as well? At eleven in the morning?"

"You're way too European to complain about the time," he said, extending a glass to her. "To new partnerships."

"Of course," he said, staring her down.

She took the champagne like she'd taken the meeting: with perfunctory insouciance.

When she didn't clink their glasses, he handled that as well and tapped them together a tad aggressively, enough that the crystal rang out with the elegance of a cowbell.

She laughed. "The glassmaker is rolling over in his grave right now at how you made his crystal sound."

"Like I give a damn," he said, taking a sip of his champagne and finding the yeasty pear notes pleasing.

He was already falling into the moment with her, every sense sharpened. It was like awakening after years of slumber.

Drinking as well, she eyed him over the flute. "You're grouchier than you used to be—but I'd heard that around the global water cooler."

That was a clever way to put industry talk. "Running a company with serious financial issues will do that to any man."

She shrugged. "Still, I won't deny you've retained some of your charm, or that you look dashing in your tailored suit."

He wanted to puff out his chest at her compliment, but he knew she hadn't finished.

"You are right, though. You inherited the problems of your older brother. While Connor was wise to leave—or you Merriams were wise to insist he do so—it has not altered the nature of your troubles."

"You would have checked out every balance sheet," he said, shifting his weight at the discomfort of knowing what the numbers looked like. "You know I need you." His heart sped up as he said the words.

"Is that the only reason you need me?" she asked boldly.

"If you're asking whether I still want you with my last breath, then yes." He drank deeply, not liking the vise around his diaphragm. "I'd hoped to keep it out of my demeanor, but since I can't, I'm going to put all my cards on the table. I need you to turn the company around. There's no one better than you, and we both know it."

She gave another Gallic shrug as the cool ocean breeze blew in from an open bay window.

"But yes..." His heart started to pound. "I never stopped loving you. You are my soulmate, as trite as it may sound. We both agreed on that point long ago. Now I know it's a family trait. All of my siblings have recognized their soulmates on sight. Just like I did with you."

She said nothing.

His mouth went bone-dry. "It doesn't have to enter

into your decision to work with me. I might have gotten grouchier, as you've noticed, but I have excellent self-control." Until she decided she didn't want him to.

Rising from the couch, she strolled past him to the large bay window. "I was afraid of this. It's been fifteen years, Quinn."

And each one of those years had felt colder and lonelier. "The poets say love is timeless." He lowered his glass to his side. "We used to read Rumi to each other in Hyde Park, remember? 'You are the root of heaven, the morning star, the bright moon, the house of endless Love.' I used to believe that. I still want to."

"Stars die, Quinn. Nothing is endless."

Her cynicism rendered him speechless. The Francesca he knew would never have said that.

She turned with enough force to have ruffled the curtains, had there been any, but her eyes didn't seek him out, instead lowering to her glass. "Let's talk business. You want my help making Merriam Enterprises profitable again."

The message was obvious: back to business. "Yes."

"It will take more than restructuring," she said, tilting her head up and meeting his gaze directly again. "You might have to sell off more divisions. I know selling the pharmaceutical arm hasn't stopped the financial bleeding."

"No, it hasn't. May we sit? I'm worried about that beautiful neck of yours craning to look up at me." At five foot five inches without heels, she wasn't a petite woman, but he was six foot four and still towered over her. He'd always teased her about that.

"Hence why I wore four-inch Manolos." She laughed, extending her foot like a ballerina on pointe. "Why don't *you* sit? Then you can crane your neck looking at me."

She paused, and he felt that old familiar beat in his blood. Her eyes tracked to his pulse point, and he could almost feel her lips on the underside of his jaw. She'd always loved nuzzling him there, saying his aftershave and skin created the most manly of fragrances, one she couldn't get enough of.

Desire shook the air between them.

God, he'd never felt so alive as when he was with her. "Stand away," he said, lowering onto the couch. "I'm happy to crane my neck to look up at you. While I may be grouchy, you are as beautiful as ever."

She raised a delicate brow but took the seat across from him on the couch, sitting sideways. "Thank you. But I wouldn't want you to need a neck brace after this meeting. You're so tense, Quinn."

No shit, he thought. "You always had remedies for that, Francesca."

Her mouth twitched. "Indeed. Now, why don't you let me tell you what I have in mind for this consultancy? Since we have a past, I'm going to be more candid than usual. You aren't going to like some parts of what I'd recommend, Quinn."

"I figured as much." He set his champagne on the coffee table and rested his ankle on his other knee. "Shoot."

"You likely have heard how I work." She lifted her flute and gestured to him.

"I have," he said slowly. "You never were one to be on call for anyone."

"I need full buy-in. Anything less won't work. My reputation for delivering results is as important to me as turning the company back around is for you. So... You and I will work nonstop on the restructuring plan until we're both happy with it."

Music to his ears.

"You'll have to create space in your schedule. I would suggest you have someone from the family take over your main duties. Flynn is on his honeymoon, I understand, and your sisters don't fit the profile. Trevor, perhaps? He's based in Ireland, I hear, but he's your lead negotiator. Otherwise, J.T. would be a strong candidate. I know he doesn't work officially for Merriam Enterprises anymore, but he's on the board. Unless your father is interested in coming back short-term?"

He winced. Asking any of them to step in would be a big ask, but he'd known he was going to have to pony up. He knew her rules, and frankly, he wanted to work with her nonstop as well. For so many reasons. "How long do you think it will take?"

"With your sole focus on the task, three or four weeks. Quinn, some divisions will need to be merged. People will need to be laid off. Those details take time. I can move the debt and the profit around to make a better engine, so to speak, but if we don't have the right person driving the car, it's still going to crash. That's why I insist on the CEO's total cooperation."

"I understand the metaphor." He fought a curse. "You don't see a way around layoffs?"

Her gaze was as steady as the ocean waters outside her house. "The only way I see that happening is if you reverse some of Connor's final decisions. His final months with the company were...erratic. Your staff isn't sure what to expect next. Investors can't read the tea leaves either, so your stock prices are at an all-time low. You've gotten away from your bread and butter, offshore oil and pharmaceuticals. Both profitable enterprises."

"I know, dammit." He shot off the couch, seeking the ocean air from the window. "Since we're being candid, I didn't agree with Connor's decisions, but I backed him."

"Because you were loyal to him as your brother and your CEO," she finished for him, coming over to put her hand on his back.

The shock of her touch tore through him, so unexpected.

"Yes, I understand such complications. The desire to do one's family duty. The need to occasionally overlook someone's personal and professional behavior out of love, as much as to maintain the peace."

Their eyes held. Her father ran their family company, and she'd essentially left Quinn to go work for him. All it had taken was a call for help, made at the right time. Having been raised with a family business, she well understood there could be an emotional subtext to profit & loss statements, no matter how neutral a person tried to be. She'd left her father's company six years ago, and while it was rumored there'd been some sort of disagreement with her father, she'd never made a public statement.

Since then, she'd traveled around the world, working with Fortune 500 executives on everything from corporate restructuring to billion-dollar acquisitions. He hoped she would tell him the full story someday. If she did speak frankly about the breach, it would be a sign of tremendous trust. She guarded family secrets more closely than even the Merriams did. "I'm glad you understand, Francesca. It makes everything easier."

"Still, you must deal with the consequences."

"You think Connor should have been removed after the Irish offshore issue, right?" His older brother had made a unilateral decision that they would no longer pursue offshore drilling after their cousin had died on a Merriam rig. As a result, he'd pushed to purchase a piece of land in Ireland for an inland rig—something that had proven problematic given the owner's adamant refusal to sell...and the fact that their brother Trevor had fallen madly in love with her. Ultimately, they'd ended up finding an alternate drilling location onshore, thanks to some fast work by Trevor and J.T.

"His best friend had just died in an accident he felt responsible for. Stripping him of his position then would have been cruel. Quinn, I know you and your family were in a no-win situation. Frankly, I think Trevor and J.T. found a brilliant solution to the issue in Ireland. But it didn't convince people of the merits of the new policy. And then there was the whole screwup in Kenya involving Connor and your sister Michaela... The ripple effects had broad reach. Selling off the pharmaceutical arm couldn't address it adequately."

She rubbed the tightness in his back, her touch exactly the balm he needed. He was stunned she hadn't pulled away, intoxicated by her nearness and her understanding.

"So you see why I need you?" he said. "I can't explain or defend all that's come before. It's been messy, and personal as hell. Francesca, Connor thought about suicide." Not that his brother would admit it, but he'd seen a picture of Connor sitting on a park bench during a Chicago blizzard, dressed in nothing but running clothes. The knowledge of what could have happened—and almost did—had preyed on him almost as much as losing the beautiful woman who was now comforting him.

"I'd wondered." Her hand pressed into his vertebrae, releasing more tension, and the gesture was so familiar it made emotion knot his throat.

"He's turned it all around now, thanks to counseling and the woman he's fallen in love with. Louisa has worked miracles, but she's the director of a homeless shelter in Chicago, so she pretty much works them every day, if you ask me."

"I'm heartened to hear it." Her hand left him then and she faced him. "All right, you put all your cards on the table, so I will as well. I did imagine what you must be facing with your family. I also know you, inside and out."

"Yes, you always did. I'm glad you didn't throw out some bullshit about people changing."

"People can change in some ways through self-improvement, but the core of who they are doesn't. That's what we call character, and I know yours. Another business consultant might tell you what you'd like to hear. They wouldn't do the job right. You need me. That's why I put you in front of others on my waiting list. You and Merriam

Enterprises can't wait for obvious reasons. So we're just going to have to figure out how to do this with everything between us."

He looked back at her, studying her somber face. "Is that guilt I see in your eyes?"

"And if it is?" She released a long breath. "I turned down your proposal and left you—for reasons that all made sense at the time—"

"Your father called—"

"It was more than that, and you know it." Her breathing changed again. "After the 7/7 bombings in London, some people hated me simply because I was Arab. Their hate hurt me—and you! Do you not remember bleeding from the wounds they dealt you? I couldn't live with it if anything happened to you."

Some punk teens had thrown stones at her, and he'd stepped in the way. The stitches had meant nothing to him—he would have done so much more to protect her—but he thought of Connor's volatile reaction to Corey's death, and something clicked. "I suppose if my older brother—who is one of the strongest people I know—can overreact out of survivor's guilt, I can't blame you for doing the same."

"I was scared, Quinn. I expected to be on edge in Beirut. I didn't expect it in London. Never had I felt unsafe or uncomfortable there. Suddenly, everything was different. It's not easy to be looked at suspiciously everywhere you go. Hated for who you are. So no, I didn't just leave because my father called for my help for the first time. I thought I'd be safer with him in Beirut, and I hoped doing meaningful work would lift my crushed spirits. Because what happened to you in London crushed them, Quinn."

Her voice was thick with hurt and grief, and he could feel the same stones weighing down his heart, this pain so much more enduring than the projectiles that had lacerated his forehead. "It's not fun to stroll down this path again, but I'm hearing you with different ears. Maybe it's because I'm older. Back then, all I wanted to do was love you and protect you. It hurt that you wouldn't let me."

She pressed a hand to her heart. "I know I hurt you. Deeply. So yes, there is guilt. Helping you will wipe the slate clean between us. It's one of my New Year's resolutions. No more guilt or regret from the past weighing me down anymore."

He stared at her. "Wipe the slate clean? Francesca, I don't want you to do this because you think you owe me something. Certainly not as some annual New Year's resolution exercise. Dammit, I want you to do this because you believe we might have something again, building on something we both love: business."

Her face fell. "I can't promise that. Don't ask me to do so. You know how important such words are to me."

Yes, he knew. Promises were the same to her as a gentleman's handshake. "Fine, then, I'll accept your help. But I'm not going to let any guilt or regret stand between us."

She took a step back from him and lifted her chin. "What if it's the only thing protecting me from possibly hurting both of us again?"

Which was as good as admitting she did care, that something else was holding her back. He took a step toward her, wanting to touch her, but she retreated and held up a hand to block him.

"Don't."

His throat thickened as he watched the agony in her violet eyes.

"Please don't," she whispered.

He took a tactical step back. She lowered her hand and released another long breath.

"Then we're agreed?" she asked. "You will find someone to take over in a week, two tops, and we will work together to restructure. In the meantime, I will email you what else I want to see and you will give it to me."

Her directness had always turned him on. Oh, how he'd love to give her everything she wanted. "Of course. Where do you want to meet? I assume we'll be working day in and day out until we're finished."

"Yes," she said, taking a step back toward the window. "We can work here if you'd like, but we can also work at another location should you wish. My personal assistant, Alice Bailey, always accompanies me. You'll like her. She's from just outside Chicago. I remember your mother is from there."

Somehow he wasn't surprised at her recollection. "You never met her." He tipped his head slightly. "My parents live in Napa, only an hour away."

"Don't get ahead of yourself."

Her pointed look had him fighting a smile. "Too late. You should interview my dad about the company."

"That won't be needed. Now—"

"Why is Alice coming along really? Is it because you don't trust me to be on my best behavior? I don't like the idea of a chaperone." Then he laughed and thought of his Aunt Clara and Uncle Arthur, who had accompanied his sister Michaela on a work expedition, along with his aunt's butler, Hargreaves, to fulfill that very role. The fact that she was now engaged to the man she'd supposedly needed chaperoning from spoke volumes.

"Alice takes care of anything I need. She will cook three of our meals per week. I expect you to handle the other three nights. We take Sundays off. No work. Our brains will need the rest."

"So Alice is kinda like your butler?"

She slashed a hand through the air. "These days we use the term personal assistant, but there are parallels. I was looking for someone resourceful and smart who was terrific with languages and people to make my consultancies easier. In some cases, she *has* served as a chaperone. Working alone with businessmen, sometimes they get ideas that require dissuading."

He sure as hell didn't like the sound of that. "Is she serving as a chaperone in this case?"

Francesca didn't answer him. "She's proficient in martial arts and speaks four languages fluently."

"Alice really needs to meet Hargreaves."

"Who?" she asked.

"Never mind," he said, tapping his foot in frustration at this unexpected obstacle. If he knew Francesca, he'd never be alone with her without this Alice around.

"She's also well versed in corporate etiquette and various cultural traditions," Francesca continued, almost as if reading Alice's LinkedIn profile. "An old business professor from Columbia contacted me about one of his MBA students who had an interest in international business and a background in hospitality, and I interviewed her the next day. We hit it off and agreed on a personal and professional scope of work. It has worked well for both of us. Don't worry. She works with me behind the scenes, amassing those balance sheets you know I pored over."

He wasn't sure it was going to work for him.

She put her hands on her hips. "This isn't negotiable, Quinn."

"Fine. You decide on the location. We can do it here, another neutral site, or at my house. I want you to be comfortable."

Her smile was all teeth. "How nice to hear."

The important thing was that she was willing to work with him. He could figure out a strategy for dealing with Alice later. "When do you think we'll have the restructuring plans completed if I have someone take over starting next week?"

"I'd say we'll be finished by the end of February at the latest."

Six weeks away. Another Merriam wedding was scheduled for February 22. Would he be drinking alone, thinking of Francesca at Michaela's wedding like he had at Flynn's this past Christmas? He couldn't do that again. "What about us?"

"I make no promises there." Her mouth lifted at the corner before falling again. "Honestly, I don't see how a relationship between us could work. You have your duties to Merriam, and from what I've heard, you work all the time. My career requires me to travel significantly."

She paused, and her violet eyes flashed with something he couldn't understand.

"But you aren't waving me off completely?" He rocked on his heels, awaiting her answer. "Even with Alice around?"

Her glare was all heat. "Could I stop an avalanche?"

"You're more of a bonfire." He unbuttoned his jacket. "Don't you see I'm already smoking in response?"

She shook her head. "This is going to be complicated. I knew that when I decided I had to help you."

He hated the guilt in her tone, but he wasn't going to dissuade her from her decision, not when it was giving him the chance he needed. "We'll figure it out, Francie."

Her brow arched, likely at his use of his old nickname for her. But she only said, "God, I hope so."

She took his hand, but it wasn't a formal handshake by any imagination. It was the intimate reconnection of two hands that held deep knowledge of each other. His palm burned from the heat coming from her skin. She kept her eyes discreetly lowered, but her touch... It slayed him.

"One thing I can promise is that we will restructure Merriam Enterprises to be great again," she said in a crisp tone. "I only need you to trust me."

Still holding her hand, he didn't hesitate. "I do trust you. I always have."

"And I trust you." She laughed. "Don't tell anyone, but I rather like this grouchy side of you. It gives you a steely edge. You're going to need it."

He took the compliment, but he knew it wasn't his edge that would see him through the challenges ahead.

It was her.

CHAPTER 2

FRANCESCA POURED HERSELF MORE CHAMPAGNE THE MO-
ment Quinn left.

"To righting past wrongs and being free of guilt and regret." Her toast echoed her New Year's resolution. She took
a fortifying sip.

Emotions long buried clogged her throat. She'd already
reached out to her father to begin clearing the past wrongs
between them. While he was still angling for her to return
as his scion, she was more interested in a personal recon-
ciliation. Their relationship had taken a hit after she left
Maroun Industries—her "birthright," as her father liked to
remind her. He hadn't spoken to her for months.

Like she'd tried to explain to Quinn, her decision to
leave him still haunted her. But her father had called her
when she felt broken, and the picture he'd painted had ignited old hopes about earning her father's approval. Leaving Quinn, she'd needed something to latch on to, and she

had focused on proving herself at Maroun Industries.

Only, her work at their family company had been a disappointment from the beginning. While she'd been prepared for her father's dominant personality and his need to have a say in every decision, he hadn't given her any independence. Worse, he'd second-guessed many of her decisions. In the end, she'd come to the conclusion that their relationship would never satisfy either of them—she would never be the son he'd always wanted, and he would never respect her. Her dream of them working well together had turned to ashes. While it had been difficult to tear herself away from the family business and her wish for her father's approval, she'd flourished as an independent consultant.

When Quinn had called her shortly after she'd made her resolution at the beginning of the year, she'd taken it as a sign that there were more wrongs to be righted. She'd steeled herself to see him again. To help him. She had lived with her own pain. But she couldn't live with the fact that she'd broken his heart too.

And yes, she had wanted to see if they could find a way to be together again. When she'd told him that she didn't see it working, she'd been *willing* him to paint her a picture. He hadn't, only talking of feelings neither of them had been able to put behind them.

Which she couldn't deny. None of her mental preparation had fortified her heart for his presence.

She hadn't expected her skin to tremble from her attraction to him, but his very presence had shaken her. At twenty-three, he'd been plenty manly; now he was thirty-eight and all alpha—hot, tough, and so built she'd fought the urge to rub herself all over him like she used to.

He'd been her most satisfying and memorable lover, and the only man to ever capture her heart.

Despite what she'd said, she knew Rumi had it right. For her, Quinn was the root of heaven, the morning star, the bright moon, and the house of endless love. She suspected he always would be.

For years, she'd watched for news that Quinn had finally found someone. But it had never happened. In the past year, all of his siblings had found love, and still no one whispered any rumors about him. Somehow she'd known he'd never gotten over her. She'd certainly never gotten over him.

But if they couldn't make it work between them, she planned to exorcise him from her system. It was past time to move on. She couldn't let another year pass regretting him and what might have been.

A knock sounded on the front door, and then Alice came bursting into the room with her contagious energy. "Check out my hair. Their stylist is a master with short layers. You're drinking! Let me catch up. The meeting must have been just as intense as you expected."

Francesca hadn't wanted Quinn to meet Alice quite yet. They'd needed to square off alone. But that was over now, and she could breathe easier knowing Alice would be within earshot when Quinn was around from now on. "You rock the pixie style. And yes, it was intense. But it's done now."

At five eight, Alice was thin as a rail with a big, bright smile that always lit up a room. Her large brown eyes were equally expressive, all the more so because they were framed by thick, dark lashes. Their friendship was just as important as their working relationship. Alice's humor, kindness, and blunt way of speaking had made her Francesca's sister of the heart.

She'd also dragged Francesca out of a depressing pattern she'd fallen into after her breakup with Quinn: working herself into the ground. Alice had reawakened her joy in celebrating life. For that alone, she owed her friend a great deal.

Alice poured herself a glass and dangled her flute against her thigh, the champagne tipping toward the rim.

"I know it's not very professional, but it has to be said. I hid behind a bush in the garden so I could check him out as he strode away from the house, and he's *hot*. I mean, I knew he had to be incredible if you wanted to marry him, but *grrr*."

Francesca laughed out loud. "*Grrr?*"

"His photo didn't quite convey his presence," Alice said, fanning herself with an endearing grin.

"No, it didn't." Her mouth went as dry as the champagne just thinking about the way he filled out his suit. "We're a go for the consultancy. I'm going to need you to do your best chaperoning. I had a hard time resisting him, Alice. I expect it to get worse."

"Who can blame you?"

"He seems determined to win me back," she said, smoothing her hair behind her ear, striving for a cool she didn't feel.

"Are you going to let him?"

She laughed. Could she stop him? "I'm still on the fence."

"There's no rush." Alice took a long drink of champagne. "It's a big decision, and you need to know how it's going to work before you jump in. You are the master of taking the big picture and bringing it to life—"

"One action step at a time," she finished for her friend, chuckling softly. "I love the details too." Details made her feel safe, her crutch after being born into a country often in volatile, uncertain conflict.

"Make him work for it then. At least he ponied up straight away. He brought Dom. Your fave... And is that jasmine I smell?"

"Yes, the variety we have in Lebanon." When she'd seen those star-shaped yellow and white flowers, she'd gone weak in the knees. She'd often told him about picking them outside their home when the flower was in bloom and giving them as gifts to welcome guests. As a young girl, she used to greet her father with fragrant bundles on days when he stayed particularly late at the office. But she'd stopped the tradition after seeing him cast them aside. Despite all his talk about loving his family, he'd never been sentimental. When she'd told him once he was a hard man, he'd scoffed at her, telling her he was simply acting like a man should. They'd never understood one another.

"Wow! It's hard to come by this variety." She would know—Francesca had asked her to find them before. "Impressive. But don't worry. I'm going to chaperone the hell out of you."

She downed the rest of her champagne. "Thank you."

"It won't be anywhere near as bad as that time at the Saudi palace, when I knew that prince was going to sneak into your chambers, and I had to sit in front of your doorway all night in lotus position. Remember how embarrassed he was to be caught in his Calvin Klein underwear? *Haram.*"

Alice's Arabic wasn't fluent yet, but she had a good command, and her use of the word that meant shame or forbidden made Francesca utter an unprofessional giggle. "Do princes even wear Calvin Klein?"

"I didn't check the label or anything," Alice said. "I'll bet Quinn Merriam doesn't wear— Forget I went there."

"No, he doesn't wear anything to bed." Francesca fanned herself for real, making them both laugh. "And that's enough of that."

"So what's the plan? Where are we going to do this?"

Francesca looked around. She rather liked the privacy and nature around her at their rented house. "Let's start here, I think. I like the spa and the dining options on the property. Speaking of... I have something for you."

She walked over to the envelope the hotel staff had delivered and held it out to Alice. Her friend set aside her champagne and tore it open.

"You got me a private chocolate cooking course!" Alice

launched herself at Francesca, who caught her with an oomph. She smiled as she hugged her friend. They might be ten years apart and culturally different in many ways, but they were sisters.

"We're in Ghirardelli chocolate territory, and I know how much you want to make your own chocolate." Francesca kissed both of her cheeks, and they smiled at each other. "I was sad your friend had to cancel on your chocolate cooking school in Bayonne around the holidays."

"Me too! The French capital of chocolate, and Sarah cancels because her boss can't do without her last minute."

"Sounds like someone else I know," Francesca said softly, "but I hope you know I'm not really your boss." This wasn't the first time they'd talked about it, but she still brought it up from time to time. She knew what it was to feel unappreciated, and she never wanted Alice to feel that way.

"What am I, stupid? Deciding not to take a boring office or hospitality job and travel the world with you and meet awesome people—that Saudi prince aside—was one of my best decisions *ever*. Don't we have the most magical partnership? Man, I love you, Francesca."

She'd only ever said those words to her mother and Quinn, and they were dear when she spoke them now. "I love you too."

"Didn't you tell me this was going to be a super emotional trip?" Alice rubbed her throat. "Thank you for this gift. I'll never forget it."

"You're so welcome, *habibi*," Francesca said, a catch in her voice. "Thank you for taking such good care of me."

Alice waved the envelope in the air. "We take care of each other. Girls gotta do that, right?"

"Right." She nodded and then walked over to pick up both champagne glasses. "Come, let's have a toast. Then we can go downtown and do a little shopping before I hunker down with more P&L statements."

"Your eyes turn sad every time you talk about restructuring this company. Working with CEO Hotstuff isn't going to be easy. You need to keep your center. Whenever you feel yourself slipping, you find good old Alice, and I'll get you back on track."

Alice was good at that, and Francesca never failed to be grateful to the fates that had brought them together.

"To cleaning the slate of the past and being set free for good," she said as Alice took the flute from her hand and clinked their glasses together.

They drank, and Alice made a humming sound of delight. "My turn. To new adventures. I don't know, but I have a feeling monumental change is in the wind. Hold on tight, Francesca. I'll do the same."

Hold on tight, indeed.

After fifteen years of being away from Quinn Merriam, she wasn't sure she was ready for monumental change, but neither was she certain she or Alice could stop it.

CHAPTER 3

QUINN NEEDED TO OUTFOX FRANCESCA'S CHAPERONE, BUT his first attempt hadn't gone over well. He'd texted Francesca on the way back to the office, asking if she'd have dinner with him to celebrate their new working arrangement, and her reply had come as he settled behind his desk.

Thank you, but Alice has a lovely meal planned. I'm glad we could come to an agreement to help your company. I'll email you shortly with more specifics. Including my price.

Her money talk made him scowl. He hadn't asked because he knew she was fair and her advice was worth its weight in gold. But that wasn't the point.

Have dinner with me, Francesca. Please.

No.

Dammit, she wasn't going to make this easy.

Pretty please...

Her response wasn't as immediate this time.

Again. No.

Tomorrow night then?

Quick as a lightning flash, she responded: *Alice and I have tickets to a local event. Enjoy your afternoon, Quinn.*

He didn't bother replying. She wasn't going to budge, and it was clear she intended to keep sidelining him with Alice. Which gave him an idea.

Why not bring in his own chaperones, the ones who'd proven they were much better at matchmaking? He could tell Francesca that he was so concerned about her comfort level he was bringing in his own chaperones to alleviate her fears. Not just one, but three: Uncle Arthur, Aunt Clara, and Hargreaves. She'd be a sucker for the family angle.

Secretly, he intended for Alice and his family chaperones to hit it off, giving him and Francesca plenty of time alone.

The whole plan was genius if you asked him. Aunt Clara and Uncle Arthur would be flying out to California in a few weeks anyway for Michaela's wedding; he'd just have to convince them to come early.

But first he needed to call J.T. and see if his brother would be willing to take over his duties as CEO for a few weeks. Perhaps he could also enlist his brother's help with the matchmaking trio. They lived in the same small town of Dare Valley, Colorado. J.T. could bring Aunt Clara her favorite bottle of gin and schmooze her over a martini.

He asked his assistant to hold his calls and pick up lunch for him, and he turned his email notifications off to give himself a few minutes of unwavering focus. Then he called his brother.

"J.T., my friend," he said when his brother picked up the call.

"*My friend*? Okay, what do you need? You've been a bear lately. No way I believe you're simply calling during the workday to say hello."

Grouchy, Francesca had said. "Fine. I need a favor, and it's a big one."

"With Flynn on his extended honeymoon, Trevor and I thought you might be calling one of us about taking over for a while if you hired Francesca Maroun. I assume she agreed. For bragging rights, am I the first or second choice?"

"Who told you about Francesca?" he asked, sitting up in his chair.

"She's the best out there," J.T. said, "and Connor mentioned you might be bringing her in to help restructure."

"He did?" Surely he hadn't told him the rest of it...

It had shocked Quinn to learn Connor knew about his relationship with Francesca. He hadn't explicitly told anyone in the family. At the time, he'd wanted to date Francesca longer before he made the introductions. Another part of him hadn't been comfortable talking about how he felt about her. He was the sort of person who was accustomed to regulating his emotions, and his love for Francesca had always been far out of his control. But Connor had known enough to guess, and apparently it was the reason he'd supported Quinn's request to be stationed out of London, where she often worked, rather than the company headquarters. Of course, he'd found himself back at headquarters anyway.

Quinn had always hoped fate might throw him and Francesca back together, but it hadn't happened back then. His pride had prevented him from taking a more active role in seeking her out. But Connor's words had finally moved him to act. His brother had warned him to not let running Merriam Enterprises become his whole life like he'd done. Now it seemed as if the perfect storm facing him had unleashed the possibility of winning Francesca back. He wasn't going to waste it.

"Hiring her isn't a board decision per se, but everyone knows you need to bring someone in to help restructure. The stock prices and public concerns aren't looking good."

"I know, and I'm more than relieved she agreed. She'll do a great job, but I need to work with her full time on the plans. It's not negotiable."

"Trevor told me. He's known a few execs who have brought her in. It's her rules or no consulting. I can't blame her. Restructuring is time-intensive, and it could drag out for months without a high-level commitment. She's like a corporate scalpel, they say. Her surgery is painful but successful, and it's fairly fast. How long did she say it would take?"

Leave it to Trevor to have done his homework. "Three or four weeks. Given our problems, it's fairly impressive."

"No doubt. So... Am I first or second choice?"

He gave a hearty laugh. "Your twin thing knows no bounds. You'd both be perfect, but I called you first since Trev's in Ireland. You're closer geographically, and Caroline doesn't have to fortify herself to get on a plane to see you like Becca does with her agoraphobia."

"I thought as much. Trev feels a little guilty about being so far away, but that's just the way it is. Did you consider asking Dad?"

When Francesca had suggested it, he'd winced, and he did so again. "I've weighed it from all angles. Bringing Dad back in would stabilize some concerns. People know what his leadership means. But I worry it would undermine my leadership in the long-term. It would be like I called in dear old Dad to swoop in and save the day."

"Yeah, we thought of that." J.T. sighed. "Well, I guess

I'm it. Caroline and I talked about it, and she can handle the museum stuff on her own for a while. I'll have to get used to those insane hours again. Frankly, I love having a job that allows for more work-life balance. But it's only temporary. Unless Francesca identifies you as part of the problem, right?"

His brother's laughter ignited his own. "Right. That would suck." Or would it? He'd been struggling under the weight of the new position, and yeah, he knew he was a bear to get along with lately. Working nearly twenty hours a day with endless meetings and answering over a thousand emails daily was driving him crazy.

How had Connor done it? How had his dad? Asking them seemed like a pussy move. He would buck up and do what needed to be done. But J.T. was right. If he won Francesca back, he'd want to marry her. How was he supposed to enjoy their relationship when he worked nonstop? She'd alluded to him working all the time this morning, and he hadn't been able to deny it.

He was going to have to do some serious thinking about that during the restructuring.

"I can be out there in four or five days," J.T. said. "You can brief me on the major stuff over email or phone beforehand. I'll assume you'll be on call if I have any questions or need your take on something. While I'm on the board, I don't know jack shit about the day-to-day business. I imagine rumors will start flying when people learn you're working on a special project, and I'll do my best to allay their fears. Other than that, I don't see much new happening in the interim."

"Exactly, and yes, I'll be on call for anything you need. Also, Francesca doesn't work on Sundays, so I can catch up then and pinch hit anything you need help on."

"Not work on Sundays? Good God, what kind of a consultant is she?"

Again, J.T.'s laughter had him joining in. "A smart one.

She realizes our brains need to rest, or so she said." Truthfully, he was already hoping she'd agree to go on a drive through wine country with him on their day off.

Which made him realize he might need to pony up the truth about his feelings for Francesca to J.T. Once the family heard he was issuing an invitation to the infamous matchmaking trio, the jig would be up anyway. J.T. was backing him. He deserved the full truth.

"J.T., I also need to disclose something personal."

"Okay..."

His tone made Quinn shift awkwardly in his seat. Sharing his feelings had never been easy for him, not even with his family. The fact that none of them knew about Francesca said everything. Except somehow Connor had known. Had others guessed? His mother had her special radar. Well, he supposed he would find out.

"I met Francesca fifteen years ago in London at a party." He loosened his tie. "Everyone says the Merriams know their soulmates by sight. I knew she was mine."

"You're kidding! Wait. You aren't kidding. How did I not know this? Did anyone know this? Okay. Forget about that. *Fifteen years ago.* Quinn, what the hell happened?"

He gave his brother an abbreviated account, and by the end of it, he could feel his anger and hurt rising again.

"Quinn, man, I'm speechless. And more than a little sick for you. That's awful, bro. Totally and completely awful. God! I...I don't know what to say except I'll fill your shoes as long as it takes. You restructure Merriam and you win back your soulmate."

The conviction in his brother's voice had his chest tightening. "Thanks, man."

"God, if Trev knew this, he'd be on the first plane out from Ireland to pitch in. Everyone will want to help. I assume you're calling in the matchmaking trio. They'll be pissed if you leave them out of this."

He smiled. "I was going to call them next. In fact,

Francesca has brought a chaperone assistant of sorts, who sounds an awful lot like a female Hargreaves."

"Really? I can't wait to meet her. I told Caroline I want my own Hargreaves. I mean, that guy is seriously cool. He knows lost Julia Child recipes from his dad's old spy days. Martial arts. Flamenco guitar. Is there anything he can't do?"

"Hargreaves is the man. We'll have to see how this Alice Bailey stacks up. She has to be pretty special if Francesca thinks so much of her."

"Maybe we can all have brunch at Mom and Dad's house and get acquainted. Now, you need to call the matchmaking trio, and I need to do a Google search on Francesca Maroun." But he was apparently too impatient to wait because he almost immediately said, "Wow, bro. She's gorgeous."

He thought of how she'd looked in her Valentino suit, oozing both smarts and sex. "Yeah, she is."

"Way too elegant for you, though." J.T. whistled. "There's a photo of her at a gallery opening in Stockholm. She's wearing Valentino. Oh, man, I already love her."

Art and fashion *would* win his brother over. "She wore Valentino today, in fact. Wait until you hear her talk business. She talks like a Merriam."

"She'd have to, being Georges Maroun's daughter. He's the shit. One of the biggest builders in the Gulf and beyond. We didn't cross paths, but when I worked on Merriam Oil & Gas issues in that part of the world, his name came up often. He is well respected. Even a little feared, I might say."

That tracked with what Francesca had told him. Quinn had also met the man in the flesh, once, while dating Francesca, and although he'd known many powerful men, none of them had prepared him for her father's charismatic ruthlessness. His takeaway about her father's character was one of the reasons he'd never told Francesca about that singular meeting. How did you tell the love of your life that you thought her father was a dick? "I figure he'd have to be a little intimidating to be successful in that part of the world. Francesca can be tough too, but she wears it differently."

She wasn't ruthless.

"I'd say so. Bro, you'd better have a good game plan. This isn't a woman who will give you an easy second chance."

He knew it. "I'm ready."

"If you need a romance consultant, I charge a hundred an hour. Family rate."

Quinn laughed. "Good to know."

"You sound less grouchy already. She's good for you. It's clear as day."

Quinn realized he did feel lighter. This conversation proved it. He also felt an excitement for life he hadn't had in a while. "I can't disagree."

"We're going to help you win her back. Anything you need, bro. Remember I can be charming. I'll roll out sweet stories about you being my older brother."

"You have stories like that?" He blinked in surprise.

"Yeah... Sure. I mean, you were the one who put me on my first bike and ran beside me until I could balance it alone."

The bike had been blue, he remembered, and J.T. had begged him for help. Since he loved the freedom of riding a bike himself, he'd stepped up. "You were a natural. Trevor, not so much."

"Yeah, his balance was awful back then," J.T. said, laughing. "Let's hope his kids don't get that gene. Thank God he grew out of it."

He didn't often think of those easy days, growing up with his sisters and brothers in their family home in Napa—and he sure as hell didn't dredge them up out of nostalgia—but he found he was grateful for them. "Mom and Dad did a good job by us."

"Mom mostly, but Dad is trying to catch up. Did you know he's talked Michaela and Boyd into letting him go on their next trip to Kenya? He wants to visit the Maasai village that protects the Valley of Stars flowers." The elusive healing flowers had drawn Michaela and the others to Kenya. Aunt Clara and Uncle Arthur were allies of the village, and Michaela and Boyd were developing the flower's healing properties. But not for Merriam. "Can you see Dad trekking in the bush?"

"Not really, but you have to admire it somehow."

"Yeah, you do. Hey! This was...good, man. We should do this more often."

Quinn knew what he meant. "Yeah. I'll have you over for steaks when you arrive. We can do a whiskey tasting. Anything you want."

"That would be great. Okay, call your matchmakers, man. Your woman beckons. Ah... Any problem with me telling Trev about her and you? Or are you planning on telling everyone individually? The minute people hear about Aunt Clara and Uncle Arthur, they'll know something is up. Since you're usually so private about things, I'm not sure they'll ask you directly."

No, they might not, he supposed. Some of his family members might be upset he hadn't said anything about her, but he'd never been good at expressing his emotions, and it had only become worse after Francesca had left him. If it had been daunting to share how much she meant to him, it had been more so to communicate how badly losing her had destroyed him. Shutting off that side of himself had helped dull the pain. So had work. "Tell Trev. Sure. Saves me a call. I'll deal with the others if I need to."

"You make it sound dire, man. They're going to be happy for you—and they'll feel the same kind of righteous indignation I do about what happened to you two in London fifteen years ago. I wish... I wish I'd known, man. I'd have come to London and taken you pub crawling or something."

He got choked up, hearing that. The grief of losing her had nearly broken him, and he'd borne it alone. "All right, enough of all this brotherly love. If we keep it up, I'll have to move Merriam HQ to Philadelphia since it's their motto."

"Being a sap looks good on you, Quinn," J.T. said, laughing. "See ya, bro."

"See ya, J.T., and thanks."

He ended the call and noted his assistant had left a message for him to call her. Marian Fong and he were still learning each other's rhythms, but he appreciated her brevity and efficiency, exactly as Connor had described it. "Yes, Marian?" he said when he rang her.

"I have the background piece on Alice Bailey you requested, sir," she said crisply. "I also emailed it to you."

He didn't say she'd managed it faster than he'd expected. It would insult her. "Your impression, Ms. Fong?"

"She is a unique person with a rare and diverse skill set. Incredible academic performance. Numerous awards for everything from cooking classes to martial arts and foreign languages as well as debate and chess. She notes additional training in high-level business contracts, mergers, and acquisitions. She is also well versed in business and personal etiquette and has high-level training in hospitality management."

Francesca had always had an eye for talent. "I'll look forward to seeing her file. Any family?"

"No, both her parents passed away in a car accident when she was in college. She's an only child."

"Thank you, Ms. Fong."

"You're welcome, sir. Anything else?"

"Not right now. I have another call to make. Then you can release my schedule again. Let the wolves in."

She didn't laugh. Was it because he'd inherited Connor's nickname of the Big Bad Wolf? "Very good, Mr. Merriam. I'll stand by."

When he hung up, he pulled up the email and read about Alice Bailey. She was another girl from the Chicago area—much like his mother and Connor's fiancée, Louisa. He knew what that meant. She didn't look tough, but then again, neither did his mother or Louisa at first glance. But looks could be deceiving. They were both as tough and loyal as they came.

The picture surprised him. Alice looked like a corporate pixie. He could see the intelligence in her big dark eyes, but the twinkle in them was equally apparent. That twinkle suggested she enjoyed celebrating life as much as Francesca always had. Was that why they worked so well together? And was she really capable of blocking him from being with Francesca romantically? He supposed he'd find out.

Now all he needed to do was bring the matchmaking trio on to handle her.

CHAPTER 4

Arthur Hale had never much cared for yoga.

At least not until he married Clara. Three mornings out of the week he sipped his coffee and pretended to read the newspaper, but he mostly watched her twist herself into pretzel-like configurations. Never had he imagined they would be so tantalizing, but at eighty, he was old enough to know life threw out surprises from time to time.

Her phone started squawking, interrupting his good humor. "Clara, can't you ever silence your phone? Woman, how can your yoga inspire all that Zen stuff if you're still plugged in to technology?"

Her response was an amused look, and then she was falling forward into a headstand. He had to admire her. She was turning eighty next month, but there was no question she was living her best life.

"Will you see who it is, dear?" she asked. "Hargreaves is upstairs."

"Balderdash." Arthur set his mug down and squinted

at the phone. "It's Quinn."

"Well, pick it up. He never calls. Always working, that one."

Since she was still upside down, he scowled at her but picked up the call. "Clara Merriam Hale's phone. How can I help you?"

"Oh, Arthur," she said, folding down like a stepladder and coming out of her headstand. "Put him on speaker."

He cursed again but did as she wanted. Marital peace and all. "Quinn! You're on speaker, my boy. How are things?"

"Hello, dear!" Clara added. "I'm doing yoga. Speak up so I can hear you across the room."

"Clara, let the man get a word in." Arthur unfurled from the chair and walked over to his wife. "And stop rolling around on the floor. It's distracting."

"It sounds like you two need a break from the routine," Quinn said finally. "How about an early trip to San Francisco? I need some help."

Clara and Arthur's eyes met. Now they were talking.

"With my soulmate," Quinn added.

Clara clapped her hands and sat on her calves. "Wonderful news! Arthur, dear, you lost this bet."

Yeah, he'd expected Quinn to hold out longer. "Who's the lucky girl?" he asked.

"I'll ignore the news that you two placed a bet on my love life. She's someone I knew in graduate school and never forgot. I hired her to help with the Merriam restructuring. She's the best in the business."

"What's her name?" Clara asked, rising.

"Francesca Maroun."

Arthur watched as she rushed over and picked up her tablet, tapping in what he knew must be an internet search. "Clara, we can look her up later."

"Oh, but she's so elegant. Look, Arthur." She jammed the tablet under his nose.

He had to concur, what with all that black hair and those arresting eyes. She was a looker, but beyond her obvious elegance, he could see her intelligence and a core of steel.

"Why is everyone surprised by that?" Quinn sounded flabbergasted. "Never mind. She's a little gun-shy after all of these years, and she's brought along her own chaperone to keep me in line while we work."

Arthur let out a laugh. "A chaperone? I like her already."

"Me too," Clara said, taking the phone from Arthur and putting it closer to her mouth. "What do you want help with? Submarining the chaperone?"

"Who says that anymore, Clara? Quinn, we'll come and do our usual duties and stick around for the wedding."

"Actually, I was hoping you could pretend I'd asked you to come as additional chaperones. All three of you, Hargreaves included."

This time Arthur snorted. "Helping the woman feel even more safe from your attentions. I like it. You have my vote."

Clara settled her hands against her magenta leggings. "I don't like the subterfuge."

"Yet you were just talking about submarining the other chaperone. Clara, keep consistent."

She stuck her tongue out at him, which had him responding in kind.

"From what I know of her chaperone—whom she calls a personal assistant—I'd say she's the female version of Hargreaves. Albeit decades younger."

"Indeed, Master Quinn," Hargreaves said from the doorway in his stuffiest British accent. "I heard my name being used and decided to enter the conversation."

"Decades younger!" Arthur said, tickled by the thought of a female Hargreaves. "How young are we talking here, Quinn?"

"Twenty-eight. Her name is Alice Bailey, and she's from the Chicago area. I'll send you the particulars, but she might be a match for Hargreaves in cooking, languages, and martial arts."

"No one is a match for Hargreaves," Clara said, striding over to her faithful butler and patting him on the arm. "But send the information."

"We'll see about that," Arthur said, casting a mocking smile at the butler.

They'd become friends—unspoken, of course. Clara loved them both, and she was the glue between them. If that weren't enough, Hargreaves did everything he could to help the Merriams. He treated them as if they were his own flesh and blood. Family was everything in Arthur's mind, so he appreciated Hargreaves' devotion. It made him a good egg.

"I am eager to meet Miss Bailey as well, Master Quinn," Hargreaves said, always polite.

"I'd love you out here as early as next week. J.T. is taking over as CEO until Francesca and I finish the restructuring. No later than the end of February. Of course, the faster I win her over, the faster you can go home."

"Skedaddle, you mean." His great-niece, Caroline, would miss her husband, but if J.T. needed to help out, they'd manage it. Man, Arthur got tears in his eyes, seeing the younger generation support one another. He could die a happy man knowing they'd all circle the wagons when times got tough.

"We'll fly out with J.T.," Clara said, casting a glance at Hargreaves, who nodded.

Arthur had expected no different. When Clara set her mind to something, he and Hargreaves tagged along.

"Wonderful. I'll figure out accommodations after telling Francesca about you coming out."

"Lay it on thick, Quinn," Arthur said with a chortle. "Your woman sounds like a tough cookie."

"I know who I'm dealing with. Thank you for coming. I... *Thank you.*"

The uncharacteristic emotion in his voice had tears popping into Clara's eyes. "We'll help you win her back. I promise, Quinn."

"Make sure you get a haircut and a new suit," Arthur teased to steer the conversation out of emotional territory. He knew Quinn wasn't comfortable with such talk. The man wasn't easy hugging his own sisters, for heaven's sake, or Clara, who tended to coo while hugging the other Merriams. Arthur was okay with forsaking a hug, truthfully, respecting each man's comfort level. "Women like that kind of thing."

"Oh, Arthur," Clara said, wiping her eyes.

He dug out a handkerchief and walked over to her, dabbing at the tears. All her cooing aside, it touched him to see her love for her Merriam nieces and nephews. She may have been estranged from her family for years, but she was making up for lost time.

"My A game is ready. See you next week. Thanks, again."

The phone call ended, and Clara sniffed. "He lost his soulmate. So many years of separation. Arthur, I know what that feels like."

"Clara, we weren't right for each other when we first met. Maybe the time wasn't right for them either, back then, but it is now. Come on, there's no need to fall into despair. You won our little bet about Quinn, and I have no doubt he'll be our seventh Merriam success story." He didn't mention he'd had others with his own family. It chapped her hide to have missed them.

"We should take our talent on the road." She wrapped her arms around his neck while Hargreaves turned his head discreetly away. "No one should live out their days alone and without love."

He patted her fanny and kissed her cheek. "No, they

shouldn't."

"Hargreaves, do you think we're still safe to travel?" Clara asked.

Arthur scowled. Clara and Hargreaves were obsessed with a mysterious pneumonia-like virus in China, currently raging in a city named Wuhan. Thailand had also reported a case, which suggested it was spreading. Arthur didn't know what reports Hargreaves had access to from his father's former work with British intelligence, and he wasn't asking just yet. But Hargreaves and Clara feared it would become a global pandemic even worse than the 1918 Spanish flu. They'd dispatched small packages containing dried healing flowers from the Valley of Stars to every family member on both the Merriam and Hale sides, thirty packages in total for personal use only. The other flowers they'd gathered were being tested for public safety and consumption by Michaela and Boyd's company.

Arthur thought they were going overboard. No, he prayed they were.

A global pandemic would have far-reaching health and economic effects. No one wanted to see that happen.

He was a journalist, and something about the whole thing made the back of his neck tighten. That sensation usually hinted at a big story. So he was keeping an eye on things and monitoring daily reports.

"From my ongoing research, Madam," Hargreaves said, "the matter still seems to be contained to China with that one case in Thailand."

"I pray it stays that way, Hargreaves," Clara said, "and that everyone affected recovers."

"As do we all, Madam. Now, if there's nothing else, I will begin packing for our trip to San Francisco. Would you like me to coordinate with Master J.T.?"

"We can have him and Caroline over for dinner tonight to discuss details. Thank you, Hargreaves."

The man bowed and left the room.

Arthur noted the fear lurking in Clara's eyes, so he pulled her into his arms. Distraction was a useful remedy when she was caught up in worry about the virus. After working on some deeply upsetting stories, Arthur had come to the realization that he couldn't let the news yank his chain; it would only make for unhappy days. He'd have to help her with that.

"Well, Clara, we have our last matchmaking gig with the Merriams. Let's make it count, eh?"

She wrapped her arms around him tightly, and he stroked her long white hair. "It will be the best of all our assignments," she said, getting into the spirit of things like usual.

By God, he hoped that was true.

CHAPTER 5

THE INSISTENT KNOCKING ON THE FRONT DOOR HAD FRAN-
cesca thinking something was wrong.

It was shortly after seven in the morning. Alice must
have gone for a run, or she would have answered it. Francesca hated answering the door in her robe, but the sharp
staccato knocks suggested urgency.

When she opened it, she had to use all her diplomatic
training to prevent an unladylike curse. Quinn was standing in the morning fog, his white shirt casually open at the
collar. The sexy smile on his face was all the more provoc-
ative with his five o'clock shadow. His dark hair curled at
the ends, signaling he'd finger-combed it out of the show-
er, and those green eyes of his were direct and filled with
spice. This was his weekend look, the one she'd always
loved, and he damn well knew it. "Are you lost? Insane? I
thought something had happened. It's seven in the morning, Quinn."

"There are some details I'd prefer to discuss directly,

not through email. Since you didn't return my call and texting seemed a dead end, I had no choice but to show up here. Would you let me inside?"

She didn't need to look down at herself to know that her navy lacy robe wasn't exactly a professional outfit, and with Alice gone, she didn't have a buffer.

"It's important, Francesca. You're going to be happy with what I've arranged. I promise you."

She knew she could handle him, and now she was curious. But she was going to play her own move in this game he'd started. "Let me get dressed. You can wait out here while I do."

His face blanked. "Oh for Christ's— I've seen you in your robe before. *Without it too,* I might add." Which was beyond inappropriate, but he'd warned her about his intentions, after all, and she'd admitted she still had feelings for him too. He grinned, looking so much like the carefree young man she'd fallen in love with. "Those are some of my happiest memories of you. May I say again that you look more beautiful than ever? Always did, even more so without makeup."

She didn't want to be charmed. "You may not. Stay outside, Quinn."

She closed the door in his face, but rich laughter leaked through it. A smile snuck across her face. It felt good to hear him laugh again. This serious side of him hadn't wiped out his sense of humor.

Hurrying to her bedroom, she selected something casual and yet professional: black wool harem pants and a loose white tunic. She wasn't going to put on a full dress suit this early.

Checking her reflection in the mirror, she brushed her hair quickly and did a few things to her face to boost her usual professional image. As she applied lipstick, she remembered how often he'd told her that he loved seeing her without makeup, like he had only moments ago. He'd even talked her into letting him take a picture of her in his white dress shirt like that, which he'd immediately pronounced was his favorite picture of her.

Her hand froze, and she stared at her reflection in the mirror. Part of her wanted to come downstairs without any makeup on so she could see that look in his eyes again. Although she knew she was a beautiful woman, she'd never felt quite so sensual or powerful—or so loved—as she had with those heavy-lidded green eyes on her.

The pull of those days was as thick as the fog outside her window.

She'd take it one day at a time, she reaffirmed. Marouns didn't dive into the deep end without a plan, without details. She would see how he was now, and how she was with him. The viability of their relationship would either unfold or it wouldn't.

Alice would have her own sense too, and Francesca trusted her friend implicitly.

Feeling more empowered, she finished lining her lips with a pink nude perfect for morning and went down to open the door again.

This time, he was flanked by two silver room service settings at his feet. "Our breakfast arrived. Good thing the staff is discreet, although, man, I have a greater appreciation for how far they have to carry this stuff from the main lodge. Now that you're dressed, how about you let me bring this in?"

He'd brought breakfast? "You planned this? You knew Alice was gone. Do I want to know how you managed it? Bribing the staff is the sign of low character, Quinn."

"I didn't bribe anyone." He picked up the first tray. "Give me some credit. I checked in last night and got up early to see when Alice left."

His laughter had her stepping forward, fire licking up her spine. "You spied on us? Dammit, Quinn."

"Let me inside, Francesca. Your bread is getting cold,

and trust me, you're going to want to eat it."

She stewed for a moment. They needed to establish some stricter rules, and now was as good a time as any. "Come in then and make it snappy. I don't have all day."

"Neither do I, but I'm making time for what's important."

He cruised past her, and she picked up the other tray to speed things up.

She was halfway to the kitchen and dining area when he reappeared, taking the tray from her. Since the door was standing wide open, she went back to close it before heading back. He was uncapping the silver trays, and her heart thudded at the sight of what lay beneath. Smoked salmon was arranged in a circle dotted with dill and crème fraîche, with an artful pile of sliced cucumbers in the middle. The other tray held two lobster salads with avocado and watercress. He'd already set a basket of fresh baguette off to the right, along with a crock of freshly whipped butter.

He'd recreated their favorite Sunday breakfast.

Her throat thickened, and she couldn't stop her eyes from tracking to his. His mouth tipped up briefly and then fell again. She fought tears, remembering those happy mornings when they'd finally dragged themselves out of bed and filled their starving bodies after a night of marathon lovemaking.

"I thought our old breakfast might be a reminder of how good things used to be with us," he said softly. "I understand why you want to take your time deciding about us. In fact, I'm here to tell you how I plan to support you in that process."

He was going to support it? When she was nearly in tears over something as simple as an old meal, one she'd never had again after their time together had ended?

"I hope you don't mind me bringing up some old memories from time to time. I can't ignore the past."

What could she say to that? "I'll hear you out over

breakfast. Alice will appreciate not having to cook." That wasn't true. She loved to cook. But Francesca had to say something. All the better if it justified her desire to stay with Quinn.

"Then sit and eat," he said, pulling out a chair for her. "I'll make coffee."

Even in London, they'd both preferred coffee and not tea for breakfast. "I can—"

"I always made the morning coffee," he said, "and you made Lebanese coffee after dinner, remember?"

She gripped her hands in her lap under the tablecloth. He loved the style most people knew as Turkish coffee as much as she did, except people in her country didn't call it that. Her mother had taught her how to read the grounds in the cup, an old tradition passed on from mother to daughter. Some of her most vivid memories from childhood were of her mother peering into their cups, clucking her tongue at whatever fate she'd read.

When she was fifteen, her mom had died from a burst appendix, a shocking and sudden tragedy that had left her desolate with grief. But Francesca had found ways to stay close to her, and making coffee in the traditional style was one of them. She cleared her throat. "Alice makes it too, but I like to keep my hand in."

"I'll look forward to you making me some when you're in the mood for it," he said, measuring the coffee and setting it to brew after filling the machine with water. "Now, how about my news?"

She nodded, feeling way too vulnerable as he busied himself in the kitchen, making her remember how much he'd taken care of her in days past. "After all of this build-up, I can't wait."

He turned the chair around and straddled it, making her mouth water. God, he'd done that when they'd eaten together in pubs. He knew it drove her wild. "I'm bringing in more chaperones."

"What?"

His grin couldn't be trusted. "Making you feel comfortable is my number one job. Like I said, you obviously want to give yourself time to decide about us. I'm trying to show you I can behave. They won't be intrusive. Based on what you've said, one of them is the male version of Alice."

"There is no one like Alice."

"You haven't met Hargreaves. He's my aunt's butler. You're going to love him. He's a proper British butler, and he's been with my aunt for nearly sixty years."

"Sixty years! They must be—"

"Aunt Clara—my dad's sister—turns eighty next month. She's newly married to Arthur Hale, who's a Pulitzer Prize-winning journalist. They know how important this restructuring is, and they agreed to come out and add to the chaperone quotient. My sister Michaela's wedding is coming up anyway, so they'll just be pushing their trip up by a few weeks. Francesca, your virtue couldn't be safer."

There had to be some subtext. "My virtue? Quinn, this isn't a Victorian drama."

"Thank God. I can't stand those. Anyway, J.T. has agreed to step in. My aunt and uncle live in the same town as he does, so they'll all fly in together four days from now."

That was this Saturday.

"We can start on Monday if that suits you." He glanced over his shoulder as the coffee maker beeped, and he rose, pulling out two mugs and pouring the coffee deftly despite his large hands.

God, she had missed those hands. The things they used to do to her.

She made sure not to look at them as he set her coffee in front of her and then went back for the milk she liked to add to it. "Monday would be fine. As I've said in my emails, I already started my prep work."

He blew on his coffee, always too impatient to let it cool before taking a sip. "I thought you might want to come meet everyone at Sunday brunch. My mom will be cooking. Alice will like her. That whole Chicago thing is a big bonder."

She gave him a pointed look. "Of course, your mother has been out here since marrying your father."

The corners of his green eyes crinkled when he laughed. "True, but Mom always says, 'You can take the girl out of South Side, but you can't take South Side out of the girl.' Anyway, I also wanted to throw out the idea that you and Alice come stay at my house. Your three additional chaperones will be staying with me, and it makes sense for everyone to be together. There's plenty of space, and Hargreaves has volunteered to handle our meals on the days Alice doesn't."

She knew a used car salesman deal when she heard it. "Is J.T. staying with you?"

"No, we agreed to keep our interaction minimal so I could focus on the restructuring. Otherwise, I might be tempted to press him all the time. He's staying with my folks. But you'll meet him at brunch if you're willing to come."

The thought of meeting his family under these circumstances had her belly trembling. When they'd fallen for each other, they'd agreed to wait to meet each other's families, wanting more time with each other. Her relationship with her father had always been complicated, and Quinn said his family wouldn't keep out of his business once they knew he was in love. "Do they know about me now?"

He arched a brow. "You mean about *us*? A few of them do now, so yeah, I can guarantee the whole family knows even though they're giving me space. I don't share my personal business like that."

How funny. He'd seemed so close to them when they were dating. Beyond their Sunday brunch, he'd called his parents and sometimes Connor. What had changed?

"They'll be kind to you, Francesca. You don't need to

worry about that. They know it wasn't your fault that you called things off between us."

That rocked her back. "Is that how you really feel? That it wasn't my fault?"

"I know you feel guilty." He scowled. "It's one of the reasons you're here, right? It was hard, having you turn me down. But I understood why you did it. Your father asked for your help with Maroun Industries, a powerful ask given what you've told me about your relationship, and those kids had just attacked us in London. You didn't feel safe anymore, and I know you worried I would get caught in the cross fire. I don't blame you for leaving. I'm glad to see you're out on your own, though. You're too independent to work under your father."

His words only underscored how deeply they'd always understood each other. She swallowed thickly. "Thank you, Quinn. It means a lot to hear you say you understand."

He pushed her lobster salad toward her and gestured for them to eat. "Of course, I also think we were both idiots not to circle back to each other after things died down. I had my reasons, and I'm sure you did too."

She picked up the fork, needing something to do with her hands, and speared a sliver of lobster. "What were your reasons?"

His shoulders, usually so straight, so strong—like they could carry mountains—sagged for a moment.

"In the back part of my mind, I couldn't dismiss the idea that maybe you'd turned me down because you wanted to. That you were using the political climate and your father as an excuse. Or it had opened your eyes somehow."

Oh, she couldn't bear this. Not this. She lowered the fork and extended her hand to him.

He glanced at it for a moment, and in that split second, her heart quaked—was he refusing her gesture?—but then his hand engulfed hers and held it. She felt the burn of the contact and the pain of remembrance. "It wasn't an excuse. I loved you. If things hadn't happened as they did, when they did, I would have married you and been happy. I've never doubted that." Back then, those details had been crystal clear. They would finish school, marry, and work for their family companies remotely in London or another city they liked. Have a few children. Spend part of the summer in Beirut, if it was safe to do so, and Paris, like she had done on summers off from boarding school.

A sigh gushed out of him, and he squeezed her hand tightly. "Thank you for telling me that. It clears up a whole bunch of junk that's been rattling around in my head."

His heart too, she imagined, and it was all she could do to keep herself from crossing to him and wrapping him up in her arms. She'd never imagined he'd doubted her love for him, and that was another regret for her list. She would have to make amends for it, and she knew just how to do it.

"Alice and I will come for brunch, and we'll stay with you and your additional chaperones."

He raised her hand to his lips and kissed it sweetly before releasing it. "Thank you. Trust me. This is going to work."

They were embarking on one of the most painful processes any business could undergo, but his attention was squarely on her. On them. What if their private affairs interfered with business? The way he'd shown up here with her favorite breakfast suggested it was a valid concern.

As she watched him begin to eat heartily, she turned to her own meal. Whatever his reasons, she would give him some leeway. Their relationship was messy, after all.

Besides, the very thought of being at his house was intoxicating. She'd often wondered how he lived. Now she would see for herself. Although they'd spent more time together than alone in London, they'd never lived together. This would be their chance. She hoped it would help her form that picture she needed—a vision of their future together.

With four chaperones in attendance, her virtue would be more than safe.

But it wasn't her virtue that worried her. It was her heart.

CHAPTER 6

HIS MOTHER WAS DRIVING HIM NUTS.

But she was doing it to distract him from his nerves about introducing Francesca to his family, so instead of snapping off a prickly response, he crossed the kitchen to kiss her cheek. "Mom, I love you, but if you tell me another story about choosing wedding cake flavors with Michaela and Boyd, I may have to poke my ears out."

She patted his cheek with her wet hand and resumed washing strawberries, a blue and white checkered apron over her green dress. "Quinn, if you don't calm down, you're going to blow a gasket. Since taking over as CEO, you remind me more of your father every day."

"And they're not good memories," his father added from his prep station in a red apron covering his suit. "Are they, dear?"

"No. Quinn, will you please cut those cucumbers for me?"

There were so many cucumbers, they looked like

freshly cut logs next to a tree stump. The prep would take him forever. "Mom, I told you I could hire someone to cook today."

"In my kitchen?" She flicked her hand at him playfully, water droplets raining on the lapel of his Italian suit. "Quinn Anthony Merriam, when did I ever willingly cede cooking to someone?"

His father coughed discreetly from where he was cutting avocados.

"Shawn Merriam, are you laughing at me?" She cocked a brow.

His usually serious mouth was twitching. "I know better than that, Assumpta, especially when you have a knife close by."

She laughed, her shoulder-length gray hair dancing. "Chop, men."

There was no denying a direct order from Assumpta Merriam, so Quinn took off his suit jacket and rolled up his sleeves and chopped, just like his father minus the apron. His mother shuttled back and forth between the kitchen and the dining room. One minute she was arranging fresh flowers in pink and white, the next she was back in the kitchen, inspecting their work with the eye of a general.

When she was out of the room, Quinn glanced at his father. "She's on a tear." But his mind kept snagging on his mother's remark. He needed to make some changes in his life. Connor had warned him that if he wasn't careful he'd blink and be alone and sixty.

"Of course she is, son," his father said. "We both are. It's not every day you learn your son had a soulmate you knew nothing about."

"I knew he had a woman in his life back then, Shawn," his mother said, popping her head in the doorway. "And I'm sure I mentioned it."

Of course, she'd known. She knew all of them inside and out. "Mom, why didn't you say anything?"

"It wasn't my place to butt in. I figured you'd tell me when you were ready. That time didn't come until fifteen years later. So we're fixing that now."

Her eyes tracked to his father's, and they shared one of their knowing looks.

"Yes, we sure as hell are," his dad said. "We only know her by reputation, of course, but everyone thinks highly of Francesca Maroun. Her father, as well."

"We're excited to welcome her," his mother added. "For you as well as for the help she's giving the company. But don't worry. We'll be discreet. No personal comments. Also, just because you don't say the words doesn't mean I can't hear you, Quinn."

He almost gulped. Her mom radar had always been strong. "Understood. Thank you for cooking. Really, Mom. I didn't want you to go to all this effort."

"I'm not," she said, smiling broadly. "I have you and your father. Now, quit talking and chop. I have more for you to do." But she promptly left the room on some sort of mission.

His father slid him another cucumber with a rare mischievous smile. "Between the two of us, I'd agree your mother's on a tear. She's excited to meet your soulmate. You know how us Merriams feel about soulmates."

"I heard that, Shawn Merriam. You're supposed to be chopping."

"I can talk and chop, Assumpta," he said, shaking his silver head. "I'm glad I can say I contributed. I want Francesca to know we cooked a family meal for her. I imagine she grew up with help."

"Yeah, more than she liked having around, she used to say." He stopped chopping and faced his father. "Dad, I wanted you to know why I asked J.T. to step in and not you."

"He already knows why, Quinn!" his mother called from the other room.

"Is she standing right behind the door?" Quinn whispered to his dad.

"No, I'm setting the table," she bantered back, although the fact that she'd heard a whisper suggested otherwise.

His father's shoulders were shaking from quiet laughter. "I appreciate you trying to explain, Quinn. I hope you'll call on me for help if you need it, but I know you have everything in hand."

"The Dare Valley contingent is here!" his mother shouted.

"Wonderful." His father set aside his work and wiped his hands on a towel, which he then tossed to Quinn. "The only way we can get your mom to refocus her attention is for the company to arrive."

The playful elbow his father gave him as he passed by had him standing up a little taller. It was nice to see this side of his father. Growing up, he'd always been tense or tired or driven, coming in late from work in a suit. He'd tried to be home for dinner, but more often than not he hadn't been. Some nights, Quinn had pretended to be asleep when his father had come in after lights out to kiss him and tuck him in. J.T.'s comments—and Connor's— came back to him about his dad sacrificing so much of his family time for Merriam Enterprises. Quinn had to find another way.

Francesca was just the person to help him.

He put his jacket back on and followed the noise to the front hallway. J.T. was stepping away from hugging their father. The grin he shot Quinn should have been enough of a greeting, but J.T. opened his arms wide like Frankenstein's monster and stepped toward him with a wicked glint in his eyes.

"Come here, big brother," he said, rushing him.

"Shit," Quinn said, seeing no play other than to dash off to the dining room. Truth be told, he didn't want to resist. Their talk about J.T.'s first bike ride had stirred up happy memories of easier days as boys.

His brother's footsteps sounded on the tile floor, but Quinn was around the side of the table and had a chair out like a bullfighter before his brother could reach him.

Still, for show, he had to say, "What the hell, man?"

"You're more chill with Francesca back, and I consider it my brotherly duty to encourage you to have more fun," J.T. said with a grin. "Besides, it got us alone, didn't it? I wanted to let you know that I've got your back. Take as much time as you need to restructure and win Francesca back. Caroline and I agreed she'll fly out weekends and maybe for some longer visits so we can be together more. Trevor's on call too, if we need him. Seriously, man. We've got you."

Quinn gripped the top of the chair. "Thanks, J.T."

"Now come on. Aunt Clara will want to kiss you, I'm sure."

He hugged his brother more easily than usual and smacked him on the back for good measure. "That's because I'm the handsomest."

J.T. reached into Quinn's pants and yanked his underwear.

Quinn yelped. "A wedgie! That's really juvenile."

"Like I care," his brother said.

Quinn readjusted his briefs and chased his brother into the living room where everyone was congregating.

"Quit your horsing around and come and kiss your auntie," Uncle Arthur barked. "If I'd known you were going to turn into two hooligans upon seeing each other, I would have checked into a hotel."

"He's all blather," Aunt Clara said, hugging Quinn tightly. "It's good to see you, Quinn. Observe. I wore my best chaperoning outfit."

"Clara, you wear black to a funeral," his uncle said, "not for matchmaking. Quinn, my boy, asking your auntie to help out made her smile, and for that, I thank you."

They hugged, and then Quinn turned to Hargreaves, who stood in his standard black suit with a crisp white shirt, looking ever inconspicuous. "Hargreaves. Thank you for coming as well."

"Master Quinn," Hargreaves said, bowing slightly. "Always a pleasure."

"Well, now that everyone has greeted each other," Assumpta said, linking her arm through Aunt Clara's, "I thought we'd start with some mimosas."

"Clara likes her gin." Uncle Arthur sent her a wink.

"Oh, don't listen to him. Assumpta, I love mimosas. When are Francesca and Alice coming again? Hargreaves told me, but I'm so excited, it's left my mind."

"The first sign of dementia," Uncle Arthur said, jerking his thumb at Aunt Clara.

"Oh, you old poop," Aunt Clara said. "Assumpta, feel free to order him out of your house if he continues on like this. He thinks it's cute to tease me."

The glare she shot her husband had real heat, but there was a flicker of amusement behind it. Clearly, she thought the teasing was cute, and they both knew it.

"They'll be here at noon, Aunt."

"That's in about an hour, dear," Uncle Arthur said, grinning as she gave him another glare.

His father popped the champagne, and J.T. made a show of pouring the orange juice in first so as to not squash the bubbles, something Uncle Arthur was quick to tease him about.

Hargreaves was leaving the kitchen as his father handed out the glasses.

Quinn called to him. "Hargreaves. Please stay. I know you don't normally join family occasions, but Alice will be joining Francesca, and I'd hoped you would do the same."

"When they arrive, I would be happy to converse with Miss Bailey. Until then, I have a few things to see to. Thank you for the invitation, Master Quinn." He bowed and left the room.

Aunt Clara shook her head. "His butler etiquette is ironclad, but we're working on him, aren't we, J.T.?"

His brother clinked glasses with her. "Every chance we can get."

"To family—near and far," his father toasted.

"To family," everyone repeated, clinking glasses together right and left.

They settled into the family room with Assumpta peppering Aunt Clara with questions about everything from the Hale family in Dare Valley to the next trip out to Kenya to work with the Maasai.

Quinn did his best to pay attention, but his mind kept wandering to Francesca's arrival. The fourth time he checked his watch, his mother drilled him with a glance.

"Do you need to resume your chopping duties, Quinn?"

His father laughed and stood. "Come on, son. Let's finish prepping for brunch."

Although he didn't much feel like chopping more vegetables, he followed his father into the kitchen without complaint.

"If you need help..." J.T. called, kicking his feet out playfully.

They didn't need help. In fact, there was a companionable quiet in the kitchen. His father had moved his cutting board closer to Quinn so there was only a foot between them.

When the doorbell rang, his father gripped his shoulder. "You've got this, Quinn."

That python-like tightness was back, gripping his diaphragm, but he calmly wiped his hands. When he looked up, his mother stood in the doorway.

"Come, let's meet your girl."

When she extended her hand to him, he felt a lump in his throat. "You really are the best mom ever."

"I know." She waggled her brows. "Your Mother's Day

card tells me every year."

His father snorted at that, and then the three of them were walking down the hallway to the front of the house. His father opened the door.

Quinn held his breath at the sight of Francesca, framed in the doorway of his childhood home. Her black hair was artfully wrapped in a knot at the base of her slender neck, and in her hands was a box of traditional Lebanese sweets he knew she only brought to dear friends and family. Her violet eyes tracked to his, and she gave a brief smile, a dead giveaway she was fighting nerves too. It made him feel better, knowing that. They were in this together, even on opposite sides of the door. His mother squeezed his hand, released it, and then she was stepping forward to put her arm around her husband's waist.

"Welcome, Francesca. Alice. I'm Shawn Merriam and this is my wife, Assumpta. It's an honor to have you both in our home."

"Mr. Merriam, it's wonderful to meet you," Francesca answered. "Thank you for the invitation. It seems you already know of Alice, my dear friend and personal assistant."

Quinn studied the younger woman, aware of Francesca's use of the word "friend." The twinkle in her brown eyes wasn't as distinctive as it had been in the photo he'd seen, but there was no snuffing it out entirely. She turned her head to the side and shot him a coy smile, which amused him. *Game on, Miss Bailey.*

"I brought you some sweets from my favorite bakery in Lebanon," Francesca said. "The ones on the far left are made with orange blossom water."

"Oh, we'll have to tell our new daughter-in-law, Annie, Flynn's wife," his mother said. "She's crazy about orange blossoms and includes them in a lot of the skincare products she makes. Using them in sweets might be new to her. Thank you so much. Alice, I hear you're another girl from the Chicago area. My heart is still in South Side, although this one"—she nudged his dad—"got me to move out here for love."

"That's so romantic," Alice said, extending her hand. "I'm from Naperville myself, Mrs. Merriam, but don't hold that against me. Mr. Merriam, it's wonderful to meet you. Both of you."

"It's Shawn and Assumpta," his mother said. "Please, come inside. We've just started with mimosas, but we have a full bar. Shawn's a good bartender, but I expect my other son J.T. is better. Quinn, please show Francesca into the kitchen. We can put out the delicious sweets she brought. I'm sure everyone will be eager to try them. So, Alice... Tell me where you went to high school, dear." She linked her arm through the woman's and led her toward the family room.

His father lifted his brows and followed the two women, leaving Quinn and Francesca alone in the entryway. *Artfully done, you two.*

"You look beautiful," he said, sweeping his eyes over her. "The sweets weren't necessary, but they're a nice touch. I remember their significance."

"The sweetness of life," she said, extending the box to him. "Your mother arranged for us to have a few minutes alone. I suppose I can't disappoint her."

"What about disappointing me?" He opened his arms. "Would you crush my ego?"

"I'm still thinking it over," she said, her gaze sweeping up his body with equal candor. "The kitchen, Quinn."

Taking his mother's cue, he linked their arms and started walking.

"You could have led the way," she said, tension present in her arm. But she didn't try to pull away, and for that he was grateful.

"This is more fun. Plus, no chaperone on earth could say I'm not being a good boy."

Her laugh was as rich as the sweets in her hands. "Quinn Merriam, you were never a good boy."

"No, I wasn't. And you loved it."

"Maybe."

It was a playful response, but the look in her eyes told him it had brought up some heavy emotions, so he nudged her with his hip. "Come on. Admit it. You missed this."

Because *he* surely had.

"Some days," she said softly as they reached the kitchen.

He reluctantly let her go and went to the cabinet for a plate.

"Do you have a serving plate?" Francesca asked. "That's a dinner plate."

"Seriously? What is it with women and plates? They're a flat surface you eat off."

"Darling, sometimes I wonder about you." She glared at him. "You know what a serving plate is."

Yeah, he did. To appease her, he went over to the cabinet with the china, kept apart from the regular dinnerware. She washed her hands at the sink, and when he placed the gold plate in front of her, she opened the box and began to arrange the sweets.

"Is this one still your favorite?" he asked, gesturing to the pumpkin sweet covered with pistachio nuts, almonds, and walnuts.

"Yes. I'm surprised you remember."

The catch in her voice told him how much it meant to her that he did. He picked the sweet up and held it to her mouth. Their eyes locked, and desire coiled in his belly as her gaze lowered to his mouth.

"I can't eat the first sweet." The rasp in her voice drove him wild. "They were a gift to you and your family."

"Always polite," he said, "so let's see if you remember my favorite. I'll take the first bite, freeing you from etiquette."

"You liked all of them, but you loved the ones with dates covered in powdered sugar the best."

"Mamoul, right?" His mouth went dry as she selected the sweet and held it a fraction of an inch from his lips, the scent of semolina and dates filling his nostrils.

"You remember the word."

"I remember everything," he said in a hoarse tone, and then he leaned forward and took the sweet into his mouth from her fingertips. The sugary pastry couldn't appease his hunger for her. Not in a million years. And they both knew it.

Arousal was hot and ripe between them as he fed her the sweet, letting his fingertips linger against her lush, rosy lips. They were locked into watching each other, and it was one of the most erotic moments of his life.

He had to put his hands on her. And when he caught her hips and held them, she didn't back away. No, she looked up at him with a hungry but direct stare that told him everything he needed to know.

She wanted him to kiss her.

His head lowered, watching her. Always watching her. She kept her eyes open too, as if she shared his need to memorize this moment. When he touched her lips, her breath rushed out slowly, and he knew to take his time. Desire was rising between them, and after so long, anything could snap the control holding it back.

When their lips curled into each other in what Quinn could only describe as the sweetest, most perfect kiss, it felt like a shard of glass was being forced out of his heart. Then she put her hands on his back, and the pain dissolved. Warmth began to return to that battered part of him, and he lifted his hand to cup her cheek as they kissed slowly, learning each other again after so long.

He seemed to sink into her, and in her total surrender, he was equally filled by her. It had always been so between them, and his head spun with relief and then awe that it should still be so.

She was the one who ended the kiss, but she pressed her cheek to his for a moment, her hands still clutching at his back, before she stepped away. She looked at him, her eyes wells of emotion.

He couldn't think of a single thing to say. He also knew nothing needed saying. That kiss had said it all.

She sighed audibly, and then her freshly kissed mouth tipped up on the right. Shaking her head, she turned and walked out of the kitchen, leaving him to gather himself and bring the plate of sweets after her.

He knew he wouldn't be able to eat any more of them in front of his family. They would only remind him of what had happened in the kitchen, and those memories were for him to savor when he was alone later.

He finally had hope that he could win her back all the way.

CHAPTER 7

$\mathcal{I}$T DIDN'T TAKE A GENIUS TO KNOW SOMETHING HAD HAP-
pened in the kitchen between Quinn and Francesca.
They entered the room separately, but the air around them
burned like it did in the Arizona desert where Clara and Arthur had spent their first honeymoon.

Assumpta's arrangement of four love seats with a coffee table in the center suited a large family, but it was less
conducive to matchmaking. Francesca had taken the seat
Alice had kept open for her on one of them. The only seat
left for Quinn as he set the sweets on the coffee table was
next to J.T., on the other side of the coffee table. Strategi-
cally, Clara should have seen the problem earlier, but it was
easy enough to rectify once they moved to the dining room,
she supposed.

Clara liked the energetic Alice, but they needed to
come to an understanding about this whole chaperoning
gig. "Assumpta, let me summon Hargreaves. Maybe it was
the long flight, but I'm suddenly starving."

Arthur gave a harrumph.

She shot him a look. He knew she was full of it—Hargreaves had prepared them a lovely repast for the airplane—but he didn't need to give her away.

"Yeah, Mom, I'm as hungry as a bear," J.T. said with his usual winning solidarity.

Assumpta stood immediately. "Let's wrap up the final stages, and we can eat straight away. Shawn, if you'll help me."

Clara pulled her phone out of her pocket and texted Hargreaves.

Would you please help Assumpta finish preparing the brunch? Also, you might mention to her about seating Quinn and Francesca together. I'm going to handle Miss Bailey.

She tucked her phone away without waiting for a reply. Arthur's bushy white brows were raised when she looked at him. "I was just letting Hargreaves know he was needed."

"I'll bet."

"Alice, dear," Clara said, rising. "I wanted to introduce you to Hargreaves. Would you mind coming with me a moment? I bet we can catch him on the way to the kitchen."

Alice glanced at Francesca before standing. "Of course, Clara. After everything you've told me about him, I'm eager to meet him."

"He is equally eager, dear." She smiled at the room. "We won't be a minute. Quinn, you might sit next to Francesca while we're gone. We Merriams can be overwhelming."

"I'm not overwhelmed," Arthur said, making J.T. laugh.

"Oh, for heaven's sake..." she muttered and walked to the doorway with Alice, who looked over her shoulder and frowned as Quinn took a seat beside an amused Francesca.

Clara indicated for Alice to continue down the hallway, and they stopped outside the kitchen. The young woman was quite tall, something a picture couldn't properly convey, but Clara simply straightened to her full height and held her own. She let her eyes track to where her brother and sister-in-law were working companionably in the kitchen. She didn't wish to disturb them—or her chance to speak privately with Alice. "Hargreaves will be here in a moment. Alice, dear, I know you've heard we're here as additional chaperones to make Francesca feel more comfortable around Quinn. The Merriam restructuring is very important to this family."

Her big brown eyes were serious, her focus intent on Clara's face, but she remained quiet. After her earlier enthusiasm, Clara understood the young woman knew that a message was being delivered.

"But so too is Quinn's happiness—and Francesca's, I might add. I've just met her, but it's obvious they still love each other. I'm hoping we can find a way to give them space to see where that might go while still executing our duties. Do you know what I mean?"

"If you think I'm a pushover for true love, Mrs. Hale, and are trying to undermine my duty to Francesca, please don't. I follow her guidance on how she wants things to go. I don't act independently on that score."

No, she was no pushover. "It's Clara, and I respect that. You wouldn't be the admirable assistant I imagine you to be otherwise. But it's clear they have some things to work out, and I only want you to know our contingent will do our best to aid in that."

"Understood." The woman still hadn't smiled, which was something, for she'd done nothing but until now. "And you need to understand that my loyalty is to Francesca."

"Yes, I can see you're as loyal to her as my dear Hargreaves is to me," she said, spotting him coming down the hallway. "Clifton Hargreaves. Please meet Miss Alice Bailey."

He nodded with a slight bow. "Miss Bailey. A pleasure."

"Alice, please, and it's my pleasure too," she said, her mouth tipping up in a kind smile. "I hear we have some common interests. I look forward to discussing them. Are you a soufflé or crème brûlée kind of guy, Mr. Hargreaves?"

A butler quiz? Clara was intrigued.

"It's only Hargreaves, Miss, and if I were pressed, I would say soufflé. You can make it either savory or sweet."

"Oh, I like that answer," Alice said, her smile coming out again. "Clara, I would ask you about being a diamonds or rubies kind of lady, but from the ice on your wrists, I already know the answer."

Ah, so it wasn't only a butler quiz. "Diamonds are so much more versatile, dear. Not only are they pretty, but you can sell a bauble or two if you're on the run."

Alice threw back her head and laughed, prompting Shawn and Assumpta to look over. "On the run! That's awesome. I'll have to remember that if I ever need to flee the country."

Clara couldn't resist smiling, noting Hargreaves was doing the same.

"Shall we see what Mr. and Mrs. Merriam need to finish brunch?" Alice asked, turning to Hargreaves. "That is, of course, if Clara is finished setting the ground rules."

The girl had teeth, and Clara respected that. But she was also kind, polite, and funny. They were going to get along fine. "Absolutely, dear. It will be wonderful to get to know you better, and in the course of our time together, who knows what magic we might create?"

"Magic, eh?" Alice grinned. "I love the sound of that. I might have to buy a wand."

Clara extended her hand to Alice and they shook companionably. "We'll both buy wands then. Hargreaves will see to it. He's adept at spreading his own brand of magic."

"What magic have you worked lately, Hargreaves?" Alice linked her arm through his, and surprisingly he let her as they walked into the kitchen together. Moments later, she heard Alice laugh out loud, and Clara smiled. Hargreaves was ever so witty.

Their assignment was going to be a piece of cake at this rate.

CHAPTER 8

S HE'D OPENED THE DOOR BUT GOOD.

That kiss... It had felt like an earthquake intent on destroying every fortification she'd erected. What good were four chaperones when she'd offered herself up like the tasty sweet he'd fed her?

But God, it had been so hot.

And now she was on her way to his house. She was supposed to *live* with him for the duration of the project.

"Alice, please pull over at the next viewing area," she said abruptly. "It's so lovely along this road."

Alice shot her a look indicating she knew the view wasn't what had gotten to her, but she did as instructed, and the view *was* lovely. The hills were a lush green and blinding to the naked eye before the terrain turned sandy and flat. She loved it here. Oddly, it reminded her of home.

Home. It was the Holy Grail for her.

Feeling at home among his family yesterday had been the aftershock to the earthquake in the kitchen. His parents had been the best of hosts, keeping the conversation light even as Francesca caught them watching her every now and then. By the end, the speculation had left their eyes, and they'd embraced her with genuine warmth, their acceptance touching her deeply.

Seeing Quinn with those he loved had been equally compelling. He'd stayed mostly quiet, letting the others take the lead—Arthur and J.T. telling stories that made everyone laugh, Clara reacting with laughter or playful punches to their arms. They'd all been so at peace with each other, so comfortable. It had been touching to witness it, especially since they'd made such a point of including her. After dessert, Quinn had helped her out of her chair with an easy smile that told her how happy he was to see her getting along with everyone.

But today she could make a new resolution: to keep her mouth and hands away from him until she was more sure of what would happen *after* they went to bed together. Those details felt more critical than ever to her sense of peace. Making love wasn't the issue, really. It was what came afterward that worried her.

"Are you ready to drive the rest of the way yet?" Alice asked, tapping the steering wheel like an impatient drummer. "Or are you going to keep stewing about the kiss? I can get out and take some photos if you need more time. Maybe go on a hike or something."

She managed a brief laugh. "A hike, huh? It's not that bad."

"Isn't it? Stop blaming yourself. So you kissed him. I mean, he's not my type, but he's totally delicious. He's like Everclear ignited on that Greek cheese I love."

"He's like flambéed saganaki?" Francesca let out a gusty laugh. "Oh, you and your metaphors."

"He's flaming—but...wait, I'm hearing how that sounds. No, he's volcanic." She uttered a sound that must have been a volcano exploding, her big-lashed eyes and mouth widening to add to the comedy. "Make sense?"

She couldn't help but laugh. "Yes. Continue."

"Anyway, even Clara noticed the way he looks at you. Of course, she also noticed the way you look at him." She made another explosion sound. "Are you really, really sure you want to move into his house? We could say we changed our minds."

"No way," she said, knocking her fists against the tops of her thighs. "That would make too much of it."

"You do realize his family members aren't really chaperones, right? I figure it's a canny ruse to get you to stay with him. Trust me when I say that Clara especially is going to do everything she can to bring you two together. She made that clear yesterday. Hargreaves will follow the straight and narrow, but Arthur—"

"Is trouble with a capital T," Francesca said with a smile. "But he's absolutely adorable. Smart as a tack too."

"So is Hargreaves. If I had a grandfather, I'd want him to be Hargreaves. Okay, so we agree they're all likable. Score one for Quinn. What do you want to do? Because we've been sitting in a running car for fifteen minutes and you've barely noticed the view."

"We go." She took a deep breath. "Once I start working, I'll be more focused. Yesterday was intense on many levels. I hadn't expected to be so affected by meeting his family or seeing where he grew up." But she should have known better, of course.

The house had been filled with photos of the Merriam family at all ages, and when she'd gone to the bathroom, she'd taken a moment to look at a few. His sweet round cheeks as a baby had crushed her, and so had the recent photo of their family at Flynn's wedding. Quinn's underlying unhappiness had been evident to her. He was the only one who didn't have his arm around a partner, and the look in his eyes said he was not just alone but lonely.

"They're a good group." Alice nodded emphatically.

"I'd like them for friends and neighbors under other circumstances."

"Oh, you and your friends and neighbors talk," Francesca said. Alice was a great believer in the power of friendship.

"Family can be hit or miss, and there isn't much you can do about that. But you get to choose your friends and your neighbors. Surrounding yourself with good ones is the key ingredient to a happy life, with neighbors being the most important since they live next door. You're my neighbor, and you're also my best friend."

"And you're mine." Francesca thought about her own family. With no siblings, she'd been sent to boarding school in England at a young age. Her mother had always made her feel loved, but she hadn't been strong enough to stand up to Francesca's father. And then she'd died, and the home they'd shared had stopped feeling like a home.

Truthfully, Francesca had always envied what Quinn had. At one time, she'd dreamed about what it would be like to become one of the Merriams when they got married. Over brunch, she'd gotten a vivid glimpse, and it was tantalizing her heart again.

"I have to see this through. I owe him, and more importantly, there still is something between us."

Alice put the car in gear. "Okay, I'm pulling back onto the road. When we arrive, though, you're going to have to be clear about my role as chaperone. If I find you in serious lip-lock, am I supposed to barge in and pull him off you or something? Or do you want me to let things...run their course?"

"Lip-lock? Really, Alice." Her mind flashed back to the look in his eyes as he kissed her. Heated. Loving. A tad scared. But she didn't think he'd let anyone stop him.

She hoped not.

"You didn't answer my question."

"I know." Her phone chimed, and she picked it up to

see the caller ID. "It's my father."

She pulled a face, something she'd only done since meeting Alice, who had taught her how.

"We better stay put then," Alice said, pulling a face as well. "He only calls when—"

"He wants something," she finished, taking the call. "Hello, Father."

"Francesca." His voice was terse, the way it was every time she disappointed him, which was often. "How do you think it makes your papa feel when he hears from another source that you're working with Quinn Merriam for the next month?"

Her stomach sank. He only called himself her papa when he was about ready to put her on the parental rack of guilt. "Keeping tabs on me still, Father? You know I don't like that."

"You're the daughter of a billionaire, Francesca. I've had people keeping tabs on you since you were in swaddling. I knew about the trip to San Francisco, but I didn't put it together you might be in touch with the Merriams. Personally or professionally."

"Quinn Merriam asked, and I decided." She fisted her hand against her stomach. "I don't run my consultancies by you, Father."

"No, and the very fact that you're a consultant instead of vice president of your birthright continues to upset me. You stubbornly refuse to be a part of everything I've built for you."

"The company is yours, Father. I'm not needed. Neither of us were happy, even if you won't admit it. You run it, and it's easier for everyone if no one interferes with that. We've covered this."

"And when I die? Francesca, there are forty thousand employees who support Maroun Industries. Those jobs put bread on the table. Now Quinn Merriam is luring you—"

"Luring?" Her voice held an edge. "Father, do I strike

you as someone who could be lured by anyone?"

"Certainly not your own father. But a former lover?"

Her breath caught. They'd never spoken about Quinn. He'd never asked her, specifically, about her personal relationships. He disapproved of all of them on principle—because they weren't his choices. He'd tried to introduce her to "a man of good standing" when she was eighteen. She had made sure that disaster was not repeated.

But of course he'd known about Quinn. He made a point of knowing everything. "That's my personal life. It has nothing to do with business."

"It does if he's trying to lure you to his flagging company on the memories of a summer fling."

"It wasn't a summer fling, Father."

"Oh, boy," Alice muttered, turning the car off.

"Of course it wasn't, which is why I approached him and told him to leave you alone."

Her shock caused her to knock her knee against the glove box. How come Quinn had never told her? "Clearly that didn't go your way," she guessed.

His rude noise confirmed it. "His outright refusal might have earned him my respect except for the fact that he's not the man for you. You need to marry someone who understands you."

Oh, God, not this again. "A good *Lebanese* man?"

"After all this time, I could likely approve of a cultured European as well. If the man's from a good family, of course."

"*Of course.* Father, you know this discussion is pointless."

"You're already too long without a husband. People talk about you, and about me too. They wonder what kind of a man could let his daughter be without a husband and children and a good home. I know your mother died—"

"It wouldn't have changed my views." She gripped the phone. "Father, this conversation is tiring. I've told you. I live my own life. Make my own decisions."

"Certainly make your own money. You won't let me support my only child. Why else do I work so hard except to take care of my family?"

She reminded herself of her New Year's resolution to make peace with him. At the moment, she wanted to chuck it out the window. "Father, I love you, but we'll never agree on this."

He went silent a moment. "Merriam Enterprises is going down, Francesca. One gust of wind and they're sunk. Not even you can stop it."

"You won't touch them, Father." Her stomach quivered.

"I wouldn't be that ruthless. Besides, you would never forgive me. But you do your consultancy and see for yourself. You're planning on restructuring the company around oil, correct?"

"Father, you know that's confidential."

He made another rude noise. "It's the wise play—on paper. Return to their roots and lock in on an industry that never loses money. Only, for reasons I can't divulge, I'm telling you: *don't make this play.*"

Silence radiated over the line as her mind raced. Why not? The oil industry was tempestuous, but the world depended on it.

Of course, she'd seen the drop in oil prices when she'd done her morning industry research. Concerns about China's pneumonia-like virus were spooking some investors. Chinese officials had confirmed yesterday that they now had nearly three thousand cases, and the virus had spread from the city of Wuhan to Beijing, Shanghai, Macao, and Hong Kong.

"Are you warning me because of the virus in China?" she asked.

His grunt was audible. "The infected are a drop in the ocean in a country with over a billion and a half people.

They'll lock it down. Saudi Arabia's Energy Minister made a similar statement, but did the market listen? No, it's like a chicken in a henhouse sometimes, bawking at the tiniest noise."

He hadn't completely answered her question. Surely he wasn't misleading her as a way of causing conflict with Quinn. "You'll have to give me more, Father."

He sighed. "Can you not trust your papa this once?"

Papa again. After what he'd admitted, she couldn't do anything but call his motives into question. Plus, how was she supposed to explain any other play to Quinn? He knew it was the best plan to save Merriam Enterprises as much as she did. Everyone did. The devil was in the details. That's where others fell down and she excelled. "I'm sorry to say no, Father."

"Then I have truly failed you as a father, and I'm sorry for that."

Her heart squeezed. "Father, I'm sorry too. I want peace between us."

"Peace! What is peace? Even now our country faces tremendous trouble and hardship. I thrive on adversity, but you have forgotten your roots and gone soft. Do not let your feelings for this man cloud your judgment. Merriam Enterprises has had poor leadership since their father retired, and the brothers have run a good legacy into the ground. I don't plan for that to happen to Maroun Industries. As my daughter, I'm trusting you'll do what you've always been meant to do. People are depending on you, and so am I. Now more than ever."

The call ended, and she clenched her eyes shut as hurt and anger wrapped her up like a hot scratchy blanket.

"Breathe," Alice said in her Zen voice.

"He makes me madder than— Do you know what he said?"

"I have an idea after seeing you two go round after round on our last trip to Beirut. Anything new?"

She threw her phone into her purse and turned in her seat. Leaving out his nebulous entreaty regarding oil, she said, "Apparently, back in London, he spoke to Quinn and asked him to leave me alone."

Alice's eyes widened. "I'd have paid big money to hear that conversation."

Frankly, so would she.

Why hadn't Quinn told her? Had he known how angry it would make her? They didn't used to keep secrets from each other.

"This only drills home what we already knew," Alice said. "Your father knows everything. Remember how thoroughly he had his people check me out?"

Georges Maroun hadn't known what to make of Francesca hiring a personal assistant whom she also thought of as a friend.

In his world, everyone had a purpose—to serve his needs. She was no different. Which was why she thought his oil salvo was a ruse. If he truly knew something, he would tell her—if for no other reason than it would reflect poorly on him if she ran Merriam into the ground.

"I should never have made that damn New Year's resolution. Peace with him is impossible."

"You always say that."

She did, and that angered her too. Part of her still hoped he could change and become the kind of father who'd actually listen to her and support her wishes. But it seemed less likely every time they spoke.

Clenching her hands around her bag, she said, "He thinks Quinn is luring me to his failing company on the heat of an old fling. Like I'm thinking with my dick or something."

"Your father is a jerk," Alice said like the good friend she was. "If you had a dick, you'd never let it run your life."

"Thank you!" The force of her anger was like a champagne cork working its way out. "And how dare I work for another company and not the family's? He apparently thinks I'm good enough to help run his company, but whenever I try to do anything else, he implies I'm weak. Weak? Me? Oh, I'm so sick of his manipulations."

"I know you are, which is why you made that resolution." Alice rubbed her hand. "I hesitate to say this while there's smoke coming out of your ears, but the resolution is about finding peace with your father. It doesn't mean your father has to make peace back."

She rubbed the bridge of her nose. "You don't think we can improve our relationship?"

Her friend lifted a shoulder, her big brown eyes soft. "It doesn't matter what I think. He's not my father. Do *you* think it's possible?"

"I don't know." She gave the footrest an unladylike kick. "I've always hoped so. But after today—"

"That's the problem. Your hope is an attachment. What if he won't or can't change? That's why you need to make peace with who he is, not who you want him to be. Once you have that, it won't matter what he says or does."

"Dammit. That sounds hard."

She laughed. "If it were easy, there wouldn't be a self-help market."

Nodding, she gestured to the road. "Let's go. I'm putting one stubborn man behind me and heading off to stay with another, although at least this one respects me. Am I crazy, Alice? Maybe a glutton for punishment?"

"You're no glutton and the crazy part is negligible."

That had her smiling. "Thanks."

She put her seat belt back on and gestured for Francesca to do the same. "No problem. Before we finally get back on the road, I want to say one more thing about my matchmaking role. Usually you're crystal clear on how you want things to go. You haven't been this time, so I'll have to follow my own intuition about you guys. Are you good with that?"

"That might be best," she answered, staring out the window at the rolling hills. "He's going to press his case the minute we arrive." He would see yesterday as a victory and keep marching the rest of the way to her heart. She knew that. Respected it even. In his shoes, she would have done the same.

"Then you might consider putting your arm around Arthur when you arrive and sticking close to him. Quinn won't be able to put his hands on you that way, and Arthur is too much of a gentleman to push you toward him. I'd hold your hand, but it would look weird."

Her laughter sputtered out. "Oh, Alice. I'm so happy you're my friend."

"You know it. Now, sit back and gather yourself. We've got twenty minutes according to Google."

When they pulled into the private drive and slowed to follow the winding road, Francesca gripped her knees. Then the flint-colored house came into view, and her heart trembled. All lingering emotions from her call with her father evaporated. The two-story house sat on the ocean, its style somehow both modern and classic with several large windows designed to make the most of the view. They'd always had similar taste in architecture, but this house...

She would have chosen it for herself.

"Wow," Alice said in a breathy voice.

Francesca reached into her purse to reapply her favorite lipstick, using the simple ministration to gather herself.

"From the limo in front, I'd say his family has already arrived," Alice said. "Arthur was so funny, teasing Clara about using a limo, especially in their small town."

"He was," she said, closing her lipstick slowly and putting it back. But she still didn't feel gathered. "Everything is going to be fine. I'm a grown woman. I've consulted with the world's most powerful businessmen."

When Quinn strode out the front door with purpose, his long strides spanning the distance between them, her heart squeezed painfully.

"Brace yourself, Effie," Alice muttered.

Alice's ongoing use of the *Mrs. Doubtfire* line usually made Francesca laugh. Not this time. She found herself tensing as the car pulled to a halt and Quinn came around the hood to open her door.

"'Bout time you arrived," he said, extending a hand to her. "I was getting restless. Anything happen on the drive up?"

Other than her father's call? She thought again about her father's mention of his attempt to interfere in their relationship and how he'd come away respecting Quinn despite his feelings.

He'd been wrong about Quinn, and he was wrong about Merriam Enterprises too. She was going to prove that by saving it. Francesca had already started working on her proposal for the Merriams because she hadn't been able to stop tossing and turning last night. Thinking of Quinn's family and the way she'd felt wanted and accepted, something she'd never felt with her father.

Thinking also about that hot, tempestuous kiss...

Alice gestured at the view. "We took our time. Pulled over to enjoy the vista. It's beautiful here."

He waved his hand impatiently at Francesca to indicate she was dillydallying, and that popped her out of her reserve. "Your restlessness is evident, Quinn. But it *is* lovely up here, and your house is magnificent."

"I got lucky. Some Hollywood type was moving back to L.A. The whole thing went like clockwork. Just the way I like it. Are you going to take my hand or what? You look beautiful, by the way."

"Comments on my beauty aren't allowed when we're working," she told him, finally taking his hand and letting him help her out of the Audi.

When she tried to extract her fingers, he held firm and stepped closer. "We both know yesterday changed things."

Perhaps it was best he'd brought it up now. They needed to clear the air. "I still need some other...items answered. Nothing new came from the moment you're thinking about."

He laughed and kissed her cheek. "You don't think it counts as 'new' that we're hotter together than ever? Or that you fit in with my family like you've always known them? You're usually more honest than this."

He was right, but she couldn't admit he was right, not when the future still felt so uncertain. "You don't know... Oh, why am I arguing with you? You have a head like a bull sometimes. Let's get started. Where are our rooms? We'll bring our luggage inside."

"Not in a million years. Alice, pop the back, will ya? I'll bring your stuff in."

"I'm glad you didn't call for Hargreaves," Francesca said as he went to the back of the car.

He shot her a look of outraged male pride. "He's not my butler, and I wouldn't have asked even if Aunt Clara had given her nod."

Hefting two of their suitcases, he started to wheel them toward the front door. "You coming? I'll grab the rest in a moment. I'm glad you still bring everything you need when you travel."

He'd teased her about overpacking on their first weekend trip to the Lake District, but she'd explained why she'd taken so many things—that she'd learned to make a home wherever she went, starting in boarding school—and he'd stopped teasing her. He'd even encouraged her to pack more things on other outings.

When Alice headed to the back to secure a smaller piece, Francesca waved her off. "Let him do it. He's determined." Also, she knew he liked to take care of her like this.

Alice was biting her lip to keep from smiling. "He's something. Oh, good morning, Clara. You beat us up here."

"We settled in after brunch yesterday," Clara said,

grandly striding forward in a teal yoga outfit and kissing Alice's cheek before turning to warmly do the same with Francesca. "Ignore Quinn's restlessness. Blame it on deeper emotions that leave a man like him unsettled. Come inside. Hargreaves is preparing tea and a snack. Arthur is reading a newspaper, per his usual morning routine, while I do yoga. He pretends not to watch, but truthfully, it's flattering to know I'm more captivating than the news to a seasoned journalist like him."

"Yoga!" Alice said, following Clara to the house. "I'll do yoga with you, Clara. If you don't mind, that is."

"Not at all, dear. Hargreaves prefers tai chi and Qigong, which we do three times a week. You're welcome to join those practices as well. Both of you."

Francesca appreciated the invitation, but she was here to work. "Thank you."

"Well, you finally made it." Arthur laughed as they entered the house. "I thought Quinn was going to burn a hole through his watch after all the times he looked at it."

"I told Francesca it was a compliment," Clara said. "So, what do you think of the house? Isn't it gorgeous? I love the open floor plan."

"A man's got no privacy," Arthur grumbled, but he shot them a wink. "I'm going to have to hang out in the bathroom to find some peace and quiet."

"Oh, Arthur, you don't talk about spending time in the bathroom in mixed company."

He kissed her sweetly on the cheek. "She can't take me anywhere, but yet, we still go. What does that say about you?"

"That love is stronger than sense," she shot back, pushing him gently in the chest and making him laugh. "Hargreaves, dear. Our new friends have arrived."

Alice beamed at the mention. "Friends! I was just saying the same thing on the way up. Right, Francesca?"

"Right." She surveyed the lower level with its tall

ceilings. Decorated in sea blue and gray with beach wood accents, the different segments were set off with either a few steps or wooden beams. The family room had two steps leading down to it while the dining room was raised up two steps. Both spaces boasted gorgeous views of the ocean and the beach below. Two large beams demarcated the designer kitchen at the back with a cozy nook facing the ocean. Somehow it was casual and yet elegant.

"Do you like it?" Quinn asked, close to her ear.

She took a moment to savor the feel of him, so close, then turned and took a step back. "I do."

"Good. Come see your room." He took her hand before she saw it coming, his touch familiar yet new, comforting yet exciting. It felt right in a way no other man's hand ever had. Was it foolish of her to keep holding back?

She thought of the look of anguish on Quinn's face when she'd refused his proposal. If they couldn't think of a plan to make it work, all the way, she couldn't risk breaking both of their hearts again. She just couldn't. The last time had nearly destroyed her, and it had clearly been no easier on him.

"Yes, Alice, come and see our rooms," she called, exerting a gentle effort to untangle their connection.

He shot her a grin, but he let her hand go with a knowing look. "First room at the top of the stairs, Alice."

Her friend saluted and started up the modern rustic wood staircase, and Francesca trailed after her, very aware of Quinn at her right. The steps were a free floating design, and she liked the ladder-like feel of them. "Is mine next to yours? I hope you weren't that predictable."

His laugh was husky. "No, yours is next to Alice's. Mine is at the end of the hall. Hargreaves is between us."

Turning her head, she studied him. "You have something else in mind. What?"

He shrugged. "You and I were way too loud in the past, remember?"

Her thighs tightened at the memory of their cries blending together in their London apartments. They'd laughed more than once about it, but they hadn't been able to come together quietly.

"Plus, they're my family," he said when she didn't respond. "I wouldn't sneak around with you in the house with them here."

She shot him another look. "I know you're up to something."

This time his laughter was a rich baritone. "You're right. I kept the guesthouse on the property free."

Oh, dear Lord. She was sure her face flamed red. "I see."

"The former owner used it as a studio, but I've outfitted it with—"

"I get the picture." She could already see her legs locked around him with her back against the wall.

He paused for a moment at the top of the stairs, looking almost as vulnerable as that little boy in the photograph at his parents' house, but his gaze caught hers, and heat sparked in his eyes again. "I've arranged for vases of jasmine to be there every day. Anytime you want to visit them, you should. Hopefully, you'll let me visit with you soon."

Their eyes held, and the thudding of her heart was so loud she was sure he heard it.

He traced her cheekbone before stepping away. "Alice, does this work?"

"Most definitely! The view is totally chill."

Francesca ducked her head in, needing space. A king bed was situated in front of one of the floor-to-ceiling windows, and a small sea blue couch and rosewood desk sat in front of the other, the furniture situated to make the most of the view. "Chill is right."

"Wait until you see your room," Quinn said, nodding to the hallway.

They walked to the next doorway, and she smelled the

roses before she entered. The flowers were the first thing she noticed when she walked in—a big vase of them sitting on a side table.

"Roses are for here," he whispered behind her. "Jasmine is for there. I wanted to be clear about the flowers. I know how much significance you put on them."

He knew roses meant love while jasmine held a rich legacy. It was the flower of home and of welcome. He wanted her to welcome him back into her home, back into her heart. The gesture grabbed her throat, and she nodded. Hadn't she chosen those pastries from her homeland to convey the message that she wanted to offer him the sweetness of life again? They were both awash in romantic subtext.

"The guesthouse is to the right down on the cliffs," he continued, his voice mesmerizing. "Do you see it?"

The single-story Payne's gray house was small but perfect. Bay windows flanked the sides, and a trio of windows marked the front of the building. The door was a rich ochre, and she could already see it opening to welcome her.

"When we finally make love," he said from behind her, "I want you to smell jasmine everywhere. I want your every breath to take it in and then later remind you what it feels like when we come together."

She could already smell the thick, lush scent. Her hands clenched as she fought the images his words were inspiring in her mind. She could see them sneaking out of the main house and making love in that quaint little house, his green eyes always on her.

"Francesca, look at me."

Turning to him, she stood tall under his intense regard.

"I can't answer your questions if you don't let me in. I'm scared too. Don't...torture us both any longer than necessary."

The agony of longing was a torture she well knew. "I hear you."

Crossing to her, he kissed the top of her head and then retreated to the doorway. "I'll let you settle in."

The walls and furnishings were done in the same sea blues and grays, which only made the soft aubergine blanket on the end of the bed and the violet throw on the winter white chaise lounge by the window pop more. Purple was her favorite color.

"Do you like it?"

His quiet voice surprised her, and she turned slowly toward the door. "You said you were going."

"I couldn't." His face fell for a moment, and the years apart seemed to crease his usually youthful face. "It's good to have you here, Francesca. I thought you might like to curl up with your work on the chaise lounge. You always did like those girly couches."

"You were kind to remember," she said, her voice also laced with an emotion she couldn't control.

His smile was bittersweet. "I told you. I always remember."

He remembered the past, yes, but how did he see their future? She hoped he would tell her, here in the shadow of the jasmine-scented cottage.

But he simply said, "I'll see you downstairs," and turned and walked away.

She walked over to the roses and plucked one out of the vase. Walking over to the window, she surveyed the vast ocean. The white waves curled into the watery depths with an unstoppable power, the same power Quinn seemed to still possess over her heart.

She felt like she'd come home, and the feeling was as bittersweet to her as his memories seemed to be to him.

CHAPTER 9

WHEN FRANCESCA ENTERED HIS OFFICE, QUINN STOOD immediately, noting how she'd changed into ecru wool trousers and a red cashmere sweater. He figured his tan slacks and white dress shirt rolled up to his elbows would pass muster with her usual elegance. "I'm glad we agree on dressing more casually. I don't want to restructure anything with my tie strangling me."

"We have no audience except the chaperones," she said, her eyes scanning his space. "Besides, you used to be more creative when you were relaxed. I hope that's still the case."

"Man, so do I."

He came around the desk and noted the way her posture changed, stiffening. She thought he was going to take her into his arms. And yes, he did want to do that, but she'd made it perfectly clear she wasn't ready. Besides, they would need to remain mostly professional to complete the restructuring.

"As you and other family members have pointed out," he continued, "my grouch factor is off the charts. I *need* to relax. Will you rub my temples?" They'd always teased each other, and he wanted to lighten the air between them.

Thankfully, she laughed as he'd hoped. "You can call a masseuse for that. Now, where are we working?"

He gestured to his office. "I thought here. Hell of a view."

"No, this is your space. We need a shared space. How about the guesthouse?"

Was that a twinkle in her eyes? He was so down with more teasing. "No way. That's reserved, as I mentioned."

"But it's not in use at the moment," she said with a challenge in her beautiful violet eyes. "Shame to waste the jasmine."

He gave her a heated stare, already able to smell the jasmine as he tasted her. "It stays reserved until it's utilized. Full time."

Her nostrils flared, and the desire between them scorched the air. Good. He wasn't the only one thinking about what they would do to each other in the guesthouse.

"I should have anticipated this," Quinn said, knowing when a retreat was needed. "Okay, what kind of a space do you have in mind?"

"A cozier one than this. Although it's impressive, you reign here. I need a space where we meet as equals."

"Other than the bedroom? Don't glare. You know it's true. But I see your point. You want a neutral but cozy place. Follow me."

He waved at Uncle Arthur and Aunt Clara as he walked out of the office. They were seated on the sofa. She was knitting something in peacock blue, and his uncle was reading on his tablet. Alice waved to him from the kitchen, where she was working with Hargreaves, and he had to laugh at her audacity.

"I was wondering where these stairs went," Francesca

said as they climbed down.

"It's a partial lower level with a deck. I had the decorator treat it like an entertaining space. This has to work because I don't have any other options."

The open room had a modest bar on the far side, but the three cream leather couches in front of the floor-to-ceiling windows anchored the room. He'd often imagined having his family over to watch the sun go down. He'd also hoped to have new friends. Maybe a woman. But he'd never watched the sun go down except on moving day, and he realized if he continued like this, the space would continue to go unused.

"It will be fine," she said, walking forward and putting her hand on the couch facing the windows. "This will be my office chair."

He wanted to roll his eyes. "I'll take the one beside you so I won't be distracted by the view." That way he could give her his total focus, which was what he wanted anyway. "Anything else?"

"We'll need a flip chart and eraser board. I'll have Alice see to them if you don't mind."

"Fine. What else?"

"That's it. How about some tea? Do you have tea stocked down here?"

He scoffed. "It's a bar, not a coffee shop."

She gave him a regal look that drove him wild.

Running to the edge of the stairs, he yelled, "Hey, Alice. Can you come here for a minute? Your mistress calls."

"Mistress?" Francesca arched her brow.

He couldn't help but grin. "You're totally the mistress."

"You rang," Alice said, descending the stairs. "Francesca, what do you need?"

She gave her order, which included the office supplies as well as the items for a full tea and coffee service. Saluting Quinn, Alice headed back upstairs.

"She's not your assistant, Quinn," Francesca said,

sitting down on her office "chair" like a grand lady. "You'd best remember that."

"I was teasing you," he said, crossing to his own seat. "I might be more grouchy than I used to be, but you're more formal. What happened?"

"It's called professionalism," she said as if he didn't have an MBA from the London Business School.

He laid his arm on the top of the couch and faced her. "No, it's more than that. I can't imagine it's easy to keep business moguls in line. I remember what you said about Alice's experience as a chaperone. You've had trouble before? Overtures?"

She waved a hand. "Of course. I handle it by being clear on the rules and keeping everything orderly. I hope you'll comply. It will make things easier."

"While we're working, I'll comply." He shrugged in response to her scrutiny. "I mean it, but I'm not sure I can promise more than that. How else am I supposed win you back? The kiss we had yesterday rocked both our worlds, but I don't need to tell you that. You're backing away because it was better than ever." He sent her a naughty wink.

"Moving on..." Her voice was all crisp professionalism. "Let's restate your goals for the consultancy as a way of kicking things off."

He knew what that meant: time to get down to business.

"Easy. I want to make Merriam Enterprises profitable and respected again."

She folded her hands in her lap. "Wonderful. Improving corporate performance and increasing stakeholder confidence will be the key pillars of our approach."

Pillars? God, he found it oddly hot when she talked corporate like that. "One more goal. I also want to create a senior office structure that will support me having a life. As in seeing my wife and kids daily."

Did she gulp? The gorgeous line of her throat changed

shape briefly in the late morning light filtering in through the windows. "Organizational structure comes *after* we've agreed on the new strategic direction and functional re-alignment."

He gave her his most charming smile. "I know. I only wanted to be clear what some of my *personal* goals are as the CEO."

She unfolded her hands and laid them on her thighs like she was trying to ground herself. Good. She understood his intentions, and they hadn't failed to make an impression.

"Your goals are important in that they impact the leadership of the company."

"I don't have enough time to do anything well. Neither did Connor."

Her eyes grew veiled. "Your father and his predecessors did, however. What do you attribute that to?"

He felt the lash of misplaced pride even as he reminded himself that his father had never been home for his family. "Maybe they were giants of men. Maybe they didn't want it any different or know it could be different. Maybe the demands were different before email became so common and the speed of doing business ramped up. Doesn't matter. I'm certain I can't be a CEO and have a life, but I want to try. Do you understand what I'm saying here?"

You asked me how this would work, and I'm telling you. I want to have enough time to be with you.

"I understand, and it's noted." She sat up straighter, almost fidgeting, which was unlike her. "Let's talk about functional areas."

And so they did, only pausing when Alice brought down the tea and coffee service and set it up discreetly in the corner while Francesca continued to drill him. He'd forgotten her incredible ability to circle back to a point and recast it in a new way. To coax out someone's thoughts and feelings.

They both knew he had to reverse Connor's stance on

new offshore drilling acquisitions. Those sites brought in some of the most reliable and largest profits Merriam Enterprises could lay claim to. The company had been founded on offshore oil, and like they both understood, investors were comforted by the bread and butter.

But it gave him heartburn to think about it.

"You're worried about how this will make Connor look," she said out of the blue. "Don't. He's not in this game anymore. Besides, he'll understand on some level."

"You a mind reader?" His response was terse even to his ears.

"Only when it comes to you," she said quietly.

That cheered him in a moment of despair. "I'm sorry. I don't want to damage his rep. That's my problem, though, and my hesitation to act is probably how we got here. Let's move on. I'm committed to reversing his decision."

"Do you envision bringing it to the board?" she asked.

He set his ankle on his knee. "No. He did it unilaterally, and somehow I think it would be a show of strength to undo it the same way."

"I agree." She poured them both tea—a fragrant Earl Grey, which he'd only ever drunk with her. "Now, let's talk about what I expect will be a sticking point."

His shoulders were already knotting. "Shoot."

"You agree restructuring around oil is the way to go, yes?"

"Yes. Absolutely."

She veiled her eyes. "There were some tremors in the oil market this morning after China released more information about this pneumonia-like virus they're dealing with. Do you know of it?"

"I've read the reports too, and my aunt and Hargreaves have been following it. I think they're making too much of it. So far, the virus seems small and contained."

"It does." Her voice was modulated.

What was she getting at? He tilted his head down to try

and catch her gaze. "I checked oil prices at our last break. They took a tumble, but that's not a surprise. The Saudis released a statement saying they're confident the Chinese will contain the virus. You know what that means."

"Yes. They were trying to calm the market. So, you're not concerned?"

"When you're in the oil business—and my family has been for decades—there's always some volatility. But the world's system is built on oil. You have to ride the wave."

"Then we're on track for restructuring around oil." This time she met his gaze directly. "No hesitations?"

"None."

"Good," she said decidedly. "Then we need to talk about what to do with the skincare line."

Acid poured into his stomach. Now he understood. "You mean Caitlyn's enterprise."

She positioned her teacup calmly in her lap. "Not exclusively, although she did exceed profit expectations—and in very short time frame, I might add."

"Her perfume took off." He was so damn happy for her. "She's preparing to roll out the men's cologne as we speak with her fiancé, Beau Masters, as the spokesperson."

"He was also the spokesperson for the women's line." She drank her tea before continuing, "Was that brilliant marketing idea hers or yours?"

"All hers. I only approved the budget."

Her eyes were narrowing, and he felt like that damn python was around his diaphragm again.

"A hefty budget, I might add."

"Thirty million is hefty?" Okay, he knew it was.

"You're fortunate her endeavor worked out so well." She took another sip of tea, and he felt like she was using the tea to pace the conversation, throwing out grenades one sip at a time.

"Dammit, this is about Flynn's wife, Annie, isn't it? You know she merged her boutique skincare line with Merriam.

What you don't know is that she wants to be one of us in business. She's got damn good products too."

She traced the rim of her cup. "Valentina wouldn't have agreed to be the spokesperson otherwise."

Having an international model was bank, and they both knew it. "So what's the problem?" he asked, even though he already knew what she'd say.

"You'll have to expend a lot of upfront capital for a wide launch of Annie's products. Capital you could use elsewhere. There's also the issue of corporate identity. Do you want Merriam to be known for oil *and* skincare? Without the pharmaceutical division, you don't have enough functional legs for this to make sense to investors, Quinn."

He lurched off the couch and stalked to the window. "You want me to sell off the skincare line? Jesus. You might as well ask me to cut out my sister's and my new sister-in-law's hearts."

He heard her set her teacup on the coffee table. Moments later, her hand was rubbing the tension in his lower back. "I told you this would be hard, Quinn."

Caitlyn's cheery face filled his mind. "That lavender farm and perfume enterprise means everything to my sister. Hell, Annie gets the same glow whenever she talks about one of her products." He'd used her new shampoo for men last night, and now here he was discussing the possibility of selling off her company.

"Let's table this for now. We have plenty of time to discuss it."

Her hand left his back, but he caught it before she walked away. "I need you to help me find a way to keep them, Francie. Merriam is a *family* company, dammit. That's our bread and butter too. If we aren't that, then..."

He wasn't sure what the hell they were fighting for. Only he and Trevor would be working for it then. How could he accept that?

"Negotiating with Annie and bringing her into the

family business was one of the best damn things I'd done in a long time." He cursed softly. "Francesca, it gave me hope for the future. I can't give that up. I certainly can't betray them. We have to find another way. You're the wiz. I'm trusting you to find it."

When she faced him, her eyes were dark with sorrow. "I knew it would hurt, and I'm sorry, but I had to bring it up. It's my job, Quinn."

"I can't do it," he rasped. "I'd rather file for bankruptcy and start again if that's the case."

She nodded briefly. "Okay, we'll find another way. But Quinn... You're not making this easy."

"You told me you knew how personal this was. I'm telling you what I can and can't accept and asking you to use that brilliant mind of yours to figure something out."

"I will do my best," she said softly.

The pull to kiss her—to find comfort in her mouth—overwhelmed him.

"We should take a break," she said, her eyes tracking to his lips, but footfalls sounded on the stairs and they both glanced over.

They separated, and he watched as Alice hefted one of the flip charts while Hargreaves carried the dry-erase board.

"Perfect timing," Francesca said, stepping farther away.

Quinn wasn't sure he agreed, but he wouldn't have wanted Francesca to kiss him out of compassion. Plus, he needed to put aside this raw feeling from their talk about the skincare line.

Francesca pointed to where she wanted them placed. "Set them to the side, please. I would hate to obstruct the view."

Alice went over to help Hargreaves once she'd positioned her equipment, Quinn noted, and the man didn't bristle as she shifted the metal legs out at a greater angle. He only smiled. Alice Bailey had won him over. That was fast.

It was also telling... Hargreaves' dignity usually got ruffled if any Merriam dared to carry a drink from the kitchen into the dining room or heft their own luggage into the house. Apparently Miss Bailey was different. Was it because she was an assistant as well? No, that was genuine fondness on his face. Interesting.

"We've been wanting to play Pictionary," he told them, rubbing his hands together to shake off the lingering sickness in his midsection. "Anyone have an idea for how to draw the word *inscrutable*? Francesca has been acting that way for the past two hours."

Maybe resuming their teasing would right his balance.

Alice shared a look with Francesca before uncorking a blue marker and starting to draw a shockingly good rendition of her boss. "How about this?"

"A beautiful likeness, Miss Bailey, if I may say," Hargreaves said.

"That's incredible," Quinn said.

"I told you she was brilliant." Francesca clapped her hands briefly. "Thank you!"

Alice quietly arranged the pens in a jar. "Wait until you see what Hargreaves and I have planned for dinner."

"I thought you were trading nights cooking," Quinn said, partially alarmed by the conspiratorial gleam in their eyes.

"We talked about it over tea and decided it would be fun to cook together. It's so nice to be around someone else who loves food. In fact, Francesca, I've talked him into going to the private chocolate cooking class. I figured you would be okay with it."

"I'll be handling the expense myself, Miss."

"I'm happy to cover it," Francesca said, a soft smile on her face. "I'm glad you two have become friends."

"Me too! Come on, Hargreaves. We have plans to execute. We'll leave you two."

When she reached for the drawing of Francesca to rip it off, Quinn lurched forward. "No! I'll...handle it."

Alice froze, and Hargreaves cleared his throat. They both nodded and left quickly.

Great, he'd made an idiot of himself. He carefully tore the paper. "I couldn't let her throw it away. It's a memento of our first day working together." It was also Francesca's beautiful face, which he couldn't bear to see destroyed.

Her hand rose to her mouth to cover the emotion there, but her eyes told him everything he needed to know. She was touched and the earlier desire to kiss her charged the room.

"I should have asked her to draw *you* at your grouchiest then, since you've already had some moments today," she teased, a smile peeking around that luscious mouth.

"Inscrutable and grouchy. We're a pair."

"But we're making good progress." She checked the discreet Cartier watch on her wrist. "It's four o'clock. How about we go until six? Then we can see what surprise Alice and Hargreaves have worked up for dinner. I assume you meant for us to eat together with your family every night except Sunday. If not, Alice and I could dine down here should you wish to be alone with them."

He pursed his lips at the challenge in her tone. "I was hoping you and I could eat alone. A working dinner. But since I know you'll balk, everyone can eat together. It'll be like a big, happy family."

Her violet eyes widened uncharacteristically for a moment. "They're your family, Quinn. Although I find them all lovely."

He set the drawing down on the edge of his couch, but he left it there, preferring the original to the drawing, and sat down beside her. "Admit it. You like them."

"J.T. is utterly charming." She smoothed her hair behind her right ear, making his mouth water. "When he was talking with such passion about the new van Gogh he'd acquired for the museum, I wondered how you two could be related."

He laughed and kicked his feet out beside her. "You dragged me to every museum in London just because you could."

Her laughter warmed him, sending away the final tightness in his midsection. "Yes, I did."

Flirting clearly wasn't off-limits, thank God. Turning, he looked her directly in the eyes. "You still have that power, you know."

The rise of her décolletage, as she called it, told him he'd altered her breathing. "I need a break. I'll see you in fifteen."

She was halfway across the room when he called, "Strategic retreat?"

When she looked back, her face was as inscrutable as Alice had drawn it. "Sometimes they're necessary to keep the peace."

He rose and picked up her drawing. Even with the harshness of the blue pen, Alice had managed to make the lines of her face elegant yet bold. God, she was breathtaking. The hairs on the back of his neck rose suddenly, and he turned slowly around.

Francesca was standing at the foot of the stairs, watching him. She was so still she reminded him of an elegant statue at one of her museums, but there was nothing stony about her expression. Her eyes were full of longing, full of love. He remembered how she'd rubbed his back during their difficult discussion about the skincare line. She'd naturally reached out to him in comfort. Right now, he wanted something else, something primal and equal that would have them both begging for more.

His body tensed in the charged silence. He waited for her to say something. To fly across the room to him. To do something. Then the line of her throat moved, and she was turning and heading up the stairs quickly.

CHAPTER 10

INDIAN FOOD!

Not again. Not on the first night of this new assignment. Arthur's luck couldn't be that bad.

He detoured to Hargreaves, who was leaving the kitchen with two of the endless plates on the counters, the smell of curry, cumin, and sesame ripe in the air. "You couldn't give a guy a break, could you?"

The man bowed, but not as stiffly as usual. "When Miss Alice learned we shared a passion for Indian cuisine, her excitement was infectious. I could hardly deny her desire to cook tonight's meal with me. I have never shared such an enjoyable cooking experience. She joked and laughed and spoke in two or three languages with me. It was...uplifting."

Arthur was speechless at the man's brief pause. Hargreaves might be laconic, but he was never unsure of his words. "You really like her, don't you?"

His smile moved past sardonic to warm. "I imagine

that cooking with Alice is what it would have been like if I'd had a granddaughter."

Good Lord. The girl had turned Hargreaves to mush. And over Indian food, no less. "You need a son or daughter to have a granddaughter, Hargreaves."

That quizzical brow went up straight away. "I am well aware of that, sir." Another unusual hesitation followed, but it was clear he hadn't finished speaking. "But... Is that feeling one you share with your granddaughters?"

"I've never made naan with them, so I can't say." Then he nudged Hargreaves because the man's question had been genuine and he didn't want to tease him too much. "Yes, that feeling of comradery is what I have with Jill and Meredith."

"Thank you for confirming it, sir." He gave a grander bow this time. "Please excuse me. The food is ready. You might call the others."

He didn't think squawking that dinner was ready would be appreciated, but he fetched everyone. Well, he shouted down the stairs to where Quinn and Francesca were working. He didn't expect to interrupt anything, but he didn't want to go in blind and catch them all tangled up. When he led Clara to the table, he realized he had to play his usual role, if only for old time's sake.

"Does no one like me?" He gestured to the Indian food. "Alice, I thought you and I were getting on swimmingly."

"I didn't know that you didn't like Indian food, Arthur," Alice said, pausing as she set Hargreaves' famous naan bread on the table.

He jerked his thumb at Clara and Hargreaves, the co-conspirators. "They did."

Clara had the gall to laugh, but he supposed that's why he loved her. Hargreaves gave as close to a smirk as his manners allowed him.

"I'd be happy to make you something else, Arthur." Alice bit her lip. "Some pan-roasted chicken and green beans maybe?"

Clara pulled Alice down into the chair next to her. "Nonsense. He eats what's on the table. His bark about Indian food is all bite."

"Goldarn it, woman, that's not the phrase. It's 'his bark is worse than his bite.'"

She patted his hand. "That's what I said, dear."

He picked up his whiskey. At least he had a good drink. "She mixes her phrases up all the time. Francesca, may I assume you like Indian food? Quinn, from that silly grin on your face, I have my answer."

Of course, Quinn had a silly grin because Clara had orchestrated the seating to place him next to Francesca. Personally, Arthur would have seated them across from each other. That way they could make eyes at each other, although to be fair, they were doing a pretty good job of that anyway. He wondered how they'd gotten through their workday. The air between them smoldered, as if they were a five-alarm fire.

"I love it, Arthur," Quinn's lady said, "but you should have what pleases you. Really, Alice would be happy to fix you something."

"Not on your life," Clara said, "but it's a sweet offer. His bluster about Indian food is an ongoing joke in the family. You should have seen him when he had Indian food in Kenya. He was inconsolable. Weren't you, dear?"

Two could play this game, and he rubbed his foot against her calf, letting her know it. "I cried into Hargreaves' naan all night under the starry sky."

Quinn laughed and reached for the bread, tearing off a piece and dipping it into the plum sauce between him and Francesca. "I didn't know about this joke. I like it."

"I'll bet," Arthur said, watching with glee as Quinn extended the bread to Francesca.

"Your favorite," he added with a heated gleam in his eyes.

She leveled him an impressive glare, what Arthur would call a set down. "I can feed myself, thank you."

He whistled. "I was only trying to be a gentleman."

"I'll bet," she said dryly. "Hargreaves, your naan is truly heavenly. Equal to the best I've had anywhere, from London to Delhi."

"Thank you, Miss," he said, looking a bit stiff at the far end of the table.

Alice had suggested she and Hargreaves could eat at the kitchen table, but Clara had talked her into eating with the family. Which had induced Hargreaves to do the same. Personally, Arthur liked having Hargreaves at the table. It made him feel weird to have the man cook for him and then eat alone. Arthur couldn't care less about butler etiquette. Hargreaves had become family, after all. Not that he'd ever allow it to be acknowledged out loud.

"It's good to have you at the table, Hargreaves," he said, picking up a piece of naan and biting into it. "The bread isn't half bad. Of course, it's not Margie's famous cinnamon rolls."

"Of course not, sir," the man said without blinking. "It's naan."

Alice and Francesca laughed. Quinn's shoulders were shaking.

Clara ran her foot up his calf this time, her blue eyes twinkling with mirth. Oh, she was so going to get it tonight, the little minx.

"Your butter chicken is delicious, Alice," Clara said, making a humming noise after taking a bite. "How did you learn to cook?"

"Cooking was my way of traveling, I suppose. When I was in high school, I became friends with a few exchange students. We had them over for dinner a few times, but my mother, being a smart woman, realized they might miss their own food. One day, she offered her kitchen to them, and that was it. I learned by helping them, and it kinda stuck. I love trying out new dishes. Heck, I even thought about becoming a chef, but I loved business, hospitality, and travel more, which is why I love working for Francesca."

"We're both lucky," the elegant woman said with a smile as warm as Hargreaves'.

"It's so wonderful to have someone like Hargreaves around," Alice continued. "He enjoys it as much as I do, and he has so much experience."

"Indeed, Miss Bailey. Today's preparations were most enjoyable. I look forward to our next adventure." The old coot continued to beam that warm smile. Yes, Hargreaves was having a granddaughter moment for sure.

"Hargreaves and I are going to also take a San Francisco breadmaking class besides the chocolate one. Isn't that right?" Alice elbowed Hargreaves, who cleared his throat but smiled. "It's going to be so awesome. Sourdough and this kind of magical bread from the area called Dutch crunch."

What kind of name was that? "I hope I won't break my teeth on that Dutch one. Sounds dangerous."

"Oh, don't worry, Arthur, your teeth will be totally safe." Alice served herself some chai tea, then topped off Hargreaves' cup and extended the carafe to Francesca, who declined, picking up her white wine.

Everyone was settling in nicely together, but Arthur could feel Quinn chomping at the bit. Who could blame him? In his shoes, Arthur wouldn't give a fig about small talk—he'd want to be alone with Clara.

Arthur waited until the end of the meal to gesture to the windows. "The moon is out. How about we take a walk along the beach? Clara's always telling me that people in Europe walk after their meal." God, he hoped the sea air wouldn't be too cold, but he'd suck it up as a matchmaker.

"Like you don't know how Europe works," she muttered, but the idea took hold of her and she pepped up. "A walk sounds wonderful. Come on."

Standing, she took Alice's arm gently, and the young woman rose with her, biting back a smile. Yeah, Miss Bailey knew what was up.

"I could walk. Francesca?"

She checked her watch, Arthur noted. "Surely you aren't planning on working more," he said. "It's after eight. Quinn isn't that much of a task master, is he?"

Her smile was downright captivating when she looked her fill at Arthur's nephew, who turned in his chair, practically radiating sex.

God, Arthur didn't need to see that.

"What say you?" he asked in a voice Arthur also didn't need to hear. "Am I so terrible?"

"Too soon to tell," she said, standing up and saving Arthur from bad dreams. "I'm happy to join the walk."

"Come on, you dear man!" Clara took his arm as if she could haul him out of his chair.

"Careful, sweetheart. This is special merchandise." He waggled his brows at her.

"Oh, you blab like no one else, but I love you." Her quick kiss had him patting her on the fanny. "Take my arm. Alice, if you'd take Hargreaves'. He's not the spring chicken he used to be."

"How kind of you to say so, Madam," he said, but he extended his arm grandly to Alice, who took it. "Miss Alice, it would be a pleasure."

"That leaves you two," Arthur said, sending Francesca a sly wink. "Quinn used to be cross-eyed as a child and sometimes still stumbles. We fear for his life when he walks alone."

Alice chortled. "That's a good one. Cross-eyed, huh?"

Arthur had to bite the inside of his cheek when Quinn capitulated and crossed his eyes in the most playful exhibit Arthur had ever seen from the man. My God, Quinn had an inner clown. What next? Miming? After Hargreaves' unusual display of emotion tonight and now this, Arthur wouldn't be surprised if lightning struck.

"I actually have a bracelet to call an emergency service in case I fall down," Quinn said seriously. "My brothers and sisters gave it to me one Christmas."

"They did?" Clara asked. "Oh, you poor boy. No wonder you stay in your office all the time."

Leave it to Clara to believe it. Arthur could tell her it was a joke later.

"Being that you're a danger to yourself, I suppose I could take your arm." Francesca batted her eyes at him playfully. "You really need to find that bracelet, though. I'd love to see it."

He pulled her to him, and the dance between them turned as hot as an Argentine tango. "I'll tear apart my drawers later looking for it. Care to help?"

"You're competent enough." She threaded her arm through Quinn's, maintaining a distance used back when waltzes were illegal. "Shall we?"

They put on jackets and left the house via the patio doors to the left of the dining room. There was a bite in the air, but it was pleasantly salty and crisp. Arthur had never lived by the sea, but he could feel the call of it. The waves crashing in the distance were primal and comforting. Nature knew what it was doing even if humans didn't sometimes.

Alice and Hargreaves were happily chatting away ahead of them on the moonlit beach. Quinn and Francesca lingered behind, silent yet still a powerful presence.

"You did good with this walk tonight, dear," Clara murmured, resting her head against his shoulder. "I've never seen Hargreaves so happy."

"Except with you," Arthur reminded her.

"No, it's different with me. I suppose it always will be. But the way he acts with Alice... I never thought to ask him if he regretted not having a family of his own, if he felt the lack like I did." She tightened her grip on his arm.

Her pain over not having children had been hard on her, but she'd been filling her heart with these Merriam children and the young people in the village they worked with in Kenya. Had Hargreaves wished for children? If so, he was glad the man had found someone to help fill that void.

"It's beyond dear," Clara said, sniffing a little.

"Do I need to be worried about you falling for Hargreaves finally, my dear, now that he's gone mushy?"

She socked him gently like he knew she would, making him laugh, startling a night-feeding seagull.

"How about our other couple?" Clara looked over her shoulder with as much finesse as an elephant in an elevator. "They're obviously attracted to each other, but they've got a ways to go. Quinn's willingness to act silly around her is a good sign, I think."

"How so?"

"It shows he doesn't feel the need to be so serious all the time with her. He can let his guard down." Clara stopped and cupped his face. "Like I can do with you."

"Just don't cross your eyes at me," he said, which only made her do so.

He laughed. "Now, I'll have to buy you that bracelet."

"No, you have to kiss me to make them uncross."

She leaned her chin up and he did as she asked.

"There. All better."

"Now, how about we head back to the house and you can kiss me some more?" Her blue eyes caught the moonlight. "I think we've done enough to bring these two together for one night. The rest is up to them."

When it came to love, you could lead two people to each other, but what came next was always up to them.

CHAPTER 11

QUINN HAD PLANS FOR FRANCESCA ON THEIR FIRST SUN-day off.

Alice and Hargreaves had just left for the chocolate making class, and he knew an opening when he saw one.

In six days, they'd gone through the entire oil and gas portfolio, plugging holes and trimming operations and expenses right and left with a scalpel. The profit projections from the changes eased his blood pressure some, but they still had plenty to do.

The only lingering uneasiness was the continued news from China about this virus and its effect on oil prices. The market was running a bit scared, but he and Francesca still believed the market would level out, and Trevor, whom he'd talked to mid-week, had said the same. Still, the news was disturbing: China had quarantined sixty million people. What did that even look like? It was crazy, and he and his aunt and uncle had discussed it over breakfast this morning with growing alarm. Francesca hadn't joined them, unfortunately, likely sending a message that she planned to have a Quinn-free day.

Not on her life.

Her door was closed, which was also a message, but he knocked anyway. It took her so long to come to the door, he'd started to wonder if she would.

She was wearing casual cream pants and an asymmetrical black cashmere wrap over a low-cut shirt. Her style had always turned him on, and he cautioned himself to be patient. They'd settled into a pattern over the last week, ending each evening with a walk, arm in arm, strolling along the beach without saying anything. They'd always been able to be silent together, to savor each other's company without the need for constant conversation, and there was solace in remembering that. In experiencing it again.

But it was so hard to come back to the house after one of those walks and part ways with her. Just like he struggled not to greet her with a kiss every morning. Every day he was reminded about all the things he loved about her... and was introduced to new things to love too, like the sensual enjoyment she displayed drinking a blue tea Alice had discovered for her in Paris. He hadn't known tea could be blue, but he had to admit it wasn't bad. More importantly, she'd shared it with him, further strengthening the bond growing between them. Back in London, they'd always savored introducing each other to new things. He'd taken to Saville Row suits because of her, and she'd fallen in love with pinot noirs from California.

"Did you see the report about the first person outside of mainland China dying from this virus?" she said without preamble.

"In the Philippines," he responded. "Aunt Clara, Uncle Arthur, and I discussed it over breakfast. We all agree the news continues to be alarming." His aunt had freaked out a touch, and his uncle had needed to put his arm around her. He'd never seen fear in her eyes before, and it had shaken him.

"Closing factories in China will continue to have an effect on oil prices."

Was there worry in her eyes too? She looked nowhere near as alarmed as Aunt Clara, thank God. He couldn't handle that. "I know that, but it's short-term. They'll get this virus under wraps and things will go back to normal."

"I hope so. Now, what do you need?"

I missed you. "I see files out on your chaise." He gestured to them. "You said you take Sundays off."

"*We* take Sundays off."

"Your brain needs to rest, and so does mine."

Layoff plans were up next, and he was already dreading it. They hadn't finalized which divisions he'd be merging, but they were close. Of course, they still had to figure out how to keep the skincare line. He knew she was working on it and trusted that.

"My brain is planning to rest shortly, don't you worry." She brushed her black hair back over her shoulder, and he fought the urge to thread his fingers through it.

"I have a better idea. Come to Ferrari-Carano with me today for a private wine tasting. Alice and Hargreaves are off on their own adventure. Why shouldn't we have one?"

"That is not the agreement." Her regal stare had him giving her his best glower.

"Oh, come on. You love wine, and before you make any decisions about us, we should spend time together outside of work. We've already established we work well together." So much so he didn't want to contemplate their time coming to an end.

"You have been on your best behavior," she agreed, "and it hasn't gone unnoticed. Even at evening meals you remain incredibly amiable around the chaperones."

Like he'd had a choice, but if he had to "suffer" them, at least they were entertaining. Aunt Clara had announced she was in charge of after-work cocktails, and she presided over the time like a grand dame of Paris. Uncle Arthur grumbled about everything from the news to the smell of Indian food in the house. Much to his umbrage, Hargreaves and Alice had made it for lunch twice this week in addition to dinner that first evening. The dynamic duo continued to be a surprise, prepping food elbow to elbow in the kitchen and laughing while they sampled one of the new cocktails they'd concocted.

"Then coming with me today seems safe, right?" He leaned against the doorway. "I promise I won't touch you unless you ask me."

Her mouth quirked. "No need to worry about that quite yet."

How many times had they looked at each other this week? Too many to count, and both of them, he knew, had been thinking about that kiss in the kitchen—and a hell of a lot more. Whenever they linked arms for their walk, he could feel a frisson of tension go through her from that simple contact. Still, she'd made her boundaries clear. She had to come to him.

"But you're thinking about it. Admit it."

"I admit nothing—yet—but I am enjoying your company." Her smile was as sudden and welcome as the sun on a foggy day. "It's been good to see you again."

While the words were guarded, he considered it the highest praise. "I feel the same way. So come with me."

He took her hands spontaneously like he'd done in days past. She didn't fight him. "You'll love this place. It's very European. I want you to see how great this area is." Because he hoped they might live here together. He wanted to show her she could be comfortable in the Bay Area. Happy.

"Wine tasting in the country sounds lovely," she said, squeezing his hands briefly with a smile. "On one condition."

His mouth went dry at her capitulation. He could

already envision himself seated across from her as the wine tasting commenced, his eyes on her lush lips. "Name it."

"Invite Clara and Arthur. Maybe even J.T. and your parents."

He grimaced. "Not that. Come on, Francesca. You know you can be alone with me. It's a public place." Of course, he'd arranged for a private tasting for them.

"Still... That's the only way I'll agree. Take it or leave it."

She was fighting a smile. Yeah, she knew he'd do anything for her, and she was enjoying it.

"Fine. You win. I'll go ask Uncle Arthur and Aunt Clara, but I draw the line at a full family outing."

He'd never have a chance to get her alone. With the older couple, he could persuade them to go to the gift shop or something while he took her on a stroll on the spacious grounds of the vineyard. The weather was cool, but the sun was out.

"Let me know when it's time to leave." She already was closing the door on him, amusing herself plenty.

"See you in a bit, sweetheart," he said with a naughty wink.

When the door closed, he could have sworn he heard her laugh. Good. It would be easier to win her over if she was in a good mood.

Heading downstairs, he found his aunt and uncle sitting on the couch. She was knitting another sweater, this time in a rich purple, while he scowled at his tablet.

"You two up for a wine tasting today? I talked Francesca into coming."

Uncle Arthur let out a laugh. "But she insisted we join you, eh? She's warming up to you, but you have a ways to go yet. I told Clara you'd better make a move today with Alice out of the house. She's a dear girl, but she's always underfoot when you start stalking Francesca at cocktail hour."

He gave his own scowl. "I don't *stalk* her." Moving behind her while she looked out the large windows at the ocean wasn't stalking. He simply wanted to be close to her.

"You do a little, Quinn, dear, but it's understandable." Aunt Clara set aside her knitting. "When is this tasting?"

He'd arranged it for two and would have to call the winery to add two more guests momentarily. "Ferrari-Carano is over an hour from Stinson Beach. We could leave at one if that suits you." God, when had he become so accommodating?

"That suits us fine, dear. This one keeps mumbling at the news."

"It's depressing, Clara. Everything is going to hell in a handbasket. The more I read, the more I come around to your opinion about this virus, and I don't like it one bit."

"I don't know if it helps, Uncle, but when I talked to Trevor, he likened it to the way Ebola spreads quickly but never really moves beyond a small area, mostly in central Africa."

"It doesn't make me feel better. It's still killing people and wreaking damage right and left."

Aunt Clara patted his arm and kissed his cheek. "We know, dear. I've never been much for praying, but I'm finding it as much of a comfort as my knitting these days."

God, they all needed to get out of the house. He was done with all the doom and gloom. He had a woman to romance.

"I'll see you both in an hour."

Taking the stairs again, he strolled to Francesca's door and knocked. She opened it faster this time.

"We're leaving at one," he said. "No need to change. You look absolutely beautiful."

"Thank you, but I'll change if I decide to." She gave him one of her regal regards, although he thought he detected an edge of playfulness. "See you at one."

Feeling like a caged tiger, he retreated to his office and decided to call Connor, something he'd been putting off.

"Hey," his brother answered. "You're calling to tell me

that you're reversing my decision on new offshore drilling, right? It's the right move, Quinn."

When had his brother become so magnanimous? Right. Since he'd turned his life around. "It was hard to do."

"I imagine it was, but you're in charge. You have to make the best decisions to steer Merriam Enterprises back on track. I expect Francesca is repositioning everything around oil despite all the industry worries over this virus in China. That's a good call too. I'm sorry I left things in such a state. I'm still working on forgiving myself for that."

Forgiving himself? Man, it choked him up to hear that. Connor had already been through enough suffering and grief. "You just be happy. Keep doing good things out there. We've got this."

"You say 'we.' How is it going on the personal front with Francesca? Unless that's too personal."

"She's still deciding. The chaperones are never far away."

"That matchmaker trio has had a better streak than most professional athletic teams. Trust in them."

Oddly, he did, which was why he hadn't balked too much about including them in the wine tasting. "Will do. You guys good?"

"We're terrific. I feel like a different man. Louisa's the best thing that's ever happened to me, and I'm so glad she feels the same way about me. She says hi, by the way. Can't wait to see you at the wedding. You planning on asking Francesca? Mom, Dad, and J.T. said they loved her. I know the rest of us will too."

The family telephone game was alive and well. No shock there. He expected Aunt Clara was sharing updates about him and Francesca in her weekly check-ins with his siblings. But none of his brothers or sisters had texted or called him about it. None of them had wished him good luck. It had been so different with Flynn. Clearly, his siblings felt more reserved with him, and hell, it was his own fault. Maybe it was time to turn that around as well.

Silence hung on the line, and he remembered his brother had asked him a question. "I'm giving her a little more time before I ask," he said.

She could turn him down, after all.

No, he wouldn't think like that. He had to convince her to give him a second chance before the consultancy was over.

"I know you'll figure it out. All right, Louisa and I need to run. Her dad and brother are having us over for a bite. See you, bro."

"See you, man."

When he hung up, he took a moment to feel relief. Then he called J.T., thinking it would be good to connect with him. They'd been getting closer since he'd agreed to help out at Merriam. The call went to voicemail after a few rings, and moments after he set his phone down, he heard it ring again and picked it up.

"Sorry, Caroline's here and we were... You get the picture. What's up?"

He started laughing. "I apologize for interrupting. You go back to what you were doing."

His brother laughed too, and laughing together felt surprisingly good, even if it was only over the phone. "When Caroline got here, Mom told us we could stay in our room the entire time if we wanted, and then she laughed until tears ran down her face. Dad did too. It was weird, but kinda great. Anyway, why are you calling? You've been good about staying on radio silence. Any reason for the break?"

Shit. What could he say? *I thought I'd reach out to you and try to have a personal conversation, but it turns out I don't know how.* "Not really. Only wanted to thank you again for helping out."

"Oh, shit. You're welcome. Your executive assistant's efficiency continues to boggle my mind. Marian's awesome, Quinn. I couldn't do without her."

"I'll give her a raise."

"And a bonus," his brother added. "How are the plans taking shape? The oil market is rocky right now, but that's only because this whole virus thing is weirding people out."

He didn't want to talk about it again. "We're mostly on track. I just told Connor I'm reversing his decision on new offshore drilling."

"How did he take that?" J.T. asked.

"Good, actually. He expected it. Told me it was the right move."

"It is."

"I'm glad you agree. Layoffs are coming up, which sucks, but we're going to keep it as minimal as possible."

He hadn't told Francesca yet, but he planned to forgo a salary until they turned things around as a way of keeping more staff. Would others in his family be willing to do the same? Maybe he needed to ask them after he had a better sense about the numbers. They all had plenty of money to live on, and preserving as many of their employees as possible was the right thing to do.

"I feel for you there. You'll figure out the best way to handle it. Everyone trusts you."

Again, emotion lodged in his throat. "Thanks, man. That means a lot. Now, go back to your woman."

"She says hi, by the way. Hopes to see you on one of her other visits before the wedding. We could pop over for dinner with the family or you could come here. I know you're busy—"

"Not that busy," he interrupted. "We'll arrange something for next weekend. I'll put Aunt Clara on it."

"She's a marvel. Says everything is on track over there. Loves Alice, and I totally agree. She's terrific."

Alice Bailey was continuing to impress the hell out of Quinn too. She'd conversed with Hargreaves in French while they made beef bourguignon the other night and then monologued about how she thought *Star Wars* was the best movie of all time, quoting the movie like a total geek and making everyone laugh at her Darth Vadar impression. Uncle Arthur had said she excelled in heavy breathing.

"Glad Aunt Clara thinks we're on track. Look, you need to go and so do I. Holler if you need anything."

"So far, it's been relatively easy if a little tense. People know your absence means an overhaul. Our employees aren't stupid."

Indeed. "No, they aren't. I'll see you soon, bro."

Then he thought about Francesca again, asking him to invite J.T. And it struck him that he might have been looking at things wrong. Maybe it would be nice if J.T. and Caroline came. They could all make an afternoon of it.

"Ah... You wouldn't want to go for a wine tasting this afternoon, would you?"

"I can go if you need me to, of course. Business related?"

Hadn't his brother just said he wanted to spend the weekend closed up in a bedroom with Caroline? Why would he want to forsake a day of nonstop sex for a triple date? "Forget it. Have fun with your wife. I'll be in touch."

"Wait! Were you suggesting we hang? Quinn, I swear I need a decoder ring or something to figure you out."

Embarrassment raced up his neck. "We can hang next weekend. I'm going now."

"First Connor and now you. The poets are so right about love. It makes a man—"

He clicked off the phone, sat back, and gave in to laughter. Hadn't he read Rumi to Francesca?

His phone signaled a text from J.T., and he laughed when he read: *Love you too, man. Can't wait to hang.*

A trio of hearts followed the words. He shook his head, but a smile lingered on his face after the laughter faded. He missed this, joking around with his brothers and sisters. He'd pulled away from them, away from the world even.

But J.T.'s quick and high-spirited agreement to cover for him had changed things. So had his talk with Connor at Flynn and Annie's wedding.

He thought about texting his other siblings, but if he piled it on too thick, they'd think he was cracking up after too much restructuring. He turned on his laptop and checked his email instead, although he was aware of how open his chest felt. J.T. was right. Love had changed him once, and it was happening again. Part of him worried what that might mean, but Connor had changed for love, and he sounded happier than ever. On some level, Quinn wanted that for himself.

When one o'clock rolled around, he strolled into the family room. Francesca was having a cup of tea with his aunt.

"Quinn, dear, are you ready to go? Francesca and I were just talking about Kenya. She's been on safari numerous times. I told her she should come and meet the Maasai tribe we work with."

He raised his brow at Francesca. "I'm trying to picture you roughing it."

"I can show you the pictures," she said in a playful tone. "Shall we go? Clara thought you might drive us all in the limo since Hargreaves isn't here."

"Not on your life. We're taking my Land Rover."

"Oh, you're such a fuddy-duddy like Arthur," Aunt Clara said, making an unladylike sound. "He's off in the bedroom after I sent him there for excessive news mumbling. I'll tell him we're ready."

His aunt patted his arm sweetly as she walked past him. Then he swept his gaze up and down Francesca. "I like your wine-tasting outfit." He let his gaze run over her silk dress in a shade of purple so dark it was almost midnight.

She held out her hands. "I felt like changing. You look happy. Were you talking to your family?"

He jerked back. "How did you guess?"

"You used to call them on Sunday afternoons when we were together." Her eyes narrowed. "Don't you remember? I'd hear you laughing in the other room, and sometimes, I'd even... Never mind."

Actually, he didn't remember any of this. "What?"

She looked away, and her beautiful profile stopped his heart.

"I'd curl up on your lap and listen to you talk to them." Her mouth curved. "I loved seeing you like that. Back then, I couldn't wait to meet them. Now that I have, I understand so much more about you."

The newness of his desire to reconnect with his family was gaining momentum in him, so he asked, "What do you understand?"

She made a face before saying, "Why you were so funny and at ease with yourself. Why you were so kind and generous to the people we met out in the world, everyone from doormen to bartenders. Why you seemed so grounded."

"You used to say those were the things that made you fall more in love with me," he said softly. "The little things that filled your heart."

The line of her throat moved. "You remember that, do you?"

He stepped in front of her and reached for her hand, which clasped his briefly. "I told you I remember everything."

"Except talking to your family, it seems." She studied him. "Has that changed?"

Part of him didn't want to tell her that some of the things she'd loved about him had fallen away. The other part knew he could keep no secrets from her. He didn't want any distance between them. "I kind of opted out, you might say. Living in London, away from family, made it hard to stay close."

Her brows narrowed. "But J.T. lived in Rome then, and Trevor was in Dublin. Clara tells me many of your siblings travel to Europe. London isn't the full reason."

Shit. "I don't want you to feel guilty, so believe me when I say it was my screwup. After we broke up, I let work become my life. I closed myself off."

Sure enough, guilt flashed in her eyes, along with sadness. "I'm sorry."

He hastily said, "But I'm committed to changing that. It really does make me happy to spend more time with them. I guess...that hasn't been a goal for a long time."

"Being happy isn't a goal. It's a state, Quinn. You used to be good at it. It was part of who you were."

That younger man who'd loved her with complete focus and passion hadn't needed happiness to be a goal. It had been his entire existence. "When I lost you, something changed inside me."

This time she reached for him, and her soft touch on his bicep was comforting and arousing all at once. "It did for me as well, and working with my father didn't help. Alice helped me reclaim my life."

He heard the emotion in her voice. He'd never imagined she'd been that affected, and the knowledge of it tightened his solar plexus. "I'm glad she helped you find it again," he said firmly. "I hate hearing you were miserable. So... Working with your father wasn't what you'd hoped?" Of course, she'd left, so he knew it couldn't have been.

"No," she said, looking down for a moment. "He... didn't need me as much as I thought. Oh, let's leave this. It's old territory."

Her troubled gaze told him the memories were only making her sadder, so he didn't press. "All right. How about we go have a nice time at the wine tasting?"

She caressed his arm, her fingers lingering on his bicep for a moment before she lowered her hand. "Perfect. I hear Arthur and Clara coming down."

She turned to the stairs to greet them, and the smile on her face took obvious effort. He needed to do something about that.

Something drastic.

"Aunt Clara, I've changed my mind. Where are the keys to the limo? I've decided I'm up for a new driving challenge."

His aunt's blue eyes shot to her hairline, and a hearty laugh burst out of his uncle.

"I was only kidding, Quinn."

And he'd bit the hook but good, but Francesca was smiling beautifully now, almost on the edge of laughter herself. He had to follow through. "I won't take no for an answer. How hard could it be?"

Damn hard, he discovered within the first ten minutes of the drive. He caught Francesca watching him in the rearview mirror, biting her cheek with laughter. His aunt had a healthy grip on his uncle, something that made him want to laugh out loud. And when they came to the next curve in the two-lane road on the way to the winery, he let the car sway a little extra since no one was around and then wove back toward the center.

"Oh, good heavens," he heard his aunt mutter.

"You asked for it, my dear," his uncle said. "Francesca, how you holding up over there? Hold on to the door handle now. CEO Hotstuff up there might be accomplished in business, but he's a novice when it comes to driving."

CEO Hotstuff? He didn't want to know. "I have a new appreciation for Hargreaves."

When Quinn wove again on the empty road, his aunt called out, "Oh, Quinn, can't you drive straight? Stay in between the lines, dear."

He started whistling in response. Francesca's gusty chuckle made the rest of the trip worthwhile, as did his aunt's sharp cries in the back whenever he took a wide turn.

When they arrived at the gorgeous Ferrari-Carano winery, he took in the view as he slowly cruised toward the parking lot. The main house had Italian villa stamped all over it, and the vineyard—all three thousand acres of it—spread out around and behind it. People were streaming up the path to the tasting room as he passed it and pulled into the lot. After choosing an end space to accommodate the limo's size, he cut the engine and exited, opening Francesca's door and helping her out.

"Hope you enjoyed the drive," he said with a wink.

"More than you can know." Her laughter was light and carefree, and he was proud of himself for having earned it. "Quinn Merriam, you surprised me. It was wonderful to see that you still could."

"Well, it wasn't wonderful for me," Aunt Clara said, coming out on the other side with the help of Uncle Arthur. "I'm driving home. I have no doubt I can do a better job."

His uncle patted her on the hip. "Let him drive home, Clara. He was yanking your chain the whole way."

"He could have gotten us all killed, and I won't have it." His aunt actually stomped her foot. "If you want to drive home, you need to do a halfway decent job."

He nodded as meekly as he could. "You have my word."

"Good," she mumbled. "Now get me a drink."

They all laughed as they walked to the tasting room. The air was cold but refreshing, and he found himself feeling like he could breathe again. When was the last time he'd taken a Sunday off? He couldn't remember.

"You were terrible back there," Francesca said, falling in step with him. "But very funny. I'm glad to see your wicked sense of humor again."

He took her arm, and she didn't pull away. "That's only the beginning of my wickedness."

She nudged him playfully. "Good thing we're in a public place."

Only he could be slightly wicked in public too. Seated at a dark wood table in the private wine tasting room, he lifted the first wine sample in a toast to his aunt and uncle. "Welcome to the matchmaker wine tasting." He winked at his aunt. "I thought you two might appreciate this one."

"Is it really called that?" she asked.

Their wine educator, Bruce, nodded and proceeded to tell them about the first wine they were tasting. Quinn pushed aside the white rectangle plate in front of him with assorted treats so he could position himself closer to Francesca.

She took a sip of her wine and leaned toward him. "Hargreaves confirmed to Alice that your aunt and uncle usually show up as *matchmakers*. According to him, they've helped all of your siblings find love. Chaperones, indeed, Quinn."

Hargreaves must be getting chummy with Alice to have told her something so confidential. Usually he was the soul of discretion. "Took you long enough," Quinn said, nudging her. "I figured you'd be onto me sooner than this."

"They haven't been too obvious," she said, swirling the wine in the glass and taking another sip. "I knew they wanted us to get together, but I didn't know they'd made a profession out of it."

"I had to bring in the big guns to get you back." He turned in his seat, needing to see her. "They're the best. Like my brother said earlier, their track record so far is flawless."

She finished off her tasting portion of wine and reached for one of the seasonal bites the chef had prepared for them, a savory and sweet amuse-bouche matched to each of the wines. "Alice was impressed."

He took another of the bites she'd just eaten and offered it to her since she'd displayed a discreet show of pleasure only he would catch. Francesca Maroun wouldn't moan aloud in public over food, although he had coaxed her to do so once in a corner booth at a London bistro over a decadent chocolate cake. Of course, he'd been feeding it to her and rubbing her thigh under the table then.

When she glanced at him, her suspicious look had

heat, he was pleased to see, as if she'd read his mind. "You try it," she said, smiling when the wine educator presented her with another wine to try.

His aunt and uncle were both talking to Bruce, and he suspected they were monopolizing his attention purposefully to give them some privacy.

"Too bad it's not chocolate cake, right?" He waited until he'd sampled it before saying, "You can see why their chef is one of the best in the field." He wished he could put his arm around her, much like his uncle was doing with his aunt.

"What is *your* best field, do you think?" she asked him, her tone that of Francesca Maroun, savior of businesses. It was obvious he'd rattled her, and she was hoping to push his mind down a different track.

He was having none of it. "Loving you."

Her sharp intake had him smiling, and she busied herself with swirling the wine and then breathing it in for a few seconds. Before she could engage the wine educator in conversation, Quinn leaned close to her ear and whispered, "Let me show you again how great I am at loving you."

The air between them suddenly seemed charged with electricity, as if a storm had blown in. Her glass tipped before she set it down with precision. "I want that, despite my concerns."

"I know you do," he said, his breath hot on her ear. "What's it going to take for you to see a future between us?"

"It's like we're still walking in a fog like the one outside your house in the mornings, and I can't see what's ahead," she said honestly. "I need to see it, Quinn."

He gave her some space and tasted the next wine. "You always look before you leap. I know that. But can't you just leap into my arms this time and trust that we'll figure it out together? I still want you to do what fulfills you, and I know you want the same for me."

"That's a love affair," she said, smiling again as the wine educator poured them another wine to taste. "That's not a marriage."

Her use of the word felt like a victory. "Isn't it?" he asked, putting his hand on her arm. "Look at me. Don't you see us meeting up at the end of the day and discussing work over dinner and then later in bed like we used to?"

Truthfully, they could do that now if she let them, and they both knew it.

"I *do* see that," she said, ignoring the next wine.

He found he didn't care to sample it either. "Then what?"

"My father has been pushing for me to return—to take over for him eventually—and while I'm not enchanted by the prospect, I haven't resolved myself against it."

"But you told me earlier working with him was miserable."

"I'm hoping to find peace with him. It's another of my New Year's resolutions."

Crap. He and her father were in the same resolution boat? He wanted to curse a blue streak.

"While I'm not prone to manipulation," she continued, "his hook about Maroun Industries employing forty thousand people is...compelling. A lot of people depend on it. I know you understand."

He *did* get it, but that didn't mean he liked it. "So you wait until you can take over outright since working with him is so hard on you. You probably have a few decades before it becomes an issue. Your father is as fit as a fiddle, and you've said he'll die in his office chair in his nineties if he has his way. Why worry about it now? Our kids could be completely grown before this happens. Hell, I might be retired by then."

He would be nearing sixty, so it wasn't inconceivable.

But she was already shaking her head, her expression agitated, her hands in fists in her lap. "I'm not willing to go into a long-term relationship before I decide what I intend to do about the business. You know better than anyone know what taking over Maroun Industries would mean."

His throat tightened. "Yeah, I do. Tell me more about how it was, working with your dad."

She reached for her wine and drank deeply before saying, "At first, everyone in the company patted me on the head, not expecting much both because I was a woman and Georges Maroun's daughter. I proved them all wrong, and once I'd established myself as a power player, I told my father I was striking out on my own. Some leaders always need to be in control. I couldn't continue working under those conditions."

Her voice sounded tortured. "You couldn't breathe with him."

She'd once used that phrase to explain why boarding school, however lonely, had come as a welcome escape from her father's dominant personality. "It made our relationship worse. After my mother died, the trips home from school were hard. I was alone most of the time, what with him working."

Her loneliness was palpable. "You always said it was easier to travel somewhere during your time off."

"Yes, but part of me was still hoping my father would change and we could have a happier relationship, the kind I had with my mother. With her gone, I'd hoped he would turn to me. But I'm a fool. He might say otherwise, but he still wishes I were a boy. Of course, he can't deny we're alike."

Quinn disagreed, but he kept his opinion to himself.

"My ability to see industry patterns and make moves comes from him, and he knows it."

Okay, he'd concede that much was true. He was more like his father too, although their similarities didn't end with their approach to business.

"Only he's too controlling and old-fashioned to listen

to me half the time. He lured me to work for him by saying he needed me—for the first time—and part of the reason I agreed was because I wanted his approval. It upsets me to admit that, but it's true. Alice says I need to give up my attachment to how I want my relationship with my father to be."

That struck a little close to home. Couldn't the same be said of Quinn pushing his vision for a future on Francesca? The thought depressed him. He finally put his arm around her, because he needed to—and he thought maybe she needed it too—and pressed a kiss to the top of her head. "Working with family can be challenging."

"And yet Clara tells me your sister Michaela and her fiancé work together, and so do J.T. and his wife. Your other siblings seem to be professionally supportive of their partners too."

Trevor helped Becca with her bed and breakfast when she needed him. Connor was helping Louisa expand the homeless shelter. Then there was Flynn, who couldn't tell enough people about Annie's skincare line. "Maybe that's something to remember when you're thinking about us and our future. On some level, you know I have that capacity too."

Her sigh was audible to his ears. "I suppose you do. All right, we've discussed this topic enough for the moment. How about we catch up on the wine tasting? Then you can drive us all home in the limo, staying in between the lines this time and not weaving all over the road."

"I thought I did admirably." He rubbed the tense muscles in her neck, just like she'd massaged his back the other day, then pulled away and reached for his glass. "What are we on now? A pinot?"

Flagging down their wine educator, he gave her the space to breathe and think things through.

Because he knew it was ultimately the only way to win her back.

CHAPTER 12

FRANCESCA WAS BEGINNING TO BELIEVE SHE OWED ARTHUR a case of whiskey for establishing their nightly walk along the beach. She'd come to look forward to the end of the evening meal, when she and Quinn would turn to each other. In his eyes, she always saw the same banked longing she felt pulsing within her. Taking his arm seemed to anchor them both.

At first it had surprised her that he didn't say much on their walks, but when she'd teased him about it, he'd just looked at her seriously and said, "You always need quiet time and space after a long day of work."

So on a gloomy Friday night, after the second week of restructuring, she was oddly sad to see the cold sheets of rain outside the windows. There would be no walk tonight. A pity, because tonight she felt particularly in need of relaxation.

The coronavirus was worsening by the day. China had nearly a thousand reported deaths, exceeding the SARS outbreak in 2003, which had devasted the global market. With China's economy at a standstill, the need for oil had halted, driving prices down ten dollars a barrel. Quinn was starting to get nervous, but he remained resolute on riding it out, saying Merriam Enterprises had done so before.

But she kept coming back to her conversation with her father. He'd indicated the virus wasn't the reason she should hesitate to restructure Merriam Enterprises around oil. And yet she'd seen no other sources of trouble in any of her daily industry research.

The World Health Organization had just sent a team of experts to China. Now the first cases of the virus were popping up all over the globe. The numbers were small, but the pattern was troubling. There was a Diamond Princess cruise ship quarantined in Yokohama, Japan, due to cases of corona, and passengers who'd been quarantined on another ship were finally disembarking in Hong Kong. The entire news cycle was alarming, and she was starting to share Clara and Hargreaves' fear that the virus could indeed be as deadly as the Spanish flu. It certainly was spreading fast.

"Francesca," Alice called, bringing her surroundings back into focus. "Do you want more panna cotta?"

Tonight they'd eaten yet another meal prepared jointly by Alice and Hargreaves—this time Italian—and she'd barely tasted it. "No, thank you. It was so delicious I couldn't have another bite."

Her friend's eyes narrowed.

"Maybe you should hit the hay," Arthur said. "You two have been hard at it this week."

"We still have to work tomorrow before we can take a break on Sunday." She would rally. They were still talking about downsizing divisions, and she needed to walk him through her plan for the first round of layoffs. So far, she thought they'd done a remarkable job, but they needed to use the scalpel more and they both knew it.

She hated this part of the process but had discovered not every CEO dreaded it as she did. Some of them didn't care about their employees beyond their functionality.

Not Quinn, though. Forgoing his salary had allowed them to save jobs, and she'd wanted to kiss him for it. He'd dismissed her praise with a casual wave of his hand, a front for what she knew were deeper emotions.

He was not most CEOs. Their talk about eliminating jobs had made his shoulders slump earlier, and yet he'd remained solicitous of her well-being. He'd risen to boil her water for tea or bring her a snack of salted almonds. He'd been like that ever since the wine tasting. He took care of her in a dozen little ways while he hung back and let her decide the future of their relationship.

He was also showing her that he was very much the man she'd fallen in love with fifteen years ago.

"If you need to take the morning off," Quinn said, suddenly tense beside her, "you take it. I mean it. We can start later than usual."

"I'll be fine," she said, rising. "As Arthur says, it's probably time for me to hit the hay. Thanks again for another wonderful meal, you two."

"It's always a pleasure to cook," Alice said. "Right, Hargreaves?"

"Yes, Miss Bailey," he said, "especially with you as a partner. Would you care for a cup of tea, Francesca?"

"I'll take care of her," Alice said, rising from her seat. "Come on, Francesca. We'll see you all in the morning."

But of course Alice didn't just walk away. She kissed both Hargreaves and Arthur on the cheek before swooping in and giving Clara a hug. Alice in action was always a thing of wonder, her warmth both genuine and remarkable. When Alice looked at Quinn, he held out his arms playfully.

"No, you're not ready for one of my hugs yet," Alice said wisely. "But I'll break you down. Ask Francesca. If I can get her father to kiss me warmly European style, I can win over anyone."

Quinn's eyebrows went to his forehead. "Georges Maroun kissed you warmly?"

She preened. "It was a good moment."

"If you say so." Quinn rose, and his green eyes were somber when they met Francesca's. "Good night. Please take some time for yourself."

"You get some rest too." She wanted to reach out to him. To hug him like Alice hadn't. To do *more*, but Alice took her arm before she could make a move.

"Come on."

Waving good night as the rest of the party started breaking up, they walked up the stairs.

"My room or yours?" Alice asked.

"I have a nice chaise we can share to watch the storm together."

"I love storms," Alice said as they entered her room.

Francesca shut the door behind them. "Okay, I know you. Are you really that worried about me?"

"A little." Her friend grabbed her hands and held on tight. "This assignment is emotional enough, but the news gets worse every day. I see it wearing you down. I hate that."

"I'll weather it." She was a Maroun in that way.

"I thought you might want some happy news, though. At least, it made my day."

"Tell me."

"Quinn framed my drawing of you and put it in his bedroom."

He'd framed it and put it in his bedroom? "I can't believe he— Okay, I can believe it." God, it was heartbreaking and sweet.

"It came this afternoon from a local gallery, and they hung it. I totally freaked out. Hargreaves found it amusing, but he's like that. Of course, he told me not to peek."

Her heart was thumping rapidly in her chest. "But you

did."

"Francesca, I have to give him big points for this one. I've been dying to tell you since I saw it earlier, but you two were buried downstairs. You totally need to see it." Alice paused. "That should boost you, don't you think? Also, he's been super chill with you. I've been keeping an eye on you two, and he hasn't stepped out of line. Hargreaves concurs. That's something, right?"

"He's been giving me space." She let go of her friend's hands. "Oh, Alice. I still don't know what comes next. I mean, I still want him."

"You want him like crazy, you mean," Alice said. "I mean, smoke rises every time you look at each other. I could cook a steak with your heat."

A reluctant laugh tumbled out. "Dinner tomorrow? Oh, Alice, I trust your opinion. I figure you have one."

"I always do." She gave a comical shrug. "But what do *you* want to do?"

"I'm going crazy with wanting," she admitted. "And my heart feels stretched more and more by all the feelings I have for him. But we have a lot on our plates. If we start in on each other, I don't want to be dashing off to the guest cottage during the workday."

"If you catch up on work later, who cares? Do you really think the great Francesca Maroun won't be able to focus on her assignment because she's tearing up the sheets with her associate?" She put her hand to her mouth. "Oh, did I just say that?"

Francesca bit her lip, fighting a smile. "Yes, you did. I'm actually glad you did. And thank you for not calling him my boss," she said, walking to the windows where the storm was lighting up the sky.

"You're my boss, and we manage it," Alice said logically. "You excel in complicated relationships. You've always said that."

She thought of her father again. "Excel might be a

strong word."

"Bull. The work is going great despite the emotional component." Alice came up beside her as lightning flashed, illuminating the crashing waves of high tide.

"Yes, it is. We're...so in sync about most things. Any sticking points are only because he doesn't want to hurt people, especially family." She still hadn't figured out a strategy for keeping the skincare line, but she would. Anything else would break him.

"That's a good sign, right? All I'm saying is that it got to me, seeing that drawing in his room. I've dated a lot of losers. They wouldn't have blinked if someone tossed away a simple marker drawing of me. Francesca, he acted like I was about to trash the *Mona Lisa*."

The urgency with which he'd stopped Alice had shocked her, and so had the careful way he'd detached the paper to avoid tearing it. But still, she'd never imagined he would *frame* it. "All right, I'll look."

She would consider it more data. Oh, who was she kidding? Her heart wasn't an adding machine.

"Is this where I tell you that I also snuck into the guesthouse?" Alice batted her big brown eyes with false innocence.

"You did?" At night, when her mind wasn't being helpful, she'd lie awake and imagine what it looked like. Sometimes she could swear she smelled the jasmine.

"Hargreaves knows, but he'd never say anything. Francesca, it's like a romantic dream in there. Okay, I was dying to tell you that too. Are you going to kill me?"

She took her friend's shoulders and kissed her on both cheeks like she would a friend at home. "Never. I admire your spunk, as they say."

"Whew! Okay, I'm going down to the kitchen to get us some tea. Hargreaves has this incredible blend called the Queen's Delight."

She wanted more than a cup of tea, but it would quiet

her mind. "You're not going to be my lookout so I can sneak into Quinn's room?" The very thought made her heart hammer.

"I can do that too! Do you want to?"

While her diaphragm constricted, she heard herself say, "Yes, actually. He usually goes to his office one last time before he retires for the night. It should be safe."

Alice grabbed her hand and tugged her to the door. She cracked it open and looked out. "All clear."

They stepped into the hallway, and sure enough, Quinn's door at the end of the hall was wide open. The other doors were all shut, save Alice's.

"We're acting like kids," Francesca whispered. "Is this terrible?"

"No, sneaking around can be very fun," Alice assured her. "Go on! I'll head to the kitchen for our tea. I'll keep an eye out for him down below. Unless you want me to go with you."

"No, you intercept him if need be." If he caught her wandering around his room, she'd be mortified. "Imagine anyone finding out I acted like this."

Like a teenager with a crush.

Like a woman in love, a small voice insisted. *Like you acted with him before.*

"It makes me love you all the more," Alice said, squeezing her hand before letting go. "Walk slowly but assuredly. If anyone finds you, say you got turned around."

She had to suppress a nervous giggle. "No one would believe that, least of all the Hales and Hargreaves."

"You're right, but they'd applaud you. I'm off. Go!"

Francesca crept down the hallway with what could best be described as soft ballerina steps designed not to make a sound. Her old training at boarding school had a new purpose: sneaking into a man's room as a grown woman.

Later she would have to decide if this was a positive life moment or not.

She started when she heard Arthur and Clara laugh through their door as she passed it. Quickening her pace, she crossed Quinn's threshold and stopped short.

The framed drawing hung on the wall across from his massive king bed. Her thighs tightened, knowing he could look at it while he lay there under the white silk duvet. Oh, dear God.

He'd had it framed in what looked like gold foil with a small blue line on the inner part of the frame—the same color as the marker Alice had used. The elegant presentation had taken a simple drawing and made it something she could see hanging in the Tate Gallery in London. Alice's art had always amazed her, but now Francesca wondered whether her friend should do something more with it. Then again, Alice was a Jill of all trades. She did what she wanted when she wanted.

Francesca admired her for it. Perhaps it was time for her to try living that way too.

Someone cleared their throat, and the dark grumble of it had her fisting her hands at her sides. She knew Quinn's every utterance. Turning slowly, she felt her lips part in shock—and also admiration—before she could control her reaction.

He was in a white towel, freshly showered, his bare chest and shoulders a feast for the senses.

Her eyes traveled across his upper body, one that had matured into total male perfection over the years. His strong build stole her breath. But it was his hot green gaze that kicked off her inner trembling.

He didn't say anything. God, should she? Instead, they continued to stare at each other. His dark hair was damp and towel-dried. She wanted to spear her fingers through it and lower his mouth to hers. Her skin could already feel the warmth of his touch—across the line of her neck, her décolletage, and her thighs.

She was breathing harshly, she realized, her chest

rising and falling from the tension swirling inside her. Their eyes locked again, and it was then that she saw the aroused pulse in his neck. Desire rolled through her, hot and lush.

She wanted him.

More, she loved him.

The fog that had been taunting her finally cleared and the image of them together crystalized in her mind. He was holding her hand at their tenth anniversary party, and their children were on the edges of the screen, smiling at them. In another, he was older and gray but no less sexy, and they were working quietly on the couch with their laptops, perfectly at ease with each other.

She wanted that future, and she was going to take it.

She crossed to his bedroom door and shut it.

As soon as it was closed, they rushed to each other. He wrapped her up in his arms, his mouth meeting hers in an urgent press of lips and tongue. She banded her arms around him and gripped his back. The moan that erupted from her throat had him moaning in kind.

Suddenly he wrenched his mouth back and stared down at her.

"Does this mean what I hope it means?" he asked, his tone guttural with longing and desire.

"Yes!" Her hands dug into his lower back. "Yes, I want this. And you. Forever."

"Thank God!" He swung her up into his arms and headed to the door. "Hang on. We're going to the guesthouse."

She wrapped her arms around his neck as he strode down the hallway and then the stairs.

Alice froze at the edge of the family room, two cups of tea in her hands. "Ah... I'll just..."

"Good decision," Quinn said, walking past her.

Her friend turned around and rushed back to the kitchen, tea sloshing on the floor in her haste.

"I should be so embarrassed," Francesca muttered, but

she found she wanted to laugh. The pressure of these last weeks was gone, and she was giddy with the feeling of freedom.

"Later," he said, shifting her and opening the front door. "Be embarrassed later."

The rain drenched them as he followed the flagstone path lined with outdoor lighting. When he turned to follow the path to the guesthouse, she buried her face in his chest to escape the rain.

They were really doing this. At last!

The outside lights glowed over them—he'd left them on all this time as a beacon—and then he was opening the door to the guesthouse and striding through the small family room to the back. The scent of jasmine saturated her nose, the smell so sweet and dear. She wanted to weep from the welcome.

Her heart was officially home.

CHAPTER 13

THE FEEL OF FRANCESCA IN QUINN'S ARMS WAS GOING TO be his undoing.

Entering the bedroom, he sat on the edge of the soft bed and cradled her, his heart in his throat. There was so much emotion rising inside him he felt swept under by its force. Her wet hands gripped him, and when she pressed her face into his damp neck, he knew she was feeling it too.

The full force of their love was gathering its strength and enfolding them once more in its power.

Despite being wet from the rain, he felt a warmth radiate up his body from his loins to the top of his head, and his heart expanded so he thought it might outpace his chest. After so long, she was his again. He'd known it the moment she'd closed his bedroom door.

"I love you," he whispered. "I never stopped."

"Oh, Quinn." She gripped his nape. "I love you too. So much I couldn't stop either."

He nudged her neck with his nose, reacquainting

himself with the feel and smell of her. Her subtle perfume captured his senses even with the jasmine filling the house. She put her hands in his damp hair, the gesture so loving and poignant his chest squeezed in response. His love for her grabbed him by the throat. He pressed his face into her neck again and held on, hoping the feelings would settle.

But they only grew stronger.

So many years had passed without her, nearly bereft of hope and joy, but no more.

He heard her sniff, and it prompted him to lift his head. Tears were coursing down her beautiful face. She'd been thinking about their separation too. He lowered his mouth and kissed her again to comfort them both. But he did it lightly this time. Oh, so lightly.

The longer he kissed her, the more he was pulled by the twin urges to both take her and savor this moment for as long as possible. So he hovered over her lips, kissing her softly and gently. She continued to caress the back of his head, her lips seeking his before she pulled back slightly, lips hovering inches from his own, and just looked at him. Desire and love filled his heart, and he cupped her face in benediction. She was so beautiful, so dear, but he couldn't force the words out. Nor did he want to. The communication coming from their hearts and their bodies was stronger than any words either of them could utter right now. The silence was its own sanctuary.

When he lowered his mouth to hers this time, she opened to him completely. The kiss was lush and wet and so carnal the urge to rush surged through him. He pressed back, not wanting to rush, and kissed her softly on the jaw and the underside of her neck. Her breath rushed out when he pressed his lips to a spot that had always inflamed her, and her body moved against him.

Wanting to give her what she needed, he lowered her onto the bed and lifted her shirt. Her clothes were damp and outright wet in places from the rain, and he began to remove them. Her hands reached for his towel, and they gazed at each other as lightning flashed outside the windows, followed by a rumble of thunder.

Her body was more beautiful and womanly than ever, and he told her so in slow, gentle caresses, starting with the undersides of her breasts and then running his hands down her torso to her belly and still lower. His eyes locked on hers, he covered her with his palm. Her hips rose to meet him.

"I need you," she whispered, tracing his jaw. "Come to me now."

He cupped her cheek with his other hand, his emotions unstoppable now. "I love you," he whispered. "So much."

"Oh, Quinn." She squeezed her eyes shut. "I love you too. I missed you so badly. I felt like my heart wasn't whole anymore."

He lowered his forehead to hers. "Me too. But we're okay now."

Their time apart was over. His lips hovered over hers again, his hand still stroking her, making her arch against him.

"Quinn, please."

Her plea couldn't be denied, not when her voice caught like that. He caressed her cheek and waited until she opened her eyes. "I'm clean healthwise, but do we need to use protection?"

She shook her head. "No, I'm on the pill. My physical was fine too."

"Good," he said, nodding. "Francie..."

His throat closed again, and she framed his face. "It's all right. Come to me now."

He didn't want to lose control, but the sharp claws of desire were gripping him. She slid under him, clutching his back and urging him on. He rested his forehead against hers and slid inside her. The feel of it had him locking himself in place to keep from giving in to the madness.

Then her hips lifted and she opened to him even more. He was lost. His first thrust went deep, and she moaned low and loud. That was all it took to unleash their desire. The rhythm they found was wild and beautiful, filled with a remembrance of times past. Her cries sharpened as their thrusts grew frantic, and then she was coming apart under him, hurling him over the edge.

He pressed his face into her neck, breathing hard, as the aftermath of their desire wrapped him in an embrace. She was the only woman he'd ever felt it with, this completeness, and his heart pulsed with the power of it. Love overwhelmed him, and from the way her hands clutched him, he knew it was the same for her.

Surrendering, he held on to her and let go the rest of the way. She was the woman of his heart and she had returned to him. There was nothing else.

They continued to lie like that until she finally stroked his back and kissed the side of his face. He simply had to see her in that moment. When he lifted his head, her eyes were waiting for him, so filled with light they seemed to glow like stars. They crinkled at the corners when she smiled softly, putting her hands in his hair again.

Somehow he was still unable to speak, but her smile helped him find his voice.

"It will always be you," he whispered.

"For me too," she said quietly back. "We're going to have to figure out what comes next, but you're my future."

"And you're mine. We'll figure it out. We have to, Francie."

"I know we do," she said, pressing him to turn them onto their sides. "When I took this assignment, I didn't expect to give in this quickly."

"Sounds like you knew on some level you were going to." He fought a smile. "Did Alice's drawing push you over the edge?"

She laughed softly, the sound so sexy it had his body

hardening again within her. "You made quite a statement with it."

It hadn't started out that way. He'd only wanted to have something else of her around him, something he could look at as he lay in bed before sleep. "I'd hoped you might hear about it and understand what it meant. I'm glad you came to my room."

"You weren't in your office." She rose on her elbow. "In fact, your door was open and you'd showered. Not your normal routine. Was it a total setup?"

He lay on his back, keeping an arm around her waist. "You came into my room, remember?"

"Alice was being my lookout downstairs," she said, giving him a gentle punch. "Quinn Merriam, you are devious."

He rolled to his side and kissed her. "Admit it. The picture finally gave you permission to be here with me."

"Perhaps it did." Her mouth curved, and she leaned in and gave him a long, lingering kiss. "We'll have to set some ground rules, you know. I still have a job to do, and this can't interfere."

He snorted. "Darling, I have a job to do too, and you're damn right we won't let this interfere. Actually, I'm hoping it will enhance our working relationship. I won't have to work so hard to keep my lustful thoughts from you."

Her laughter was light and musical and so achingly familiar he found himself smiling.

"Please. You didn't do much to conceal them. I could hear your lustful thoughts from across the room. At the dining table too, I might add. I feared the others could as well." Thank God they all wanted them to get together. Otherwise, it would have been horribly awkward.

"There's not much you can do to hide a fire. But I didn't make any overtures after that kiss in my mom's kitchen. I was a damn good guy if you ask me."

"You were," she said with a small smile, resting her cheek against his chest. "What are we going to do now?"

He shifted so he could see her face. "I want to romance you a bit. I...I want to treat you like the most precious thing in the world. Because that's what you are, dammit."

Her eyes went soft, and her fingers caressed his chest. "Aside from the cursing, that was a pretty nice compliment. You're still precious to me when you're not aggravating."

"Have I been aggravating?" He traced the small of her back. "I agreed to host the chaperones, Francesca. Never forget that." Truthfully, he'd enjoyed having them around. It had been yet another reminder that he missed his family, that they brought out this other side of him—playful and mischievous—just like Francesca did.

"You get points for that. What are we going to do about them now?"

"Kick them out," Quinn suggested, earning him another nudge. "Hell, they can stay with my parents. The wedding is—"

"Two weeks away tomorrow," she said, worrying her lip. "Quinn, Alice always stays with me, and she's having such a great time, with Hargreaves especially. I don't want to break that up. When her parents died— He's become special to her and she to him."

He turned her and rose over her. "You aren't suggesting they all stay *here*?"

She waved to the room. "We have the guesthouse for privacy. Plus, didn't you want me to get to know your family better?"

Dear God, she was serious. "You can meet them all at the wedding." Most of them were coming in late next week to spend time together before the festivities, and he hoped they'd finish their work early so they could hang out with everyone.

"Are you asking me to accompany you?" Her brow rose in a regal dare.

"I was getting around to it. But yes, of course I want you to go. I didn't want to ask you until we were a sure thing."

"Like now," she said, giving him a look.

He was having none of it. "Francesca, the last wedding I went to was Flynn's, and Connor and I had a heart-to-heart about you. I walked away from the reception because I was missing you so much. I don't want to do a repeat of that."

"So ask me." Her regal dare was gone, replaced by an open entreaty.

"Will you be my date to my sister's wedding?" he asked.

"I'd love to," she said, her smile warm. "And the chaperones stay."

He groaned, knowing he wasn't going to win this one.

"Look on this as a positive. Their presence will keep us from ripping each other's clothes off during the day, which would make us have to work late into the night."

That was a positive? "Honey, I was looking forward to some naked work breaks with you. I'm tired of the damn tea time."

"Oh, look who's turning grouchy again," she crooned, making him growl.

"Is it terrible that I want to be alone with you?" He traced the delicate line of her brow. "I love you."

She was quiet for a moment. "I thought it might be strange to say the words again after so long. I told myself my heart would know when to say them. Tonight, when I saw the drawing in your room, I knew I couldn't stop myself."

"I'll have to thank Alice." Then he laughed, long and loud. "Her expression when I came down the stairs carrying you—"

"Was priceless." She laughed gustily as well. "Then you said 'good decision' when she talked about going back into the kitchen. Oh, Quinn, we must have been a sight, with you wearing nothing but a towel."

He lifted her leg over his hip. "But a hot one. I'm about to show you another sight."

"I had an inkling." She tightened her grip on him. "I can't wait."

His heart filled with love for her as he gazed into her eyes, and he couldn't stop himself from saying, "I know you like to have a plan for everything, but I also want to be clear. I want us to get married. Soon. Not in a couple years. Tell me that's what you see too."

She was quiet again, and his heart thudded in his chest as he waited for her to compose her thoughts.

"I do. I love you, Quinn. 'Soon' will need some definition, of course. You still want children, don't you?"

His throat squeezed. At one time, he had so easily seen a dark-haired little girl with Francesca's eyes holding his hand as they walked through the park. After their breakup, he'd pushed aside all of those visions. But suddenly, the little girl was in vivid color in his mind and she was smiling at him. "Of course. And you?"

"Yes," she said, her smile radiant. "Until now, I didn't see it happening. But I saw our children in a vision tonight. It...confirmed my decision."

He kissed her slowly, needing to share the emotion they both felt.

"Well..." She gave a lusty sigh when he released her mouth. "We've fallen back into it, haven't we?"

"It's like riding a bike," he quipped, but he squeezed her arm gently. "Or it's the soulmate thing."

"The soulmate explanation sounds better to my ears. Quinn, we really will need to restructure the company so you can have a life outside of work once we get to the management structure. I don't want you to work like my father did when I was growing up."

"Or mine," he added, lifting her hand to his mouth. "We're going to figure it out. And you'll need to make changes too. I mean, living around the world one consultancy after another isn't going to work. For either of us."

Would she consider working with him at Merriam?

She would make a terrific vice president. But he hesitated. It wasn't the time to ask. Not if she was still conflicted about her duties to the Maroun employees.

He couldn't imagine her father would be thrilled at the news that they were together again. After all, he'd only been with Francesca for a matter of weeks when her father had come to see him in London, warning him off. He'd known how much it would upset her, so he'd handled it.

"You're right," she said, caressing his lower back. "Besides, I felt the call of home when I arrived here."

That heartened him. "You did?"

"I did, and I feel it now, surrounded by the smell of jasmine."

"Every breath you take, I want you to remember what's between us," he said softly.

Her eyes flashed violet fire. "I always knew you were a romantic at heart, Quinn Merriam, from the first moment you brought a book of Rumi poems to the park with me."

"You weren't exactly romance central when I brought Rumi up that first day we met."

"I was protecting myself."

But now she wasn't. She'd opened herself to him, and that knowledge made him swallow back emotion. He made a glib joke. "Mum's the word on my Rumi readings. The news would be horrible for my rep."

"That part of you is only for me," she said softly, caressing him lower, making him rouse with desire.

He shifted until she was on top, wanting to show her how equal they'd always be. "Only you is right. Now you give me what I need." *Like I will you.*

"Always."

He heard the promise in her words and tucked it deep inside his heart for what lay ahead.

CHAPTER 14

CLARA WAS DETERMINED TO HAVE THE BEST DAMN VALEN-tine's Day ever.

The worsening news about the coronavirus wasn't going to dim her day—or her husband's. It was the first time they'd spent the holiday together.

"Put the tablet away, Arthur," she said, poking him in the shoulder as she sat beside him on the couch.

He threw his tablet to the side and rubbed his eyes. "Bah! Sixty some thousand cases in mainland China alone. The first one in Africa. Hell, Heathrow Airport even delayed eight flights out of London because of the virus. It's spreading fast, Clara."

The recent news downright terrified her. "I wanted to be wrong."

"Maybe it will run its course quickly."

He might be a jaded journalist, but he was attempting to be hopeful, which was the greatest gift he could give. "We can hope. I talked to Michaela earlier, and she and

Boyd are starting to worry about whether their international guests should still come to the wedding. Not only for their health, but for others. Boyd's rethinking their honeymoon plans, especially since Michaela almost died of that virus a couple of months ago."

"That's a wise decision given the news, and Boyd would know it. They've been to a lot of places with weird viruses. They know how dangerous they can be."

She thought of her eightieth birthday party in Dare Valley coming up in early March. Might it also have to be canceled?

"They're adding technicians to fast-track testing for the healing flower, but it'll still take a year at best. It's so frustrating."

Arthur snapped his fingers in front of her face. "All right. We're going to stop all this talk. Are you ready for your Valentine's present?"

She took his weathered hand. "You're mine, but sure, if you got me something."

He harrumphed. "If I got you something... Woman, you know I did. Be right back."

Clara watched as he took the stairs. Looking over her shoulder, she was encouraged to see Hargreaves and Alice in the kitchen, hunched over a cup of tea, their heads tilted together like usual. A few strains of German filtered to her, and she shook her head. They were always talking in a different language it seemed, and Alice liked teasing Clara that it gave them extra privacy in an open house. Personally, Clara would encourage them to speak in just about anything if it kept that warm look on Hargreaves' face.

In truth, privacy was easy to come by these days, because Quinn and Francesca retired to the guesthouse every night after dinner. The two had been very close-lipped about the change between them—Arthur said they were beaming so brightly he sometimes couldn't see his food and needed sunglasses—and Clara wondered why the reunited couple hadn't asked them to leave. She figured Alice had something to do with it, and since Hargreaves was so happy with his new friend, she wasn't keen for a change. Out of respect for their reserve, she hadn't asked.

Arthur appeared carrying a silver-wrapped present.

Clara gasped. "You didn't wrap that. Where could you have hidden it? Hargreaves and I packed your bag."

"Hargreaves had it. Happy Valentine's Day, my love. Thank you for making every day happier than the last."

Tears filled her eyes. "You're becoming more of a poet in your retirement."

"Bah! Love makes a man say the most crazy things." He sat next to her and placed the present in her lap. "To remind you of our journey together so far. This was Jill's idea, by the way."

As she unwrapped the present—a beautiful scrapbook with a photo of them in the lavender fields of Provence gracing the cover—and opened it, she had to admit Jill knew her audience. "Arthur Hale. You surprise me in the best ways."

She caressed the first black-and-white photo of them at a ball in 1959 and then another at Grandpa Merriam's house in the garden. The next page had photos of their wedding last summer, and then there was a page devoted to each of their trips to help matchmake the Merriam children. The final ones were of their extended families: his with the Hales and hers with the Merriams.

"Thank you for being my family, Clara."

His eyes were misty as she leaned in to kiss him. "Oh, Arthur Hale, you're going to make me cry."

He produced his trusty white handkerchief. "I'm ready for you."

She dabbed her eyes and then did the same to him. "I love you. Never forget it."

"I love you too, despite the Indian food you foist on me weekly. Did we have to have it again last night? I swear I sometimes feel like curry is my new cologne."

She laughed. "If it is, it smells delicious on you. Now it's time for your present."

She pulled up the email and handed him her phone. He'd go on about the technology, but truthfully, his blustering amused her.

He peered at the screen, his frown ferocious. "You got me an email account."

"No, look closer."

Grabbing the phone, he laughed. "You got me reckless driving lessons? With a hot mama?"

She punched him. "No, it's high-performance driving training. For your convertible. You drive like an old fuddy-duddy, and I've come to realize you have the need for speed."

"The need for speed?" He threw his head back and laughed. "Good God, woman, I only have a need for speed to keep up with you. But thank you. I love it."

"You're welcome. I'm already looking forward to all the speed you can drum up during our afternoon 'nap.'"

He waggled his brows. "Not today. We have plans for the late afternoon and evening. Part of your next present. I think it's time to call up Quinn and Francesca. Hargreaves!"

"I'll go and grab them, Arthur," Alice said, jumping to attention. "Everyone needs to get ready for their date."

He slapped his head as she raced to the stairs leading to the lower level. "And she just gave it away."

"Her enthusiasm sometimes gets the better of her, sir," Hargreaves said, coming toward them, a broad smile on his face. "It's one of her most charming assets, I believe."

"Good thing you think so, Hargreaves, since you spend every waking minute with her."

Clara noted her old friend's smile only grew. "I do, indeed, sir. We converse on any number of topics, from European history to the best technique for cooking lamb shank, and we speak in languages I haven't had the opportunity to converse in for some time. It has been stupendous."

Stupendous? When did Hargreaves ever use that word? "Maybe I'll need to hire Alice away from Francesca. I don't know how you two will be separated after this." They'd even taken to lightly sparring with each other after the yoga or tai chi Clara did with them.

That dimmed his smile, and she was sorry she'd opened her mouth. "We must all soldier on. Perhaps I will need to embrace texting and FaceTime as you have, Madam."

"Good God, Hargreaves," Arthur said with a feigned gasp. "Not that."

Alice ran back up the stairs, eliminating the need for Hargreaves to respond, but Clara saw the look on his face. He *was* going to miss Alice, and she him. Clara would have to figure out what to do about that. Well, surely she could encourage him to take his vacations. He'd rarely used the time off allotted to him.

Then she wondered if her friend needed to find a new purpose in life. He was eighty, like her, and she'd finally found hers. Was it time for him to find his own way? She clutched Arthur's handkerchief at the very thought. But if it came to it, she'd have to buck up. Hargreaves' happiness meant too much to her.

"Well, you got us up here," Quinn said, putting his hand on Francesca's back. "Is it time to unveil the surprise, Arthur?"

"Past time," he said with a nod.

"Age before beauty," Quinn said with a laugh after Francesca pinned him with one of her regal glares.

Clara really had to admire her for their execution.

"We're having a private tour of the de Young Museum," Arthur said. "Hargreaves had the idea, and he deserves the credit."

"You asked, sir," the man said formally. "Master J.T.'s reputation in the art world secured it. Miss Caroline will be joining us."

"J.T. texted me a picture of her face after he told her what we're doing." Quinn fished his phone out of his pocket and handed it to Clara.

The photo was of Caroline with her hands on her face, mouth open in a silent scream. Clara laughed. "I know how she feels. The de Young is one of the best fine art museums in the world. You all did well."

"Hargreaves started it," Quinn said. "This one used to drag me to museum after museum in London so I knew she'd like this for Valentine's Day."

"I hadn't anticipated celebrating," Francesca said, putting her hand on Quinn's arm. "It's not a holiday in my circle of traveling."

"But it should be," Alice cried out. "Forget the commercialism. How can you not like a holiday that celebrates love? Growing up, I used to make Valentine's Day cards in school for my friends and then drop in little heart-shaped candies with phrases like 'Be Mine' or 'Love you.'"

"Then where's my card?" Quinn teased, something he'd started doing a lot more of lately. "I still haven't gotten an Alice hug."

The young woman ran at him, and he uttered a heartfelt, "Oomph," as she banded her arms around him.

"Since it's a holiday and you've made my girl so happy," Alice said by way of explanation.

"The cat's out of the bag," Quinn said. "She's made me happy too. And Alice, you give great hugs. I can see why Georges Maroun let you give him one."

"Actually, it was a European-style kiss. I don't think he hugs."

Clara noted Francesca's grin faded at the mention of her father. There was a new tightness to her brow line. And although Clara knew Francesca was concerned about the virus' impact on the oil market, this tension was clearly related to her father. Not Clara's business except she was very fond of the woman.

"You can have a hug anytime from now on," Alice said. "I'm going to make some tea for me and Hargreaves. Does anyone else want a cup?"

"We need to head back downstairs," Francesca said, smiling at her friend. "I have a present for Quinn."

"During work hours?" Alice blurted out and then slapped a hand over her mouth.

Arthur barked out a laugh, and Clara fought laughter of her own. Hargreaves' shoulders shook with mirth.

"What she said." Quinn jerked his thumb at Alice.

"It's business-related," Francesca said, "but it's so great... Oh, you'll understand momentarily. Back downstairs."

He winked at the room. "I love it when she orders me around. Alice. Hargreaves. I hope you plan on joining us at the museum tonight. We've also invited my parents."

Alice seemed to melt. "When I was in second and third grade, we had a Valentine's Day dance where you could bring your father or grandfather. My dad worked nights and both my grandfathers had passed. I never got to go. Hargreaves, I would love to have you as my date tonight. We can pretend it's like a grandfather/granddaughter dance."

"It would be my honor to be your escort," Hargreaves said. "After all, I don't have a granddaughter. I can't imagine a better one than you, my dear."

Clara settled her gaze on Hargreaves again. He'd found in Alice what she'd found in the Merriam children. It struck her that Francesca probably wouldn't be traveling so much anymore now that she and Quinn were shoring up their relationship. Where would that leave Alice and her role in Francesca's life? Clara would have to do some thinking on it.

"When do the rest of the Merriam kids arrive for the pre-wedding festivities?" Arthur asked.

"They're arriving over the next couple of days, but everyone will be here by Sunday afternoon. My mother has a big dinner planned for the whole family," Quinn said.

"I could have told you that, Arthur." Clara nearly rolled her eyes at him. "I'm up on all of the festivities."

"Which Francesca and I are going to have to pick and choose from," Quinn said. "We need to finish the restructuring. J.T.'s going bananas, and it sounds like the rest of our employees are going nuts too, waiting for the plan."

"Any idea when you'll finish?" Clara asked.

Francesca gave a mysterious smile. "After today, we might have a better idea. Quinn, let's go."

As they left the room, Clara fingered her husband's present. The scrapbook represented every hope and dream of hers come to life.

She hoped Francesca and Quinn had rediscovered their dreams in each other.

Then she glanced at Hargreaves.

Was it time to help her longest friend find his dreams as well?

CHAPTER 15

FRANCESCA HAD FINALLY LANDED ON THE SOLUTION QUINN
wanted with his whole heart.

After they descended down the stairs, she broke her
cardinal rule—no mixing work with play—and pulled him
down next to her on her couch. Laying her hand on his
chest, she gazed into his beautiful green eyes.

The past week had been one of the happiest of her life.
For years, she'd tried to make home wherever she went,
but there'd always been a hollowness at the center, and
now she realized why. *He* hadn't been with her. And while
the news was bleak, experts were saying the virus' impact
on oil was nearly over. Chinese factories were coming back
online; U.S. oil production was up for the second week in a
row, and everyone from the Europeans to the Russians to
the Saudis were enthusiastic for the future. Had her father
been wrong? She was starting to think so. The possibility that he might have tried to sabotage her efforts to help
Quinn and his company broke her heart, but she wouldn't

allow it to detract from her joy.

She'd helped the love of her life solve one of his greatest problems to date.

"I know how to include the skincare line." His heartbeat, solid and reassuring under her hand, kicked into higher gear at her words. "And it's going to work even better than I could have hoped."

"Of course it is!" A quicksilver smile flashed across his face. "You're brilliant. Can you imagine how brilliant our kids are going to be?"

Words like that inflamed her every sense, like smelling the battery of spices in Istanbul's famous Spice Market. Their love was opening up so many new possibilities for her—for them—and she was eager to inhale it every day with him by her side.

"We're going to restructure Merriam Enterprises into two functional areas. Traditional Business Initiatives—TDIs—will be the bulk, and they'll include oil and gas to start. The other area will be called Speculative Ventures—SVs—allowing you and your team to bring in anything you think will make a profit and might add to your greater long-term portfolio. Once the individual venture starts rolling in profits and adding to your market share, they'll be rolled into the TDIs."

"I love it!" he said, kissing her full on the mouth. "Man, babe, you're so awesome. Tell me more."

"Let me show you." Rising, she grabbed a marker and started drawing. "Each business unit will have its own CEO. Let's take Caitlyn, for example. She'll be in charge of her perfume and product line. All units will have a controlled budget—set by you and your CFO—but the CEO will have greater autonomy in day-to-day operations. The controlled spending model ensures you can't—"

"Lose money," he finished for her, rising to stand with her at the flip chart. "Plus, it reallocates some of the management and budget responsibilities, freeing me up."

"Yes!" She grabbed a dry eraser and started to draw the new management structure. "It's a performance-driven model. You'll have a CEO for oil and a CEO for gas for the TDIs. My pick is Trevor on the oil side since it's your largest industry, but you need to decide for yourself. Then you will have individual vice presidents under that, one for offshore and onshore."

She continued outlining the draft management structure, her excitement growing.

"Delegating more authority while holding people to greater fiscal—"

"And operational efficiency," she finished for him.

They shared a smile.

"Damn, I love working with you, Miss Maroun." He put an arm around her waist.

"Back at you, Mr. Merriam. This new model will build in individual profit unit plans that take industry, customer, and employee factors into account."

"We'll have to retrain the staff around this new model, but it'll be a hell of a lot more streamlined and efficient long-term," Quinn said, massaging her back. "God, this is terrific. It's so different than what we've done before. How did you come up with it?"

"I had to look outside your industries for other models, and I took a little inspiration from a few different sources. Suddenly I could see it. Your investors will expect your SVs to be risky, but they're not a significant portion of your overall operation, and it'll be pure bonus if they work."

"Freaking genius," Quinn said, shaking his head.

"Thank you. Plus, it shows you're cutting edge and innovative. With Caitlyn's growth rate, she could be rolled into the TDI arm in two years. Annie would be on a similar track. I would put her as a CEO of her skincare line with a smaller controlled budget. Someone in the company can mentor her. Your father might be a good person if he's willing. Clara told me they get along well. You brought him in to do the assessment of her company before she merged with you, after all."

"Good idea. Dad's been looking for ways to connect and contribute."

"And mentoring is a terrific way of doing it," Francesca said. "Lastly, I think you need to consider making Flynn a CEO of what we'll call Technology Initiatives. I don't think you're utilizing him enough. Tech is a growing market, and if you want Merriam to stay competitive, you need more products and initiatives in it."

Quinn rubbed his chin, his eyes sparkling. "If I make the other Merriam family members CEOs in this new model, it'll send a message: we're as much a family business as ever, but it's in a controlled fiscal model that respects growth, innovation, and accountability."

She knew he'd get it. "Exactly!"

"Francesca, you have exceeded all hopes for this consultancy," he said, framing her face. "God, I love you. Now I have something to ask you."

From the look on his face, intent and hopeful, she knew it was important, so she repressed the urge to kiss him. "Shoot, as you Americans say."

"Come work with me at Merriam. Let's find a way to do this—you and me—every day. Francie, we work so well together. Wouldn't it be wonderful to live together, work together? Tell me you see it. More, tell me you want it."

Oh, why did he have to bring this up right now? She'd been so overjoyed to give him this gift, knowing how much it would mean to him. "I love that you asked me, but Quinn, it took me three weeks to come up with this new plan. We've only been back together for one. Can't you give a girl a little more time?"

The excited gleam in his eyes receded some, and it hurt to see that, to know she'd caused it.

"You're right." He kissed her slowly. "I got carried away."

"I love that about you," she said, her throat thick with love for him. And oh, she wanted to soften the hurt she could feel emanating from him. "This news calls for another break in my cardinal work rules. Come to the cottage with me."

His eyes blinked at that. "Now?"

"Yes, Quinn. Now." Taking his hand, she led him to the door that would take them to the path to the guesthouse.

When she'd imagined leading him there earlier, the fantasy had shown them running with glee to the guesthouse, awash in excitement, but the reality was different. There was no spring in his step, or hers for that matter.

He feared she would leave him again, and she needed to reassure him that wouldn't happen.

Inside, the welcome scent of jasmine brought tears to her eyes. She undressed down to her matching black bra and panties and kicked off her heels. Approaching him, she lifted his shirt off him, unbuckled his belt, and slowly slid it out before she unzipped his pants. Taking him in her hands, she caressed him lovingly, wanting him to understand what her words couldn't convey.

They had a future together.

He just needed to give them time so the details could take shape.

"Trust me," she finally whispered.

His eyes locked with hers. "I'm trusting you all the way, babe."

Her heart squeezed, and then he was arching into her hands in total surrender. She understood the message, and her earlier joy took shape inside her.

Yes, they would figure it out. They were stronger and wiser than they'd been in their youth, and they would find a solution.

Wanting to express her love and her gratitude for having him back in her life, she sunk to her knees in front of her and took him into her mouth. He groaned and threaded his hands in her hair as she loved him.

When he was nearing the edge of release, he lifted her head. "Come. I want to be inside you."

Turning, she let him unhook her bra and undress her the rest of the way. And then he took her by the waist and pulled her on top of him.

Again, she knew the message he was sending. She would always be his equal and he respected her.

Lowering herself onto him, she began to move. She closed her eyes as he filled her, again and again. God, it was so good. How had she been without him all these years?

He pressed his hand to where they were joined, and she picked up the pace, feeling the urgency between them. Opening her eyes, she found him watching her. They held each other in their sights as they both came.

The love on his face as he gazed at her took her to new heights, and she leaned forward and gripped his shoulders, wanting to be closer to him as the tide rushed over them.

Panting, she kissed him in short, quick, loving bites. His arms caressed her back and encouraged her to find a place on his chest to rest.

As she fitted herself onto him and let the warmth spread through her, she nuzzled his neck and said, "I love you."

He responded quietly, "I know, and I thank God for it."

They lay there for long moments, not talking, only caressing. When he turned them onto their sides, his carefree smile was back. He'd pushed aside his disappointment about his business proposal, and she was grateful for it.

"About the museum visit," he said, kissing her cheek with lingering emotion. "I'm driving my own car, and we're leaving early. I know you. You'll fawn over every damn painting in the place, and after hearing you talk to J.T. about art at my parents' house, I can already envision you talking to him—and Caroline, whom you're going to love— more than me. I'm heading it off. Call it your Valentine's

Day present to me. I know you already gave me a terrific one, but I hope you're feeling extra generous. Especially after I give you mine."

He untangled from her and rose from the bed, crossing to the closet. When he pulled out the large rectangular present, she pulled up the sheet and inched toward the edge of the bed.

"I thought this might help you imagine our future," he said, resting the present by her side.

She tore away the wrapping and her breath caught. The painting was in her favorite style—Impressionist—and it showed a family walking on a beach holding hands. Their backs were to the viewer, allowing one to imagine being in the scene. The sun was setting in a bold orange, and the water was brilliant blue, but it was the way the family held hands that captivated her. The couple's clasp was strong and seamless, as if nothing could come between them. And the way they were holding the two children's hands hinted at playfulness and whimsy.

"I love it," she whispered, lifting her eyes to his.

"This is us, babe," he said in a deep voice. "When you need more clarity about the future, you can look at this. Or ask me to draw what I see for us. I can't draw as well as Alice, but I'd draw stick figures of a family surrounded by a bunch of hearts."

Oh, how she loved this man. They very act of drawing would be humbling for him—he only liked to do things he excelled in—but he'd do it for her.

"I'd love to see that," she said. "Perhaps that's the drawing I would frame and put across from my bed."

His mouth tipped up and he leaned over and kissed her deeply. Her heart turned over in her chest.

"I'll keep that in mind." His expression serious, he said, "There's nothing that I wouldn't do for you."

"I know that."

Now she had to show him there was nothing she

wouldn't do for him.

She prayed the solution she found for her future work was as brilliant as the one she'd landed upon for Merriam.

CHAPTER 16

THE WEEK LEADING UP TO MICHAELA'S WEDDING WAS ONE of the best of Quinn's life.

In fact, he was basking in a sea of positivity. The rest of the restructuring had fallen into place quickly after Francesca's brilliant solution, which had made their night at the art museum feel like even more of a celebration. Spending time with his siblings and introducing the rest of them to Francesca had only added to his good humor. They loved her, of course, and teased him good-naturedly about having held out on them by not introducing her fifteen years ago. Having her by his side at the evening get-togethers with his family felt right, and from her ease and ever-present smile, he knew she felt the same way.

The news about the virus continued to be alarming, but he wasn't going to let it spoil his mood. There still hadn't been a single case in San Francisco, but fear was swirling locally, just like it was in the global market.

Still, he was nervous as he stood by the bay window in

his parents' living room and waited for his family to join him. He'd left a copy of the restructuring plan with his father and siblings last night, wanting to give them time to review it before the wedding, which was tomorrow. Surely they'd all read it by now. Uncle Arthur and Aunt Clara had been given their own copy, although neither had commented on it this morning.

Someone suddenly slapped him on the back, and he turned around to see all of his siblings save Connor grinning at him alongside his father. Annie was also in the mix, which was only appropriate given she would be a CEO in her own right in the proposed restructuring plan.

"Man, you and Francesca outdid yourselves," Trevor said, bear-hugging him. "We all finished reading the report. Damn! It's ridiculous."

"I'm *underutilized*," Flynn said, pulling a face. "Quinn, prepare for an onslaught of tech initiatives that are going to make bank."

"Bring them on," he said with a laugh.

"You're lucky I'm cool having two CEOs in the family," Flynn said, nudging his wife. "Right, Annie?"

"Like it changes anything," Annie said, but she was beaming. "Thank you for your support, Quinn. It's all so exciting."

"The board is going to love it," J.T. said, stepping forward and man-hugging Quinn. "As a member, you have my vote. But seriously. Well done, man. Both of you."

He wished Francesca were here to hear this praise, but she was off with his mother, Aunt Clara, and Alice in town. Something about showing her the shops. Meanwhile, Boyd had taken some of the in-laws and Annie (and now Flynn's) girls on a special botanical tour at the University of California at Davis that morning along with Hargreaves.

Quinn had decided to stick around his parents' house and hang with his family, thinking it would be a good opportunity to discuss the plan with them.

"You two did great!" The bride-to-be grabbed him and kissed his cheek. "J.T. has my proxy for the vote, but I'll be thinking about you guys next Tuesday."

"Sorry we had to call an emergency meeting while you were on your honeymoon," he said, watching as her eyes darkened.

She and Boyd had decided not to go on safari in South Africa due to the virus. Boyd didn't want to chance anything, and while Michaela had agreed, Quinn knew it was a disappointment. To bolster her spirits, he and his siblings had arranged for a chef's tasting at the mountain resort they were going to in Jackson Hole, Wyoming. There was an abundance of wildlife there, and Boyd had joked it would be their domestic safari.

"You need to move forward with the plan," Michaela said. "It's a good one, and I know everyone at Merriam has been dying to hear it."

His dad came forward and extended a hand to Quinn. "Everyone who's served as the president of Merriam knows what a tough job it is to steer the company out of troubled waters. You've made us all very proud with this plan, Quinn."

He shook his dad's hand, oddly emotional. "Thank you, but it was all Francesca."

"You brought her in, and that makes you smart," Caitlyn said, putting her arm around him. "Also, thank you for believing in me."

He kissed her cheek. "You believed in yourself and wrote a kick-ass proposal. I'm glad I funded it."

"Me too," Flynn said with a shake of his head. "Otherwise, I would have had to kick your butt. Frankly, Quinn, while you've been pretty grouchy lately, you've also made some really good decisions. I look forward to seeing how much better you're going to do with your woman by your side. She looks good on you, bro."

His mouth twitched. "Yes, she does."

Then Connor came down the hall with Louisa, and Quinn went still inside. How would his brother react to hearing about the plan? Never in a million years did he want it to hurt him.

But his older brother just crossed to him and shook his hand, and he knew what it meant. Connor was assuring him he needn't have worried.

"I don't know the details, but it's good to hear everyone's happy with the restructuring plan. Congratulations, bro, on a job well done. When Francesca returns, I'll have to tell her the same."

Caitlyn wiped tears from her eyes, and Flynn took her hand in comfort. They all knew how hard it was for Connor to approach him—all of them—like this. Quinn was just glad his brother didn't try apologizing again. They were done with that chapter of Merriam Enterprises.

"If I had something to drink, I would give a toast." Quinn looked around at his whole family. "To all of our futures. May they be bigger and brighter than we ever imagined."

"Sounds like we all need some champagne," their father said. "Come on. It's happy hour somewhere, and this calls for a celebration."

Quinn dug out his phone and texted Aunt Clara.

Get my woman back here STAT. We're toasting the restructuring plan, and she should be here for it.

She responded quickly.

You always were bossy, but that's a Merriam for you. Message received.

He followed the rest of the family into the family room, smiling as multiple champagne corks were popped. More toasts went around once everyone had a glass, and he took a moment to savor the feeling of being among his family. All of his worries had disappeared this week—mostly. Sure, he had to initiate layoffs, but they'd reduced them by half with Francesca's brilliant solution and also because his siblings had decided to forgo their salaries too. He still didn't like the prospect of eliminating jobs, but he could live with it.

"I heard we were missing a celebration," their mother said, entering the family room some twenty minutes later, carrying a blue gift bag. "Quinn, your father walked me through the major points of the restructuring plan before we came downstairs for breakfast. You did good, son."

He lifted his flute in her direction. "Thanks, Mom."

Francesca came in laughing with Aunt Clara and Alice, and the colors in the room suddenly seemed more vivid. She lit up a room by being herself, and he drank in the sight of her in an asymmetrical red cashmere sweater and navy wool pants. Soon, he'd ask her to marry him again. As far as her work plans went, he trusted she'd come up with the perfect answer. She had always exceeded his expectations. This time would be no different.

"Finally!" He crossed the room and kissed her sweetly on the mouth. "Everyone has been toasting me for the restructuring plan, but they should be toasting *you*."

Her regal brow rose. "I've told you before, Quinn. When you lead, all the successes or failures rest on your shoulders."

What a crock of shit. "I wouldn't have been able to come up with any of this without you."

"Are you two really going to argue over this?" Aunt Clara rolled her eyes. "I thought this was a celebration. Where's my champagne?"

"Coming, Aunt," J.T. called, filling more glasses and then enlisting Annie to help him pass them out.

"Let me show you how this is done," Aunt Clara said, giving him a set down and lifting her glass to the room.

"Arthur, Hargreaves, and I didn't do much matchmaking this time, but these two have found their way back to each other. I'm calling that a success. To another Merriam finding his soulmate. May your love make you more joyous each and every day."

"Hear, hear," Trevor and J.T. shouted.

Francesca clinked their champagne flutes together, reminding him of that day, a few weeks ago now, when she'd held back. "I believe we're both being called to more graciousness. How about a toast to our mutual success?"

He loved it when she talked like that. "I can jump on the bandwagon of anything mutual when it comes to you, babe," he said so only she could hear.

Except Alice bit her lip, and he knew they'd been overheard. Well, with everyone underfoot, he'd gotten used to it. The other day, his mother had walked in on him kissing Francesca in his old bedroom and said, "Have fun, you two. Only next time close the door."

He hadn't needed to be reminded twice.

"Now, to Francesca," Aunt Clara was saying. "I read the plan well into the night with Arthur snoring beside me, and I have to say, it is downright ingenious. You two make an incredible pair."

"I couldn't agree more," his father said, lifting his glass.

They all toasted Francesca, and he squeezed her waist as they sipped their champagne. Seeing his family's pride in the woman he loved filled his heart.

"It's nice when your partner brings out the best in you," Flynn said, smiling at his wife.

"To love," Caitlyn said. "It brings out the best in all of us."

"It does?" Uncle Arthur said, stepping into the family room with Boyd and the rest of their party.

The girls ran through the room, chattering about finding a snack. Boyd had his bridegroom glow on, but Beau and Caroline looked green, which puzzled Quinn.

"News to this old journalist," he said, prompting Aunt Clara to let out an unladylike noise and cross the room to her husband and poke him in the belly.

"You know it does," she said, kissing his weathered cheek. "You missed me, I bet."

"If I did, I know better than to say so," his uncle said. "You drinking already? It's not even noon."

"Yes, it is," Aunt Clara said. "How was the tour? I was so conflicted about what to choose, but Assumpta was persuasive."

"Boyd could have left out the snakes." Uncle Arthur shuddered.

"Oh, I'm sorry I didn't go!" Aunt Clara said with real regret. "You know how much I love snakes."

Michaela grinned as she crossed to her soon-to-be husband. "You just couldn't resist the temptation, could you?"

He kissed her full on the mouth. "Nope. I'm like your aunt. Something about them just appeals to me. Maybe I was a snake charmer in another life."

"It was terrifying," Caroline said. "I may never be able to hike in Dare Valley again. Good thing Beau offered to go outside with me. I think we were both green when we came across one eating a mouse."

That explained it. Quinn would have been green too.

"It wasn't my favorite moment," Caitlyn's fiancé said with his usual low-key humor.

"Oh, yuck, babe," Caitlyn said, taking his hand. "I'm so glad I stayed home to read the report."

Is that why his siblings had stayed home? He knew it impacted their jobs too, but he still felt all kinds of choked up anyway. Francesca rubbed his back, as if sensing his emotional response. The smile she gave him settled him some.

"I loved the snakes," Becca said, putting her hands to her face. "They're right fearsome creatures though, especially the ones that puff up. We don't have them in Ireland, you know."

"Another reason I love Ireland," Trevor said to his wife.

"No offense, Boyd, but I think it's time to head off more snake talk guaranteed to give me and others the heebie-jeebies," Flynn said, clapping his hands. "Time for the real fun. Louisa and I dreamed up the perfect way to get everyone excited for your wedding day. Hargreaves! We're ready when you are."

Louisa came forward and gazed around the room. "You missed the fun in Chicago," she said in her best pro-wrestling announcer voice, "but you heard about it. Said you'd have joined in—"

"Oh, no," Quinn said out loud, because he suddenly knew where they were going with this. Francesca didn't, though, and she turned her head and gave him a puzzled look.

Caitlyn started clapping with Flynn, and Louisa and Connor joined in.

"It's time for Merriam karaoke!" Louisa cried out, pointing to the doorway.

Hargreaves wheeled in the portable machine, his usually inscrutable smile completely absent.

"Cool!" Alice cried out.

"Not karaoke!" Uncle Arthur smacked his hand to his forehead.

"We have every song from your favorite soundtrack, *Sleepless in Seattle*, all primed and loaded for you," Louisa said, doing a happy dance.

"I love it!" Michaela jumped up and down like a little kid. "Boyd, what first?"

"How about 'A Kiss to Build A Dream On'?" he asked, then kissed her slowly on the mouth and waved his hand in the air to the crowd, signaling they should applaud as it continued.

"Boyd's certainly getting into the spirit of things for tomorrow," Flynn said with a lopsided grin. "It's the only time you get to kiss like that in public and have people clap. Kinda weird when you think about it."

"I think it's great," Caitlyn said, leaning her head against Beau's chest. "I can't wait for our turn. We might need to practice."

"Anytime you want, sweetheart," Beau responded.

Quinn thought about practicing with Francesca. He liked the thought of kissing her unreservedly whenever he felt like it, and he patted her hip to let her know.

Michaela and Boyd gave an endearing rendition of their chosen song, and Louisa had apparently taken on the master of ceremony duties, because when they finished, she took the mike and held it out to him and Francesca.

"Are you two ready for your duet? I was thinking 'We Are The Champions' by Queen might be the perfect victory song. Will you accept the challenge?"

Quinn had watched the last Merriam karaoke in Chicago from the wings, just like he'd experienced most family events in recent years, and everyone knew it. He planned to change that. He turned to Francesca, who was pursing her lips. Was she in shock or trying to hide her amusement? "You game, babe?"

The elegant Francesca Maroun he'd fallen in love with wouldn't have been inclined to participate in karaoke any more than the old Quinn Merriam. But her eyes flashed, and suddenly she was taking the mike from Louisa. "I love Queen, but how about something more apropos. Do you have DJ Khaled's 'All I Do Is Win'?"

Hargreaves entered in the search and started nodding within seconds. "Yes, Miss, we do."

"Then hit it, Hargreaves," she said.

"Oh, my God!" Flynn said, tapping his chest. "I love her. Quinn, you'd better step up your game because your woman has serious swag."

"Serious," Trevor agreed as the song started playing.

Quinn couldn't believe it, but she pointed to the screen

showing the lyrics in that commanding way of hers and he joined her. He knew the song, of course, and really liked it. He hadn't expected Francesca to go for it, but she started jamming to the beat, making his family start jamming along with her.

Trevor whistled, followed by an answering catcall from J.T.

Quinn was bobbing his head, close to Francesca's, and he realized he was having the time of his life.

That sense of celebration continued in the house into the wedding the next day. Michaela and Boyd's ceremony was heartfelt and touching. When Aunt Clara read a love poem written by one of the Maasai children, inspired by Michaela and Boyd, there were few dry eyes in the house. Quinn's throat had grown thick at the line about Boyd sitting by her bedside night after night during her illness. To the little girl who'd written it, his vigil was the greatest act of love any one person could ever give another. He saw Francesca wiping a tear and took her hand.

The absence of most of the international guests was felt, especially at the reading of the Maasai poem. Quinn caught sight of Evan Michaels and Chase Parker, who owned and ran the company where Michaela and Boyd now worked. Selling off the natural health division to them had been a necessary step to ensure Michaela and Boyd could work together on the miracle health cure they'd found.

He felt a pinch about that decision. Their subsidiary would have fit wonderfully under Francesca's new scheme. Maybe in a few years when profits were back up, he could try and bring it back under the Merriam umbrella. It would be nice to have another one of his siblings working with the company.

At the reception, he bypassed the dancing and led Francesca out into the vineyards. He'd thought of this moment for weeks, ever since she'd agreed to go to the wedding with him.

The weather was cool, but she'd wrapped an ivory silk scarf around her shoulders in a fashionable knot. Her elegant navy velvet dress had a sexy slit up the right thigh that inflamed his imagination.

"Where are you taking me?" she asked, her eyes shining like starlight.

He stopped between the vines, where the breeze couldn't touch them, and pulled out his wallet. She reared back as he opened it, and for a moment his heart hurt. She'd thought he was going to propose, and she wasn't ready.

Anger spurted through him.

Give me some credit.

If she hadn't figured out her work future, she wasn't ready to be asked. The next time he asked her, he wanted to be damn sure she was going to say yes.

He pushed his hurt and anger aside and took out the picture of her that he kept in there. Handing it to her, he shifted his weight. "When Flynn got married after Christmas, I came out here and stared at your picture. I know this might sound weird, but I've kept it in my wallet for fifteen years. I couldn't bring myself to take it out."

Somehow it was easier to say that than to use the words to describe the pain and sorrow he'd felt after their breakup.

"It helped me feel like you were still with me. Even after all that time, I was still missing you." He swallowed thickly when she raised her head, the strain on her face noticeable. "Connor found me. I might have mentioned that he urged me to win you back. I wanted to bring you out here and rewrite the scene, so to speak. The last time I was out here, I didn't have you. Merriam Enterprises was in trouble, and I didn't know how the hell I was going to turn it around— personally or professionally."

She pressed the photo to her chest, her eyes somber. "I remember this. I didn't have makeup on, and knowing you thought I was sexy like that made me feel...giddy. And so loved."

"Well, you were. You are. I love the hell out of you, Francesca." He blew out a pent-up breath. "My talk with Connor was over a month and a half ago. I wanted to bring you here to cement how far things had come for both of us."

Taking one of her hands, he squeezed it gently.

"We can move mountains together, babe. I can't wait to see what else we accomplish together. That's all." He raised her hand to his mouth and kissed it.

She smiled at him, a look so full of love and intimacy, he bathed in it. "I'm glad you came after me, Quinn. And may I add... It was about damn time."

"You're going to bust my balls?" He laughed. "Even after this past week? Oh, Francesca, you hold my feet to the fire like no other."

"That's why we work," she said, looking at the photo again. "I didn't know you kept this. Quinn, I... Thank you for showing it to me."

He took it from her and tucked it carefully back into his wallet. "I think I'd like to get a new photo. Of you in one of my shirts and nothing else. Also without makeup."

She linked her arm through his as they walked back toward the music. "That could be arranged. Quinn, I love you. And I'm so glad I'm here with you. I'm truly happy in a way I couldn't be on my own."

Pulling her to him, he kissed her softly. "Me too, babe. Now, let's go join the party. At Flynn's wedding, I'm ashamed to say I sulked away and kept to myself." He'd actually drunk a lot of whiskey, watching his family have fun on the dance floor. Not this time.

His life was never going back to that sorry state. And fairly soon, he and Francesca would be dancing at their own wedding. He could already smell the jasmine.

He only needed to give her a little more time to figure things out.

CHAPTER 17

IT WAS UNANIMOUS. READY THE CHAMPAGNE. I'M COMING home early to celebrate.

Francesca's work was officially done. Merriam's board had approved the restructuring plan.

Quinn had invited her to be a guest at the board meeting, but she'd turned him down. This was his moment, and it made a stronger statement for him to present the plan on his own.

Alice and Hargreaves were sitting in the kitchen, their heads huddled together like usual. Arthur and Clara were with Shawn and Assumpta and the remaining family in town. She'd passed on going over there, wanting to take some time for herself after a whirlwind weekend with Quinn's family. She'd enjoyed every minute, and his family had been wonderful to her.

The quiet gave her time to think, the silence punctuated by Alice's explosive laughter and Hargreaves' quiet chuckles. With the Hales leaving on Wednesday, Francesca knew it would be a letdown for Alice not to see her new friend every day. It hadn't escaped her that any future she decided upon professionally would impact Alice.

"It's done!" she announced. "The plan's been approved. No dissenters." Not that they'd expected anything else, but it was still a relief.

Alice lurched out of her chair and threw her hands up in the air. "Awesome! Bubbly?"

She rose and walked into the kitchen. "Quinn is coming home early, but I think we can have an early celebratory glass."

Without further ado, Alice had three glasses poured and handed out. "To killing it like usual," she said, hoisting her champagne flute. "Francesca, you rock, girl."

Hargreaves lifted his glass in her direction. "To rocking it, as Alice says."

There was a delightful incongruity between the words he spoke and the formal British accent in which he uttered them, which only further demonstrated the impact Alice had had on the man.

Then again, she had transformed Francesca too. "To rocking it. Thanks, you two, for making everything so comfortable here. A relaxing space always ushers in the right creative inspiration."

They clinked glasses, turning to look out the windows at the ocean. The sun had burned off the early morning fog and was shining brightly, causing the water to look positively sapphire.

Goodness, she loved this place. Soon this would be her home, and her heart filled with peace when she thought of it.

An hour later, she was working in her room when her phone rang, and dread crept through her at the sight of her father's name on the display. "Hello, Father."

"I was informed of the press release outlining the Merriam restructuring plan and the board's approval." His sigh was harsh on the line. "I'd hoped it would take you longer to complete it. I warned you against oil. You should have listened, but there's nothing for it now. You should leave San Francisco ASAP."

The sick feeling in her stomach returned. "Why? I rocked this consultancy. Even you have to admit the plan is genius."

Another deep sigh. "It is, daughter. Or it would be under different circumstances. Come to Milan. It's time to talk about you returning to the family company."

She pushed aside a rising tide of anger. He didn't truly think she'd made a mistake—he was playing the same old game with her. Rather than snap at him, which would only lead to an argument, she murmured something noncommittal.

"You love fashion week," he pressed. "It would be good for you to leave town now that you've completed your assignment. For reasons you don't understand. The news about the virus is troubling enough. There are several flights a day between San Francisco and China."

More vague allusions? "According to the news, there are no cases in the Bay Area. Father, you aren't being discriminatory, are you?"

He scoffed. "Can a father not be worried about his daughter's well-being?"

"Dozens of towns in northern Italy are in lockdown, yet you want me to go to Milan with you." She and J.T. had spoken just last night about what was happening in Italy. He'd made Rome his home for many years, and he was deeply worried for his friends and colleagues there. Venice had even halted its annual carnival. It was all so difficult to believe.

"Italy only has around a hundred cases so far. Officials would have closed fashion week if there was just cause. You should come. We could talk."

"And yet Armani presented its line to an empty

showroom and streamed it on the internet yesterday, which was unprecedented." Realization dawned. "Wait a moment. You're already there. Your current mistress wanted to go, didn't she? Were you hoping we would all have dinner?"

"Don't shame your father. She's a lovely woman, and it's not as if I'm a married man. I needed a break from all the squabbling and tension in Lebanon. Much like I need to see my daughter. Things are bad at home, Francesca."

Her heart hurt at the sorrow in his voice. They both knew the financial crisis was worsening. Protestors had taken to the streets. "I keep hoping for a miracle on that front."

"Miracle? We need sweeping changes. Don't get me started. Come to Milan, daughter."

She decided it was time for complete disclosure. "I'm staying here. With Quinn. He and I have fully reconciled, Father."

"Then there is nothing more to say. It won't last, especially when your restructuring plan fails. I did warn you. Goodbye, Francesca."

She stared at the phone after it went dead. That's all he was going to say? She hadn't expected him to be pleased to hear about Quinn, but the cryptic warnings he'd spouted didn't sit well. Her fear and discomfort returned. If he was playing her, would he do it this thoroughly? Usually he tried a tactic to sway her, and if it didn't work, he tried something else.

She pulled up the news on the oil industry again, searching for information. Oil prices had tumbled four percent this morning as concerns over the virus grew. Iran, South Korea, Japan, and Italy were reporting growing infections and a few deaths. The world market continued to be concerned about shrinking oil demand in the face of China's closures.

But her mind kept going back to her first call with her

father. He'd said the virus wasn't the reason for his concern. She rubbed the space between her brows. He had to be privy to something not yet public.

Well, there was nothing she could do about it. If it happened, she and Quinn would deal with it.

When she checked the markets again, her gut wrenched. The Dow was dropping heavily in the U.S. stock market.

She and Quinn had drafted a press release about the restructuring to go out right after the board's vote. News about the restructuring was supposed to shore up Merriam Enterprises' stock price.

Only that wasn't happening. It was caught in the downward market spiral with all the other companies.

She texted Quinn, sick at heart.

You see what's happening with the stock market?

She waited a few minutes for his reply.

We just can't get a break. Our stock is tanking like everyone else's. Jesus. I'm with Trevor, seeing if there's anything we can do. I won't be home early like I thought. Sending you a big kiss.

Part of her wanted to be with him. To work beside him and feel like she was making a difference. Powerlessness wasn't her friend, but they both knew there was nothing they could do on a dive like today.

They'd announced the restructuring. All they could do at this point was hope that investors saw the new plan as a positive and started showing more confidence in the stock after the dust settled. But she feared it wasn't done, what with the virus and her father's dire warning.

A feeling of foreboding bore down on her, and she left her room to find Alice. The door was cracked, but Francesca could see Alice on FaceTime with her best friend, Sarah.

Descending to the first floor to make herself some tea, she smiled when she found Hargreaves seated at the kitchen table, a James Patterson paperback in hand. She would have expected him to favor heavy biographies, so it was delightful to see his interest in a popular suspense novel.

He set it down immediately and rose. "How may I help you, Miss?"

"I was going to make myself tea. I'm a touch restless."

He set his book aside. "I confess to feeling the same. Usually a gripping novel commands my full attention, but the house feels rather empty today. I've spent much of my life alone except for Madam, of course, but I've discovered that I rather like having company."

Her heart melted at the honesty. "I confess I'm missing people as well, Quinn especially. He's been delayed."

"May I recommend an elderflower and chamomile tea?" Hargreaves suggested. "Alice and I developed the blend together. It's been calming for me, especially in light of the news."

She tilted her head and asked, "You and Alice are going to miss each other quite fiercely, aren't you?"

"We will. Her company is most delightful, but we plan to be in touch."

He was already filling the electric kettle with water, and she decided it would be silly to step in. Silly, and likely not appreciated. "She is one of the most positive and enthusiastic people I've ever met. I'm glad she's taken to you so. After her parents died, she found it hard to let people in. Did she tell you?"

"Yes," he said gravely. "She said it was a dark time in her life. Death is very hard, especially when it is so unexpected. You were the first person she decided to accept as her new friend. Then you reached neighbor status."

She thought of Alice talking to Sarah upstairs. They'd gone to grade school together, so their lives had been intertwined for many years. "What a lovely way to put it. I expect you've reached it as well. Do you ever think about retiring, Hargreaves? Sorry, that was an abrupt question. It's only, I'm thinking about what's next for myself—and Alice—since we've been working together for some time."

She'd only given herself a few moments to think about it, but there was one point on which she felt great clarity. She couldn't consult with anyone who was a competitor to Merriam Enterprises. That wouldn't be fair to Quinn. But not knowing what areas Merriam might move into under their Speculative Ventures arm, how could she help other companies? At some point, she might find herself helping a future competitor. Ethically, it didn't feel right.

"I expect you will know what is best for you," Hargreaves said. "If there is one thing you've more than demonstrated, it's that you have a good head on your shoulders. Alice respects and trusts you. You should decide what's best for you and you alone. She wouldn't want it any other way. Perhaps it will give her the room to make her own decisions about the future."

Hargreaves was right. Alice needed space to decide what was next as much as she did. "I appreciate your thoughts, Hargreaves. And you?"

He measured out a teaspoon of loose tea and spooned it into a blue teapot. "I am still musing over my life. These past months since Madam reconnected with her family have been the most exciting time in my life. They have a way of expanding what you believe is possible, simply by being who they are. I admire them for it."

Expanding what you believe is possible. Yes, that's exactly how Quinn made her feel. Hadn't his words in the vineyard been a call to her soul? "I do as well."

He set the teapot to boil, and she gestured to the chair across from her at the table. They both sat.

"This virus is also causing me to ask deeply buried questions inside myself, I must add. The more it spreads across the globe, taking lives as it does so, the more I feel the call of Horace's phrase 'carpe diem.' What do the people facing death wish for in their last moments? I'm terribly sorry if that's too macabre for you, Miss."

She waved her hand. "Please, don't apologize, Hargreaves. It's a very good question." Her mother had wished for more time with her as she lay dying, she remembered. "You know... I haven't let myself think of the human toll this virus will take. When I do, my heart breaks. I was born in 1982, and my earliest memories are of the Lebanese civil war and the toll it took in human terms. I was eight when it ended, but by then, despite my parents' best efforts, I'd seen people killed on the streets. As you said earlier, death is hard."

Hard was an inadequate term for it. She'd trembled at night as the bombs and gunfire kept her awake. Her father, she remembered, had instructed her mother not to comfort her, saying it was a fact of life she needed to become accustomed to. He didn't want a weak daughter.

"Living can be hard too," Hargreaves said, pouring them both a cup of tea. "My father used to say that, and it's stuck with me. He lost his brother in the war, along with many other close friends. He admitted in a moment of rare candor years afterward that he used to wish he'd been one of the brave men who'd been taken. Living had been more difficult, he'd said. Rebuilding was hard."

She thought about Lebanon's rebuilding, something her father and Maroun Industries had been a part of. She admired him for the role he'd played, something else that factored into their complicated relationship. "My father helped rebuild my home country. He isn't the kind of man to talk about his emotions, but I know it took a toll on him."

Hargreaves sipped his tea, lost in thought for a moment. "I imagine so. Your father and mine would have understood each other, I imagine. But I find I've benefited from Mr. Hale's wisdom, although I'd never say so aloud."

She smiled, having observed their playful relationship.

"Mum's the word."

A shaft of sunlight cut through the windows, making his silver hair gleam. "He talks about a man making his own fate, circling the wagons with loved ones, and pressing on and on until undesirable elements are gone or defeated. Certainly his life is a testament to such sentiments. It's given me much to think about."

In her short time with Arthur, she'd seen ample evidence of his unflappable grit. "He is a wise man," Francesca said, "and so are you, Hargreaves."

"You are too kind, Miss."

"Wouldn't you please call me Francesca? I've heard you call Alice by her name."

"Mostly when it's only us two," he said, and then he smiled. "Since it's only you and me for tea, perhaps I can ease up on the restriction. Alice thinks it distances me from people, not using their given names. Her argument is what led to me breaking stringent butler protocol."

Alice had a way about her. "You can't argue with her on points like that."

"No, Francesca, you can't," he said with a winning smile, settling back into his chair, more comfortable now.

She'd won plenty of victories in business, but somehow this felt more momentous. Later she would have to tell Alice. "Thank you for taking tea with me, Hargreaves."

He met her gaze directly, warmth in his brown eyes. "I look forward to doing so again."

They quieted and sipped their tea, watching the sun light up the ultramarine ocean. Francesca relaxed into the companionable silence. Her hard-earned wisdom was to live in the moment, especially when things looked like they were coming apart.

She'd made a new friend, and in times such as these, that gift was priceless.

CHAPTER 18

Arthur Hale had never been one for Doomsday prophesies.

Yet he started every morning by reading a dozen or so trusted papers from around the world—his own included—and they were all painting the same picture: things were bad and getting worse every day. When he talked to Meredith and Tanner, they further confirmed it from their sources. For only the third time in U.S. history, the stock market had finished down more than a thousand points. As if the virus' continual spread around the globe weren't alarming enough.

"Poor Quinn," Clara said, fingering her diamond bracelets. "And poor Merriam Enterprises. Their stock closed down twenty percent when Quinn was hoping for at least a ten to fifteen percent increase. Shawn had to take a walk he was so upset, and J.T., Trevor, and Flynn all headed into headquarters to be with Quinn."

Arthur surveyed the family room at Shawn and

Assumpta's house. Caitlyn's brows were scrunched together, but she was making a valiant effort to carry on a conversation with Annie, who looked equally troubled. Both of them knew how badly things had shifted after this morning's success with the board.

"Arthur, I'm not sure we should leave on Wednesday," Clara said. "A few of the Merriams are talking about staying on longer to see how things shape out with the company."

Only Connor and Louisa had left as planned. Her work with the homeless didn't allow for many vacations. Everyone else had stayed on for the board meeting except for Michaela and Boyd, of course, who were on their honeymoon.

"We'll stay for moral support if you feel it's best, dear," he said, patting her hand.

She released a long breath. "Thank you, Arthur."

He wanted to assure her everything would turn around, but he didn't know if it would, and he wasn't a man for false promises. "Family sticks together in times like these. We'll stay as long as we're needed."

He only wondered how long that might be.

"Mr. Hale," a little voice said suddenly, and he looked over to see Annie's youngest standing beside the couch where he and Clara sat. "Why do you look so upset? Do you need a hug?"

His five-year-old friend Amelia was the apple of his eye, and he smiled to offset the worry around her mouth. "I'll always take a hug from you, Amelia."

"Good! Because I've got plenty for you. Aren't you lucky we live in the same town now so I can give you a hug whenever you need one?"

"I'm the luckiest," he said, enfolding her gently.

Personally, he was delighted Flynn and Annie had decided to move to Dare Valley. He could never have enough little people around him. Amelia always smelled like the orange blossoms her mother loved, as sweet as the girl herself.

"Where are your sisters?" he asked when she hugged him tightly one last time and then released him.

"Iris and Eloise were braiding their hair again, and it was taking *forever*. They tried to catch me, but I can't stand having my hair pulled that tight. It hurts my head."

He tapped her cute little nose, her cheerful sweetness easing his heart. Little ones had a way of pushing the troubles of the world away. His granddaughter, Jill, used to distract him like that when she was younger. Not his other granddaughter, Meredith, though. She used to fret alongside him, reading the newspaper with him from her perch on his lap. It was no wonder she was the one who'd assumed his role at the newspaper he'd founded.

"Your hair looks fine flying free. No need to scrunch it all up like that. Right, Clara?"

"What?"

His wife was fretting too much to listen, which meant one thing. He pointed to her. "She could use a hug too."

"I could, yes," Clara said and leaned forward as Amelia gave another one of her sweet hugs.

"Everyone is reading the news an awful lot, Mr. Hale," Amelia said, pulling on her purple overalls. "Are there lots of articles right now that talk about bad things?"

She'd become his little journalistic pupil a couple of months ago, when he and Clara had gone out to Ohio to help Flynn romance Annie, leading up to their recent marriage. Amelia had black ink in her veins, it seemed, and while her canniness delighted Arthur, he wanted to protect her some now. "There will always be stories that upset us, stories about things we don't want to see in the world. All we can do is try to focus on the good."

She nodded and peeked over her shoulder at her mom before gazing up at him. "But the bad stories are about all the people getting sick from this virus, right? It's called the coro-something—I don't know how to say it."

Clara squeezed his arm in what he could only feel was shock and alarm. He kissed her on the cheek. "My dear, why don't you find Caroline? I believe she was helping Assumpta and Becca make dinner." They were chopping up a storm for kebabs, he knew, channeling their worries into something productive.

Her mouth twisted, but she kissed him again and then stood. They both knew she didn't chop. "I'll see you later, Amelia. Thanks for the hug."

"Anytime, Mrs. Hale," she said, but her tone wasn't quite as bright and cheerful as usual.

"Come on up here," Arthur said, helping the little girl onto the couch next to him. "Seems you're turning into a good little journalist."

"You taught me how to research a story." She swung her feet, which dangled off the end of the couch. "Who, what, when, where, why, and how. Those are the questions you ask. I remember everything you taught me, Mr. Hale. Remember the story I wrote about the twins?"

He'd helped her with that story, hoping she would feel less left out by her older twin sisters. His idea had worked. "You outdid yourself, Amelia."

"Then will you tell me why so many people are getting sick?" she whispered, leaning on his arm. "I heard Uncle J.T. say he was worried about some of the people he knew in Italy getting sick, and I had Iris and Eloise look it up on the tablet, but Mom found us and took it away. She said it would only scare us and not to worry. But I know something's going on. She and Flynn have the news on a whole lot right now."

He cast a furtive glance at Annie, who was watching them out of the corner of her eyes. Of course she was scared. They all were. The Merriams had friends and colleagues in Europe and Asia and beyond. The virus had been growing there. Now it was at America's door. Texas had just announced its first cases, and so had other states recently. It was starting to hit home, and what parent wouldn't want to protect their children from that? "Come on. Let's go for a walk."

Surely Annie would trust him to talk to Amelia. She was a smart girl, and he couldn't bear for her to be scared. Better for her to know the basics of what was going on than to have unanswered questions preying on her mind. At least a person knew what they were dealing with when they were informed.

She took his hand, and he made sure to smile as Annie and Caitlyn lifted their heads. "We'll be back in a bit. Gotta escape the braiding twins."

Annie made a strong showing of a smile. Caitlyn wasn't capable of mustering one, which told Arthur how stressed she must be.

He paused for their jackets in the front coat closet, and then they hustled outside. The path to the vineyards was familiar to him, and he led them there. Amelia wasn't skipping like usual, so when they reached the stone wall at the edge of the vines, he propped her up on it and gathered his thoughts.

"I don't want you to be scared," he told her, "and neither does your mom or Flynn or anyone else."

"Mom isn't scared very much, Mr. Hale, and Flynn is always joking and laughing. But he hasn't been doing much of that lately. I've seen him rub his forehead right here." She pointed between her brows. "And he frowns a lot. Even Iris and Eloise have noticed. I know it's not just the family company because I've been listening—like you told me to."

Eavesdropping, he imagined. Hadn't he said she was a budding journalist? "You see more than the average bear, so I'm going to be straight with you. There is a virus, and it's kinda like the flu."

"We got flu shots last year." Her nose scrunched up. "I don't like getting stuck with needles."

"Neither do I," he said, resting against the stone wall beside her. "This virus doesn't have a shot yet, which is why people are getting it."

"Can animals get it? Like my pony?"

It was still early days, but Arthur hadn't seen anything to that effect. "No, I don't think Carrot can get it. Only people."

"Are many of them dying like my daddy did?" she asked, her blue eyes enormous in her little face.

He stroked her blond hair. Any child who'd lost a parent young was changed by death, and it made them older in years somehow. "Yes, they are."

"How many?" she pressed.

"A fair amount," he decided to say. Telling her the hard figure he'd seen reported today—more than twenty-six hundred—wouldn't be helpful.

"I feel bad for all the kids and mommies and daddies. They're going to cry a lot like my mom, Eloise, and Iris did. Things like this shouldn't happen, should they, Mr. Hale?"

She'd always repeated phrases she'd heard from others, and this one struck him as such, even if it was plain truth. "No, honey. It shouldn't."

"I don't want anyone to die, Mr. Hale. Not you or anyone."

Tears started to stream down her face, and his heart tightened upon seeing them.

"Oh, now, let's not start crying." He put his arm around her as she gave a little wail that tore him open.

He'd faced down death recently with his heart attack this past summer, and while he'd made peace with the prospect of moving on, marrying Clara had been a game changer. She talked about them living until one hundred, and he'd signed on, wanting to enjoy their every adventure and see their families continue to thrive and grow. As news of the virus continued to filter in, he felt a new fear lurking in the back of his mind.

He wasn't ready to go yet. And he didn't want anyone else he loved to go either.

Amelia was sobbing now, and he held her to his chest. "I'm going to tell you a journalist's cardinal rule, Amelia. You don't cry until something bad has happened directly to you. We're supposed to observe and report the news. Not cry over it every day. Be hard to do our job otherwise, right?"

He raised her sweetheart-shaped face, and she wiped her nose. "I don't want to cry every day. I just want to play with my sisters and Carrot and laugh with Mom and Flynn and talk to you. But it still makes me sad, Mr. Hale."

"If it didn't make you sad, I would worry about you, Amelia. Only good people worry about other people like that. But we're reporters, so we have to set our emotions aside and focus on the questions we need to ask to get to the truth."

Nodding, she wiped her nose again, her tears finally stopping. "I have a question. If we can't get a shot, then how do we not get sick?"

He sighed. Did she know about the healing flower Clara had given her family just in case? Should he even mention it? Drat, there weren't enough healing flowers for every sick person in the world, and he felt guilty they had something that might help and couldn't distribute it. Still, there was so much they didn't know. It had healed Michaela from a tropical virus, but who knew what—if anything—it would do for the coronavirus? The testing phase was in its infancy in Michaela and Boyd's new company.

"That's an excellent question," he said instead, "proving how smart you are. Right now, there isn't much of an answer."

A few countries were testing people for the virus and implementing masks, much like he'd seen done during the SARS outbreak in 2003. Arthur had no idea if anything else was effective because he hadn't looked. The go-to seemed to be handwashing, and that just didn't seem to cut it.

Her direct gaze locked him in place. "That's kinda scary, Mr. Hale. You always say there's an answer to every question when you look hard enough."

Caught by a novice reporter. "Then we'll have to look harder, won't we? Thank you for reminding me."

"You're welcome," she said, scooting over on the wall until she could lean her head against his chest. "I'm going to do an article too. You said before you might publish it in your newspaper if it's good enough."

He had said that to her at Flynn and Annie's wedding. "That's our deal."

"Then it will be the best article ever," she said, her blue eyes reminding him of her mother's steely-eyed gaze whenever she talked about her business. "I just want everyone to stay healthy and strong. Grandma Loudermilk prays for that for me and my sisters every day. She told me so. Isn't that nice?"

"The nicest." June was a sweet woman, and he'd enjoyed becoming friends with her on their trip to Ohio. She'd planned to visit them in Dare Valley this summer, but now he had to wonder if that would happen. Travel was starting to slow down in Asia and Europe. Wouldn't the virus affect the U.S. in the same way? It seemed inconceivable, and yet he was reading more articles about its impact daily.

He kissed Amelia on the top of her head. "You are bright as sunshine, Amelia, my dear, and I'm so happy you and I get along so well."

"We're friends, Mr. Hale," she said, hugging him. "I'm happy you answer my questions. I don't like not knowing things, and I'll try not to cry when I do my research."

He wasn't sure he wanted her to read the news directly, without any kind of oversight. "How about you let me take the lead and you can work with me on finding some answers?"

He'd have to talk to Annie and Flynn about it, but you

couldn't hide anything from kids. They always knew something was going on, and if you refused to tell them what, they made up stories to fill in the blanks. Better to help them understand things in a way that made sense for their age.

"Okay. We're good partners. I also asked Iris to help me with my reading so I could research anything. When I read, I understand things better."

Simple, yet profoundly true. "You're prodigious."

She looked up at him. "What's that?"

He thought learning a new word might spike her curiosity and turn her mind away from the virus—if only temporarily—so he told her what it meant. While he was glad he'd been able to comfort her some, he didn't have enough answers yet to allay his own fears. Certainly not Clara's or anyone else he loved.

That didn't sit well with a Pulitzer Prize-winning journalist like Arthur Hale.

CHAPTER 19

H E'D BEEN POISED FOR ONE OF THE GREATEST VICTORIES
of his career. Instead, Quinn was nursing a whiskey with Trevor, J.T., and Flynn in what could only be described as a war room party.

"You guys should head back to Mom and Dad's," he
told them, finishing off his drink. "I can't thank you enough
for pitching in today."

Seven o'clock had come and gone. They'd all been on
the phone nonstop to senior Merriam executives, industry partners, and market insiders. While their restructuring plan was largely seen as strong, some were thinking it
was too late.

With oil prices taking another dive along with the giant
plunge of the stock market, Quinn couldn't blame them.
Merriam Enterprises was in more trouble than ever. Even
Francesca's genius hadn't been able to save them.

He couldn't imagine how upset she must be. When he
got home, he'd have to assure her somehow.

"We need to show some strength here at headquarters," Trevor said, clapping him on the back and finishing his own drink. "I'm staying on to help you, Quinn. Caitlyn and Beau said they'd fly Becca back to Ireland tomorrow on their way to Provence."

"Annie said she'll fly home with the girls so I can stay longer too," Flynn said, only adding to the constriction in Quinn's throat. "We're still getting into the new normal with their school."

"Caroline will go with them," J.T. said. "I'm not leaving until we dig our way out of this ditch. Jesus. This virus is killing us."

It was literally killing people too, but no one wanted to voice that.

"It's hurting everyone's stocks," Trevor said, rubbing his eyes. "We have to remember we aren't alone in this bleed."

"True, but we were in a weak position going into today," Quinn said, "and current global conditions aren't helping any."

"No, they aren't," Flynn said, flicking open the button of his jacket. "Dammit. Francesca's plan rocked. It shouldn't have gone down like this."

"It did, and we deal." He was sick of complaining about it even if he wasn't sure what to do about it. "Oil prices haven't just been free-falling. They rose before. Let's hope they do again."

Hell, when had he become an optimist?

"All right," Trevor said, clapping him on the back again. "You head on home to Francesca, and we're going to get back to Mom and Dad's place. See you in the morning."

He faced his brothers. "Thanks for being here."

They'd gone beyond their duties to the company tonight, and they all knew it.

"It's what family does, bro," J.T. said. "Later, man."

He man-hugged him, and his other brothers did the

same.

"You enjoy pounding me, Trev?" he asked, rotating his shoulder jokingly.

"Am I treating you too rough?" his brother responded with a laugh. "Maybe Francesca will kiss it and make it better."

"She'd skin your balls if she heard you talk like that," Quinn said, but he was smiling.

"I love that about her," Trevor said. "You might consider hiring her on a more permanent basis. She has a reputation for excellence, and having her on board might bring in extra market confidence fairies."

"Your time in Ireland has made you daft," Quinn shot back. And then, because he couldn't duck the suggestion without comment, no matter how much he might want to, he added, "She's figuring out her next steps professionally now that we're back together."

J.T. cleared his throat. "I see. Hang in there, bro. Okay, now we're out of here."

They left the room, and he rubbed his brow. Truthfully, he did wish Francesca would decide to join them. Him. But after the bath they'd taken in the market, he hated asking her to board a leaky ship. And hadn't he promised he'd give her space?

He had to keep his promise. A person's word meant everything to her.

When he arrived at his house, it was nearing ten o'clock. Entering from the garage, he let himself into the lower level and stopped short at the sight of her standing in front of the windows.

When she turned, the devastation was obvious in the tense lines of her mouth and around her eyes. "It was a tough day, and I'm sorry. I had a glass of champagne with Alice and Hargreaves to celebrate. Before the market took a tumble."

He crossed to her and pulled her into his arms. "Yeah,

and I've had a belly full of talking about it. The only thing I need to say is this: your plan is still genius. We're just dealing with a global situation that's unprecedented. Okay?"

She tightened her grip around him. "I know that. Still, I'm sorry. I can't imagine how you felt today. When I tried to put myself in your shoes, I felt sick."

"I was sick," Quinn said, "but my brothers came in and helped me make some big calls. It helped more than I would have thought. They're staying on for a while longer. Trevor's calling it a show of strength."

Pressing away, she caressed his face. "He's right. You need to show you aren't concerned about what's happening. People respect strength, especially in moments like this. You stand tall. Keep your chin up. The market responds to it."

He uttered a derisive chuckle. "Usually. Now? Hard to call. Come on, I need to grab something to eat, and then I want to go out to the cottage. How was your day other than all of this?"

"Some things good. Others not so much. But my biggest victory was unexpected. Hargreaves used my first name today. Only don't tell him I told you."

"Your people skills remain nothing short of miraculous."

She kissed him slowly on the lips. "They worked on you, didn't they? I seem to remember a terribly grouchy executive at my door only last month."

Was he heading back to grouch territory with all this doom and gloom? God, he didn't want to go back to that. "We'll try to keep him in the past. It might help if you kiss me again."

Winding her arms around his neck, she tipped his head down to hers and gave him a thorough kiss, one that had him reconsidering a late meal. He deepened the kiss and thought about breaking his own rule about sex in the house.

When she started to unzip his pants, he realized she was of a similar mind. Eyeing the stairs, he decided no one was likely to come down. Usually everyone in the house was in bed by this time. No one would have any reason to venture all the way down here.

He was glad she was wearing a loose skirt. His mouth had watered as she'd rolled up her thigh-high stockings this morning, a tantalizing way to send him off to the board meeting. His hand found her center, and sure enough, she didn't have anything on.

"You planned this," he whispered, stroking her slowly.

"I knew where you'd come after parking your car," she said, opening her legs wider. "I thought you might want to be alone with me. Plus, this is where we finished our assignment. I thought it apt for us to make love here."

He hoisted her up onto his hips, savoring the tantalizing feel of her legs wrapping around him. "Full circle. I like the way you're thinking."

Kissing her deeply, he walked them over to the windows facing the ocean and pressed her against the glass after checking to make sure it wouldn't be too cold for her skin. Then he looked her straight in the eye and penetrated her. She moaned, low and long in her throat, and then he started thrusting slowly in and out.

"I love you," he said in a low voice.

"I love you too," she said, tightening her legs around him. "Come with me now."

When she raised her hands over her head, he grabbed them and held on tight. Their pace became frenzied, both of them meeting thrust for thrust. When she came, he pressed his mouth to hers to cover her moans and followed her over the edge.

Panting against her neck, he stared out at the ocean below. It was churning, the tide high. The world felt like that to him right now, and he didn't know what to do to hold it back.

"I'll make some calls tomorrow on your behalf," she said, kissing him on the cheek. "If that's all right with you."

Her offer to help had something hot burning in the back of his throat. He didn't need to ask who she'd call. Her connections were on point and strategic. "I'd love that. Thank you."

"I promised to help you make Merriam Enterprises profitable again. That goal still hasn't been achieved, so I hope you don't mind extending my contract when I go into headquarters with you in the morning. I always finish the job."

Pressing his forehead to hers, he was shocked to feel the burn of tears behind his eyelids. God, he had to be exhausted to feel this raw. "Done. Francesca, I—"

"You don't have to say it," she told him, cupping the back of his nape lovingly. "You don't need to say it."

"Yeah, I do. Babe, you can't know how much this means."

"My reputation is at stake too, after all." Her voice was hoarse as well. "Can't let people thinking I did a half-ass job."

He imagined she meant it as a joke, but he realized it was true. Some industry analysts might genuinely feel that way. More weight settled over his shoulders. He had to make this right for himself and his family and employees, but he needed to do it for her too.

And he could. He *would*. With her support, somehow everything would be all right.

It had to be.

CHAPTER 20

FRANCESCA WENT TO THE OFFICE WITH QUINN THE NEXT day, wanting to support him with her presence, and he'd offered up the conference room so she could make some calls. But she hadn't been in there for more than a few hours when she heard the breaking news. It was shocking enough that she stopped what she was doing and immediately walked into Quinn's office.

"The mayor of San Francisco has just declared a state of emergency in the city," she said without preamble, prompting him and his brothers to turn their heads her way. "We're going to need to find somewhere else to work. Draft a plan for Merriam Enterprises here and prepare one for the branch offices overseas to either work at home or close. It can't be put off anymore, Quinn. Not after today."

"But we don't have a single case of the virus in San Francisco," Quinn said, jerking on his tie. "Yesterday there was a dog-and-pony show in Chinatown encouraging everyone to visit, saying there was no cause for alarm."

"Seems your mayor feels differently," Francesca said. "You need to prepare people to work from home wherever possible. Flynn, I assume your tech team can help set that up. Trevor, given where things are going, you might want to halt oil production on the rigs for now. I've talked to a few people who are taking that approach."

They were all staring at her. Except for Quinn, who was sitting back, an amused smile on his face.

"Sorry, did I overstep? That did sound rather—"

"Authoritative," Flynn said, crossing and kissing her cheek. "I love it. Man, you're an awesome team player. Bro, seriously, you have so scored with this one."

Quinn's eyes lifted to hers, and she saw the love and warmth in them. "I know it. All right, let's get the plans drafted. Hell, closing down headquarters physically right now—"

"Will suck and make our job harder," Trevor said, shaking his head.

But the tide was changing. The first case was announced in San Francisco the next day, and another county in California declared a state of emergency.

"I don't think we can wait," Quinn said as he sat with his brothers and Francesca at the round work table in his office. "Something doesn't feel right. A few days ago, a senior official was encouraging travel to Chinatown. Then the mayor declared a state of emergency, and the very next day we're hearing about an actual case. What's going on behind the scenes?"

"We need to be proactive and make good decisions for ourselves and our people," Trevor said.

"I agree," Flynn said. "I've created a software program to do some data mining on the virus. We need to see the real numbers."

"Numbers are only going to get us so far given there are so many countries, politicians, and international groups involved," Francesca said. "I've seen countries quibble over lesser things. What we need to do is find a safe place to work, with good internet access. I would recommend somewhere remote. An urban center doesn't feel right after everything I've seen in the news. I don't think we need to worry about being in the same time zone as headquarters since your people work all over the world."

"How about Ireland?" Trevor asked, resting his elbows on the table. "The Wild Irish Rose Inn has plenty of rooms right now since it's low season. Becca's had a few people cancel bookings already because of the virus. We have an in-house chef and lots of space. We could take it over."

Francesca had checked out the inn online after hearing about it from others in the family, and it looked captivating. But it wasn't her call. Quinn had his hand over his mouth, and she sensed his brother's offer had touched him deeply.

"Also, it would ensure we can be on the same video conference calls together when needed," Trevor added. "Plus, Buttercup."

Clara had showed her the original video of Trevor fleeing from the animal, and she'd laughed so hard she'd cried.

"That alpaca would be a boon right now," Flynn said with a lopsided smile.

"It feels important for us all to be together," J.T. said. "Caroline and I have been talking. If things worsen here like they have in Asia, museums will close. We won't have anything to do, and I'm sure as hell not sitting home when I can help you with Merriam."

Francesca grabbed Quinn's hand under the table.

"You never could sit quietly when you were a kid," Quinn joked, but his voice was thick. "I'd love to have your help. I've gotten used to it over the last month."

J.T. gripped Quinn's shoulder. "Yeah, I know you love me. Flynn, what about you and the family? I know you're getting settled in Dare Valley right now and the girls have school."

Flynn tilted his head back and studied the ceiling. "Annie and I have been talking about this. With the company still in trouble, her merger, and this virus... You don't want to make a bad move here. I mean, hell, it would rip my guts out if Annie or the girls got sick."

Tears burned in Francesca's eyes. She thought of her father going to Italy. Even with their rancor, she didn't want anything to happen to him. Beyond that, she hadn't let herself think about the possibility of Quinn or one of the Merriams falling sick. Quinn squeezed her hand tightly, and she glanced at him. His mouth tipped up encouragingly, and she made herself smile back.

"Well, hell, man," Trevor said, punching Flynn lightly in the shoulder. "Aren't you worried about me? I thought we were close."

Flynn uttered a harsh sound and let his head fall forward. "I wish I could laugh, Trev. Believe me, I do. Of course I worry about you guys. But I'm more worried about Mom and Dad and Uncle Arthur and Aunt Clara. From what China is reporting, most of the people who've died are elderly."

"I wouldn't call any of them elderly to their faces," Trevor tried to joke again, but it fell flat.

"Sorry," Flynn said, letting out an explosive breath. "This isn't what we were talking about. Let's get back on track."

"We need to talk to the rest of the family," Quinn said. "The others might not be as involved in the post-board issues, but we should still ask Caitlyn to join us. France had their first known death over a week ago, and being so close to Italy—"

"People are still traveling," Francesca said. "Fashion week in Italy involves a lot of attendees from France." She thought of her father again.

"The lavender farm is remote, at least," Quinn said. "But I think we're better off sticking together."

"I agree," Trevor said. "Beau won't be going on the road for his upcoming concerts, one would imagine."

Entertainment could come to a standstill. Again, the feeling of the surreal settled over her.

"What about Mom and Dad and Aunt Clara and Uncle Arthur?" J.T. asked, his brow knit with worry.

Quinn stood up and helped her out of her chair. "We ask them what they want to do. Should we call Michaela and Boyd, do you think?"

"I hate to interrupt their honeymoon," Trevor said, rising as well, "but I'm glad they switched it to Wyoming. With Michaela being so ill only a few months ago, we need to protect her health at all costs."

Francesca couldn't agree more. People with weakened immune systems were one of the high-risk groups. "Maybe they should extend their honeymoon."

"It'll be like a love quarantine," Trevor said, making another attempt at a joke. "They sure as hell won't be traveling around the globe for a while."

"I think we still ask them to come after their honeymoon," J.T. said.

"We ask everyone, then," Quinn said, turning to Francesca. "Will you ask Alice?"

She nodded. Usually she took a couple of weeks off between consultancies to clear her mind. She and Alice would jet to Paris or London for a much-needed break. Not now. She expected her friend already knew that, but they hadn't talked about it yet.

As for the companies on her waiting list, she'd had a few inquiries on timing. There was a lot of fear in the market, especially since the Dow continued to decline. She'd told them her schedule was still occupied at the moment.

"All right," Quinn said. "We should go to Mom and Dad's now."

The other Merriam brothers had driven in together, and she and Quinn had come in his car. "We'll see you there," she said. "I want a minute with your brother."

After they left, he set his hands on her waist. "Why do I have an idea you're about to tell me something I may not like?"

She laid her hand on his lapel, removing one of her hairs. She'd have to be more careful about kissing him in his business attire. "If you're going to ask your family to come to the inn and help the company—as well as stay safe—you should have a role for your father. It would be hard for any man to sit on the sidelines and watch the business he'd poured his life's blood into crumble. Your father might be retired, but he had pull with the market and he's smart. I think you should include him."

He pulled her to him. "All hands on deck. I suppose you're right. J.T. is coming back on board. Why not him?"

"It doesn't undermine you," she said softly. "It shows strength and wisdom. Why wouldn't you use an ace when you have it in your hand?"

Kissing her cheek, he framed her face. "You're right. How about Aunt Clara? I was going to ask them to come anyway, and she's the one who came up with the idea of spinning off the plant science division after we had trouble in Africa. At this point, I'll take everyone's help."

"Within reason, of course," she said, knowing sometimes more opinions were harder to manage. "Asking her for help is a wonderful idea. She grew up with the business at its glory. She's also a canny woman."

"Do you believe she and Uncle Arthur will come?" he asked, rubbing his brow. "They have family in Dare Valley too, and Uncle Arthur might not want to be so far away from them for an indeterminate amount of time. Especially at such a pivotal time. I imagine he'll be tempted to help out some with his newspaper, retired or not."

A light flicked on in Francesca's head. It occurred to her that newspapers—news in any form—would only become more important in the months ahead. "You just gave me an idea. I'm going to look into the media sector and see if there are any companies we can cheaply acquire for your Speculative Ventures Initiatives. We might be able to add some profit quickly that way."

"Because information will be more critical than ever in the months ahead," Quinn said, kissing her flush on the mouth. "You sure you don't want to be the CEO of SVI? You're already thinking like it."

She caressed his face to soften her answer. "Let's keep my role as it is for now. But I'll keep the possibility in mind."

His face fell. "But you said you weren't going to think about your future while working with me. I find I want it settled—for both of us."

She did too, but she also knew better than to rush when so much was at stake. "So much is changing daily. Staying current needs to be our focus."

"Our future doesn't take second fiddle to anything." He took her hands. "Not even business."

And yet, business ran through their blood; it nourished the roots of their family trees. "We're together, and I'm going to Ireland with you to work. The rest of it will unfold. We have to keep Merriam and everyone's safety as our priority right now. Our future is here and now."

His mouth twisted. "Here I'd envisioned everything would fall into place as soon as we finished our plan. That we'd be able to go away for a week somewhere with a beach. All of that seems impossible right now."

"We'll have time together in Ireland," she said, holding him tightly.

But she well knew they had their hands full, and time was of the essence.

CHAPTER 21

WHAT IN THE WORLD WERE SHE AND ARTHUR GOING TO do?

Clara wasn't prone to sleeplessness anymore. Her restless and lonely nights before reuniting with the Merriam children and Arthur had disappeared. Until tonight.

A large contingent of Merriams was going to Ireland. Flynn and Annie had said they needed to think it through more. Clara and Arthur had been invited too, but they hadn't decided yet. He'd been so drawn by the end of the family meeting, she'd told him to go to bed. His exhaustion had produced some uncharacteristic snoring on his part, and every deep rumble of it seemed to shake her heart.

What were they to do?

His family was in Dare Valley, and she loved them with all her heart. But her Merriam family had become more important to her than she'd ever imagined. Furthermore, Quinn had suggested he wanted her to contribute to keeping Merriam afloat with her "strategic business sense."

How was she to refuse?

A loud snort sounded next to her, and Arthur rolled onto his side. His warm hands reached for her under the covers. She settled back against him, her mind spinning. His breathing changed and his hand left her and reached up to rub his face. Usually that meant he was trying to wake himself.

"You can't sleep, huh?" he mumbled, kissing her neck. "God, I was out. Did I snore?"

She smiled in the dark. "It wasn't displeasing. I envied you the rest."

"Everything caught up with me," Arthur said, his voice growing stronger as he woke. "As the young people might say, 'shit got real.'"

"Yes, it sure did." She squeezed her eyes shut. "What are we going to do? I wish we could be in two places at once."

He rolled onto his back and tucked her against him. "But we can't. If we leave, it would mean canceling your eightieth birthday party."

"I know that," she said, her heart aching a touch. "I'll be with family, and that's all that counts."

His harrumph wasn't more than a murmur. "So you want to go then—to Ireland."

For the first time in her marriage, she felt an uncertain gulf between them. Part of her wanted to qualify her answer or say something like *what do you think*? But if she'd learned anything in the past months—and God, wasn't she turning eighty in two days on the twenty-eighth?—it was that she had to be honest and speak from the heart. "Yes, especially after Quinn said he'd welcome my help. But I know you have your own family to think about."

"You're my family too, Clara, gosh darn it," he grumbled, rubbing the arm she had on his chest.

"Arthur, if there was ever a time for brutal honesty, it's now." She rose on an elbow, wishing she could see his face. "You've had them for a lot longer than you've had me. We've never thought in terms of 'step' this or step that. You know I love them as if they were blood relatives."

"And I love your Merriams," he admitted. "Dammit, woman, you know that."

"Yet the world is falling apart quickly, and we have to decide where to circle the wagons, as you say. Arthur, do you see us being apart for this? You in Dare Valley and me in Ireland?"

His harrumph was both heartwarming and heart-wrenching. "No, dammit. I don't want to be without you. You're my wife, my life, my heart."

She pressed herself to his side, tears filling her eyes.

"But so is my family in Dare Valley...and the same is true of your Merriams. Oh, Clara. We should feel blessed to have so many people we care about and the means to even talk like this."

Nodding into his chest, she took a breath. "I know. We are lucky. For so long, I only had Hargreaves." She thought of her dearest friend, who'd changed so much over the last month. He would go wherever she went, but still, she would free him to make his own decision.

"You have a whole bunch of people on your side, so don't let those past maudlin thoughts sneak in. You hear me?"

His bluster couldn't have blown a piece of paper down, but it was still comforting.

"I know Meredith and Tanner will be okay," Arthur said. "Tanner worked in warzones, and Meredith showed her true grit when she came back to Dare Valley and rebuilt her life. It's Jill who worries me. After my talk with Amelia, I realized I wasn't asking some important questions about health and wellness. Clara, I can't find jack shit about the virus' effect on pregnant women and their babies."

"Lucy is pregnant too," Clara added, her heart sinking.

"At least Andy's a doctor," he said. His great-nephew

might be a generalist, but he was a good one. "God, he lost his first wife so young. It just can't happen again."

"Arthur Hale, you stop those thoughts right now," she said, putting steel into her voice. "You're thinking worst case when nothing has happened yet."

"But it's coming, Clara," he said, finally sitting up and turning on the bedside light. "You were right about that."

In the soft glow, his wrinkles seemed to define his face, almost like a map of the life he'd lived. One of her old friends in the Maasai village had taught her about the meaning of wrinkles. The longer, deeper ones marked the good times and good choices, especially those around the eyes and mouth, while the shorter, broken ones showed choices one regretted.

Clara had watched her wrinkles change since being re-united with Arthur and her family. The smaller, broken ones had healed through her smile and newfound joy while the others were softening into signs of wisdom. She didn't want this new threat to stamp its presence on her face. She wouldn't tolerate it.

"You can feel it every day," Arthur said, his blue eyes troubled. "Before I met you, I had a feeling of peace about death. About moving on. But you changed things for me. Dammit, I want to reach one hundred and then some with you, and I want the rest of our family to do the same."

She bit her lip. "So do I. We have the healing flower from Kenya that saved Michaela's life. I just wish we had enough for the entire world."

"Yeah, I've thought about that. It's hard for me to rec-oncile—as both a human being and a journalist. Healing shouldn't be anyone's exclusive domain. But there's the red tape to think about. Even with fast-tracked testing, it's still too slow. And even if everything goes well, the flowers will still need to be grown. Bah! What's the use of having a heal-ing flower that's not ready to help the world?"

"You're right about it taking too damn long," Clara

said, cursing uncharacteristically.

"The hands of time are clicking loudly right now," Arthur said. "I hate dancing to the tune."

She hugged him. "Don't fret too much. It's probably not good for your blood pressure or your heart."

"Bah! I'm as fit as a fiddle and plan to keep it that way. In fact, I wanted to tell you... Tomorrow, if you and Hargreaves are doing one of your exercise things, I hope you don't mind me joining you."

"We'd love that!" she cried out. "Oh, Arthur Hale, you dear, dear man."

She wouldn't focus on how scared he must be to suggest such a thing. This was a victory.

"Only I want to be clear about a few things," he said, a twinkle coming back into his eyes. "I'm not sure I can or want to get into that downward dog thing."

Suddenly the urge to laugh was upon her. "You do the poses you want to. Yoga is about freedom."

"I also won't stand for Hargreaves adjusting my poses like he does with yours."

As if Hargreaves would ever presume, but she nodded again, laughter close to the surface. "I'll put my hands on you if needed. How about that?"

"I'm always up for that," he said, extending his cheek. "How about you give me a kiss?"

Her hand cupped his face and she planted one sweetly on his mouth.

"You missed, but I like your target. Got any other targets in mind?"

His cheeky request suggested their underlying tension was gone. "Before I do, have we decided anything? Or do we need more time?"

"I go with you, my dear, and you need to go to Ireland. For your family and for the business. I don't see it going any other way."

She squeezed her eyes shut as conflicting emotions

surfaced. "Are you sure you can live with that?" Her mind tossed up a horrible image of something happening to one of his relatives in Dare Valley. How would he feel if he wasn't there? Jill was having her baby in mid-May. Surely they would be home by then.

"I live with my choices, and this one I make freely," he said gruffly.

"I love that about you," she said, kissing him slowly on the mouth. "Thank you."

"Don't thank me. We go together. Always. I'll be able to touch base with the Hales on that dratted FaceTime you use so much. You'll have to help me with it—and the texting. Jill loved to text me before I put her on a monthly plan."

He'd insisted his granddaughter could only text him three times a month—a rule he'd instituted after an onslaught of memes. But Jill had only gotten more inventive. She texted Clara endless pictures of the twins for her to share with Arthur. He might bark, but he looked at every single one.

"And the newspaper?" she asked.

"Meredith and Tanner will see it through these times and report the hell out of everything. If they need me, they know how to reach me. I imagine I'll have an Op Ed or two to contribute. And Amelia and I are working on an article together, remember?"

She did, and she kissed him again for being so dear with his little assistant. Annie and Flynn had agreed with his approach, knowing they couldn't stop Amelia from pursuing her story. Also, they didn't want to. She might be young, but she was also smart. They wanted her to live without fear, and if this helped, so be it.

"Well, back to Ireland," Arthur said, fitting his arm around her. "We experienced plenty of magic and miracles there on our first two visits. Do you think it has more to share with us on that score?"

God, she hoped so. Becca had made the Wild Irish Rose Inn a haven for herself since the world had been so scary for her. She'd suffered from agoraphobia for years, and only in recent months had she managed to leave the grounds of the inn. How ironic that she'd conquered her fear at a time when the world was growing scarier by the day. "If I have to scour the countryside for every rainbow and fairy to find that magic, I will."

"So will I, my dear."

As she slowly drifted off to sleep, her worries keeping her awake, she found herself imagining the inn. Situated on the sea, it seemed far away from world events, a place out of time, some would say.

Now it would be a haven for the Merriam family while they tried to save the company and keep the family safe from the virus.

CHAPTER 22

QUINN HAD NEVER THOUGHT OF HIMSELF AS A SENTIMEN-
tal man.

At least not in the years he and Francesca were apart.
She'd brought out that piece of him, alongside a surprising tenderness. Seeing her surrounded by the family who
had come to Ireland in the Wild Irish Rose's dining room
evoked heart pangs. She was sitting next to Trevor, twirling
a lock of her black hair like she used to in graduate school
when studying a particularly complicated problem, as Buttercup—his brother's lovesick alpaca—bobbed her head
outside the window. The animal's forlorn cry had everyone
laughing, including his father, who sat beside his mother
at the next table.

"Quinn!" Alice called, appearing beside him, presum-
ably coming from the kitchen where she and Hargreaves
were cooking with Becca's French chef for Aunt Clara's
birthday dinner. "Have you tried Aileen's scones? They're
ridiculous!"

Aileen O'Shea often made the scones when Becca had other duties, and he had to concur with Alice's assessment. "I hope you saved me some."

"She made like ten batches with our entourage showing up. She told me your brother's record is ten in one sitting. Maybe we should have a scone-off to relieve all the tension. I'm so glad we're here. I was just telling my friend Sarah how awesome it is here. I mean, if the sixty rabbits weren't cute enough, there's Buttercup. I think I'm in love."

Alice seemed to be a ray of sunlight regardless of circumstances. Francesca had commented on her friend's unbelievably positive nature, something she'd honed after her parents' deaths. Quinn could respect that kind of grit. "Don't tell Trevor. He and Buttercup have a thing going."

"Don't they just?" Aileen said, coming out of the kitchen and wiping her floured hands on her apron. "Have you had your scones yet, Quinn? I've just taken a fresh batch out of the oven."

He inhaled deeply, taking in the smell of butter and rich baked goods in the air. "I haven't had breakfast yet. I had a few calls to make with our European partners."

Aileen gave him a gentle shove toward the tables. "Well, go on with you now. I'll make you a fresh plate. Come on, Alice. Let's get back to the kitchen. It's not every day a woman turns eighty."

Alice winked at him, and then Aileen was putting her arm around the woman and ushering her away. As the door swung open, Quinn could hear the excited French coming from Chef Padraig Buckley, followed by Hargreaves' reply. Alice joined in, and the trio laughed. Since Chef Padraig— trained at the Cordon Bleu and an award-winning restaurant in Paris—was known for his seriousness in the kitchen, Quinn had to scratch his head. There was something about Alice and Hargreaves these days. They'd become a force of nature, capable of getting a laugh or a smile out of nearly anyone.

Laughter was a commodity right now, and he wished he could store it up like scones. When they talked business, there wasn't any such sound, only the gnashing of teeth and the popping of jaws.

"How did your calls go?" Francesca asked, having left the table to cross to him.

"About how you'd expect. Investor confidence is the lowest I remember seeing it. But people are more worried about themselves than they are about us. They didn't ask how we were faring. They assumed it was bad news."

She laid her hand on his shoulder in a show of comfort. "Come and eat," she said, leading him to the table. "You'll feel better afterward."

He greeted everyone and sat down, and to his surprise, he ate heartily. Buttercup's grunts and cries through the window were the background music, adding a bit of much-needed cheerfulness.

"This isn't the kind of birthday celebration anyone imagined for Aunt Clara," J.T. said to his right, tearing apart another scone. "We were all supposed to fly into Dare Valley and give her the time of her life."

"At least we're together," Caroline said, her face taut with tension. "Alice and Hargreaves are baking her an incredible chocolate cake named after a queen."

"A *reine de saba*," Francesca supplied.

"I haven't wished her happy birthday yet," Quinn said, noting his aunt and uncle's absence. "Where is she?"

"Uncle Arthur took her on a walk to see the rabbits after they ate breakfast," Caroline said. "She was wringing her hands terribly this morning after reading the news."

"Her face looked drawn," J.T. said, cursing under his breath. "She's scared."

"We all are," Caroline said. "I talked to a couple of my sisters last night, and everyone in the States is holding their breath."

Quinn stood, tired of the doom and gloom. "I'm going

to wish her a happy birthday. Then let's get back to work."

Francesca stood with him. "I'll come with you."

Pride swelled in his chest—it still came as a shock, a delight, that he had her support and love. He took her hand, and they walked to the coat closet together. "I was going to ask you."

"You were in your take-no-prisoners mode," she said, tugging on her coat. "I also know you're struggling with all of this dire talk."

"Do I need to be more patient?" he asked, shoving his hands through the sleeves of his jacket. "Understanding? There's nothing to be done about any of it except what we're already doing."

She framed his face, her hands cold. "Agreed. But yes, you might want to be a bit more understanding. Everyone's emotions are stretched to the limit right now."

He studied her, noting the worry lines around her expressive violet eyes. "Yours too." He reached up to touch her brow. "The worry never goes away anymore, even when we make love." He'd looked into her eyes in the aftermath last night, but there'd been no sign of her usual peace and lassitude. He felt powerless to help her. Powerless to improve the situation or allay anyone's fears.

"It keeps it away long enough," she said, "and that's something to be grateful for."

"I want to slay every damn worry for you," he said, pulling her toward his chest.

"I feel the same," she said, tightening her arms around him for a moment. "Come on. You might want to try holding a rabbit this time. They're wonderful for stress reduction."

Like hell, he thought. "If I end up holding a rabbit for comfort, commit me. I won't be fit to do anything."

She led him out of the inn. "Oh, you tough guys."

The wind was bracing when they cleared the house. In the distance, the sound of the waves crashing against the cliffs signaled a potent fight between the land and the sea. He wondered if either side ever won or if the fight continued daily without a clear victor. Oddly, that battle was something he understood. He could batter himself against the market daily and still not feel like he'd won anything.

"You're thinking," Francesca said, tugging on his hand. "Set your worries aside for a moment and take in the view. Aren't we fortunate to be here? The sea is so powerful today; the inn is breathtaking, and the company is *magnifique.*"

Her use of the French wasn't lost on him. "Next you'll be in the kitchen, talking in French and cooking with the others."

She smiled. "Maybe I will. I haven't made you Lebanese coffee yet."

A punch of memory hit him: Francesca sitting on his lap in nothing but his shirt as they drank coffee after dinner. "Maybe a private drink in our room is in order."

Her eyes sparkled. "Maybe."

Hours later, she made Lebanese coffee for his entire family after Aunt Clara's special birthday dinner. He helped arrange the cups so she could pour. They weren't the traditional small cups, but Francesca had declared them a perfect substitute. "You didn't have to do this."

She slowly filled the cups, one after another, careful not to pour out the grounds in the bottom of the saucepan. The brew was a redolent mixture of milk, coffee, sugar, and a touch of cardamom.

"I was happy to," she said. "She deserves all the good cheer we can give her. Your gift was lovely."

He set the filled cups on the silver tray Aileen had provided for them. "I shopped at Becca's yarn shop. It was a piece of cake."

More than that—it had been enjoyable, something he wasn't ready to admit out loud. The first time he'd met Becca was an unmitigated disaster. He and Connor had come to the inn in a chopper, not knowing she had severe agoraphobia triggered by the sound of helicopters. She and Connor had established a sort of camaraderie on the family's last visit, but Quinn had never really had a moment alone with her. He appreciated the trouble she'd gone to in the shop—she'd brought out a bright red yarn she'd only just finished, something that wasn't available for sale yet—and they'd ended up talking for half an hour. She'd attempted to give him the yarn for free, knowing it was for Clara, but he'd insisted on paying, something she'd declared she would only agree to in exchange for a hug. So he'd hugged her, and when he pulled away, he could tell both of them were feeling the emotion of it.

"Speaking of cake," Francesca said. "I might need some more of the *reine de saba*. Hargreaves and Alice outdid themselves."

"I heard Hargreaves say it was one of the cakes they learned how to make at that chocolate cooking class back in San Francisco."

"I hadn't heard," Francesca said. "How nice! I knew Alice would love the class. Chocolate makes everything better, she always says. Come on, let's take these trays out to everyone."

When they entered the dining room, each bearing a tray of coffee, he saw Aunt Clara had changed into the sapphire blue cocktail dress Caitlyn had gotten her.

"Clara, that looks wonderful on you," Francesca said, approaching the first table and going from person to person to allow them to choose their cup while Quinn did the same at the adjoining table.

"I can't wait to see what adventures you have in it," Caitlyn said, but her smile dimmed before she finished the sentence.

Quinn knew what she was thinking. What adventures were they likely to have? Europe was talking about locking down, and the U.S. was sure to do the same.

"Tonight my adventure is being here, at the Wild Irish Rose Inn," her aunt said, running her hand along the fine cloth. "In fact, I'm going to dance with my beloved husband. Becca, my dear. Would you pull up a song on your speakers so we can dance?"

His sister-in-law picked up her phone and brought it over to the music console. "How about 'As Time Goes By'?" she asked, plugging it in. "I loved hearing that at Boyd and Michaela's wedding."

"That sounds lovely," Aunt Clara said, pulling their uncle from his chair.

He spun her slowly in a circle. Trevor whistled, followed by J.T.'s piercing catcall, as Louis Armstrong belted out the song. After distributing the coffee, Quinn and Francesca brought their own cups to their seats. He pressed his thigh against the woman he loved, and she settled her hand on his leg under the table, stroking it sweetly.

Beau started to sing softly, and Caitlyn joined in, prompting a few more people to add their voices to the mix. Soon everyone but Quinn was singing and swaying to the tune, including the woman next to him.

Quinn sipped the coffee and thought of the long, cold years he'd spent without Francesca. They'd been apart for far too long. And he also thought about the strange march of time during this global crisis. Clocks seemed to tick too loudly right now, each passing minute bringing worse news. He'd actually extracted the batteries from the bedside clock in their room. When they were there, he wanted no mention or presence of the outside world.

The song's final verses were upon them, and Francesca gazed into his eyes, singing softly alongside the rest of his family.

He finally added his voice to theirs. "As time goes by," he sang, gazing into her eyes. It was his way of telling her that one thing hadn't and wouldn't change in this ever-evolving world: his love for her.

She leaned closer, and he kissed her softly on the lips. The warmth he saw in her eyes had him whispering, "I love you."

She whispered back, "I love you too."

As the next song began to play—"I Love You For Sentimental Reasons" by Nat King Cole—Aunt Clara gestured to the middle of the dining room. "Come, everyone. Let's dance and hope for better times ahead."

His middle tightened, but he took Francesca's hand and led her to the newly crowded dance floor. His parents were already on the dance floor, along with Becca and Trevor and J.T. and Caroline. Aileen and Liam joined them, he noted, and Hargreaves grandly led Alice out onto the floor, executing what Quinn could only describe as a flawless ballroom frame.

At the end of the next song, Aunt Clara approached Hargreaves, causing everyone to stand back.

"You and I have never danced, Hargreaves," she told him, flicking her diamond bracelet his way. "I hope you will remedy that tonight on my eightieth birthday."

The butler's smile was filled with warmth. "It would be my greatest pleasure, Madam."

"It's Clara, tonight, and I'm going to call you Clifton." She extended her hands to him, and he smoothly took her into his elegant ballroom hold. "In fact, since I'm eighty now, you might want to indulge me and start calling me Clara from now on."

Quinn's eyebrow wasn't the only one that rose at the command in his aunt's tone.

"I might very well consider it," Hargreaves said, turning her grandly and leading her into a waltz.

"I suppose you could call me Arthur," his uncle called out. "Master never sat well with me."

Hargreaves' mouth twitched. "With me either—Arthur."

"It's like we have front row seats to a miracle," Alice

said, coming up beside Quinn and Francesca. Her joy was infectious. "I've told Hargreaves to lighten up. I mean, if you can't dispense with formalities when the world is in peril, when can you?"

Quinn grated at the mention of the word "peril," but Francesca laughed. "Peril, indeed? That makes me want to open more champagne."

"Let's grab some from the icebox in the kitchen," Alice said. "Chef Padraig brought a special vintage up from the cellar."

They shared a conspiratorial smile, and Francesca said, "We'll be back."

Alice repeated the phrase but in a horrible impression from *The Terminator*.

The dancing continued, and so did the champagne drinking—much later than Quinn had imagined it would. Alice and Francesca were dancing to a Beyoncé song Quinn didn't know well, clearly having the time of their lives.

He turned over his coffee cup, which he'd put facedown on the saucer after finishing the brew, and studied the pattern of the remaining grounds. Francesca was the one who read the cups, and he wondered what she'd see.

When the party finally ended and everyone hugged and kissed one another and went off to bed, he drew her back toward their cups.

Her hair had slightly more volume than usual after the dancing, and there wasn't a trace of lipstick left on her luscious mouth. She'd never looked more beautiful.

"What do you see?" he asked, extending the white teacup to her.

She looked into it, and her eyes flashed dark before she blinked and set the cup back on the table. "Tonight's a night for champagne, not Lebanese coffee. Come, let's take a bottle up to our room and drink and make love until sunrise."

Her dismissal of the teacup made his stomach quiver.

He wasn't usually a superstitious man, but her readings had always been surprisingly on point. Moreover, he knew she set stock by them. He wanted to dismiss it. But as she kissed him impulsively and dashed off to grab a bottle of champagne, he found himself picking the cup back up.

What had she seen? And, more troubling, why wouldn't she tell him?

CHAPTER 23

THE CHAMPAGNE COULDN'T ERASE THE DIRE WARNINGS
she'd seen in Quinn's teacup.

She was pragmatic in most things like her father, but
she had her mother's whimsy in this one area. As she
poured champagne on his belly and drank from it, she
struggled to stay in the moment. Usually the defined angles and muscles of his body captured her full attention,
but tonight her mind kept floating back to his coffee cup, to
the design formed by the grounds.

He flipped her onto her back and loomed over her.
"You're having trouble being here. Let me help you."

When he lowered his mouth to her core, she finally
surrendered. She laid her hand over her eyes as he used
his lips and tongue to make her come again and again and
again.

When she was floating in the aftermath, she felt him
slide into her. Her body arched, so sensitive to his touch
now, and he started to move. Moaning aloud, she pressed

her hands to his back and rose to meet him again and again until they both came in a rush, calling out each other's names.

He gathered them to their sides, and then she was falling asleep, her eyes heavy with fatigue.

The next morning, she awoke to an empty bed. The sun was visible out of the window over the sea. When she opened it a crack, the wind whipped pleasantly at her face.

She needed to set aside what she'd seen in his teacup.

Part of her wished she'd looked at her own. Then again, it might only have inflamed her fear. They were linked, so whatever befell him affected her.

She very much prayed the predictions in his teacup would be wrong.

Over a week later—on March 8—everything she'd seen in his cup came true, only it was worse than she could have imagined. Oil prices plunged twenty-four percent.

Her father had been right. Dear God.

The week leading up to it had been alarming enough, with the Saudis starting to sell off crude oil after Saudi Arabia and the other OPEC members failed to come to an agreement with the Russians on oil production cuts.

"We're dead in the water," Quinn said, his face gray.

They were sitting at the dining room table with his father and brothers, including Flynn, who'd flown his family to Ireland after Colorado had announced eight coronavirus cases.

"It's the worst plunge since 1991," Quinn's father said, rubbing his forehead. "I can't believe they made this move. It's going to cripple every oil-dependent nation and all of the producers, us included."

But Francesca knew they were capable of it. The Saudis played the oil market like Bobby Fischer played chess...and her father had known what they were planning.

"We can't recover from this," said Trevor, his tense jaw covered in two days' beard growth. "We don't have the financial reserves to hold until prices go back up, assuming they even do. This virus is killing demand right and left. Italy has already gone into lockdown mode, and the other E.U. countries will almost certainly follow. No one will be driving or flying anywhere."

"It's catastrophic," J.T. said, patting his dad on the back when Shawn leaned onto the table with his elbows.

"Everything we've built will be gone. I don't see it going any other way." Shawn rose slowly, showing his seventy-two years. "You all have done an incredible job, and I'm proud of you. In other times, the restructuring would have worked. These simply aren't those times. I'm going to find your mother."

As Francesca watched him leave the room, she tightened her hands in her lap. Shawn was wrong. If she'd listened to her father like he'd asked, she wouldn't have restructured the company around oil. This could have been avoided. *She* could have avoided it. All her hopes of buying into the media sector for a quick profit were impossible now.

"It's my fault," she admitted. "My father told me not to restructure around oil. Quinn—all of you—I'm so sorry I didn't listen."

Quinn whipped his head in her direction. "Your father told you about this?"

His voice shook with anger, with *accusation*, and she felt herself wither a little. "No. He wouldn't give any details. He only told me not to restructure around oil and said it wasn't because of the virus."

When he stood slowly, he seemed to tower over her. "Why didn't you tell me? Dammit, Francesca."

"At first I thought he might be trying to sabotage you—us." Her own voice turned hoarse. "I kept looking for a sign in the market, but I couldn't see anything."

"Jesus," Trevor uttered. "He had insider information."

"Of course he did," J.T. said bitterly. "He's Georges

Maroun. He's always been tight with the Saudis."

They were right. Her father's Saudi connections went back to his early schooling at Oxford. But she'd had no reason to believe him at the time, nothing but his say-so, and he'd proven he would lie or stretch the truth to influence her. "I didn't suspect anything until this week when talk between the Saudis and Russians escalated. But I would never have imagined something like this."

It was unprecedented. Every oil market analyst was saying so. The impact to the market—and to the people who worked in it—was going to last years. Hundreds of thousands of people would be laid off. Businesses like Merriam Enterprises were going to fold.

"You should have fucking told me!" Quinn said, his hands fisted at his sides. "At least we would have had a chance to look into it. Trevor and J.T. have good connections with the Saudis. Dammit, Francesca!"

She shot out of her chair. "What would you have asked your sources exactly? Can you please confirm a vague and scurrilous warning by Georges Maroun? There was nothing you could have asked that would have elicited any information. It might even have hurt your reputation to ask. Or it would have blown back on my father. Trust me. They kept this shut up so tight no one outside of the inner circle knew."

"And yet, your father is in that inner circle," Quinn shot back. "That's why I hired you. Because *you* have access no one else does. You failed to disclose a critical piece of information during a major restructuring of our family company, our heritage."

His eyes drilled into her, hot with anger, rich with hurt. Her heart squeezed in response.

"What do you want me to say? That I'm sorry? I am. More than you can ever know. Do you think I *wanted* this? I've failed your family and you—and I love you so damn much." Her voice cracked on the words. She felt all too conscious of the eyes on them, of the fact that they weren't alone.

His hand closed around her arm, and he stepped closer, his scent engulfing her, bringing more attention to the distance now between them. "Then why not tell me? Babe, I thought we shared everything."

She shook her head slowly. "Like you told me that my father tried to warn you off fifteen years ago? Quinn, my father didn't want me helping Merriam Enterprises, and he certainly doesn't want to see us together. I couldn't trust his motives. Even if I'd told you, would you have heeded the warning? Restructured the company differently simply on Georges Maroun's say-so? Please! We both know better."

Quinn's mouth twisted.

"Tell me." She gestured with her hands, entreating him. "What would we have restructured it around instead?"

He looked away, his jaw ticking, and while it broke her heart to say the rest, she knew it had to be done.

"Oil was the only major area you had left," she said, making herself speak like a market analyst. "There was nothing else to do other than what we did."

"She's right, Quinn," J.T. said. "I wouldn't have trusted a vague bullshit salvo from Georges Maroun given his feelings about you, and neither would the rest of us. No one could have imagined this play. Right, Trev?"

His brother took a moment to respond, though, and he only jerked his head.

"You're the queen of improvisation when it comes to business, Francesca," Quinn continued. "That's what makes you so great at what you do. Surely we could have done something."

"Let it go, man," Flynn said. "It's not her fault. The whole damn world is falling apart, and everything with it. Our company is just another in a long line of collateral damage."

Quinn whipped around and faced Flynn. "That's why you're the tech guy and I'm the CEO. I can't just say, 'too bad, tough shit' and move on."

"Hey—" J.T. said as Flynn lurched out of his chair.

"Fuck you, man," Flynn shot back, his eyes glittering. "You're not the only one who's upset here. I get that this is horrible. I'm Merriam Enterprises too. But there's more at stake here. Your relationship with Francesca for one."

The gesture fell on deaf ears. Quinn didn't look at her. He hadn't so much as glanced her way, she realized, since she'd told him about her father.

God, she ached.

"We have people who depend on us," Flynn continued. "Acting like a dick isn't going to help. Did you see Dad? This has fucking crushed him."

Everyone went still at the anguish in his usually carefree voice.

"He's right," J.T. said, standing up, regret in his eyes. "We have to take care of our people as best we can. We need to plan for bankruptcy and give people as generous a severance as possible."

Quinn strode over to J.T. and shoved him back. "I'm not fucking filing for bankruptcy."

Francesca gripped her chair, aware of what that would cost Quinn.

He whipped around to her and pointed in her direction. "You broke it. You fix it."

All the life seemed to leave her body as she stared at the angry man she loved. She'd thought him grouchy the day he'd walked back into her life. He was furious now, and it was the kind of fury that could give way to hate. She had to be honest, and her heart cracked, knowing it could end them. "I don't know how."

His green eyes glittered. "Figure it out. I can't—I won't—accept defeat."

Her throat was hot with tears. "I can't fix something

this globally dependent. I'm not a miracle worker, Quinn."

He looked away again, and it felt like he was withdrawing from her. From the future they'd envisioned together. From that family walking together along the beach.

"Do you want me to leave?" she made herself ask.

His head fell forward, and he said, "No, I don't want you to fucking leave. If you do, we're done, and I can't take that."

The words were wrenched from him, and tears burned behind her eyes in response.

"I just need some time. Excuse me." He strode out of the room, his shoes slapping the floor harshly in the ensuing silence.

She turned to his brothers. All of them were looking at her, a mixture of grief and anger in their eyes. Their shoulders sagged with it.

"I'm sorry," she whispered again. "I'm so sorry."

Seeing no other choice, she fled the room.

CHAPTER 24

SHE'D BETRAYED HIM.

Quinn couldn't erase that thought from his mind. He locked their bedroom door, then scooped up her red silk robe from the bed they'd shared last night. It had always tantalized his senses. Now it made him more sick at heart. Her scent wafted to him as he tossed it into the wardrobe where the rest of her clothes hung. God! Why hadn't she told him?

He picked up his phone and called the only person he knew he could turn to right now. Connor picked up right away, almost like he'd been waiting for his call.

"I didn't know if I should reach out given what's happened," his brother said, his usually baritone voice even deeper with emotion. "I feel like this is all my fault."

He rocked on his heels. "Yours? *I* restructured the company. Did you know the Saudis were going to dump oil? Moments ago, I learned Francesca had been vaguely warned about it."

"By whom? No one saw this coming."

"Her father," Quinn said, picturing the bastard and imagining him being his personal dartboard.

"Georges Maroun knew? I suppose that's no surprise given how tight he is with the Saudi royalty. What exactly did she know?"

Recounting her side of things had him needing some fresh air, so he crossed and opened the window as he spoke. The gray sea thundered in the background, bashing itself against the cliffs in the distance.

"She didn't have enough information to make a different decision on the restructuring in my opinion," Connor said when he'd finished. "Flynn gave me a copy."

He hadn't known that. Then he thought about how he'd launched himself at his brother and shoved J.T. back. He'd wanted to rip something apart, and he'd gone after them. His brother was right. He was a dick. A total dick.

"But she didn't tell me. How can I ever trust her again? She betrayed me. Us. Our family. You should have seen Dad. And everyone else."

I failed them too.

"Ah... Quinn, I love you, so I'm going to be as honest as I can be. As Louisa says, I think you need a different perspective."

"Why do I sense this is going to feel like getting kidney punched in an alley?" He leaned his elbows on the windowsill and let the cold wind cruise over his hot face.

"How you feel about it is up to you. You might ask why she didn't think she could trust you with the information. What haven't you given her that allowed for this breach in intimacy? God, you can tell my therapy is working. I sound like a combination of my therapist and Louisa."

"You think it's my fault she didn't say anything?" Quinn wanted to rip the window off the wall. "Are you fucking kidding me, Con?"

"You're pissed, and I get that. And you're crushed

because Merriam probably isn't going to make it. Oil prices will continue to plunge, and there's nothing you or anyone else in the industry can do about it. I get what that must feel like. It's gut-wrenching. But you haven't let the family down, and Francesca hasn't let you down. From everything I've heard, she's had your back. Her solution for keeping Caitlyn and Annie's ventures was brilliant."

Hadn't he thought so too? But it hadn't worked. Merriam Enterprises was going down, and he couldn't take that. "You didn't see Dad walk out today. Hell, Trev couldn't even respond other than to jerk his head. How am I supposed to live with this?"

"I felt that way when Corey and our other employees died in the offshore accident in Asia, and the decisions I made out of guilt and grief caused a lot of damage for a lot of people, myself included. Quinn, I'm telling you. Don't follow that path. And whatever you do, don't lose your soulmate over this. I'm going to use a non-therapy phrase now. That would be a stupid move, and you're not stupid."

"You sound like Mom," Quinn said, clenching his eyes shut.

"Mom has always had the most common sense of any of us," Connor said. "Maybe you should talk to her."

How could he face her? She was likely comforting their father. "I can't right now."

"Don't cut yourself off from everyone," Connor said in a hard tone. "I did that, and you almost decked me for it later. Don't you remember berating me? You're going down the same path."

"So maybe you can deck me when I see you," Quinn said, rubbing his eyes.

"Are you hearing me, bro? I can't up and leave Chicago to come kick your ass right now. We've got our hands full with the homeless and this virus. It's going to hit them particularly hard. Plus, it's still winter here. Cold as hell for a human being, especially kids."

Louisa had been homeless as a kid, and her mother had died on the streets during a Chicago snowstorm. Quinn snapped out of his own tunnel vision and thought of what Flynn had said. There was more at stake here than just Merriam Enterprises. People were being hurt by this virus, both their bank books and their health, and it was going to get a lot worse before it got better.

"I'm hearing you, Con." He let out a tortured sigh, one he would never have normally let anyone hear. "How do I take all this and not get crazy or sick or aggressive with everyone?"

"You have to forgive yourself for any personal responsibility you feel. Then you have to do the same with Francesca. Because the truth is there's no one to blame here. You're only mad this went down so badly. Sure, she didn't tell you about her dad, but why didn't she? That's what you need to ask her."

He thought again of the reasons she'd given him. They'd been a combination of personal and professional, but maybe Connor was right. Maybe some other current writhed underneath. He'd have to ask her.

"I'm going to go figure this out," Quinn said. "Try to do what you said. But one last thing. Do you have any ideas how we can save Merriam Enterprises from bankruptcy?"

"I've been racking my brain since the news broke." His brother paused, and there was a death knell in the silence before he said, "No, I don't. God, I wish I did. Does Dad have any ideas?"

His dad's haggard face swam into his consciousness, and his throat knotted with emotion. "No, I don't think so. I don't think anyone knows."

"What about Francesca?" Connor asked.

His mind flashed to the moment she'd told him she couldn't fix this. She'd been ashen, her voice strained with a hurt he hadn't heard since she'd turned down his proposal. "No, she doesn't have any ideas either."

"Well... You know what you need to do then."

How could he give up? It wasn't in his nature. Francesca had left him, and he'd spent fifteen long years hoping she'd come back. No, he wouldn't give up so easily. He had to give it a few days. Surely someone would challenge the Saudis. He almost laughed at himself. Hadn't the Russians done that? The Russians were as feared an entity in the oil market as they came, and look at what had happened there. Flynn had said they were collateral damage, and while Quinn had snapped his head off, he was right.

God, he was going to need to apologize to a whole bunch of people, Francesca first among them.

"All right. On that fucking depressing note, I'll let you go. Promise me you and Louisa are being safe. Jesus, I don't like knowing you two are on the streets most days, but with this virus out there..." He shuddered.

"We're implementing strict safety protocols, but I've finally learned there is only so much you can control in life," Connor said. "The rest you have to lean into with courage and love. My parting words, bro. I love you, Quinn."

Jesus. His eyes burned. They'd worked together for years, side by side, but they'd never talked like this. They weren't the kind of men who did. And yet, his chest was tight with emotion from it. "I love you too, Con. Don't make me deck you for stupidity either. Got it?"

"Got it. You tell everyone I love them. I know the whole family is going to need a lot of comfort in the coming months. I wish I could be there, but I need to be here. See ya, bro."

Quinn wanted to hurl the phone at the wall. Comfort? How was he supposed to provide that? Patting people on the backs and telling people everything would be all right in the end wasn't his schtick.

Besides, it was total bullshit, and he couldn't lie. Their beloved family company was going to be wrenched away from them. He'd worried about cutting jobs, but now hundreds of thousands of their employees would be out of work. Many wouldn't find anything new for some time in this market.

What in the hell was he supposed to do? He'd be a failed CEO, just like Connor, in the industry's eyes. There was no coming back from that.

And Francesca? This was her first defeat. Would her reputation as the most sought-after consultant to the Fortune 500 take a hit?

God, the future depressed him.

Francesca's phone started ringing, and he crossed to her bedside table to see who it was. The name on the display was simple: Father.

He knew he should let the call ring through. But rage pumped through his system, giving him a kick of adrenaline. Georges Maroun deserved an ass kicking, and Quinn Merriam was just the man to do it.

"Georges, you bastard," he answered.

The man didn't laugh. He gave a rumbling cough instead. "Answering my daughter's phone. How surprising."

He went for blood. "It shouldn't be. It was lying next to our bed."

"You're angry with me, and who could blame you? I was calling my daughter to give her my condolences. I thought about her reaction all day. Did you blame her as I've been imagining?"

Dammit, he hated being predictable. "Is that what you wanted all along? Why else give her the vaguest snippet of nothing? You wanted to drive a wedge between us. Did you even think about her reputation in the market? Or all of the people Merriam Enterprises employs?"

It struck Quinn that it might serves Georges' purposes for Francesca to suddenly lose street cred as a consultant. Maybe he hoped it would drive her back to the family company.

"You flatter me. Your company was in dire straits

already. Do you think Chevron or Exxon won't make it through these dark days? Please, Quinn, at least show enough honor to admit responsibility for your actions. My daughter did an admirable job, all things considered. It was only an old man's fancy that led me to warn her in the first place."

"Now who's flattering himself? You don't give a fuck about your daughter and her wishes. If you did, you'd have supported her wish to be with me—then and now. All you care about is your own agenda."

More coughing sounded over the line before he managed, "I do care about my daughter. I work like a dog every day for her. She's my heart, my legacy."

"She's a woman who wants to live her own life. I don't know why I'm wasting time on you anyway. I have more pressing concerns than your bullshit. I have to find a way out of this." Part of Quinn hoped Francesca's father might drop more information, like breadcrumbs, and he hated himself for it.

"You won't," Georges said, coughing again. "No one can stop what's coming. Not even my daughter. Tell her to come back to Beirut. Her father, Maroun Industries, and her country need her."

There it was...

Quinn knew the trouble Lebanon was facing right now. The economic picture grew worse daily. Of course Francesca was upset. She loved her country.

"Like the Irish say, 'I'll tell her when pigs fly.' Goodbye, Georges."

He hung up, and the rudeness relieved some of his anger. No one treated Georges Maroun like that, and he just had.

Still, her father's words sounded like the proverbial nails in the Merriam Enterprises' coffin.

Somehow it didn't matter. He couldn't give up.

CHAPTER 25

THE WILD IRISH ROSE INN MAY AS WELL HAVE BEEN A FUneral parlor to Arthur's mind.

Sure, there were none of those cloying lilies that seemed to pile up around the dead, but it stunk to high heaven all the same. Not even the nonstop batches of scones Aileen was pulling from the oven and setting out in baskets in the gloomy dining room lifted the mood.

As the older Irish woman passed his table, he gently snagged her arm. "You're a dear to bake for them, but I think they have enough scones."

She clutched the basket. "I didn't know what else to do for them."

The resident Merriam brothers save Quinn were huddled at a table, their faces grave. Caitlyn was sitting next to Beau, her face buried into his shoulder. Annie had taken the girls out to play with the rabbits. Shawn and Assumpta had gone for a long walk on the cliffs despite the cold wind rattling the windows. Clara was knitting up an inferno in their room after talking to Michaela and Boyd, who were still holed up in Wyoming. No one on their honeymoon should be bombarded with this kind of news, but that was the way of it, Arthur supposed.

Bad news waited for no man or woman.

As a journalist, he knew that firsthand.

Alice had gone off in search of Francesca, and Arthur was glad the woman had such a good friend. How in the hell could anyone think this was her fault? That was ridiculous. J.T. had filled him in on the latest developments before leaving him alone with his ever-present tablet, the headlines screaming up at him.

"It's horrible," Aileen said, patting his shoulder after placing the basket of scones in front of him. "There's nothing worse than losing something you love, and their company was built on the blood and sweat of generations, much like our beautiful inn here."

Everyone was acting as though bankruptcy was inevitable, and while Arthur was no expert, he had never been one to accept defeat.

"It's not over yet, Aileen. I'll be back in a bit. If they start singing some funeral song, come find me."

The corner of her mouth tipped up. "If I hear even the beginnings of 'Down By the Salley Gardens,' I'll find you straight away."

"That's Yeats, right?" he asked, making her eyes sparkle momentarily.

"You know your Irish poets."

"I know good writing. Be back in a jiff. I'm still a match-maker, and this whole situation is bollocks, as you Irish say."

Clara might have forgotten their task in the thick of her grief. He'd give her time to get her head back on straight or he'd help straighten it for her, but he wasn't straying from their goal. Quinn needed to get his head out of his ass, and Francesca needed to know she had allies.

He closed the tablet he hadn't been reading and strode off to Alice's room. She was in the Queen Maeve suite next to Hargreaves, who was in the Kings of Connacht suite. Usually Arthur enjoyed brushing up on local mythology and history, but current events occupied his every brain cell these days.

He knocked on Alice's door and did his best to smile when the woman cracked it open, her sweetheart face devoid of its normal smile. "I'm looking for Francesca. Any ideas?"

Alice opened the door the whole way. Francesca was discreetly wiping tears, sitting on the mustard-colored sofa against the wall in the small anteroom. Hell, he thought. Of course she was crying.

"These Merriams can be real jerks sometimes," he said without heat. "Can I have a moment? I wanted to say something."

Her oval face was so strained her high cheekbones made it almost gaunt-looking. "Of course. You're always welcome, Arthur."

"That's sweet of you," he said, coming in and sitting next to her as Alice closed the door. "Then again, you're a sweetheart."

Alice perched on the couch's arm beside her friend. When Arthur rose to give her his seat, she waved him off. He let her. He was feeling every day of his eighty years.

"I'm sorry you're hurt," he continued, "and it's understandable given some people's actions. Quinn's being a complete butthead, as my granddaughter Jill would say."

Thoughts of Jill pained his heart. She was starting to worry about the virus now that cases had been reported in Colorado, and being pregnant wasn't helping. He needed to call her more often.

"Butthead is right," Alice said. "Hargreaves said I would love Jill."

"She's as bright as they come and completely immune

to bullshit," Arthur said, "but we're straying from my point. Francesca, you need to know I have your back. Anything you need, say the word. I might not be at my fittest, but I imagine I could sneak a punch in on Quinn. If he's asleep."

She let out a shaky laugh and then leaned over and kissed his cheek, delighting him. "You really are the dearest man. But it's Quinn's right to feel betrayed and angry. That isn't in anyone else's control."

"Love always wins," Arthur said, grabbing her hand. "You need to trust in that."

"I'm a bit weak on it at the moment." She combed back her black hair. "Maybe love isn't enough."

"Bullshit! Excuse me. At my age, my opinions spurt out like nobody's business. Only hear me out."

Alice put her hand on her friend's shoulder, and they shared a glance. Yes, she was a good friend.

"You shovel the shit in the way. Love always wins when you do it. I expect you know Quinn's a handful sometimes."

"Stubborn. Grouchy. Completely unreasonable." Her violet eyes flashed.

"Yes," Arthur said, "but there has to be some reason he's your soulmate. Didn't you know it when you met him?"

Her scowl was fearsome. "Maybe I was dropped on my head as a baby."

"Or the doctors used forceps to pull you out," Alice added. "Oops, sorry. Continue, Arthur."

"Thank you." He worried the button on his cardigan, wanting to say his piece right. "It's only... In times like this we need to remember why we love the people in our lives. Because when things get rough, it can be hard to remember."

"I'll have to make a list—in a week or so—when I'm calm."

When her lashes were dry again, Arthur thought. He didn't imagine she was a woman often brought to tears. "Now, with the soulmate reminder behind us, there's something else I wanted to ask you. About the business."

Her eyes narrowed, the wariness evident in her stiffened frame. "Shoot, as you Americans say."

"My newspaper fell into some debt this past summer, and I worried about going bankrupt." He wouldn't bother her with the details. "Someone decided to bail me out, and while it chapped my hide, I let them. I couldn't allow my pride to stand in the way. That would have been stupid, and I don't do stupid."

"I like that phrase," Alice said. "I might have to borrow it."

"It's not trademarked," Arthur responded. "Assumpta is fond of it too. Let's talk about Merriam Enterprises. Everyone thinks the company is finished. Isn't there a bank that could bail them out?" Hell. Didn't he remember Lee Iacocca's bailout in 1979?

She shook her head. "Merriam Enterprises isn't the only company impacted by this, Arthur. The entire oil industry took huge losses, and this Saudi-Russian price war is only going to worsen. Add in the news around the virus—"

"I read that Italy just announced it was placing sixty million residents in lockdown." He ran his hands through his hair. "It's unbelievable. Their cases have run up higher than anyone would have thought possible given the time frame."

Alice gasped. "Francesca, what about your dad? He was just there for fashion week."

Arthur's brows rose. He'd heard about Georges Maroun's role in this current rift between Francesca and Quinn. "Is your father well?"

"We haven't spoken," she said, her brow knitting. "As for the news, I expect global stocks will tank tomorrow. It will be chaos. The financial losses are unimaginable."

"Are you saying there's no bank the Merriams can turn to?"

"I haven't done the loss projections, but if oil continues to plunge, and I think it will, it will cost more to pump it and store it than its true value. Arthur, you won't be able to give it away."

He couldn't imagine that world. Oil drove politics and every facet of life on the planet, for better or worse. "What about a government then? Who would want to buy a bunch of oil now on the cheap?"

She ticked off a number of countries in Africa and Latin America before trailing off. "But that doesn't help Merriam Enterprises long-term. They have no company without oil. The other ventures like Caitlyn's, for example, are chump change in comparison. Nothing against perfume, but against oil, it's like—"

"Comparing David with Goliath," Arthur finished.

"But David won," Alice said, perking up so much she almost unbalanced herself from the couch's arm.

"In a two-person fight, yes," Francesca said. "But this is a global fight with tons of players."

"All the more reason to think there's someone out there who could help." Arthur stopped there. He'd planted as much of a seed as he could. If it wasn't possible to turn Merriam Enterprises around, then it wasn't. But he was the only one thinking clearly, it seemed, and he was going to share his ideas until they nailed the company coffin shut. Only then would he join them in singing Yeats' funeral dirge.

"In a crisis, people close ranks," Francesca said. "It's a risk-averse market and getting more so by the day."

"Understandably." He stood and gave her what he hoped was an encouraging smile. "I'm still trusting in the human element. I've covered the news since I was a young man. Watched it when I was a boy. People and their sparks of vision always surprise me. And they've changed their communities and the world with them."

Because humans were more than flesh and bones.

They were heart.

He thought of the Civil Rights Movement and Selma and the march on Washington, where Martin Luther King's "I Have A Dream" speech had boomed across the Lincoln Memorial. He thought of Lech Walesa organizing the 1980 strikes in Poland against the herculean Soviet Union and later winning the Nobel Peace Prize and becoming the first democratically elected leader of his country. He could see the Berlin Wall coming down, brick by brick, as angry protestors dismantled it on the night of November 9, 1989. He remembered Boris Yeltsin climbing on a tank and delivering a speech that routed a Soviet coup and made him a Russian hero of the new post-Soviet state. Rosa Parks filtered through his mind, and so did the Mothers of the Plaza de Mayo in Argentina, who'd stood against authoritarianism.

There were so many examples of people stepping up in dark times in their communities and spheres of influence. He'd penned more than one opinion piece on such matters, joining his voice to those pressing for freedom, democracy, women's rights, worker's rights, civil rights, and *human* rights.

Dammit, he knew people were going to rise again in this current situation. They had to. The world needed them. In the business sector too. Maybe the Merriams could find a way to be heroes in their own camp.

"I'll see these old bones out." He smiled more easily. "You keep in mind what I said. I see you as a hero with a vision, Francesca."

A fire flared in her eyes. He let himself out as Hargreaves came down the hall with a tray of tea service.

"You might bring something stronger, Hargreaves. I just lit a fire under Ms. Maroun."

The man smiled. "Good to hear, Arthur."

Hearing his friend finally call him by his given name sounded pretty damn great. "Take care of them, Clifton."

He received a glower, followed by a warm smile.

"Being mushy looks good on you, Clifton."

Whistling, he took the stairs and let Boru, Becca's dog, outside. "Let's take a walk, shall we? I feel years younger."

Reminding himself of the human spirit seemed to be the ticket.

CHAPTER 26

HE WENT LOOKING FOR FRANCESCA, AND INSTEAD FOUND Uncle Arthur sitting with his tablet in the dining room. His uncle stood before he could walk past.

"I've been waiting for you."

He cocked his head, and Uncle Arthur chuckled humorlessly. "I'll tell you what no one else will. She's in Alice's room."

"Thank you." He immediately turned in that direction, but his uncle put a hand on his shoulder. "Fix this. Don't be a dick. She's your soulmate, you idiot. Companies can be rebuilt. My friend and the founder of the company, your Grandpa Emmits, would knock your block off for thinking bankruptcy means failure."

Quinn raked his hair back. "How can you say such a thing? Grandpa Emmits would hate seeing his life's work come to this."

"Bah! Do you know how many times he thought he was going to go bust in the early years? You might ask your father about it. He'll remember. If not, come back and find me after my nap. You Merriams are exhausting me."

He thought about Arthur's slow progress out of the dining room as he went to Alice's room. She opened the door in response to his knock, but she was already shaking her head. "She doesn't want to see you quite yet."

The door snapped shut in his face.

He hung his head. Yeah, he imagined she didn't want to talk to him. Returning to his room, he grabbed the Wild Irish Rose Inn stationery and wrote a note to her.

I know you're angry, and you have every right to be. I'm sorry I hurt you, but you hurt me too. Please come talk to me and let's make this right.

I love you.

Quinn

He delivered the note to Alice, who took it with quick efficiency, but Francesca still didn't come to him.

Dinner was a somber family affair. Even Amelia was quiet, sitting in her mother's lap, her fingers tangled in Annie's hair. No one stated the obvious. Alice and Francesca weren't joining them. They'd all watched as Hargreaves took a tray through the dining room and out toward the guest rooms. He'd returned empty-handed and resumed his seat at Uncle Arthur and Aunt Clara's table.

"Flynn," Uncle Arthur said when Aileen set out dessert. "You didn't happen to bring a karaoke machine, did you?"

A few people closed their eyes, almost as if the very idea made them ill. Quinn understood. He thought of him and Francesca singing "All I Do Is Win." They'd lost, and he feared her ongoing silence might mean he'd lost more than Merriam Enterprises.

After pushing around his Carrageen moss pudding—a travesty to dessert everywhere—he stood. He wasn't going to take this anymore. "Good night, everyone."

Aunt Clara wiped her mouth and said, "You about done with this status quo?"

Everyone was suddenly looking at him. It wasn't comfortable. "I don't know what you mean."

She tossed her napkin on the table like a gauntlet. "We're all waiting to see if you're going to be the one to lose your soulmate a second time. Like I told Arthur after he woke up from his nap, you can lead a horse to water, but you can't make it drink."

Horse metaphors in the worst moment of his life? "Are you serious right now?"

"Completely," she said, rising, the diamond necklace she'd worn to dinner flashing fire. "No one has wanted to say anything to you after how you attacked Flynn and J.T. earlier, but we all feel the same way."

Jesus, everyone knew about that. No wonder no one was speaking to him. He glanced at his mother—whom he could usually count on to call him out on his bad behavior—and all he saw were sad eyes and a tight mouth. Shit.

"I said something," Uncle Arthur said, shaking his head. "Boy's as stubborn as they come."

"I went to talk to her," he found himself saying in front of the entire room. "I even wrote her a note. She's stonewalling me."

His mother let out a rude noise.

Finally. The relief he felt surprised him. "Mom. Do you have something to say?"

She stood up, her hands braced on the table. "I thought your father and I raised you to understand what's important in life. It pisses me off to discover we didn't. I love you, Quinn, but sometimes... Excuse me."

She walked right out of the room. Caitlyn's eyes were as wide as quarters, and Trevor slapped his forehead as if in disgust.

"Perhaps this is a good time for me to say something," his father said, crossing to him and putting a hand on his arm. "Your mother is right. The company has always been a gift—to all of us—but it's the people that count. This family counts. I forgot that for many years and put Merriam Enterprises above your mother and this family. But it's only a company, Quinn, as hard as that is for any of us to swallow."

He watched as his siblings took their partners' hands and nodded to each other. God, was he the only slow one?

"The woman you want to marry, however," his father said, "you need to move heaven and earth to keep her. If I hadn't had your mother all these years, my life would have been nothing. You kids too. I'm sorry I wasn't a better father to you, but I'm trying now. Maybe the silver lining here—as your Grandma Anna used to say—is remembering what's really important. Now, I'd better go after your mother."

Then he hugged Quinn briefly, shocking him even more, and left the room.

The staring match continued with his family, so he held out his arms. "Anyone want to take a swing at me?"

Amelia started to cry, burrowing her face into her mother's neck. "Don't hit him. Please."

Shit. He'd made a little girl cry now. This was an epic low. Retreat seemed the best approach. "Flynn. J.T. I owe you an apology. The rest of you too. I'm deeply sorry for my behavior."

He strode up the stairs of the inn, thinking about his first trip to Ireland. He and Connor had made such a mess of things with Becca that their mother had needed to fly in to negotiate peace among the Merriam siblings.

God, he really was a dick.

How else could he have gone after Francesca like he had? She was the delight of his heart. She'd done everything she could to save his company. As for attacking his brothers… That was the calling card of a complete asshole.

He'd done the very thing Connor had warned him not

to do.

He'd let Merriam Enterprises come between him and what he loved.

Boru whined at the sight of him and padded down the hallway in the other direction. God, even Buttercup would probably flee his presence. He wouldn't ask what Becca's cantankerous cat, Hatshep, would do. Probably barf up a hairball on his bed.

At Alice's door, he knocked again. Softly. She answered in pink flannel pajamas covered in dancing flamingos. He shouldn't have been surprised. "Does Francesca have pj's like yours? I'd like to see them sometime."

"She's still deciding," Alice said, her stare hostile. "I believe the term 'you're in the doghouse tonight' is apt. Good night, Quinn."

His patience snapped. "Are you really going to keep hiding, Francesca? This kind of cowardly act is beneath you."

"Oh, brother," Alice muttered. "You'd better stop right there, buster."

When she started to close the door, he stopped it with his hand and called out in pure desperation, "No way. I'm done with this crap. I'm sorry. I'm a dick. A complete asshole. I've alienated my family. Hell, I even made a five-year-old cry. I don't deserve your forgiveness, but I'm asking for it all the same. I love you. You're my soulmate. I'm not giving up on us. Don't you dare either."

"You made little Amelia cry?" Alice asked, crossing her arms over those gaudy flamingos. "You really are a complete asshole. See you in the morning."

When she pushed the door this time, he let it close.

"I'll sleep out here all night if I have to," he yelled back.

Would he really? Hell, yes, he would. She had to talk to him. Situating himself in the doorway, he tried to get comfortable. Only his hard head didn't like the door as a pillow, and his long legs stuck out into the hallway.

Of course, the sight of him lying prostrate in front of Francesca's door delighted a few of his siblings who were down the hall. J.T. made a show of stepping widely over his legs, and Flynn put him in his place by stomping way too close to him for comfort. He didn't call his brother out, and when Flynn looked over his shoulder, his mouth quirked into a half-smile. They were going to be okay.

No one came and brought him a blanket, however. Not even Aileen, who walked past him as she made the final rounds. Nor Hargreaves, who brought Alice and Francesca a tray of bedtime tea. Quinn just let the stalwart butler step over him. He wasn't moving a muscle, and he hoped Hargreaves would tell them as much. When the man left without a tray, he only shook his head at Quinn, a very unbutler-like action to his mind.

He finally slept and awoke when something situated itself on his lap. Jerking upright, he noted Hatshep curling around him. "You've got to be kidding me. This is my magical pet moment?"

Every one of his siblings had experienced a magical pet moment in pursuit of their soulmate. Buttercup for Trevor. A goat, Chou-Chou, for Caitlyn. Boyd's lizard, Marvin, for Michaela. (Of course, Marvin had died. Another depressing thought.) Connor's animal moment had come courtesy of the homeless shelter's literacy-minded guinea pigs, which Louisa insisted were cute although Quinn couldn't see it. Now, here he was with Becca's usually prickly cat on one of the worst nights of his life.

If this was meant to be a sign, he wasn't buying it. Seeing an angel or a ray of light would be a sign. Or being in Ireland, seeing the fairy people. But this cat? No. Quinn was a realist, a cold-hearted cynic...

And yet, he tugged Hatshep more comfortably onto his lap, stroking her soft white fur. When she started purring, he almost grimaced. This is what he'd been reduced to? Finding comfort from a Persian cat on the doorstep of his soulmate in the middle of the night? He should go back to his room. His leg was falling asleep, and he was losing his Man Card by the minute. But the cat nudged him in the belly when his hand stopped caressing her fur, so he continued.

His eyes closed again, and then he drifted off.

When the door opened, he jerked awake. Alice's flamingo pj's were gone, replaced by neon green yoga pants and a sapphire tank top.

"Now I've seen everything." She stepped over him and the cat, leaving the door open, which had to be a good sign, right? "I need to go to class."

Every morning, he watched the brightly clad exercise crew do yoga, tai chi, or Qigong in the front hall. Well, everyone was dressed like a nightclub's hot electric light display except for Uncle Arthur, who wore loose pants and moaned and groaned to high heaven as he followed Hargreaves or Alice, who usually led everyone else.

"Enjoy." He took one of his hands off Hatshep and saluted her.

Then he coughed as cat hair rained down on his face.

"My God, Hatshep, you're the hairiest cat I've ever met, but I like you."

"I've always heard cats don't mind ornery people being that many have an ornery streak themselves," he heard Francesca say.

Turning his head against the doorjamb, he winced as his neck popped in three places. "Hatshep must have a huge one then, because I'm a complete asshole. I'm sorry, Francie. Are you ready to hear how much?"

She dropped a file in his lap instead. "These are my suggestions for how to save parts of Merriam. The oil sector is unsalvageable based on recent losses and my projections for the continued price of crude falling in the coming months. You can pay out good severances and reinvest the money. I recommend you spin off Caitlyn and Annie's

ventures into one company. Maybe Merriam and Merriam. Build from there. Not everything has to be lost."

Then she stepped over him and the cat.

"I...thank you." He set Hatshep aside and pushed off
the floor, wincing as his muscles groaned in response. "You
didn't have to do that, but I'm grateful. I don't want to talk
about Merriam right now, though. I want to talk about us."

Her level gaze reminded him of the kind of look a strike
negotiator would give a shitty boss. He was about to get his
ass kicked. And he deserved it.

"You want to talk about us? You blamed me for everything, Quinn."

"Unfairly." He took her arm gently.

She eyed him dubiously but didn't pull away. "Continue."

Oh, how he loved the regal mandate in her tone. He'd
lain out here all night, but now he struggled for what to
say. Then he remembered his conversation with Connor.
"I want to ask why you couldn't trust me enough to tell me
about your father's warning. It's hard for me to accept that.
But I realize there is something about our relationship that
makes you not trust me all the way, and babe, I really want
to fix that. I don't want to lose you over this."

"You think this was about me not trusting you?" Her
head turned ever so slightly, almost as if she was trying to
figure out a puzzle. "It's my father I don't trust."

"Okay... Hearing that helps. I thought you'd betrayed
me—"

"That sounds more like it."

He held up his hand. "That was my hurt talking. Dammit, I hate talking about my feelings." He put his hands on
her shoulders. "My knee-jerk reaction was to cast blame,
and I'm sorry. I've always thought I was up for personal responsibility. Maybe I'm a coward."

She snorted. "Like hell you are. Stubborn is more like
it. I was the one who hid in Alice's room. Not my finest

moment either."

"I bunked down with a cat." He gestured to the front of his shirt. "I have the evidence to prove it."

"Yes, you are covered in white fur." Her smile was subtle, but it filled him with hope. "It might be your best look yet. You won some points last night. I never expected you to lie across my doorstep. You didn't even do that when I turned down your marriage proposal."

His mouth parted. "Did you want me to?"

She looked away and stroked her neck. "I'm honest enough to admit I would have liked it if you'd fought for me more." Something flashed in her eyes and she sought out his gaze. "Yes, dammit, I would have loved it if you'd slept in my doorway and told me you refused to take no for an answer. But I also don't know if it would have changed my mind. I thought I was protecting you. That I was doing the right thing, going home when I thought my father needed me."

Shit. That still hurt. Talking about her father would only stir a hornet's nest, especially since Georges Maroun was trying to come between them again. "Let's leave the past where it is. How about we return to me winning some points? What else can I do to fix this? Maybe I should rephrase that. What else can I do to help you trust me all the way?"

His breath was ragged as he finished that question, but so was hers. They stared at each other.

"Why didn't you tell me my father had contacted you when we were dating?"

So much for leaving Georges out of things. His shoulder came up in defense before he said, "I took care of it. I know how upset he makes you. I didn't want it to hurt you."

"Is that all?" Her astute violet eyes were trained on him.

So they were going to poke the hornet's nest after all. "No. Fine. I didn't want to tell you what I thought of your father."

"*And?*"

She wasn't buying it. "I worried you might listen to him. About me. He has a hold on you, after all."

"I've been working on that for a long time." She sighed. "Our relationship is confusing. Clearly, I have a ways to go. But I'm not running when he calls. I don't even trust him, and Quinn... That makes me sad too."

He remembered what his parents had said to him at dinner, first his mother and then his father, and how it had affected him. "I suppose we all have confusing moments with our parents. I just don't want him to come between us. I'm sorry I didn't trust you in that moment. It was a knee-jerk reaction. Losing the company hurts." *I played right into his hands.*

"I know it does." She stepped closer and put her hand on his cheek. "Oh, Quinn. You've always been right for me. After I set aside most of my hurt, that truth remained. Of course, it hurt to realize that because I wasn't sure you trusted me anymore."

"I do trust you," he said, putting his hand on her hip. "I'm sorry I struck out. I did it to my brothers too. Francesca, when I say I can be a complete asshole, I mean it. I promise to do better. I've hurt my entire family. That's not how I want things to be. Shit, maybe I need therapy. It's worked wonders for Connor."

"Working on yourself always produces incredible results," she said, stroking his face.

"I imagine you know someone who can help me," he said, his mouth tipping up. "I'll do it too. I don't want to hurt anyone anymore—or end up sleeping in a doorway with only a cat for a friend."

She glanced around him. "Your friend seems to have disappeared. She must have realized you were past your crisis."

"Are we?" He framed her face in his hands, letting her see all of his messy emotions. "Because I love you, and I want you, and I need you. I lived without you for fifteen years, and it was horrible. I don't want to do that again. Ever."

"Me either." She pressed their foreheads together.

His feeling of failure, his grief for the family business, his worry for the future—they felt like tiny shards of metal stabbing him, but his heart and the love he had for her eased them out. As he held her, he felt lighter. The warmth in his chest overtook the hurt, and when she softened her body against him, he knew it was the same for her.

"I love you," he whispered. "Don't ever doubt it. No matter how stupid I might act sometimes."

"If you're really willing to work with a therapist, I bet those moments will become few and far between," she said, chuckling and wiping the tears leaking down her face. "I love you too. Trust is a choice, and I promise to trust you."

His entire body expanded with that one comment since he knew she wasn't someone who made promises lightly. "I promise too, which is why I'm going to tell you that I talked to your father yesterday."

She jerked back. "You did?"

"He called your phone, and I'm not proud of this, but I was so angry, I picked it up." Shit. In hindsight, he knew it hadn't been his best moment. Would she forgive him for acting on impulse?

"What did he say?" she asked, her brow knitted.

He gave her a more detailed account than normal because he was trying to turn over a new leaf. The light that had returned to her violet eyes was gone by the time he finished, and he was sick at heart.

"Did he sound all right?" she asked.

"Meaning?"

She worried her mouth. "Did he sound well?"

Quinn thought back to their call. "He coughed a few times. It sounded like he had a cold."

Her eyes closed and she shook her head. "A cold…"

"You think he's sick?" he asked.

"He was in Italy for fashion week," she told him.

His gut tightened, knowing where she was going with this. "You're thinking he might have the virus. Francesca, I hate to say it, but if he had it, you're the first person he'd tell. He'd hope you would go rushing back to him, right? Don't overthink this."

From the set of her shoulders, he knew she was doing just that. Again, he thought of the hold her father had over her. Would she rush back?

"You're right," she simply said.

He let it end there. She'd admitted her reactivity to her father was a work in progress, much like Quinn's way of lashing out when he was angry, and they loved each other. They could work through anything together.

"Come on." He rubbed her shoulders. "Let's go back to our room. I want to show you how much I love you. Afterward, I need to make some more amends to my family. Any chance you and me might be able to find a karaoke machine to rent in Ireland?"

"Are you planning to sing Elton John's 'Sorry Seems to Be the Hardest Word'?" But her joke didn't hide the worry darkening her eyes.

"Seems tailor-made for me, right?" He wanted to slay the dragon facing her down, that beast made of worry and helplessness, and he knew only one way to do it. He kissed her and led her back to their room.

Putting her pleasure first for hours, he held back, wanting her to understand how much she meant to him. Finally she pushed past his strength and they rode the waves of love together.

When they were holding each other, her arms tightened around him. The tension signaled a return of her worry. He wanted to reassure her, but how could he?

The world seemed to change hour by hour.

CHAPTER 27

HE NEWS ONLY CONTINUED TO WORSEN AND, WITH IT, Francesca's fears about her father.

The World Health Organization had declared the outbreak a pandemic.

A state of emergency had been called in the United States, and each day, each hour, brought news of new lockdowns, the places precious to the people harboring in the Wild Irish Rose Inn.

San Francisco.

New York.

France.

Dare Valley.

Lebanon.

Ireland.

The list grew rapidly as global infections and deaths began to soar.

When Francesca finally reached out to her father, he scoffed at her concern. He had a cold from working too much—nothing more. *Don't spread scurrilous gossip like this, Francesca. You know better. Such news would have a catastrophic effect on the company's financial health.*

She wanted to be relieved, but she couldn't dismiss a vague, lingering sense of unease. Her mother would have read her father's coffee grounds to see, but that wasn't possible for Francesca. Besides, a part of her would be terrified to look. What if she saw something terrible, like she had in Quinn's cup, and couldn't do anything to change it?

The Wild Irish Rose Inn became the Merriams' whole world. During the day, she and Quinn worked with key family members on the bankruptcy and spin-off plans. Oil prices hit twenty dollars a barrel at the end of March, down more than fifty percent, and each day brought new, and worse, projections for the virus' impact on the global economy.

As Quinn and she lay in bed after an evening of karaoke—Flynn had ordered a machine and emceed the event with forced cheerfulness—he turned on his side to her and said, "Anything else you want to do besides business? Because I think getting out might be a wise course."

He'd tried to infuse some teasing into his tone, but she heard an undercurrent of sadness. Her mind whirring, she said, "I've always thought weaving cloth might be nice. I've told Becca I'd love to help her sometime."

Frankly, right now they were all grateful for any kind of distraction. Annie and Flynn's girls were going stir-crazy, although everyone tried to entertain them beyond the usual pastimes of movie-watching and the visits to the rabbit shed and alpaca pasture. Assumpta had joined the global breadmaking craze and produced more perfectly crusty bread every day than they could eat at dinner, as if Aileen's never-ending batches of scones weren't enough. Alice and Hargreaves, more inseparable every day, continued to make chocolate desserts to pass the time, expanding the dinner menu with Chef Padraig's approval. Flynn had installed Zoom on Uncle Arthur's phone so he could keep in touch with his Dare Valley family.

Seeing Arthur after those calls was painful. The grooves around his mouth and eyes were harsher than ever, and even Amelia's hugs couldn't put an easy smile on his face.

Francesca was grateful for long walks around the inn and the extensive property, either alone with Quinn or with other members of his family. Becca had made her a dashing red pullover, and she donned it on a sunny Wednesday in preparation for the surprise outing she'd planned for her and Quinn. They needed a break to lift their spirits.

"Where are you taking me?" he asked as she pulled him out of the inn.

If she told him, he'd likely bolt. This kind of fun wouldn't make Quinn's top hundred list, but something told her it was exactly what he needed. When they reached the rabbit shed, she heard sweet giggling, and her heart immediately lifted. Annie had said Flynn was taking the girls up there to give her some time alone.

What was it about children laughing that raised the spirits so? Alice had taken to watching baby videos along with a few of the others for a heart boost, as she liked to call it, and Francesca understood the appeal.

"We're stopping here," she told Quinn, who looked sexy if not a bit haggard in an Irish sweater from Becca's shop paired with rust-colored slacks.

He peered inside the shed. "The girls are here with Flynn, playing with baby rabbits."

The three girls were in a huddle on the ground, giggling as they cuddled baby rabbits, a floppy-eared white one tucked under Amelia's chin. Flynn was sitting with his own lapful of rabbits, laughing right along with the girls.

"Listen," Francesca said. The infectious sound had already pulled a smile from her, and her heart felt lighter. She squeezed Quinn's hand, and sure enough, his mouth tipped up.

"All right, it's cute. I've gone all mushy, as Uncle Arthur says. Now what?"

Oh, she almost socked him like Clara did with Arthur. "We're going to join them."

He rolled his eyes. "You expect me to hold a bunch of baby rabbits? I can tell you what I'd rather do. Kiss every inch of you in our room."

"Afterward," she said, putting her hands on his face. "Quinn, we both need a boost. Give it a chance."

He kissed her slowly in response. "I'm only going to allow this indignity," he said as his mouth hovered over hers, "because I need practice with this kind of thing for our kids."

"I love that idea." She gave him a long kiss, her heart melting at the image he'd created in her mind.

"Are you two going to keep kissing or join us?" Flynn called out. "We have plenty of rabbits for everyone. Come on, Quinn. I've got Flopsie right here for you."

Quinn uttered a groan but grabbed Francesca's hand and strode into the shed. "Flopsie! Flynn, I need a more manly rabbit than that."

Amelia giggled. "Don't be silly, Uncle Quinn. Rabbits aren't manly. They're sweet and fuzzy. Right, Flynn?"

"Exactly so, sweetheart," Flynn replied, patting the ground next to him for his brother. "They're soft and cuddly. Like Uncle Quinn here."

Laughter spurted out of Iris and Eloise, and Francesca had to bite her lip as Quinn leveled Flynn a glance before arranging himself on the ground next to his brother. "I am so soft and cuddly. Ask Francesca."

"He really is," she agreed out of loyalty as she sat beside him. Amelia immediately leaned over and handed her a fluffy baby rabbit. "Goodness!" she said as the animal nuzzled her. "What's your name?"

"Mr. O'Shea said it's Noodles," Amelia said, her blond hair peeking out from under a green woolen cap, another of Becca's creations. Each of the girls wore one. "Don't know why. Maybe he likes noodles like I do."

"Rabbits don't eat noodles, silly," Eloise said, petting a gray bunny.

"Maybe they want to," Amelia said and fell back laughing like only a little kid could. Iris took the opportunity to put her three rabbits on Amelia's tummy. A black one jumped off, and another's pink nose twitched, moving its whiskers.

"I think we should ask Aileen to make some delicious noodle soup so we can test your theory," Francesca said. "What do you think? Would Noodles eat it with a spoon or fork?"

The twins laughed, but Amelia giggled until her face was dark pink. "Rabbits can't use silverware, silly."

Francesca looked at Quinn, who was finally smiling and, sure enough, stroking the baby rabbit he held against his stomach. "They do in *Alice and Wonderland*."

"That's a storybook," Amelia cried. "It's pretend!"

"Is it?" Francesca shared a conspiratorial look with an amused Flynn before miming a piece of flatware and offering it to Noodles. The rabbit peered at her finger before hopping forward to investigate. "See. Maybe she's a friend of the White Rabbit. He used silverware."

"Nah," Amelia said, lowering herself close to the rabbit's little face. "That's silly."

"Yes, it is," Iris said. "Francesca, you need to meet Teacup. He's the sweetest."

She took the furry brown rabbit with a smile, grateful the girls were so willing to include them. "Teacup, eh? What kind of tea does he drink?"

"Strawberry tea!" Amelia called out. "Mrs. O'Shea let me have some, and it's delicious."

Flynn made a slurping sound and pretended he was drinking a cup of tea. "I rather think he prefers Earl Grey," he said in a British accent. "Quinn, what do you think?"

He pursed his lips, fighting a smile, before saying, "Troublesome Brothers Tea. It's made from the bones of younger brothers who disobey orders on a pirate ship."

Amelia's eyes widened. "That's really scary, Uncle Quinn. But I like the part about the pirate ship. What's it called?"

His blink was momentary, and then he said in a reasonably good pirate impersonation, "It's called the Jolly Princess, and it only takes nice girls like you and your sisters on its voyages."

She gave him a winning smile as he resumed stroking Flopsie.

"I like the name of that ship," Amelia said. "Where is it going?"

Quinn gave Francesca a pleading look, but she nodded at him encouragingly. This was the man who read Rumi and other poems to her, after all. He let so few people see the creative side of his soul. His ears turned red in embarrassment as he paused, but Flynn's nudge to his side dislodged an answer: "To Mermaid Isle. It's only three leagues from Becca's Inn, by the north cliffs of the sea. But you can only see the mermaids when the sun is setting. Otherwise, they're in the water, looking for treasure."

And so, Quinn Merriam ended up telling a pretty decent tale about pirates and mermaids to three little girls cuddling baby rabbits. Francesca fell a bit more in love with him, something she hadn't imagined possible. That future she'd envisioned for them, still so hazy in some ways, was crystal clear when it came to him and the family they would form together. She could see him sitting beside a pair of twin beds, spinning a story like this one. Or perhaps telling their children about the day he'd held a baby rabbit on his chest.

When they put the rabbits away, Flynn smacked his brother on the back. "Hey! You did great with the girls. Love does the most amazing things to people. First Con, and now you. Keep it up. I like this side of you."

Quinn gently shoved his brother in the chest. "Back at you. Mr. Fashion. You have rabbit fur all over your designer sweater."

Flynn laughed. "This is a designer *sweatshirt* from a label in Denmark you wouldn't know, and it's washable. We all make changes out of love. Right, girls?"

"Right!" all three of them shouted.

"Come on," Flynn said, getting into a runner's crouch. "I'll race you back to the inn. Everyone gets ice cream."

The older girls took off, and Flynn scooped up Amelia, who giggled as he jogged after them. She waved to them over Flynn's shoulder. "Bye!"

Francesca put her arm around Quinn's waist. "See. Don't you feel better?"

He pulled her flush against him. "Yes. Perhaps I should start a rabbit petting room at corporate for stress release."

His face darkened as he remembered. There wouldn't be a place for that anymore.

She hugged him tightly. "Stay in the moment with me. Or I'll go back and get Flopsie. She can be our new roommate."

He buried his face in her neck. "I have a different type of stress relief in mind. Race you back to our room."

She found it easier to smile again as he shot off, clearly needing to expend more stress. Looking back at the shed, she felt grateful for Flopsie and all of their new rabbit friends, for the laughter of children, and for a man who could set aside his worries for long enough to tell a story to three little girls.

CHAPTER 28

CLARA HAD KNOWN HARGREAVES A LONG TIME, BUT SHE could count on one hand the number of times she'd heard him raise his voice in anger. Only once with an aggressive delivery man who'd almost broken a Ming vase. She rose from her chair in the dining room, where she'd been having a cup of tea after chatting with Michaela and Boyd, who were clearly restless and frustrated in Jackson Hole. They'd been in touch with the team of researchers working tirelessly on research and testing on the flower and working remotely themselves, of course, but there were no new developments; nor would there be for some time. Michaela had vented her frustration. Not her usual.

Everyone had had a moment where they hadn't quite acted like themselves. Lockdown grated on the mind after a time. Apparently this was Hargreaves' turn.

She paused in the doorway, observing her dear friend facing off with Alice in the entry hall.

"I'm going with you." His words were almost a demand.

Clara worried her bracelet, not wanting to intervene. But seeing these two at odds was painful when usually they were so chummy.

Alice put her hands on her hips and gave him her best fighter's stare. "We've gone through this."

"You've taken the last two turns at the store," Hargreaves accused, his back ramrod straight. "It's my job as butler to buy the groceries. Today is my turn."

Oh, Hargreaves.

"I've explained to Aileen and Liam that I'm going to be the only one going to the grocery store from now on. I thought we'd had this conversation."

"You informed me moments ago that I am too elderly to go out to other stores," Hargreaves said, his hurt obvious.

"Everyone over sixty is high-risk—including Aileen and Liam—so yes, I'm going to make all the runs now. I'm young, and I never get sick."

Clara gritted her teeth at that kind of talk. There was no denying it was accurate, and she'd agreed to stay at the inn, but who liked to be reminded of such things?

"That is unacceptable," the man said stiffly, his fists uncharacteristically clenched at his side. "I won't have you endanger your life for mine."

"Well, too bad! I'm not letting you outside the inn's grounds."

Hargreaves yanked on his black jacket. "I won't allow you to usurp my duties."

Alice put her hand to her heart. "I'm not usurping anything. I'm only trying to protect you."

"Don't!" His voice had a harsh edge, and Clara felt tears pop into her eyes.

"Clifton," Alice said, her tone softening. "You're like a grandfather to me. I'm not losing you. Please let me do this for you, but also for me. I do it out of love, okay?"

Even from the doorway, Clara could see the tears

tracking down Alice's face.

Hargreaves' mouth bunched. "You have come to mean so much to me as well. But I can't let you do this. I feel guilty as it is, but if something happened to you..."

"I have my mask." She pulled it out of her jeans pocket. "I'm in and out of the store, zip, boom, bam. Okay?"

"Hargreaves!" Clara finally called, unable to witness more discord.

He spotted her, and his entire demeanor bristled.

"Alice, dear," Clara said, crossing the entryway to pull her into a brief hug. "All of us appreciate you going to the store, and I heard Trevor say he wanted to go with you. There are a lot of people to cook for, and there's no need for you to do the shopping all by yourself. Trevor's as strong as an ox and never gets sick. Go find him."

Alice touched Hargreaves' arm before leaving the hall.

"My friend," Clara said, "it's been decided. Anyone high-risk is not to travel outside the inn's grounds. That includes you, despite your duties to me and this family. You are too dear to us. Would I send Arthur or Shawn or anyone else outside this property right now? No. You stay here with me and have some tea."

His face seemed to fall all at once, the usually angular features dropping. "But, Madam."

"It's Clara, remember?" She put her hand on Hargreaves' arm. "We've been together for too long to quibble over something this small, especially during a pandemic. Don't make me fire you, Clifton."

The right side of his mouth tipped up. "Spare me that indignity, Clara."

She nodded crisply. "Fine then."

"Perhaps this is an opportune time to tell you that retirement might be in my future," Hargreaves said.

Clara hugged the man, and although it took him a few moments to respond, he put his arms around her too.

"I'm overjoyed to hear that, Clifton. It's more than past

time."

They shared a watery look before Hargreaves extended his arm to her like a gentleman of old. "May I escort you to tea then?"

"I'd be honored," Clara said, quickly dashing at her eyes.

When she let herself back into their room after a quiet tea with Hargreaves, she braced herself. Arthur was on Zoom with Jill, and his granddaughter was crying.

"You don't need to worry about my investment in Brian's restaurant one bit, Jillie!" Arthur was gripping the edge of the table on which his tablet was propped. "It's only money. You just take care of yourself and your family. Getting upset like this isn't good for you and the little one."

She bit her trembling lip and nodded. "Grandpa, I don't know what Brian will do if he loses the restaurant. I have a job at the hotel when it reopens..."

"Hey, now!" Arthur took Clara's hand, although she remained out of sight. "Brian will figure out something. Takeout seems viable. Plus, there are loans, and people are still going to want to eat out in the future. This damn virus can't last forever."

But it felt like it would, Clara thought, and its weight was the ugliest specter she'd faced.

"I just want it to stop." She lowered her head and sobbed. "Grandpa, I don't want to have the baby right now. Not like this. I'm trying to be brave with Brian, but I'm scared."

Usually Jill was so goofy and full of laughter, and it cracked Clara's heart to see her so upset.

"Women have been having babies since the dawn of time," Arthur said. "You're tough and strong, and you'll have Meredith and any of the Hale cousins you need to help if you decide to have the baby at home and not the hospital."

"Brian can't be with me, according to the new rules at

Dare Valley General. I can't do it without him. Grandpa, I don't want to. He should be there. It's our baby."

Clara had to bite her lip to force back her tears. She'd read horrible accounts of mothers being forced to labor by themselves for hours. And she was worried about the virus' impact on their small town. Although Arthur's nephew, Andy, had told them there were several cases at the hospital, they only knew one of the patients so far: a regular at Arthur's bingo night, a lovely man in his eighties who'd once been in city government. She knew it was unlikely to stay that way.

Arthur made a shushing sound, the kind of sound a person might make to comfort a small child. "If that's still the policy, Andy told me he has a plan. He's going to train Moira and Blake in basic home delivery for you and Lucy."

Right now, they weren't sure if Andy's duties would allow him to be with Lucy, regardless of the rules. He was living in his mother's house alone now, so he wouldn't risk bringing the virus home to his family from the hospital. His mom had moved into Arthur and Clara's house for the time being.

"I know, Grandpa, but Lucy shouldn't be alone either. Andy should be there."

"Okay, now, sweetheart. I know it's not fair, but Andy's a doctor and Lucy understands. He'll be there on Zoom if not in person. Let's focus on what a good plan B we have. Wasn't Blake a great coach for Natalie when she had their baby? Heck, he coaches a football team. One baby will be a piece of cake. And Moira is rock solid. It's not like you're having twins again. This baby will be a piece of cake."

"I hope so." A jumble of cries sounded in the other room. "That's the twins waking from their naps. I need to go. Sorry I lost it. I love you, Grandpa. You stay safe."

"Love you too, Jillie," he said gruffly.

The call ended and Arthur folded over the tablet, his head down. She leaned over him and wrapped him up. His shoulders shook for a moment, alarming her, but he was overdue some tears. They were all coping with so much right now.

When he raised his head, he rubbed his wet eyes. "That call about did me in."

She kissed the top of his head. "It's no wonder. I had my own moment with Hargreaves. He was fighting with Alice about her going for the groceries."

"He's not the only one who feels like shit over that," Arthur said, pushing up from his chair. "I've always fought my own battles, and dammit, it chaps my hide to have other people facing down the virus for me while I hole up in this picturesque inn, hiding out because I'm old. Bah! Then I get so mad at myself for not being grateful for Alice and Trevor and this place when so many people are facing hardships. Hell, old people are hanging out in parking lots, hoping some Good Samaritan will buy their groceries. We have it cushy, Clara."

She ran her hands through his hair, which relaxed him. "Yes, we have it cushy, but it doesn't diminish how we feel. Dammit, Arthur, people are scared and hurting all over the place. You just cried, for heaven's sake, and I had to swallow my own tears with Hargreaves. You feel what you feel. Yes, be thankful, but be honest too."

"Like 'the whole world is going to hell in a handbasket' honest?" He made a raspberry sound. "I wanted to help Jill, but what the hell do I know about having a baby at home? All I felt was helpless, and I hate that most of all."

She opened up his tablet and hit the keys almost hard enough to crack it. "Then let's do something empowered, dammit, because I feel helpless too, and I hate it as much as you do."

"Enough of that talk." He tipped her face and kissed her softly on the mouth. "Does kissing make it better?"

She gave him an answer, and the slow kiss helped ease the constriction in her heart. "Yes, it does. So does giving money to various causes."

Hence her attack on the tablet.

When she wasn't knitting, she was finding—and funding—GoFundMe campaigns for medical personnel, restaurant workers, and face mask drives.

"There is so much need," Arthur said. "Unemployment is... I don't have words for it."

"How about we sit here together and find a few organizations that help people with their rent and mortgages? That sounds like a lovely way to pass the time. I've reached my breaking point with knitting. Arthur, if I don't have an intervention soon, I might start to bake banana bread."

"Good God, no! Not banana bread. Clara, you've never baked a damn thing in your life. Plus, Clifton would have a fainting spell."

She thought of what her dear friend had told her. "He's going to retire soon, Arthur. He said so."

"About time," Arthur said, rubbing her back. "You knew it was coming. Did he say what he was going to do? Curl up on a beach somewhere and write a novel?"

She resumed her typing. "I suspect he and Alice will do something together, but I'm only guessing. They seem to be enjoying their chocolate making."

In fact, their chocolate making had reached artistic levels. Although food didn't tempt her much these days, she'd still closed her eyes in ecstasy after trying their most recent creation: a lavender and Earl Grey-infused truffle.

"They do indeed," Arthur said, "and it's encouraging to watch anyone create anything right now. Hey! Maybe after this pandemic is finished and Hargreaves has settled into his new life, we can use our matchmaking skills to help him find his soulmate."

The ropes squeezing her heart loosened, and she experienced a warmth so great she pressed her hand to her chest. Imagine! Helping her dearest friend find love, like she had with Arthur. "How wonderful would that be?"

"Pretty wonderful," Arthur said, sitting and pulling her onto his lap. "You hold on to that image, my dear. Those kinds of plans fill a person with hope."

And hope was the most treasured of gifts during the pandemic.

CHAPTER 29

QUINN SOUGHT OUT HIS FAVORITE MATCHMAKERS FOR AD-
vice.

He and Francesca had been working almost ceaselessly
on a phase-out timeline and bankruptcy plan for the company, with help from key family members. News in the oil
market continued to be bleak, and he'd grown numb to seeing the price of crude oil. They both needed a break—family dinner and karaoke nights had grown stale, sadly—and
he wanted to do something romantic for her. He couldn't
take her out to a candlelit restaurant or fly her to the Costa
del Sol for a weekend getaway, but he wanted more good
memories for her, for them, in the midst of all this anguish
and horror. She'd given him the idea with her rabbit outing.

When he knocked on the door to his aunt and uncle's
suite, he tapped his foot impatiently. Although he'd gotten
better about opening up to others, it still didn't come easily.

"Quinn!" Aunt Clara's glowing face had a crease on it like she'd been sleeping.

"Were you napping?" God, he knew what that code word meant.

"We're just up," she said, gesturing for him to come inside to their small sitting room. "Arthur is getting dressed."

Something he didn't need to know about, although he aspired to still be "taking naps" at their age. "I'm sorry to intrude, but I need some ideas for a romantic evening with Francesca."

He'd thought about asking Alice for help, but she worked for Francesca, not him. It would have felt weird and uncomfortable to ask her for romantic help. Alice would probably laugh at him for that, but that was fine by him.

"Romance," Aunt Clara said. "What is that again? It's hard to remember the easy days of going out for dinner or a movie or even taking a long drive in the country."

The Irish government had decreed citizens couldn't travel more than twenty kilometers from their home, and while Quinn could understand the measure, it sucked.

Of course, they had more outlets than most people did. The property was large, and they always took long walks before dinner. God knew he'd seen the videos of people holed up in their apartments, trying Zumba and other exercises for the first time in their living rooms. As far as he was concerned, the compulsion to film such a thing and share it indicated people really were at their breaking point.

"Do I need to ask someone else?"

"You came to the right place," Arthur said, coming out of the bedroom. "We are the masters of romance. We were just taking a romantic break now, weren't we, Clara? Not that you want to hear about it, but I figure having sex right now is a sign of sanity, if not sheer will."

"Thank you, Arthur." Aunt Clara made a rude noise. "It's nice to know I'm helping you work out your lockdown crisis."

"I'm helping you too, dear." He snapped his suspenders and laughed. "We have to find humor wherever we can. If I focus on one hundred thousand people dying from this damn disease, I'll want to punch something."

Quinn understood. The infection rate and death tolls were rising. New York was being crushed, and Caitlyn and Flynn continued to hear about people in their network who'd caught it. So far no one had died, but they were waiting for the other shoe to drop. Dammit, he didn't want to keep thinking like this.

"Back to romance." He put his hands on his hips, ready to get down to business. "What can I do for her?"

"You could write her an ode," Aunt Clara suggested. "The Irish poets are quite inspiring. I've been reading some Yeats myself."

"I suck at writing poetry." Hadn't he tried once, hoping to match Rumi? What a fail. "Moving on."

"He needs a practical suggestion," Arthur said, crossing to the electric kettle on the side table and flicking it on. "Next you'll suggest he paint her nude. For God's sake, Clara."

The idea made him smile, at least. But he couldn't draw for shit. "She loves things like museums and the theater and restaurants. All closed."

"But she also loves food," Arthur said, ripping open three tea bags and dropping them into matching blue cups. "Cook for her. Dress up. Did you bring your tux?"

"To plan for bankruptcy? Who am I, James Bond?"

Aunt Clara laughed until tears streamed down her face. "Oh, I must be stretched to my limit to find that so funny. Did you bring any baby blue swim trunks like Daniel Craig wore in his first Bond movie? I imagine Francesca would love to see you in those."

Arthur guffawed. "I'd love to see him wade into the Irish Sea in nothing but a tiny pair of swim trunks. His other bits would shrink to nothing too."

They laughed so hard they had to hold each other up, and Quinn wasn't sure how he felt about them laughing over his *bits*. He opened the door. "I'll see if I can borrow Trev's tux and figure out something to cook. I'll leave you two to your hilarity."

"Thanks for the laughter," his aunt managed to spurt out. "I needed it today."

"Happy to help." He closed the door and shook his head, realizing he felt lighter as well. Maybe he should don a swimsuit and face the Irish Sea. *Nah.*

The kitchen was crowded when he entered. Aileen dropped an unbaked scone she was handling. Alice nudged Hargreaves, who was piping another chocolate creation onto parchment paper in the shape of a flower. God, Amelia was going to love that. She exclaimed over every shape they created, and the pure innocence of it always brought a smile to his face. Chef Padraig sprinkled the last of the rosemary on a giant leg of lamb.

"Sorry to bother you, but I was hoping to cook something for Francesca and myself tonight." He shifted on his feet, feeling an unusual flush coast up his neck. "Like for a date. If you could point me toward the icebox."

Chef Padraig picked up his knife and extended it like a saber in his direction. "You wish to cook in my kitchen?"

No, I'll build a fire outside like a caveman and hope Buttercup doesn't lick me. "Yes, if you would be so kind." Should he have asked Becca first?

"You can work over there." He pointed his knife regally to the station to the right of Alice and Hargreaves. "You will be quiet."

"Of course. Thank you."

"Pour l'amour, on fait ce qu'on peut," he replied with a shrug.

When he reached his assigned space, Alice leaned closer and said, "Chef Padraig said, 'for love, one does what one can.' Don't worry. He usually warms up to people after a while."

Quinn didn't plan on being there that long. "I only need to cook dinner for tonight." Of course, who the hell knew how long they were going to be in lockdown? Maybe he'd have to do this again. Better to be on his best behavior.

"Let me show you what we have," Alice said, wiping her hands on her apron.

"A capital idea, Quinn," Hargreaves said, giving him a firm nod. "Flynn was talking about something similar."

"I told that dear boy I'd be happy to cook for him and Annie," Aileen said. "They have their hands full entertaining the girls even if they are the sweetest angels alive. Who can blame the little ones? I'm going stir-crazy, and my days aren't much different now than before this horrible virus started plaguing us, God help us all." She crossed herself.

"Would you cook for me?" Quinn brightened at the very thought.

"Ah, boyo, it's Flynn who's stolen my heart after your dear brother Trevor." She made eyes at him. "Maybe after I get to know you better."

Turned down flat. Wasn't that his luck these days?

"Come on," Alice said, grabbing his arm. "Clifton and I will help you."

"Indeed, Master—Quinn." Hargreaves—Clifton—gave a sardonic smile. "Old habits are hard to break."

"But you're doing marvelously," Alice said, picking up a semi-soft truffle and popping it into her mouth.

"There she goes again, Clifton," Aileen said, clucking her tongue. "She'd eat all of them if you turned your back."

"I'll only make some more," Clifton said, his brown eyes warm as he glanced at Alice.

"She's a vixen and a chocolate thief," Chef Padraig said with a gruff laugh, "but she's so sweet you can't be mad at her. Come here, *cherie*, and taste the mushrooms I will serve with our beautiful lamb."

Alice made the expected humming sounds, making Chef Padraig offer her another piece. Quinn had to stop himself from tapping his foot. He wasn't a man who liked waiting, and he didn't savor being the outsider in another's space.

When Alice showed him the choices, he went for the steaks. "Those babies. They'll be easy to grill."

"Are you going for easy or for romance?" Alice asked. "Francesca's top ten dishes don't involve steak."

"Not even if they were served with the best Parisian *frites*," Chef Padraig said and then muttered something in French Quinn imagined wasn't flattering.

Other than the breakfast they both enjoyed, Quinn realized he didn't know many of Francesca's favorite meals. She loved fish and shellfish and she'd eaten beef, pork, and chicken in his presence. He asked with dread, "You aren't going to encourage me to cook Indian food, are you?" A cold sweat started to coat his skin.

Alice and the others began to laugh, and again, Quinn felt a flush coat his neck. Dammit, this was getting embarrassing.

"Indian food!" Alice cried out, laughing. "I'd love to see that. Right, Clifton?"

"I expect Quinn can cook anything he puts his mind to," Clifton said diplomatically.

No, not Indian food. The taste profiles were much too complex. They were insane, perhaps hopped up on the gas coming from the warming stove in the corner. "Thank you for the vote of confidence, Clifton. Perhaps I need to do some research and plan better." Or beg J.T. or his mother to cook. Surely they would take pity on him. Or he could pay them. Anything at this point.

"How about we make some beef bourguignon together?" Alice said, clapping her hands, her brown eyes flashing. "I'm sure Chef Padraig would give us a few of his precious mushrooms."

"Maybe," the chef said with a mock glare.

"Oh, please!" She rushed over to him and kissed him on the cheek, and he laughed.

"For you, *ma belle*," Chef Padraig said. "She's irresistible, this one. A siren in the kitchen. I don't know what I will do when she leaves. Perhaps, she will stay here forever with us. *N'est-ce pas*, Aileen?"

"That would be grand," Aileen said, setting the scones in the oven. "Clifton as well. The kitchen will be too quiet without them."

"I thought you liked a quiet kitchen, Chef Padraig," Quinn said.

"Only guests must stay quiet." He kissed Alice again on the cheeks. "These two have become family."

Which seemed to be everyone's reaction to the duo. "All right, Alice, if you're willing to help me."

"I'll do what your mother did with you for our first brunch at their home," Alice said, grinning now. "You can chop."

He had to give her credit. There was something charming about her. So he chopped the ingredients he was given, grateful for her and Clifton's help. They debated the amount of red wine to add after the beef cubes, mushroom, *lardon*, and onions had been sautéed with garlic, thyme, and bay leaf. Chef Padraig hotly debated the absence of carrots in the dish, and Quinn learned Alice and Clifton were passionate about it adding a sweetness to the dish they disdained. *Disdained*. When had he ever acted like this around food? Oil prices, certainly, and the stock market. He supposed to each their own.

After the wine issue was resolved, Alice patted him on the back. "Now, we leave it to simmer. Do you want candles tonight? How about eating in the wine cellar? It's private and so cozy. Flynn's idea—I can't take credit."

Flynn was Mr. Pandemic Romance, it seemed. But did he have a tuxedo? He doubted it. After thanking everyone in the kitchen, he went to find Trevor. His brother was in the dyeing shed with Becca, and they were stirring a pot of beet-colored water.

"We can't wait any longer to shear the sheep, Trev," Becca said. "I swear I saw a few of the sheep glistening with sweat in the sunlight. It's been warm for this time of year."

"We'll have the shearers wear masks," Trevor said. "Farming is considered essential, so it shouldn't be a problem. I'll talk to Liam about arranging it."

Quinn had been so caught up in Merriam Enterprises that he'd forgotten Trevor had other concerns. He was glad Trevor had a role to fulfill at the inn, but would it be enough for him after the company folded? He realized he wasn't ready to ask that yet, of his brother or himself. Or talk with Caitlyn or Annie about the logistics of planning the spin-off Francesca had envisioned.

He'd been content for Caitlyn and Annie—and Flynn, for that matter—to work remotely in whatever way they could right now. Company operations were different with their employees working from home, if they had roles that allowed it. Some were furloughed, of course. None yet knew the plans Quinn would soon reveal about the end of Merriam Enterprises as they knew it, and the spin-off. But he imagined anyone with a brain who looked at the market and their stock price would know they were headed to bankruptcy.

"Should we invite the others to watch? I would feel horrible if anyone became ill after coming to the shearing," she said, blowing out a breath.

"We have a little over a hundred cases here in Cork," Trevor said. "We'll keep being smart, Becca. It's our only defense."

Was it? Quinn still wasn't so sure after reading the news. He was starting to believe the virus would spread regardless of what anyone did to stop it. "Excuse me."

They spun around, Becca lifting a hand over her heart.

"Goodness, but you gave me a fright, Quinn."

"Sorry," he said, a now familiar rush of embarrassment cresting up his neck. "Trev, can I speak to you for a minute? It's not about business."

His brother crossed to him. "What's up?"

"I'm doing a pandemic date night. Do you have a tux? Uncle Arthur thought dressing up—"

"I've read about people doing that." His brother's lips twitched. "Are Aunt Clara and the singing mice going to make Francesca a ball gown?"

He gave his brother his best sneer. "Only after Uncle Arthur blows the glass for her slippers."

"Nice one." He slapped him on the back. "Back in a jiffy, babe. Romance calls."

They left the shed and headed to the Grace O'Malley tower where Trevor and Becca made their home. Hatshep met them at the top of the stairs and wove figure eights around Quinn's feet.

"She likes you," Trev exclaimed. "Holy shit. I can't believe it."

"She likes you, doesn't she?" He wasn't going to admit he'd spent the night with Hatshep in his lap. The three people who knew—Alice, Hargreaves, and Francesca—had shown remarkable restraint.

"Of course. I'm charming." Trevor pushed open the deluxe closet.

"*I'm* charming," he protested, admiring the rows of Becca's handknit fashionwear. The bold colors were like a rainbow on a waterfall. God, he'd been in Ireland too long.

"You're something, all right." His brother pulled out the tuxedo, hanging on a wire hanger. "It might be a little loose on you—especially in a certain area."

Were they back to third grade and who had the bigger dick? He welcomed the normalcy somehow. "In your dreams. If I rip the seams down under, I'll have it repaired."

"Hah!" His brother pressed the hanger at him. "That

will be the day. You can change in here later if you want to keep it secret."

"Thanks, man," he told Trev. "I have to check on dinner now."

"Don't burn it," his brother joked as they walked out together, Hatshep mewing softly as they passed her.

"I still can't believe she likes you," Trevor said.

Quinn only smiled, and to his surprise, his smile held steady the entire way to the kitchen. The aroma of stewed meat, garlic, and wine was redolent in the air, mixed with the buttery deliciousness of the scones.

Alice jumped up from the table she was sitting at, her teacup wobbling until Hargreaves righted it. "Good! You're back. I was hoping you wouldn't bail."

"Never." He made his face very serious.

She laughed. "Okay, let's check this baby. Then you can peel the potatoes and we can talk about dessert."

He settled on chocolate mousse after Alice made a passionate argument for it being one of Francesca's favorites. Beating the egg whites ended up being easier than separating the eggs. Alice had spooned out the egg yolk he'd broken and then taken over in a polite but officious way that was impossible to deny, not that he had a mind to. Clifton had watched with a fond smile he couldn't quite conceal.

When everything was ready, Alice volunteered to get Francesca dressed and down to the cellar. Clifton took over the final touches, allowing Quinn the opportunity to get spiffed up too.

As he was going back through the main hall, having dressed in the tux in Trevor's room, someone whistled. "Looking good, Quinn Anthony Merriam. Hot date?"

He looked back and spotted his mother at the top of the stairs, a warm smile on her face. "Yeah. Come down. I need you to fix my tie."

He didn't, but it was a happy reminder of his first prom. She'd been the one to help him. His dad had worked late, he recalled, missing the whole event. He'd been oddly disappointed.

"Where's Dad?" he asked.

She sighed, a shadow crossing her face as she made it down the stairs and crossed to him. "Watching the news like usual. I keep telling him there's nothing he can do about it and becoming too embroiled isn't good for anyone. But does he listen?"

They were all acting a bit obsessed over the news, but it was changing constantly, and no one knew where the bottom would be—or when they would reach it. "How are *you* holding up, Mom? Really."

She drilled him with a quiet stare before retying his bow tie. "I'm hanging in there like everyone else. Making the best of things. Counting our blessings. I know things seem hard right now, but we have each other, Quinn. That's everything."

"Truly?"

Her hand was comforting when she touched his face. "You're so like your father. You and Connor always were the closest to him in personality. My serious boys, so ambitious. Yes, that's everything. So long as we all stay healthy, that's all I care about. The rest of this... We'll weather it. And when I need reminding, I look at one of my mother's letters to my father during the war. There's a lot of wisdom in there. I was so glad Trevor brought them out. They helped Becca, you know, with her fears, and many others. If you need them, they're yours, Quinn. Your grandfather made a great life for himself after the war took everything. So did your grandmother. You remember that."

When she kissed his cheek, he held her to him longer. "I love you, Mom." He realized he didn't say it enough.

"I love you too," she whispered. "This time together is hard, but we'll remember the karaoke and the family dinners and the laughs and the tears. It's life, sweetheart. We take what comes and steer ourselves forward. Always together. Have fun on your date."

She paused then, and something flashed in her eyes. He knew that look. She was about to deliver one of her mother smackdowns. "I probably shouldn't butt in, but since you're like your father, I'm going to trust my instincts and give you a push. Are you finally going to propose to Francesca again?"

He could feel himself drawing back in response, old fears rising up. "Now?"

She kissed him again on the cheek. "The only way to find out is to ask. With the world being as it is, in such a state of uncertainty, my perspective is: if not now, when? Don't you agree?"

Oddly, he did, but Francesca had wanted a clearer sense of her future career before she fully committed herself. And yet, the future wasn't clear for any of them. There was no predicting what would happen next month or next year. He was going to take his mom's advice. She'd never steered him wrong. "I'll just head back to my room and grab the ring I bought," he said.

She laughed. "I was hoping you were prepared, Quinn Anthony Merriam. A man should have a ring when he proposes marriage, but I was willing to lend you the ring your father gave to me the night he proposed."

He was deeply touched and hugged her warmly again. "Thanks, Mom."

"We take care of each other. Go get 'em, tiger," she said and sailed off, whistling.

He detoured to their room, checking to make sure Francesca wasn't inside. Retrieving the ring from its hiding place, he tucked it into his jacket pocket and let himself into the hallway.

His gaze tracked down the hallway to his parents' room. His mother had said he was a lot like his father, and he knew it was true. Did Francesca have to work overtime to pull him out of his funks? *Yes, you idiot*, his mind supplied. She'd taken him to a rabbit shed, hadn't she? He vowed to do better. Before he could chicken out, he started walking toward his parents' room.

He knocked, and after a brief wait, his dad opened the door. "Where's the party?"

"Date night with Francesca." He brushed his shirt front. "Trev was good enough to loan me his tux."

"Looks good." His dad's hair, which had been silver for years, had whitened at the temples in the past few weeks.

"Actually, I'm going to propose tonight." His stomach quivered a touch, but he kept his face impassive.

"Good decision. She's a wonderful woman and the perfect match for you."

"Thanks, Dad." He smiled when his dad put a hand on his shoulder in an unusual display of affection. "Hey, maybe you should take Mom on a date. I mean, she mentioned it sounded like fun. I'll let you get back to the news."

He was turning when his dad said, "Thanks, Quinn. A date with your mother would be nice. Think Trevor would loan me his tux?"

"Sure. I'll make sure it's cleaned and pressed for you."

"Perfect." His dad shifted. "Good luck tonight."

"Thanks. See ya, Dad."

"See ya, son."

There was a warmth to the word that made it sound like an endearment, and it touched him. His mother was right. There *were* parts of this lockdown he would remember fondly for the rest of his life.

He was about to make it even more memorable.

CHAPTER 30

DRESSING FOR DINNER SOUNDED LIKE THE PERFECT ANTI-dote to the ever-present blues in the inn.

As Alice clucked over her red silk harem pants and ivory cashmere sweater—her dressiest and still warmest outfit for the changeable April weather—she held up the silver heels she was thinking of wearing.

"Yes!" Alice cried out. "Make sure you wear one of your darker red lipsticks. Tonight is going to be so much fun."

"You look terrific," Francesca said, gesturing to her friend's soft peach sweater and black wool pants.

"Clara was a peach—bad pun—to knit me a thank you present for helping Clifton blossom. I mean, he did all the unfurling."

"You encouraged it by being you," Francesca said, slipping on her heels. "Much like you did with me. You know... I don't know what's next for us, so if there's something you really want to do, you should go ahead and do it. You don't need to hold back on my account."

"Like open a chocolate shop?" Alice cried out, her rapid response proving she'd given it plenty of thought. "Sometimes after yoga when I'm meditating, I can see the door opening and a glass counter filled with chocolate: truffles, cakes, brownies even. Then I fall back to earth. Opening a shop seems like a crazy idea right now. Why would anyone venture into a chocolate shop during an outbreak?"

But her excitement was obvious, and Francesca truly did think she could do anything, so she found herself saying, "You would find a way to make it work. Besides, aren't you always saying how healing and uniting chocolate is? I figure we're going to need a lot of both in the days ahead. Have you thought about asking Clifton to join you?"

Alice inhaled a deep yoga breath before blurting out, "I can see him behind the counter when I'm meditating. It's so cool and sweet and weird. He's like a grandfather, friend, and neighbor rolled up in one person. Francesca, he's become family."

"I know," she said softly. And no one deserved a loving, doting family more than her sweet friend.

"But I'm delaying us. We need to get to dinner. Come on."

They were out the door before Francesca could ask more questions, and Alice tugged her hand like a woman on a mission. Except she took her down a side hallway instead of to the dining room.

"We're having an aperitif in the wine cellar first," Alice said, her black boots sounding on the small wooden steps as they descended.

"Oh, how lovely!" A punch of excitement broke through, the kind she used to feel when she and Alice would try out a new hot spot in London or Paris or Prague. This was something *different*.

When the door opened, she felt a spark of attraction, of appreciation. Quinn sat there in the candlelight, wearing a tux and looking impossibly handsome. He unfurled slowly from his chair, giving her plenty of time to check him out.

"Welcome to date night," he said, gesturing to the golden room. "Alice and others helped me cook. I wanted to do something special for you—for us."

"I'm outta here," Alice said, giving her a side hug before slowly backing out. "Quinn, text me when you want me to bring the food down."

He crossed to Alice, sending Francesca a cheeky wink as he passed her. Then he whispered something in Alice's ear, and her friend shrieked and launched herself at him. "Okay, you're officially my friend now! I am so outta here."

Francesca watched as Alice raced up the stairs, sounding like a herd of bulls during Pamplona's famous run. "What was that about?"

He gave a sardonic smile. "She liked my suggestion for dessert." All jokiness leaked out of his expression. "Come here. I really want to kiss you. God, you look beautiful."

She held out her hands and he took them. "You look handsome and hot and deliciously sexy. Did you bring a tux with you?"

He laughed. "No, this is Trevor's. He's a sucker for romance now. I probably need a tutorial from him and Flynn. Flynn is going to do date night with Annie tomorrow, apparently. I beat him to it."

Her hands curled around his nape, and she loved the smell of his crisp cologne washing over her. "I could get used to date night in a wine cellar in a historic Irish inn. You still got game, Quinn Merriam."

"I'm glad you think so, Miss Maroun, because I've got a little more to show you. I don't think I can wait until dessert, after all."

Before she could process what that might mean, he stepped away and reached into his jacket pocket. She gasped as he lowered onto one knee.

The heart he'd captured started to pound in fast, insistent beats. He was opening the box, and she had a flash of another time, when he had opened a red Cartier box. The ring was different, of course, but just as magnificent. The ruby was surrounded by diamonds in one of her favorite settings.

It was perfect for her.

"You managed to find the perfect ring twice, Quinn," she said, her voice a little breathless.

"That's a relief, what with it being a different jeweler and all." He swallowed thickly. "Let's not talk about last time. Francesca... I know you wanted to wait until you had a clearer picture of your career, but the future seems pretty hazy right now. I figure two people who love each other shouldn't wait to be together, so I'll continue... If that's okay?"

He was asking for her permission to propose? His thoughtfulness moved her, and his words spoke to something deep inside of her. She found she didn't want to wait either. Hadn't she spent most of her life waiting for one thing or another? "Please do."

He blew out a long breath. "From the very first, I loved you and knew we were meant for each other. I know it's been a long road, but there's no doubt in my mind that you're the person I'd like to walk beside. Always. Will you marry me and be mine forever?"

Be his forever. "Yes, Quinn Merriam. I want that too. I missed you horribly when we were apart. Whatever comes, and I know it's hard to predict the future right now, I'm yours. For better and for worse." She stopped the rest of the vows because he was slipping the ring on her finger, standing, and taking her into his arms.

"For better, babe. Always for better." Then he was kissing her senseless, and she was kissing him right back.

His lips cruised down her neck, and she cupped his face, awash in love for him. "You and I have been through it, Quinn, but we're coming out on the other side."

She'd more than fulfilled her New Year's resolution

regarding him, she realized. She only wished she could have saved all of Merriam Enterprises too. Her heart still hadn't made peace with the loss of their core business. Quinn wouldn't have a role in a small skincare company, and he didn't know what was ahead either.

But that was the last thing she should be focusing on right now. They'd agreed to spend the rest of their lives together. She tightened her arms around him, forcing the swell of dark thoughts aside.

"More than," he said, kissing her lightly on the lips. "How about we make love, and then I can text Alice?"

She eyed the sturdy wooden farm table. "Make it quick but good because I want to share our news with everyone. We could all use happy news."

He laughed. "You've got to be kidding. I always make it good."

It certainly wasn't quick, but she wouldn't have had it any other way. He stripped her down to only her bra and boosted her up onto the edge of the table. She arched toward him and moaned as he penetrated her, his hands cupping her hips. They started to rock, and she locked her ankles around his waist as he began thrusting deeper, harder. Soon, she was lying back and gripping the edges of the table, eyes closed as their passion built. When she came, she heard him cry out and follow her, his hands clasping hers.

"Jesus, if this is what engaged sex is like, I'm all for it." He lowered his upper body onto her and kissed her sweetly. "I love you. I promise to show you how much every day."

Needing to touch him, she threaded her hand through his hair, which was an inch longer than usual since most hair salons were closed. Personally, she liked it that way. "I promise too. Come. Let's eat. Then we can celebrate with your family."

"Prepare to be blown away by my chopping prowess," he joked, picking up his phone and texting Alice. "Get dressed. She'll be here like the wind."

Sure enough, Alice was there five minutes later, balancing a silver tray alongside Clifton, who carried one too.

"We're engaged!" Francesca cried out, holding up her left hand.

Alice set her tray down and grabbed her up in a bear hug. "Way to go! I was so excited when Quinn told me. I love that he couldn't wait until after dinner."

"Congratulations," Clifton said, a warm and rather unprofessional smile on his face. "It's marvelous news. If I may..."

He set his own tray aside and approached Francesca, kissing her on both cheeks. "Welcome to the family, my dear."

"Thank you, Clifton." She shared a look with Quinn. Yes, she was officially joining the Merriams. How lucky was she?

After they supped on the scrumptious meal Quinn had expertly chopped and then scooped up every last spoonful of chocolate mousse for dessert, they ventured upstairs to share the news with his family.

She was passed from Merriam to Merriam for kisses and hugs and congratulations. Shawn brought out champagne with Aileen's help, and everyone lifted their glasses as she and Quinn stood in the center of the dining room.

"To true love and the long tradition of Merriam soulmates," Shawn said. "May it always be so for generations to come."

Francesca thought of the children they would have as she lifted the glass to her lips. Never had the champagne tasted so perfect, the bubbles so delicate and buoyant.

Quinn raised his glass again. "I want to toast Aunt Clara, Uncle Arthur, and Hargreaves for being our family matchmakers. You did a hell of a job."

"I'd say," Uncle Arthur called out. "Some of you were easy as pie while others were downright bears. You know who you are."

"Bears?" Amelia asked, holding on to Flynn's leg. "Where's the bears?"

"It's a metaphor, sweetie," Flynn said. "I, for one, was easy. Speaking of... We should call Connor and Louisa and Michaela and Boyd, right? Not that it's my news, but—"

"Great idea!" Quinn said. "Let's call Louisa and Connor first from our makeshift conference room." Since Connor had nudged Quinn in Francesca's direction, it seemed only fitting.

They all piled into the formal parlor—what had become their war room—and Flynn took over on the tech side.

Louisa picked up after a few rings, her face gray. "I was thinking about calling you, but I was going to wait a little longer until we knew for sure."

"What is it?" Assumpta asked, stepping toward the large screen.

"Connor started to run a fever," Louisa said. "He's congested suddenly. It happened so fast."

Francesca's stomach dropped. She took Quinn's hand, and he gripped back like it was a lifeline.

"You think he has the virus," Assumpta said, her voice filled with steel as Shawn walked forward and put an arm around her waist.

Louisa nodded her head slowly. "Yes. A few cases have come through the shelter despite our safety policies. I've been praying it wouldn't spread, but it's so hard to know. The doctor my dad sent over performed a test, and we should know in a couple of days. It usually takes a week for results to come back. Isn't that insane?"

If it was a serious case, he could be dead before the results came back. Francesca had read other accounts of that happening.

"Give him the flower," Clara said, coming closer to the screen. "There's no use waiting for the results. If he's sick with fever, he has something. Boil the water. Put the flower in the bottom and let it steep for fifteen minutes. How awake is he?"

She pressed her hand to her mouth. "In and out. He keeps waking up saying he's tired and achy. I've...been giving him broth and tea. It only started this morning. He went to sleep early last night, saying he was tired, but I didn't think anything of it. We've both been working non-stop. But he was burning up this morning."

"It's going to be fine, dear." Clara's voice had the same steel in it as Assumpta's. "That flower saved Michaela. It will do the same for Connor."

"All right," she said, wiping her nose. "I'll give it to him once we get off. I...had to get tested too. If I'm sick, I'll take care of him as long as possible. The doctor said no one else should come into the apartment. If the fever worsens, we might have to go to the hospital, but not yet. My dad said he's going to leave groceries and whatnot for us outside the door, and Boxer is going to step up with the shelter. But—"

"Take one thing at a time, Louisa," Assumpta said, "and let others help you. Take care of our boy, okay? And yourself. We love you both."

"And we love you too," Louisa said, her mouth tight. "I'll push and prod him to get better. I'm not losing him to this. I've been telling him so."

Francesca felt the burn of tears and held them back. Crying right now wouldn't help anyone.

"Go get the flower, honey," Assumpta said. "Keep us updated."

"I will," she said with a hard shake of her head.

The screen went blank, and a shock rolled through the room like a dark cloud.

"Not Connor," Caitlyn said, starting to cry. Beau wrapped her into a tight hug, and as Francesca found solace in Quinn's arms, she noted the other siblings were all holding their spouses or partners. Clara and Arthur were of course holding each other too. The only exception was Assumpta and Shawn.

"I have to go to him, Shawn," she said.

"The doctor said no one should enter the room," her husband said. "He's my son too, and I want to call the pilot and fly over this minute. But this isn't a normal illness. Let the flower do its work, Assumpta."

Tears flooded Assumpta's eyes, and all of her children paused at the sight.

"He's right," Clara said, rubbing the woman's arm. "The flower will heal him. I know it will."

"And what if this virus is beyond its power?" Assumpta said. "Boyd and Michaela said there was nothing conclusive about its use for the virus yet."

"Testing is in the early stages," Clara said gently.

"I can't let my boy go through this alone. I just can't." She strode out of the room.

Shawn lowered his head, putting his hand over his eyes, and Clara hugged him to her.

"I'll go talk to Mom," Trevor said, wiping his nose. "I've thought about this a lot. What I'd do and how I'd react if one of us got sick. I'll lay it out for her. That's all we can do."

He left the room, and Quinn bowed his head to Francesca's shoulder and whispered, "I don't think I can take this."

She didn't know what to say to him, so she didn't say anything. She just wrapped him in her arms. The mood was somber as many of them took up vigil in the dining room. Annie and Flynn had left to tuck the girls into bed, but they returned an hour or so later. Trevor had come back too, saying their mother had promised to consider his perspective. He'd pulled Hatshep onto his lap, and Becca was sitting next to him with her hand on his thigh.

"It's finally hit home," J.T. said, rubbing his face. "I wonder how many people are doing the same thing we are tonight, waiting for news of someone they love."

"You trust in that damn flower," Arthur said gruffly. "You don't give up hope. Connor is strong. He's going to pull through."

Francesca recalled the symptoms she'd read about. At least Connor's lips weren't blue. That particular symptom sounded like a death sentence.

They waited through the night with Alice and Hargreaves and Aileen bringing in pots of coffee and tea. Assumpta finally came downstairs with Shawn.

"My husband and one of my sons have pointed out that it would hurt this family even more if I went to Connor and became ill myself."

Francesca's throat grew tight, hearing the proud woman's voice break.

"It goes against a mother's every instinct to not run to her child's side—no matter what their age. But Shawn pointed out that I have other children too, and I know you guys need me. He does too. I'm staying here, although it really pisses me off, and I'm not sure I can forgive myself if something happens. I wouldn't care if I got it, but Trevor told me that's stupid, and we don't do stupid in this family. Right, Trev?"

Francesca couldn't imagine anyone saying that to Assumpta.

"Right, Mom." He crossed the room and pulled her to him. "We all want to be with him, Mom. I'm sorry I had to say those things."

She stroked his hair. "Oh, honey. I'm proud you did. No man but your father has ever talked to me like that."

J.T. stood up and walked over to them. "I'm glad you're staying, Mom."

Then he wrapped his twin and his mother into a group hug, and the other Merriam children rose and joined them, Quinn included. Shawn was the last to join, and Francesca brushed tears aside as the proud man wiped away his own tears as he embraced his children.

She shared a glance with Arthur, who was also wiping tears. In fact, there wasn't a dry eye in the house. Alice and

Clifton were there too, as intent as the rest of them, and Clifton's mouth was tight with his battle to keep his tears from dropping.

The hours passed, and time seemed to slow. Francesca was sure that if she went to the window, the tide coming in from the sea would be in slow motion. Louisa texted a few updates to Assumpta, which she read stoically to the group. She'd given him the flower brew, but there was no change yet, and Francesca's hands grew cold.

What if this mythical flower she'd heard about couldn't cure the virus? Michaela and Boyd had been stricken, hearing about Connor, and they hadn't been able to offer any reassurance about the flower. They didn't know if it would cure him.

What if nothing could?

Needing to use the lavatory, she decided to wash her face and change her clothes. She kissed Quinn and left the room. Every motion was an effort. By the time she reached their room, she was crying silently. Glancing down at her engagement ring, she pressed it to her mouth.

Last night was supposed to have been a celebration.

As she was changing clothes, her cell phone rang. She finished pulling on her clean shirt and crossed to the bedside table. It was her father, requesting a FaceTime call. The rarity of it made her hasten to answer.

When his image flashed onto the screen, she almost cried out. He was in a hospital bed, his lips a terrifying bluish tint, plastic tubes in his nose cresting over the ears he'd always said were too big.

She tumbled down a rabbit hole of despair.

"Oh, Father," she cried out.

He lifted a weak hand. "I thought I was invincible after the war, but the damn virus got me."

His voice was whisper-soft, and she turned up the volume of her phone only to realize it was at the loudest setting. "Where are you, Father?"

"A private hospital in Beirut." He expelled a dry cough, and it sounded like he was choking. "Listen to me. I have few words left."

She nodded, fighting the tears pressing hard at the backs of her eyes.

"The doctors say there's nothing left to do but put me on a ventilator. My chances of recovery go down significantly. I'm going to spare myself that indignity."

She was chilled by his answer. "What if I send you something that might help?"

He gave a harsh shake of his head. "It's my time. Do you think I learned nothing in the war? I know when death is at the door."

The desire to argue with him surged within her. *Why don't you let them put you on a ventilator? Why not try? Live, dammit! We have so much to reconcile.* But she knew it was futile. He'd made up his mind, and listening had never been his strong suit. She didn't want their last words to be angry ones.

"I've left you everything as planned, the company included. You are now CEO of Maroun Industries. I know you didn't want it, but perhaps you will be happier taking the reins without me in your way."

She pressed a hand to her mouth. "Don't talk like this."

"Don't argue. Listen. Your mother is calling me, and I'm going to take her hand when I see her next. I want to go to her. Do you understand, daughter?"

Thoughts of her mother calling him home brought tears to her eyes. "I understand."

She couldn't think about the company right now. This was her last chance to speak to him. She lowered her hand from her mouth and pressed it again to her heart.

"There's so much I want to say to you," she whispered.

His violet eyes, so like her own, welled with tears. "And I, you, Francesca." He broke into another coughing fit, and this one went on for so long a masked nurse appeared and extended a plastic cup with a straw to his mouth. He drank and sputtered and drank again.

He pushed the cup aside and pinned her with his gaze. "I love you. I hope you will remember some of our good times, especially when your mother was alive. Losing her changed me, although I always had rough edges." More coughing came from deep within his chest, and his body seemed to spasm with the fight for oxygen.

"You suffered because of them," he rasped after the fit subsided, "and I'm sorry for that."

"We both suffered, Papa."

He bowed his head, and the tears he'd been fighting so valiantly streamed down his gray face. "Now you say it. Thank you. I should go. You remember what I taught you and what you know. I don't have to ask you to honor the Maroun family. You always have. I love you, daughter."

The energy on the line went still, almost peaceful, and she felt a gentle hand on her shoulder. Could it be her mother? Then she smelled a waft of sweet, spicy jasmine, and she knew for sure.

"I love you too, Papa."

The assertive hand that cut toward the phone held the strength of the Georges Maroun she knew, and then the screen went blank.

Her tears couldn't be contained. She knew she would never see her father again, and it hurt. She lay on the bed, tucked her feet under her, and cried—for herself, for her father, for the man she loved and his family, and for the world. J.T. was right. There were hundreds of thousands of people going through this right now. Some were already living with the virus' devastation and still more would experience it soon enough.

It felt like the end of the world.

Quinn found her like that, and he wrapped himself around her. "Hey..."

"My papa called from the hospital. He's dying from the

virus." She made herself say the rest. "There's no hope."

"Oh, babe." He rose to look at her face. "I'm so sorry."

"He left me the company, Quinn."

Shock rolled over his face, but he remained silent.

Fresh tears filled her eyes. "I don't know what to do."

His face darkened. "You'll figure it out. Here, let me hold you."

"Any news on Connor?" she asked as his arms went around her again.

"Louisa called back and said his fever reached one hundred and five degrees. We could hear him calling Corey's name. It scared the shit out of me. She just called an ambulance."

"Oh, Quinn. It's all so terrible."

He pressed his face into her neck, and she felt his tears.

All they could do was hold each other. She said a prayer for her papa, and for Connor too. While it didn't make her feel better, at least it was something. Afterward, they rejoined the Merriam vigil and waited for news.

Two days later, Connor recovered. Miraculously, the doctors said. Clara praised the flower along with Michaela and Boyd for having led them to it. Assumpta broke down and left the room with Shawn, only to return some time later. Francesca was so happy for them, but her heart ached at the thought of her father dying alone in his hospital bed. It felt wrong not to be there, and yet there was nothing she could do. Even if she flew out to see him, she wouldn't be allowed into his hospital room. The call came only a few hours later, confirming the news she'd expected—he was gone—and Quinn and his whole family comforted her.

The announcement of her father's death sent shock waves through the industry, just as she'd known it would. His perfectly timed press release, published the same day, named her as the new CEO, something that shocked her even though she'd known it was coming. Quinn read it aloud when they returned to their room.

My daughter, Francesca Maroun, will assume the full duties of Maroun Industries as its CEO. Her market brilliance and leadership abilities are well known, and I could not be a prouder father. I only wish I could see where she will lead the company, but I know it will be to brilliant shores. I expect every friend of Maroun Industries to welcome her and extend her every courtesy they ever gave me.

"That's one hell of a statement," Quinn said after he'd finished, his jaw clenched.

She could only nod in agreement. Her father had done everything he could to pave the way. The emails and calls started to come in. Over and over again she was reminded of how dire the global financial picture was and how many people depended on her. Some of them even reached out to thank her for continuing to take care of them and the other employees, saying times in Lebanon and beyond were tough enough without the further complications of the virus. They trusted her. Her ascension to CEO was like an answer to their prayers.

It wasn't an answer to hers.

CHAPTER 31

QUINN WAS FINDING IT HARD NOT TO RESENT A DEAD MAN. He didn't know if it was a new low or simply a matter of honest feeling. Georges Maroun had fucked with them yet again. It had been his last act, and Quinn feared that he'd managed to separate him and Francesca for good.

Unable to listen to Francesca handle Maroun business in their room, he'd detoured to the kitchen to ask Becca if he could use her office to work on the list of employees they'd be offering severance. He could add more names. His family had collectively decided last night to donate a portion of their personal wealth to help their employees. It made him feel better to know they'd be providing for people, but it didn't feel like a silver lining just now.

Except Becca was crying with Trevor's arms around her. Alice and Aileen were wiping their eyes too, and Clifton sat in a chair by the butcher's table, his face in his hands.

"What happened?" he asked.

Trevor's face was green. "Annie just learned her former

mother-in-law—the girls' grandmother, June—died of heart complications a day after having the sniffles. It was virus-related."

Shit.

"Flynn and Annie took the girls to the rabbit shed to tell them. Uncle Arthur had to take Aunt Clara to their room because she was crying. God! She didn't even know she had the virus. Now she's gone."

"I'm sorry," he found himself saying and excused himself.

He passed his mom and dad on the way to Becca's office. His mom's lashes were wet, but she gave him a tight hug and he returned it. When his dad did the same, his throat clogged. That could have happened to Connor or anyone in their family. It still could.

He strode to Becca's office, prepared to focus on work. There was nothing he could do to help anyone. He hadn't known June, but he hated that his family was hurting. Those girls...

Jesus, he couldn't handle it. He buried himself in the severance list, focusing on the lives he *could* help.

When Francesca found him in Becca's office a few hours later, he could see the final decision on her face. Dammit, it shouldn't have come to this.

"I have to go to Beirut," she told him, approaching the desk. "I don't see how I can't. I've looked at it from every angle, Quinn. I can't abandon the company and the people it employs. You know how it is. You're working on helping yours this very minute."

He set his pencil aside and tried to stay calm. "I do know. But taking the leadership of Merriam Enterprises was my choice. Your father didn't give you one."

Anger flashed in her eyes. She didn't like that either, although she hadn't said so. It was clear she didn't want to resent his final manipulation. "No, he didn't. But that's not our employees' fault. They shouldn't be punished. If I don't take the reins as announced, it would be catastrophic. I'm not sure Maroun Industries could survive it."

"And what about us?" He stood up.

She took a deep breath before saying, "I figure I can usher the company through the global waters for six months to a year and then turn the reins over to someone I've trained."

He walked over to the window and opened it, letting in the fresh sea air, his calm unraveling. "Traveling is unsafe—"

"I'll be extra careful," she interrupted.

His control snapped. "I don't want to lose you, dammit!"

She flinched. "You won't. I have a strong immune system, and I have the flower."

His scoff burned his throat. "I'm not willing to test it. Francesca! Dammit, Annie's former mother-in-law died of it last night."

"My God," she said, her hand flying to her mouth. "They must be devastated."

He'd heard the girls crying when they'd come back from their walk with Flynn and Annie, and he'd had to shut the window, hoping to drown out the sound of their grief. But he couldn't. It carried on in his head. "Yeah! She was supposed to visit Dare Valley this summer. Not now. Her life was snuffed out like that." He snapped his fingers. "That could have been Connor too!"

Her lips trembled before she clenched her mouth. "It took my father too."

"But you're still thinking about going off to Beirut for six months. Hell, it could be a year with the way the virus is going. Maybe even longer. I understand you wanting to go to the funeral, but people are watching the service remotely because of the virus."

"I'm going, Quinn."

Yes, she was. "Do you want me to come with you?"

She shook her head. "No. As you said, travel is unsafe. I also have to stay for the business."

He could already feel the wall rising between them. "I understand attending the funeral, but Francie, you're putting something else before us and our future. Dammit, we did that before and we lost fifteen years. I'm not doing it again."

Her face went to that cool, controlled mask he hadn't seen in months. "What do you propose? That I not take over?"

He stalked over to her and cupped her shoulders. "Do you *want* to do it? You told me you didn't want to take over because you knew what it would be like. Because you barely knew your father growing up, and you don't want that for your children. But you're doing it anyway. During a fucking pandemic, no less, in a country that grows more unstable by the day. Since you don't want me to go the funeral, I assume you don't intend for me to come at all."

She looked him straight in the eye. "I considered it in a moment of weakness. But it's not a good idea. I'll be working all the time. What are you going to do? Hole up in a country you don't know, whose languages you can't speak, during a pandemic, and what... Wait for me to arrive home late each night? Hell, I wish I could hire you to help me, but we both know that wouldn't be well received either."

She might as well have slapped his face. "Because I'm the CEO of a bankrupt company?" He curled his lip. "I know how it looks. Do you think I don't? You could be my vice president, but I couldn't be yours."

"I'm not trying to hurt your pride. Don't take it that way. You're an outsider. That's why it isn't a good idea. Times of transition require long-standing relationships based on trust. My people don't know you. Quinn. Please don't make this personal."

"Personal? *Personal?* Babe, this is about as personal as it gets. You're already thinking of them as your people.

They're employees—your father's."

"I can't abandon them."

His jaw locked. "Your father finally got what he wanted."

She flinched, but that mask slid back into place. "I can't focus on that. It is what it is."

He got in her face. "Bullshit!"

"Have it your way!" She threw her hands in the air and her mask cracked. "Quinn, something always seems to pull us apart. Before it was the London bombs, and now it's my father dying and the pandemic and all of the people who would be hurt if I failed to do my duty."

"Soulmates in times of crisis," he said, swearing and stepping away from her and detouring to the window. "I hate that narrative. I want you to pick me this time. Stand up to your father. You're a market wizard. Craft a press announcement noting for personal reasons you will be choosing another CEO and mentoring him or her. You can use the pandemic as an excuse. But if you go to Beirut and sit in that chair, I don't know if you'll be able to leave it. Don't let your father entrench you in something you don't want. Babe, I love you. Don't do this to yourself. Don't do it to us either."

She fisted her hands at her sides, gathering herself. "No one can do a better job than I can right now. We both know what the market is going through. You're not being fair, Quinn. Maroun wouldn't survive. Everyone expects me to take over. Wouldn't you kill to have Merriam Enterprises survive?"

He shook his head after thinking it over. "I've learned my lesson. I wouldn't lose you over it. I'm past that. The world is falling apart. The people you love are the only things that matter. I finally get it."

She pressed her hand to her heart, tears in her eyes. "I'm glad you can see that. It shows how much you've grown. But other people matter too. You were just working on the severance list. Quinn, I have the opportunity to do something good—something positive in this long-suffering world. How could I stand down?"

She was going to debate him until he bled out. "Then start something you want to run!" he raged. "Rehire the people Maroun employs. Only, don't do it in an unstable country and on your father's terms."

She shook her head. "Start something now? That's a mad scheme if I ever heard it. We're talking about a billion-dollar company here. Not some small venture."

He set business talk aside and played the only card he had left. "I love you, and I want to marry you." He pointed at her. "You said yes. Dammit, my ring is on your finger."

"I don't see another play," she whispered.

He watched as she took off his ring and extended it to him. Pain gripped his heart again, but he couldn't reach for the ring.

The hand holding the ring started to shake. "I guess we'll have to call this now. Maybe the third time is the charm for us? When the pandemic is over and everything is stable again..."

God, he couldn't stand to think about that. His eyes narrowed to slits. "You don't believe that, and neither do I."

She set the ring on the desk. "I hate this too."

He couldn't look at the symbol of the future they would never have. "Yet you're still going."

She crossed to him and kissed him on the cheek. "I'm so sorry, but I don't see another way."

When she left the room quietly, he sank onto the couch. He thought of the painting he'd given her of the family on the beach, the one he'd told her to fix her gaze upon whenever she needed help imagining what their future would look like. He should have brought it to Ireland.

But in his heart of hearts he knew it wouldn't have helped. She'd lost her vision of them, and there was nothing he could do to help her find it again.

CHAPTER 32

NOTHING MADE SENSE TO CLARA.

June's sudden death had shocked everyone. Her new friend—the one who'd just taken steps to start living her best life like Clara had—was gone. The life she'd reclaimed was already over. Now Francesca was leaving for Beirut to support the people who relied on Maroun Industries for bread on their tables.

"It's so unfair, Arthur." She eyed the martini Clifton had made for her, his heart in his eyes at the news of June's death. "I want to change it all, and I can't do anything except pat people on the backs and donate money."

"You do more than that." He curled his fingers around hers. "We both do. But I know it doesn't feel like enough right now. June's loss... They say death comes like a thief. I want to rip his face off. Amelia and her sisters can't stop sobbing. God! If I can't make sense of it, how can they? The article I've been working on with Amelia more than stalled when Connor became ill. I'm not sure it would be wise to resume it after this. "

Clara nodded in agreement. "They lost their father, and now June. It's too much. It's simply too much. Doesn't God or the Universe have some kind of overload understanding?" Then she stopped herself. Bad things happened every day to people who'd had enough of them.

"Quinn's going to lose Francesca a second time." Arthur cursed uncharacteristically.

"And she him." Because it *was* a loss. Clara had seen the woman's face before dinner. She'd sat with a somber Alice and with Clifton, who hadn't spoken a single word. There'd been no sign of Quinn.

"I want to bash their heads together, but I understand the untenable position her father put her in. She can help a lot of people experiencing horrible times. Even before the pandemic, Lebanon's economy was in shambles. Women were trading dresses for baby formula and diapers, for heaven's sake."

"Women need formula and diapers in the U.S. too." The online stories she came across daily were heartrending. She fingered her diamond bracelet absently and then looked down at the gems sparkling like Irish rainbows after a storm. God, who was she to be wearing diamonds with the kind of economic suffering in the world? When she started to take them off, Arthur stilled her hand.

"You don't stop being who you are or living your life," he told her, his blue-jean eyes steady on her face. "You like to wear diamonds and you can. Besides, what are you going to do? Give all your money away? You've given half to bail out more Merriam employees."

Even with everyone donating from their personal fortunes, they were only going to be able to give everyone a one-thousand-dollar bonus, plus whatever severance they were due. "It isn't enough. What will become of them?"

He touched her cheek. "Clara, if there's one thing I've learned from covering tragedy, it's this. It's important to have compassion—empathy even when it's possible—but the world isn't better for anyone if we *choose* suffering. Wearing diamonds brings you pleasure, and selling them won't do much to someone who's lost a job, a company, or a loved one. Your guilt won't help either. So maybe you don't buy any more diamonds. Fine. But instead of focusing on what you perceive as your flaws, try thinking about all the good you've done. All the good you're *doing*. I'm proud of you, love."

She closed her eyes, feeling a little weepy. Not her normal. Arthur pulled her onto his lap and held her. She inhaled his cologne, a mix of bergamot, leather, and orange, crafted by Caitlyn's perfume maker, Ibrahim. Something was missing. "You haven't been chewing red hots much or handing them out."

His sigh gusted out. "Maybe it's my version of diamonds. I usually hand them out to comfort people, but candy seems like such an insignificant gesture right now. It can't make hurts this deep better."

She felt something inside of her shift as she smoothed his hair. "You bring those red hots back, Arthur Hale. I miss them, and I'm sure I'm not alone. They not only inspire connection; they inspire comfort and normalcy."

"Well said, my dear." He kissed her softly.

"Where do you have them tucked away?" she asked.

"In my sock drawer, where I put everything else," he said, patting her backside as she rose.

His handprint was warm on her fanny, a touch which had her mouth curling. Oh, how she loved this man. She found a bag of red hots in his sock drawer. She grabbed a handful and returned to the sitting room. "You put these in your sweater pockets and start handing them out again. But I would like to have one first."

"You would, eh?" He extended one to her and shoved the rest in his pocket, secreting one for himself.

They unwrapped their candies and popped them in

their mouths. She sat back on his lap, the cinnamon firing her every taste bud, ones that had been dead lately even amidst the nonstop onslaught of delicious food and drink from Clifton and Alice and the others.

"Are we really going to do nothing to help Quinn and Francesca?" she asked after silently musing. "Are you not the Matchmaking Jedi?"

"I don't know how to help there," he said, the candy clacking against his teeth. "Their problems are beyond anything we've faced."

"Except when Michaela fell ill, we hiked into the bush to find a healing flower to save her."

He crunched his candy angrily. "The path seemed clear. This one doesn't."

"No, it doesn't," she answered, biting into the red hot herself in frustration. "Do you think Clifton might have an answer? He's been ever so helpful in these matters."

"We can ask him. None of the Merriams know what to say either—not even Assumpta."

And her sister-in-law usually saw matters of the heart in black and white.

They were doomed.

CHAPTER 33

FRANCESCA BRACED HERSELF TO HAVE THE SECOND HARD-est conversation of her life.

Her bags were packed and stored in Becca's office, thanks to Clifton's stealth. He set down a tea tray on the small burnished rosewood coffee table in front of the couch she was sitting on.

"I'll go for Alice," he said, his face somber and a touch gray.

"It's for the best," she told him, her bones already aching with her choice. "I'm trusting you to help her understand that after I leave."

"I'll do my best." He folded his hands in front of his body and regarded her. "It seems a great tragedy, however. I wonder if your father truly intended for you to lose both the man you love and your best friend and sister."

His face in the hospital rose in her mind. He'd said nothing about Quinn even though he knew they were together again. She might try and lie to herself, but he hadn't thought about her happiness. To a Maroun, family and duty were more important. "I agree, but right now, it doesn't seem like I have another choice. People are counting on me, Clifton."

"Quite." He pursed his lips before saying, "I had a complicated relationship with my father as well. I followed his footsteps into service without another thought. Reflecting back, I realize it didn't occur to me to do anything else. Our family had served in this field for hundreds of years. A wise man doesn't look back on his life with regret, but... Perhaps I am not so wise in these turbulent days."

She poured two cups of tea and handed one to him, knowing what an honor it was for him to disclose his personal thoughts. "Please have a final cup with me. Alice and I won't be able to drink any."

His skin turned a shade grayer, but he sat next to her on the couch and took the teacup, sipping quietly with her. She thought again about her decision not to say goodbye to the Merriams. How could she put herself or them through it? Especially with June's death still so fresh? "I have a letter I'd like you to read at dinner tonight. The one for Quinn... I'd appreciate it if you would deliver it after my car leaves."

They hadn't spoken since he'd left this very office, leaving the ring on the desk where she'd put it. She withdrew both letters from her bag with a trembling hand. The beautiful ring Quinn had given her had already perforated the envelope she'd sealed his letter in. She couldn't take the ring. It was a promise. A promise she no longer knew if she could keep.

"Of course." He set his half-empty cup down and stood, smoothing down his black jacket. "I will go find Alice now. It has been a pleasure and an honor, Francesca. If there is ever anything I can do to help you, I would gladly do so— as a friend."

Fiery tears burned her eyes, and she stood as well,

embracing him warmly. "It was good to make a new friend in you, Clifton. You and Alice look after each other and this family. Open that chocolate shop she sees in her meditations."

He withdrew from her, his mouth tipping up. "I see them in mine as well. We will take good care of each other, like family does. Be well, Francesca."

"You too, my friend."

When he left, she brushed the edges of her eyes and attempted to steel herself for what would come next. She could get through this next part. She had to.

When Alice came in, her face crumpled immediately, and fat tears spilled from her large brown eyes. "I knew it when I saw Clifton. You think you're leaving without me? Like hell."

Francesca laid her hand on her friend's rigid arm. "You know it's for the best. How can I take you to Beirut with me? Our arrangement was for short-term consultancies around the world in places of stability. My new job as a CEO in Beirut meets neither of those conditions. You have a new life ahead of you. Clifton is part of it. You see it yourself. I can't take you with me simply because I love you. Alice, I'm not even doing that with Quinn."

"You're both being idiots!" Alice stomped her foot in a rare fit of anger. "I know you inside and out. I've seen you pull off brilliant turnarounds for other people. Why aren't you trying to work out a solution for yourself? For the Merriams' entire company? Why have you given up?"

Her heated words knocked Francesca back. "I'm giving up everything I want to make a difference the only way I can. Do you think I don't want to help the Merriams keep everything? It's not easy for me to admit, but I *failed*, Alice, and I'm losing the man I love."

"Maybe I've been stewing too long over this, but I agree with Quinn. You need to stop letting your father call the shots. Look at how he played you. He didn't even ask you about taking over."

"He was dying of the virus!"

"If he'd died before the pandemic, do you think he would have set things up any differently?"

She rolled her neck, which had stiffened with tension. "No, probably not. In that case, I might have made a different choice. But in this pandemic—"

"This pandemic sucks, and it hurts. Every day more people are getting sick or getting screwed. I get it. But you don't have to be one of the casualties. I love you too much not to say it. I don't want to see you taking this path. I know you. All you'll do is work for others and sacrifice yourself. That's how you were when you left your father and Maroun Industries last time. You'll be a burned out shell in a couple years. Wait!"

Francesca watched helplessly as her friend dug her phone out of her pocket and started swiping angrily at the screen. When she held it back up, Francesca found herself peering at an old photograph.

"That's you a month after I started working for you." She waved the screen. "Do you see how drawn your face was? Your cheekbones looked like they were going to split your face. Your eyes were too big because you were practically starving. Don't go back to that."

Her lips started to tremble. Was that thin, sallow-faced woman truly her? Was that going to be her life now? "I won't let it become like that this time," she said to Alice, and to herself.

Alice shook her head and shoved her phone away. "You've already started looking like her. It happened the moment your father died and named you CEO without your consent, and it's only worsened since you broke your engagement off with Quinn."

She remembered how she'd looked when she'd applied her makeup this morning. She'd had to pad on more foundation to cover up the dark circles under her eyes. "I hear you, okay? And I know you're saying this from a place of love, but Alice... I need you to have my back here. I need my friend to support me."

Tears streamed down Alice's face. "I love you too, which is why this hurts so much. I will always support you. I just can't support your choice. I wouldn't be your friend if I did."

Something wet tracked down her face, and she realized she was crying too. "Will you at least hug me and wish me well? My car should be here."

Alice dashed at her and pulled her into a tight hug. "You figure something out, dammit. Don't make me fly to Beirut after you, because you know I will. You have three months to figure this out. After that, all bets are off. I mean, if you can sacrifice yourself for the greater good, why can't I? Working for you in Beirut would mean I get to help a lot of people through you. How could I not come?"

Her friend's uncanny argument pinged her vulnerable heart. She tightened her grip and inhaled the scent of chocolate clinging to her friend, a scent that had become as redolent of home as jasmine. "I love you. I'll call you. Every chance I get."

Alice leaned back and cupped her cheek, bringing fresh tears to Francesca's eyes. "You'd better. And eat, dammit. Eggs every morning. Okay? You skip lunch when you get going, and you need something in your stomach to last you until a late dinner."

She might have chuckled, but her chest was too tight. "I'll have a bowl of almonds on my desk at all times."

"And fruit! You have to take care of yourself. I won't have you chuck all the progress we've made out the window. I'm texting you that photo. Don't you ever go back to looking that miserable or starved again."

"I have to go."

Alice nodded. They left the room. Clifton was standing in the hallway.

"The car is here and your bags are loaded. Quinn is in the main hall waiting for you."

Her knees knocked. He was working, and she'd hoped her escape would go unnoticed. "Fine. Thank you, Clifton."

She embraced him again, the scent of chocolate and bergamot engulfing her. Then she embraced Alice again, her heart breaking a second time. Wrenching herself away, she walked to the main hall, dashing at tears she couldn't seem to stop. God, where was her control? Her usual comportment?

"Well, at least you're crying," Quinn said, his jaw granite hard as she entered. "Where's Alice?"

"She's staying, of course. Did you imagine I would take her?"

He looked away, his face darkening. "Honestly, I don't know what you'll do right now. Part of me feels a little better knowing you're leaving her behind, but the other part of me wants to smash something. God, I wasn't going to do this, but then I saw your bags being loaded in the car from the upstairs windows. Are you really going to allow your father to separate you from everything and everyone you love?"

She quivered in place. "This talk isn't helpful to me," she said, needing to cut him off. "I've left you a letter with Clifton. I didn't expect to see you before I left."

He stormed over to her and took her by the shoulders. "Didn't want to, surely. Well, too bad. I've seen you, and I'm going to remind you of everything you're throwing away."

Then his mouth was on hers, moving in heated desperation. It was a kiss she imagined would only be possible in wars or pandemics, the ache was so strong, the longing so great. It was the kind of kiss a person knew might be their last. She gave herself over to it completely. By the time he wrenched his mouth back, they were both breathing hard.

He took her face in his big hands. But anger glimmered in his eyes when he saw the look of devastation in hers.

"You can kiss me like that and still leave? Damn you."

Then he was striding off toward the back of the inn. She brushed her tingling mouth. Drew her shoulders back. A cough sounded at the top of the stairs and she spotted Arthur.

"Don't make these old bones come down and say good-bye to you."

She dashed up the stairs, and he wrapped his arms around her the moment she reached him. "You stay safe. I won't tell you to do a good job and take care of your people because you will, of course. I have something for you to remember us by."

He released her and moments later pressed something into her hand. A red-colored candy enclosed in plastic.

"This my version of the sweetness of life," he said, his blue eyes swimming as he regarded her. "I remember you bringing that symbol the first day we met you at Shawn and Assumpta's home."

That morning seemed so long ago. My God, how the world, and hers with it, had changed since then.

"You don't forget what's important to you, or that this family loves you. Okay?"

She clutched the candy in her hand. "Okay. Goodbye, Arthur. Tell Clara and everyone..."

Her voice broke so she couldn't continue, and he crisply nodded, clearing his throat.

She descended the stairs, fresh tears filling her eyes.

She walked out of the Wild Irish Rose Inn, the whole world around her a blur.

CHAPTER 34

OFFERS WERE COMING IN TO BUY THE OIL AND GAS DIVIsions of Merriam Enterprises—the bulk of what had been their company.

Under different circumstances, Quinn might have popped a bottle of champagne in Becca's office, but the offers were for the current value of that section, since they still intended to spin off the skincare line. So instead he paced the small space, sucking on one of the red hots Uncle Arthur had started handing out as frequently as other people doled out hand sanitizer. Trevor and J.T. were with him, presiding over yet another dark moment in Merriam Enterprises' recent history.

He supposed he couldn't blame the opportunistic behavior by his competitors. The price for a barrel of crude oil, set by West Texas Intermediate (WTI), the benchmark for U.S. oil, had fallen below zero for the first time ever, and the vultures were circling.

Who could have imagined a moment like this? Their oil

was officially worthless, and their gas claims hadn't fared much better. In addition to the Saudis' power move, oil demand had evaporated. Unused barrels were backing up and killing an already dead market. They'd lost four hundred million in the second quarter alone due to the virus.

If they sold, they'd have money to pay most of their debts but not employees' severance. Layoffs would still happen. The companies offering didn't need all of their personnel.

He wished he could call Francesca and ask her what she thought of this possibility. She'd only been gone a week, but it might as well have been five years. "Trevor, do you think you can work your magic and get us more?"

His brother threw aside the most recent offer. "When they have us over the barrel, unlikely."

J.T. gathered up the papers. "We could sell some of Grandpa Emmits' art. I haven't wanted to go there, but maybe—"

"The art?" Quinn's voice, which had remained steady throughout their discussion of the dismal offers, went hoarse. "But that's for the museum. It's your dream, J.T."

"It's only art," J.T. said. "I didn't think about it before, but Caroline mentioned it last night after much nail biting. She'd seen a recent newspaper article about someone selling their art because they'd lost big in the financial crisis."

"Yeah, even billionaires are hurting," Quinn scoffed, rising and opening the window to the unusually warm spring air Ireland was experiencing. "Millions of people around the world can't make rent or pay for groceries. We're a disgusting lot to complain."

"Exactly. Only... We've kinda donated it to Emmits Merriam University, but Trev could get us out of it."

"I'm not sure I can take another Merriam giving up on their dreams right now," Quinn said, looking at his brother's ashen face.

J.T.'s mouth worked before he said, "Jesus, man.

You're crushing me."

"Me too," Trev mumbled, scrubbing his face. "Maybe we should look at the numbers for the art. Maybe—"

"It would take a while to unload the art, right?" Quinn waved his hand. "I don't know how long we could wait. I was committed to bankruptcy. I'd given up hope on getting any offers."

None had come in until now. Francesca had mused there were only a few corporations in the industry that still had the cash reserves to make an offer on what would be left of Merriam Enterprises after the skincare spin-off. But the oil business had a few mavericks still around who understood the boom-and-bust times. Those were their two offers.

"Quinn," J.T. said, coming over to sit next to him on the couch. "We could unload the big names fairly quickly, I think, in an online auction. Flynn could set it up."

"He's helping the girls grieve," Quinn said. Grieving was something he understood, although his grief wasn't over a death, but over a lost future—the life he'd imagined sharing with Francesca. Alice had tried to talk to him, comfort him actually, but he couldn't share how he was feeling with her or anyone. Not even his mother. It hurt too much, and he didn't like being raw and emotional period, least of all in front of anyone.

Trevor shook his head. "Flynn could use a break. Mom can step in a little more and so can Caitlyn. With much of the perfume work scuttled or postponed, she's got some time."

"The girls aren't as close to them," Quinn said, but it sounded like an excuse to his own ears. He wasn't ready for this extreme.

"Dammit, Quinn!" J.T. snapped. "Run the numbers. People are more important than art. Jesus, we almost lost Connor. You lost Francesca. I won't mention June again although I didn't know her well. What the fuck good are a bunch of canvases painted by a bunch of dead guys right now?"

His rant rendered Trevor and Quinn mute.

"I'm going for a walk." J.T. stalked to the door and yanked it open. "You do it, dammit!"

After he stormed out, Quinn found his throat was thick. Trevor pressed his fingers to his brow.

"He's never talked like that," Trevor said. "I mean, the guy once waxed poetic about the pastel blues of this famous French portrait painter for something like thirty minutes while I was trying to watch the World Cup. Liotard, I think. I almost killed him. But dammit, that's why I love him."

Yeah, which was why Quinn was so touched by his offer. "I hear you. But shit. It's hard for me to admit this, but I don't know what to do."

"And it's not like you can call Francesca," Trevor said, reading his mind. "We're too close to this one."

"We don't have a lot of time either," Quinn said.

"Screw that." Trevor stood up. "I've lost my touch as a negotiator if I can't at least stall them. Talk to Dad. I'll buy us some more time."

His belly quivered. "You want me to talk to Dad? You have the easy job, man."

"That's why I'm a good negotiator." His brother gave a maniacal laugh, which made Quinn's lips twitch.

"Don't quit your day job." Then Quinn sobered. "That was poor form. I'm sorry."

"No, I'm trying to embrace sheep shearing. Maybe we'll buy some cows. People will always need milk, right?"

God, he hoped his brother was joking. "That's what we thought about oil."

"Right. Shit. All right. I'll tell Dad you want to talk to him. Later."

He was out the door before Quinn could stop him. Hell, maybe they should spin the bottle or flip a coin in the air to decide on the best course. Too bad all their options sucked.

His father came in, his usually groomed hair ruffled at the back as if he'd been running his hands through it. They all needed a haircut, he supposed, but in the scheme of things, who the hell cared?

"Trevor said J.T. had an idea." He stood inside the door, shifting on his feet.

His father's antsiness, and his own, reminded him of when he was little—of those nights when he'd pretended to be asleep when his father had come into his room to tuck him in. They still weren't completely comfortable with each other. Perhaps it was time to fix that. "Come sit down. Maybe we break open some whiskey. It's happy hour somewhere, right?" It was only ten o'clock in the morning.

"I don't think I could stomach it," his dad said, but he took a seat in the chair across from the couch. "What's up?"

He folded his hands and watched as his father did the same. Had their mannerisms always been so similar? "J.T. suggested we sell the art for the Merriam Museum as a way of helping the company. I know you've read the offers that came in by now."

His father nodded. "They'd get us for seventy percent less than what we were worth in January. It's tough to swallow. But it's tougher to imagine trying to stay afloat in this market. I'd never imagined a day like this, Quinn."

"No one could."

"I'm sorry it fell in your lap." His dad looked down. "I wish I'd still been in charge in some ways. I could have spared you this. Plus, I'm an old man. You have your whole life ahead of you. I feel like I've hamstrung your career, son."

That python was back, squeezing him to death. His father felt like that? He found himself putting a hand on his dad's arm. "Connor said he felt guilty too, but neither of you are to blame, Dad. We make our own choices."

"Your mother and I raised you to make your own choices and be your own person. But as a parent, I'm finding I want to cushion the hurt right now. Maybe years too late. I've asked the other kids, and perhaps it's time to ask you."

Oh, God. He wasn't sure he was ready for this, but he nodded.

"Will you forgive me for not being there for you when you were growing up? I know you're your own man, but I want you to know you can always come to me. With anything. I'm going to be there for you kids from now on."

"Sure, Dad," he found himself saying, that damn python doing its job around his middle. "There's nothing to forgive. I mean, it's not like I'm a saint."

His dad's mouth curled. "This might be a good time for all of us to move past those old habits and commit to supporting and loving each other. Almost losing Connor... I love you kids. I'm sorry I haven't shown you how much."

Oh, hell. "I love you too, Dad."

His father gripped his arm. "So how much does J.T. think we could get for the art? I think Grandpa Merriam would be on board if it helped Merriam Enterprises, this family, and its employees. He knew the value of people. We can ask Clara too—and Arthur. They both knew him."

"I wish I had."

"You have his likeness and some of his ways. He wouldn't have gone down without a fight."

That settled it. "Let's go talk to J.T. and run some numbers."

His heart told him to fight until his last breath. But he still wished he could ask Francesca if it was the right move.

CHAPTER 35

SHE WAS ALONE.

While she had been surrounded by people all week, whether in socially distanced meetings or online conference calls, no one stood beside her at her father's funeral. It only heightened her sense of loss.

Usually a death of this magnitude would have packed St. Louis Cathedral, one of Beirut's largest churches downtown, but not in these times. The few mourners she'd invited—key Maroun family members, friends, and business associates—were spaced two meters apart at the gravesite. There would be no gathering afterward, and that suited Francesca fine. She'd elected to have no one speak to minimize the ceremony. Pomp and circumstance weren't called for during the pandemic, only reverence for the ones who'd passed.

Remembering her father quietly as the warm Mediterranean breeze flirted with the black lace covering her upswept hair, she realized she was exactly where he'd wanted her.

Not where she wanted.

Anger flared within her, so powerful she was sure the candle flames in the clear glass vessels surrounding the grave danced in response. Since she'd last seen her father in his hospital bed, she had not shed one tear over him. Rage had burned them away—all except for the tears she'd expended for Quinn and Alice and what might have been.

Because she knew they were right. She was still dancing to her father's tune.

The ceremony ended, and she nodded as people quietly left the churchyard. They'd already paid their respects, although it still felt strange that no one had kissed her or embraced her in the customary fashion. My God, everything was truly upended when no one physically connected at a funeral.

After looking at the coffin one last time, she walked down the path past fresh graves of the newly dead. They were covered in bright flowers, and her throat thickened as she read the gravestones: a man of twenty-five, beloved son; a woman of fifty-three, beloved wife and mother; a man of seventy, much like her own father. So many lives had been snuffed out by this virus—over two hundred thousand globally by the end of April—and she did not know when it would end.

The beginning of May had proven a turning point in many places, thank God, but Lebanon's troubles continued. Germany, Spain, Italy, Denmark, Thailand, and New Zealand looked to be coming out of lockdown. Ireland had extended its lockdown another few weeks, she'd seen, and of course she'd thought about the Merriam family ensconced in the Wild Irish Rose Inn.

All she wanted was to be back at the Inn with her beloved and the family who loved her for who she was and not what she was supposed to represent: a legacy. What if she became ill too? Would she have regrets as she lay dying? She'd always said life was meant to be enjoyed, but she wasn't following her own wisdom.

As she neared the end of the graveyard, she sighted one of her father's oldest friends. "I missed you before the ceremony," Joseph Khouri said, looking sharp in a dark suit. "I wanted to see if there was anything you needed. Before your father passed, God rest his soul, we spoke. He asked me to look after you. Help you usher the company through these dark times should you need assistance."

The company had lost money like almost every other corporate entity, save titans like Amazon or Google that would come out of this richer. "We're doing as well as can be expected. These times have stretched us all."

"Indeed," he said, nodding. "I hesitate to mention this as your father lies here only meters from us, but he would respect a business offer even in these moments. I've heard there are offers on the table for Merriam Enterprises' oil and gas platforms. I know you recently were helping them restructure. I was wondering if you might query your contact there and see if he'd be open to an offer."

She lifted her brows. They both knew making an offer at a funeral was unusual. Based on the rumblings she'd heard, there'd been other offers. There was also gossip that the family might sell some, or all, of the prized art they'd intended to display at the museum at Emmits Merriam University. She'd paced the floors in the middle of the night when she couldn't sleep to keep herself from calling Quinn and discussing his plans. That they would sell the art...

Something must have happened.

"Who would the offer be from?"

His elegant jaw moved as a smile spread across his face. "Myself. The Merriams own oil wells in strategic geographic locations around the world, notwithstanding the gas reserves. Such an acquisition would be a crowning glory to my company."

"Indeed." She knew Starquest Industries' portfolio as

well as she knew her own. They didn't have the capital to make such an offer. "Joseph, who lent you the money?"

His smile was as guarded as the name of his Italian tailor, whom he'd always refused to reveal to her father. "You know such things are not discussed."

That could only mean one thing. He was getting money from the Saudis. Other than Russia and China, they were the only ones with the reserves to loan billions right now. She returned his smile. "Of course not. Forgive me. It must be the grief speaking."

They both knew it had not been.

He inclined his head and made a move to kiss her in the customary fashion before he stopped himself. "Old habits. Well... I will leave you. Should you need anything, come to me. Your father and I weathered many a storm through the civil war and all of the unrest in this region. You will do the same."

She'd been assured that all of Maroun Industries' construction contracts would resume and not be canceled. For that, she was grateful. "Yes, I will. Thank you, Joseph."

After he left, she located her car. Usually she would have had a driver, but not in these times. Deciding to return home and not the office—it was a day of mourning for the company, after all, and she didn't want gossip—she rolled down the window. The back of her neck prickled, a sign she had come to know well in her years of working as a consultant.

She was about to see the solution to a problem.

When the sweet smell of jasmine greeted her as she walked up the steps to her three-story villa in Achrafieh's Golden Triangle area, she stopped short. Today she did not fight the powerful images that fought to the forefront of her consciousness. She closed her eyes and was back in Quinn's guesthouse. They were making love, and the warmth of his body was covering her as her every breath was filled with jasmine.

Tears filled her eyes when she finally returned to the present. The warmth she'd felt wasn't from his hands but the rays of the sun shining down on her from an untouched blue sky in her front garden. She would never feel the warmth of Quinn again unless she did something differently.

If she didn't, she would die alone here in Beirut. There would be no loving husband or children to mourn her.

This was not the life she wanted.

She unlocked the door and let herself inside. The smell of jasmine followed her all the way to the sitting room with the arched ceilings. Suddenly the solution was before her, as clear as the mirror on her north wall. Pulling out her cell, she made a call that would rock the market and change her life.

Joseph would have to forgive her.

When it was finished, she found a bottle of champagne in the ice box and drank her last toast alone. She'd finally made peace with her father.

Then she called her pilot and gave him their destination.

Satisfied for the first time since coming to Beirut, she brought her champagne upstairs and started to pack.

The plane ride was uneventful save for the flickering lights on the runway leaving Beirut due to the electricity shortage and rolling blackouts. While her masked flight crew had been surprised to be called in only hours after her father's funeral, she didn't care. The five hours passed quickly. She pulled her phone out only once to text Alice as they took off.

Can you have someone pick me up at Dublin airport or arrange a car? Cork is closed. It's a three-hour drive. BTW, this idiocy is done.

Her friend's reply came only minutes later.

Finally! And before the three-month deadline I gave you. Did your father's ghost speak to you as you buried him today, absolving you of your duty or something?

She texted back:

Creepy, and no. I'll tell you more about it when I see you. Ah... How will my return be received?

She waited with a vise around her middle until Alice responded:

With open arms by most. You're back in a week, and that's going to mean something. As for Quinn, he's like a grouchy boiled egg these days. No hard shell—all wobbly with feelings—and he doesn't much like it. But he's been kind and he's fighting hard to help their employees. The move to sell the art is heartbreaking, but I respect it. I thought you might hear about that and come a-calling.

She almost laughed.

No, it wasn't the art. Or the offers. I have something new to put on the table. Wait until you hear. It might be my most brilliant idea yet.

Alice texted a trio of emoticons—a dancing woman, a fist bump, and hands clapping—followed by:

That's pretty brilliant then. I'll talk to Trev about arrangements and text you back with deets. Love you, and hot damn, I'm so proud of you. You were killing me here.

She'd been killing herself, exactly as her friend had predicted. Sending back a trio of heart emoticons herself, she lifted the champagne her masked attendant had poured for her and toasted herself. Alice had told her she needed to come to peace with her father, and she'd finally done it. She'd come to peace with herself too. He had never been the father she'd wanted, but she didn't want to blame him anymore. If she'd let him decide her future for her, she would have held it against him for the rest of her life. This move absolved all the ties he'd placed around her, and my God, how freeing it felt.

She could only hope Quinn saw the brilliance in her plan.

CHAPTER 36

T HE SIGHT OF FRANCESCA WALKING INTO THE DINING ROOM stopped Quinn's heart.

A collective gasp of shock went through his family, who were pushing around the chocolate pudding Alice and Hargreaves had made for dessert, comfort food for the girls who were still mourning their grandmother.

"Hello, everyone," she said rather formally, the black traveling outfit making her pallor more stark. "Quinn, can I see you for a moment?"

His heart resumed pounding, and part of him wanted to sit back in his chair and leer at her. *See him*? She'd fucking walked out on him.

"Quinn," Alice said, striding over to him. "Go listen to her. You won't believe what she's cooked up this time. Trust me. Give her a chance."

"She flew here after burying her father, Quinn," Uncle Arthur said from the next table. "Least you could do is give the lady an audience."

"Would you like a cup of tea?" Clifton asked. "I've secured your bags in the Honeysuckle Cottage so you can quarantine yourself."

Quinn lurched to his feet. "You did what?"

Hargreaves—Clifton, he mentally corrected—gave him one of his narrow-eyed looks. "Earl Grey, Francesca?"

"That would be excellent," Francesca said, cupping one wrist with another hand, a nervous pose if he'd ever seen one. "I can share the news with the whole family if you'd prefer, Quinn. We don't need to do this alone. I was only suggesting it given your role as CEO and our history."

"Oh, for heaven's sake," Aunt Clara said, crossing to her.

Francesca held up a hand. "Maybe wait fourteen days before hugging me. I've been careful, but Clifton's right. We should probably socially distance until it's clear I'm Covid-free. My driver—thanks for arranging that, Trevor—and I wore masks in the car on the way here. And I had my airline crew do the same on the flight. I did too."

Her account made Quinn realize just how idiotic he was being. She'd traveled through a pandemic to reach him. Trevor had even helped her get here, although he hadn't said a damn word.

"How about we talk in Becca's study?" he asked.

"Fine," she said, touching the bun she'd put her hair in. "Socially distanced, of course."

When he neared her, he muttered, "Don't piss me off."

"Same goes for you," she said, raising one of her elegant brows at him. "Until it's clear I'm Covid-free, we're keeping the proper distance."

He didn't like that one bit. Even though he was mad as a hornet at her for leaving, she was back and planning to stay. The last thing he wanted to do was stay six feet away from her. "Fine."

Inside Becca's office, he pointed to the couch and pulled the adjacent chair back six feet even though part of him thought it was ridiculous. She smoothed her pants, her hands pressing on the tops of her thighs. Again, her nerves were evident.

"All right," he said. "Let's hear this mastermind plan."

"After Clifton brings the tea," she said.

He growled. "You broke my heart a week ago and waltzed back in tonight like nothing happened, and now you think I'm waiting for fucking tea service? You're crazy."

"Possibly," she said, smoothing her hands up and down her thighs again. "Given what I'm planning, most assuredly. How have you been, Quinn?"

Small talk?

"How do you think?" he asked stonily.

"I heard about the offers and the sale of the art." Her usually luscious mouth went flat. "It didn't dawn on me to consider those assets."

"Me either," he said, wanting to growl again. "J.T. insisted, and after my dad and I talked it over, we agreed Grandpa Emmits wouldn't want us to hold on to it when it could help more people. The offers—a polite term, trust me—would beggar our severance packages."

She nodded as a discreet knock sounded on the door. Clifton entered and set the tea tray on the coffee table in front of them, keeping his distance from Francesca. "I'll pour," she said, giving him a smile Quinn had dearly missed. "Thank you."

He watched as she poured each of them a cup. Like he could stomach anything at the moment.

"All right, you have your tea. What's your news?"

She eyed him over the rim of her tea cup, those beautiful violet eyes sparkling. "I have the loan I need to purchase your company at pre-crash value—if you're willing to entertain my unconventional offer. It involves you and I working together."

He fell back against the chair. "A loan? No way! Who would give you a few billion for a loan? No one has that kind of money right now."

"Some of my father's friends do, and as friends of his—"

"They are friends of yours," he finished, seeing where she was going with this. "My God, you're not kidding!"

"I can make good on my promise to you when we started all of this," Francesca said, setting her teacup aside and fisting her hands in her lap. "I've asked for enough capital to weather the next few years, since we don't know how long we'll be dealing with this, and the payment plan doesn't begin for some time. You'll remember I'm a hell of a negotiator."

He needed some fresh air to clear his buzzing head, so he rose and opened the window. "I know you're good, but this good? What did you promise? Your firstborn child?"

"I would never promise *our* firstborn child. In my part of the world, long-term relationships yield the most amazing miracles sometimes. I made a five-minute call after I returned home from my father's funeral. It was rather easy. I don't know why I didn't think of it before. Well, I do, although you don't want to hear it."

He leaned against the wall beside the window. "Your father told his friends to give you cart blanche."

"Yes, and it's also in their interest to support Maroun Industries and its new CEO," she said, her gaze assessing. "How do you feel about that? Some idiots in the market who refuse to give women their due will say it's an emotional decision even though it will open up Maroun Industries to an entirely new field of play and profits. Including the skincare line, since the paperwork for the spin-off is still forthcoming."

"Others might say a woman saved my ass," Quinn said, chuckling. "You think I'm still that proud? Do you know how many jobs this is going to save? Sure you do. You went over every name with me."

"It will save your job too. And Merriam Enterprises," she said, reaching for her teacup again and then withdrawing, another nervous gesture. "I would like you to remain the CEO. I want you to know that I considered a merger for a second, but *that* would be an emotional choice."

"It would be stupid to merge with a company on the verge of declaring bankruptcy." Quinn wanted to stride over to her and pull her off the couch. "I wouldn't let you do that to Maroun Industries."

"Thank you." She looked him directly in the eyes. "I would like to discuss our personal merger if that is acceptable to you."

"Pitch away." He resumed his seat, crossing his ankle over his leg. "And make it good. I will negotiate hard if need be."

The right side of her mouth tipped up. "I look forward to hearing your counterdemands. First, I am sorry for leaving and dancing to my father's tune, as you said. I would like to remind you that I only did so for a week."

She looked so defensive he almost laughed. "This week felt like an eternity. I won't grant you too many points on that one."

Her brow crinkled. "Fine. It was a lifetime for me too. About our location... I thought we might move Merriam Enterprises and Maroun Industries to London as our permanent headquarters. Of course, you can keep regional operations intact, as will I. There are employees with lives and homes to consider. Is that acceptable?"

"More than," he said with a firm nod. He had hoped he wasn't going to have to fight her on that point.

"Wonderful," she said, her voice tipping back into consultancy mode. "Next point. I would like Merriam's Special Ventures Initiatives to come under my umbrella so I can add to it too."

"Hence stopping the skincare spin-off. I'm more than happy to keep Caitlyn and Annie's ventures in our company."

"As am I. I have also some ideas on permaculture, for

example, that we could fund under that umbrella. Also, with this loan, I'm toying with reaching out to Evan Michaels to see if he might sell back Michaela and Boyd's company. It would be nice to have all the Merriams under the same global umbrella, so to speak. Of course, it would be an emotional decision for him, but Evan has been known to make them for a good cause."

My God, he'd love that. "More agreement on this side."

"That flower is important to the world. We would continue to support scientific testing for a vaccine for COVID-19 based on the flower's healing abilities."

"Of course we would. We need to stop this damn virus."

"Precisely," she said, making a slashing motion with her hand for emphasis. "Switching to the personal—I'm not going to let world events come between us a second time, and again, I'm sorry I let it happen for a moment. I'm a work in progress, as Alice likes to say."

"You look pretty good from this end," he said, gazing at her loveliness from head to foot. Savoring the fact that she was here, that she'd come back to him. "Are you finished with your points?"

She nodded. "I believe so. Except that I love you. I want to be with you. I never plan on leaving you again. I'm also going to hire the best vice presidents ever so I can delegate responsibilities and have a real life with you and our children."

Well, hot damn. "Let's make that official." He stalked to the door. "I'll be right back."

He almost ran into Alice in the hallway, and she bit her lip, seeing him. "Oops. I thought I'd be within earshot in case Francesca needed me."

"Did you think I would chew her out or something?" he asked, putting his hands on his hips.

She lifted her right shoulder and pulled something out of her pocket. "No, I thought you might want the engagement ring."

She'd guessed right. He grabbed it from her hand. "Did you look through my room?"

"Trevor did," Alice said, crossing her ankles and swaying in place. "He said he legally has the right to search any guest's room in the Wild Irish Rose as one of its proprietors. If it makes you feel any better, Becca helped."

Laughing, he gave into the impulse to hug her. "Thank you."

He was opening the door when she smacked his butt. "Go get 'em, tiger."

Glaring at her over his shoulder, he watched as she pressed a hand to her mouth to cover her laughter. As he closed the door, he heard her whisper loudly to someone, "He took the ring!"

Shaking his head, he came into the room. "I don't want to do this next part socially distanced."

Her smile flitted across her face before it faltered. "Me either, but we have to. I won't risk you, Quinn."

He flashed back to the first time he'd proposed, when she'd turned him down for that very reason. Not today. "Yeah, that's how all this started." So he sank to his knee six feet away from the woman he loved. "This is the third time I've done this. I don't plan on doing it again."

"I told you that the third time might be the charm." She bit her lip. "Sorry, I couldn't resist. I'm nervous."

He realized he wasn't. After everything that had happened, he knew she wasn't leaving again. *Nothing* could tear them apart now. "I love you, Francesca. I'm glad you came back to be with me. I'll never forget that."

His throat tightened, and so did his grip on the ring. God, he was getting way too emotional. When had he ever felt like this?

"Take your time," she said, and he noticed tears were streaking down her face.

Jesus, that almost destroyed him. "Will you marry

me?"

Her head moved slowly in assent, her tears making her even more beautiful. "Yes. I will marry you and love you forever."

Forever was so messed up right now—a concept he couldn't begin to wrap his head around—but instead of letting that thought mess him up, he extended the ring to her.

"Put it on the table and back up," she said, dashing at her face.

Put it on the table? "Dammit! I want to put it on your finger and kiss you senseless. I hate this!"

"I hate it too," she said, waiting until he'd done as she'd asked. She slid the ring on herself, sighing a little as she did. "But I would rather know we're taking every precaution. It's only for fourteen days. We made it fifteen years. This will go fast."

❀ ❀ ❀

It didn't.

On the eighth day of her quarantine, Quinn paced outside Francesca's cottage, going out of his mind.

Which was how Alice found him. "You might serenade her," she suggested. "Beau could play the guitar. Do you know any love songs? I'll bet Flynn has a karaoke playlist we can check out."

His brother hadn't done much singing lately, what with his family's grieving over June. Of course, news of their engagement and the loan Francesca had secured to buy the company had lifted everyone's spirits, as had the news of the healthy arrival of Jill and Brian's baby boy born at home. Uncle Arthur and Aunt Clara had cried tears of joy over FaceTime. Even Quinn had to admit how sweet the baby looked cuddled up against his beaming mother's side.

The scene had made him think of Francesca and the babies they were going to have. But being six feet apart and then some from his own fiancée wasn't going to get that job done any time soon.

"Find Beau. I'll do anything to romance Francesca."

And that's how he ended up singing Chicago's "You're The Inspiration"—Alice's suggestion—outside of her cottage after a few good rounds of Irish whiskey. Beau played guitar, and J.T. and Trevor served as his backup singers.

Francesca kept the light on all night after their serenade, which, according to Alice, was a Spanish custom acknowledging the one who'd serenaded her was her man. Of course, the way she'd called out to him and said she loved him amid her laughter and tears earlier had been enough.

He was waiting outside the cottage when Francesca finally emerged on the fourteenth day, and he grabbed her to him tightly.

"I'm never letting you go," he whispered right before he claimed her mouth.

She wrapped her arms around him, kissing him back fully and freely. "You better not. I love you so much!"

He framed her beloved face in his hands. "And I you. We have the rest of our lives ahead of us. I'm trusting it's going to be a long and fruitful one."

"Me too."

Cheers sounded above them, and they looked over to see his family waving from the windows.

"Come inside!" Aunt Clara yelled. "I want to hug you, Francesca."

"Me too," a whole chorus of people cried in unison.

"Oh, let them kiss each other a little more," Uncle Arthur said. "Plenty of time for us later. Go take a nap, you two!"

"Yes!" Alice cried. "A nap!"

"A capital idea," Clifton called out. "I'll refrain from bringing you afternoon tea, Francesca."

"Make it champagne," she said, gesturing grandly. "I'm in the mood to celebrate."

So was he. Quinn grabbed his beloved's hand and they rushed back to the cottage.

Shutting the door, he watched as the inside of Honeysuckle Cottage lit with golden rays of sunshine. Quinn had been in Ireland for long enough to start believing in magic. And as he was learning, much to his newly discovered delight, love and magic worked together.

After all, hadn't he and Francesca finally found their happily ever after?

CHAPTER 37

THE PANDEMIC HAD BEEN NO MATCHMAKER'S IDEA OF A good time.

But they'd gotten through it, Arthur reflected. Quinn and Francesca had walked down the aisle an hour ago, married in a service officiated by Clara.

That meant their mission as matchmakers was complete.

The first dance between the couple began in the front yard of the Wild Irish Rose Inn in the center of the circle of tables he and the rest of the family were occupying. Champagne was bubbling in the glasses in anticipation of the first toast to the couple. Swathed in a lace gown designed and made by Becca—an act that had prompted the couple to suggest that Becca design a fashion line for the company—Francesca was a showstopper as the couple whirled around in their first dance. Quinn's complete, intense focus was on his bride, his eyes glued to her face as surely as his hands were to her waist. She was laughing at something, and when he threw his head back and laughed with her, Arthur couldn't help but smile. He knew they were going to be happy together.

All of the Merriam children had been well matched, and that delighted his heart, a feeling he treasured even more in these troubling times. Much like he had at the other Merriam wedding yesterday.

Beau and Caitlyn's ceremony hadn't been what they'd planned, but it had been no less joyous for it. They'd been married at the Wild Irish Rose Inn as well, also with Clara presiding. Like today, that beautiful late June day on the cliffs had been awash in Irish green, ocean blue, and sunlight. Ibrahim had been able to come from France now that travel to Ireland was open to tourists, and Michaela and Boyd and Connor and Louisa had joined them too—after observing quarantine, of course.

When Cole Porter's "Night and Day" ended, Quinn wouldn't let Francesca go, and she tipped her head up and kissed him lovingly, causing the crowd to cheer and whistle. He had to give them both points. They hadn't once broken quarantine in the two weeks after Francesca's return from Beirut.

He put his hand on Clara, who sat next to him at the white-clad table, because he could. Touching her wasn't something he'd ever take for granted again.

She laid her hand over his and continued talking to Alice, who was sitting beside her with Clifton on the other side. He shared a smile with his friend. Arthur even thought about making a joke about looking forward to their next feast of Indian food, but that was taking the whole wedding euphoria way too far.

The tinkling of a fork against a glass had conversations hushing. Quinn was standing at the head table with his bride, champagne flutes in their hands.

Arthur grabbed his quickly. He'd been slow to the draw.

"Usually the best man gives the toast and so on," Quinn

said, "but these are unusual times. Francesca and I wanted to be the ones to give the first toast."

She lifted her glass toward the crowd. "The past few months have been harder than any of us could have imagined, and we seem to have a ways to go yet. But if one thing has become clear, it's that love is the most important thing any of us can hold on to and search out. This family has been so loving, so welcoming to me. I'm grateful to be one of you. I love you all so much. We both do. Thank you for being here today. We look forward to celebrating more good times ahead."

"Hear, hear," J.T. shouted.

Quinn extended his flute. "All right, my turn. I don't have to tell you how uncomfortable I used to be talking about love or even expressing it. But even a formerly grouchy, stubborn guy like me can change, I suppose. Like my beautiful bride said, these past months have been tough. Times might still get tougher, but we have each other. I've never been more grateful for this family or the woman I love. So... To love and family."

Everyone repeated, "To love and family," and then everyone clinked glasses and drank. Arthur's vision was a little blurry after that speech, to be honest. Who would have imagined Quinn speaking so openly about his feelings? Well, the pandemic was changing people right and left, and Arthur continued to hope for the best.

They danced and supped, and he and Clara took more than one turn on the dance floor. Of course, Michaela and Caitlyn talked him into dancing, as did Alice and Amelia. His budding little reporter was still grieving her grandmother and likely would for some time, but she was getting stronger every day.

She pulled him to the side and tugged some folded papers out of the small purse Caitlyn had let her borrow for the wedding. "I finished my article, Mr. Hale, since you needed more time."

He almost laughed. That was one way to put it.

"Iris and Eloise helped me, and Iris handwrote it since she has the best penmanship. You read it and tell me if it's good enough to be published. I'm going to have another piece of chocolate cake before Mom sees."

She ran off in her purple dress, and he had to shake his head. Yes, she was a little reporter, all right. Even her own tragedy hadn't stopped her from writing her article, and she'd beaten Arthur to the punch. Whenever he sat down to pen an opinion piece, his prose was angry, accusatory even. He wanted to bash so many heads together. Wasn't that part of the problem? Everyone was yelling at each other and no one was listening. He hadn't been ready to say anything constructive yet. But little Amelia had found the words he couldn't. Wedding or not, he had to read them.

Detouring to the table, he tapped Clara on the shoulder. She finished what she was saying to Alice and turned to him. "Fancy a walk?" she asked.

He smiled—she'd read his mind like usual—and twined his fingers around hers and helped her out of the chair. They often took a moment to have a final matchmaking roundup at parties like this.

The music coming from the wedding was faint as they paused near the cliffs. The sea was a deep gray flecked with white diamonds of foam. The sky was light until near midnight some nights, and Arthur loved it.

"I noticed little Amelia handed you something," Clara said, proving she was always watching.

"Her sisters helped her write an article." He pulled the three pages of three-holed paper out and started to read aloud:

My friend, Mr. Hale, used to run this newspaper. He said I could write an article about the coronavirus sometime. I was too scared and sad to do it before. But good reporters stay strong. They report the facts. My sisters helped me. Here's what we want to talk about.

Some people are saying the coronavirus is made up. Like pretend.

I don't know how people can believe that. My grandma died of it. One day she was fine. Then she was gone. It's real. Otherwise, I would still be able to talk to her and tell her about my day.

Other people don't want to wear masks when they go to shops or other places.

They say it's wrong to tell them what to do. And that a mask doesn't stop the virus. I don't understand that either. If you sneeze or cough, you're supposed to cover your mouth. I'm five years old and I know that. Because this virus is so bad, we have to wear something stronger to keep our germs in. It makes sense.

I wish everyone could have been wearing masks before my grandma died. Maybe she wouldn't have gotten the virus.

A lot of people are talking about whether kids should go back to school. I think the virus has to be gone from the area where the school is. Some people say kids can't get it, but my sisters and I found articles about kids getting sick. They've died too. This virus can kill anyone, and that's really scary.

My sisters don't want to go back to school if the virus is still hurting people. I've waited to go to kindergarten forever. I really looked forward to meeting my new friends, and I don't want to only see them and my teacher on the computer. I also don't want to get sick. I could hurt my sisters and my mom and stepdad. I would feel horrible if anything happened to them. I hope every school makes the right choice. For us kids, and for our moms and dads, because they're scared too.

I've heard my mom tell my stepdad that she's scared my sisters and me aren't getting to act like kids. Like when it was safe and I could hug anyone I wanted. She's kinda right. Before this virus came, we used to go into town and eat at a restaurant or see a funny movie. I like Disney ones like "Frozen." Now we don't go anywhere. We stay inside a lot. Maybe soon we can go somewhere, but we'll have to wear a mask. It will be weird. I hope I don't get scared if I see someone coughing in the store.

I want to tell my mom I'm strong. She wants me and my sisters to be independent. And happy. She put signs like that all over our house to remind us. It's hard to be happy after losing Grandma, but my sisters told me they got happy again after our dad died. It's possible. I mean, they cried a lot and were sad for a long time. They still miss him. I don't remember since I was a baby. But I do remember my grandma. I miss her. I know I'm going to be sad for a long time. But I'm going to be happy too.

My sisters and I made a pact. We're going to be safe. Stay inside when we have to. Wear a mask when we have to. Follow the guidelines. Like we would at school. All I want is for my family to be safe and not get sick.

I want every person in the whole wide world to be safe and not get sick.

We need this virus to stop hurting us.

He wiped his eyes and tucked the papers back into his jacket. "Out of the mouths of babes."

"My God," Clara said, coming over to him and hugging him. "You have to get Meredith and Tanner to publish that, Arthur Hale. It's beautiful."

There wouldn't be a dry eye amongst their readers. "She said it better and with more heart than I could."

"I'm so glad you're mentoring her to be a reporter." Clara took his face between her hands. "Remember how you told me I was doing enough? That little girl and this article is you doing your part. Don't you forget it."

He gave a watery laugh. "Yes, ma'am."

She released him and sniffed, but the sound had

backbone, like she was putting her emotions behind her. "Now... Let's do our roundup. I wish I'd brought my champagne so we could toast each other. We've managed to help all seven Merriam children find their soulmates. That is some feat, and I'm proud of us."

He gave a hearty laugh. She was stretching it just a little. "You are, eh?"

She socked him, something she didn't do as often lately with all this heaviness around. He'd have to tease her more, he realized.

"I am. But I don't think we're finished."

Hadn't he been ready for this? For her, he would have crossed a desert. "No?"

"No." She nodded her regal head firmly, as if she'd decided something absolute. "We must help Clifton, dear. And then there's sweet Alice. Finding their soulmates during this horrible pandemic is going to be tough, but I know we're more than up for the challenge."

He took out a red hot and handed her one. "I didn't think we'd decided anything about leaving Ireland yet, what with some parts of the States getting hot again and Ireland coming out of lockdown and doing so well."

But they couldn't stay here forever, although the Wild Irish Rose Inn was closed to tourists all summer like many bed and breakfasts in Ireland. Becca and Trevor hadn't seen a safe way to host guests. Everyone had a place for as long as they wanted it. No one knew how long that might be yet. Everyone could work from afar, except for Connor and Louisa, and arrangements for the girls' schooling were premature in these times.

Still, he wanted to see his new great-grandson, Benjamin, and Lucy and Andy's baby girl, Mabel. He wanted to hold Jill and the rest of his family. His home was in Dare Valley, and many of the Merriams had returned to it too. But the future they'd anticipated had been upended. Hell, Arthur's retirement had been nothing as he'd expected.

Instead of quietly reading in his old green chair and sa-voring his golden years—whatever the hell that meant—he'd been to Ireland, Provence, Kenya, Chicago, San Francisco, and now back to Ireland again. He didn't have a clue when it would be safe enough to return to work with the Maasai in Kenya, nor did Clara.

"Being flexible seems important right now, doesn't it?" Clara worried her mouth. "I want everything to be normal again too. It's only…. I'm not sure when that will be or if the meaning of 'normal' has changed forever."

"Then we stay together here and remain nimble."

She nudged him, and he waggled his brows in response.

"*Nimble*? Arthur Hale, all of this yoga you're doing is making an impression on you."

Rolling his eyes, he put his hand on her fanny. "If you think yoga is what has me nimble, you're underestimating yourself, my dear."

She gave a bright smile and kissed him softly. "For me too. Also… I want to mention—"

Oh, dear Lord, what now?

"In addition to our matchmaking duties—which we agree will continue—I want to add officiating marriage ceremonies to my résumé. I absolutely adore it."

Next, she'd be onto midwifing with her diamonds on, helping usher in the next generation of Merriams. That had to be next, right? Sure, no one thought these troubled times were ideal for bringing a baby into the world, but life went on.

Always.

Love made bad times more palatable, and on nights like this, it could even bring joy to the heart of an old man like Arthur.

Yes, they would weather this. Everyone would. Somehow the world would come out stronger and learn from it. He would keep believing that. Hope and love were gamechangers. His life was a testament to their power.

"My dear," he said, kissing her again. "If I had champagne, I would make a toast."

She mimed a glass in her hand and he did the same. "To the love of my life and to our next adventures. Whatever comes, I'm happy to spend my every day with you."

"To our next adventures, my love. May they be even bigger and brighter than before." That was a pretty tall order, but he was down for it.

He only hoped Clifton was prepared.

Epilogue

His resignation letter to Clara Merriam Hale rested on the rosewood table in front of him.

He signed it grandly with his full name, Clifton Timothy Hargreaves, and sat back. His chest felt light, and he anchored himself in the peace surrounding his decision. It was time. They both knew it.

He hoped he had conveyed his gratitude to Clara, as he thought of her now, thoroughly and yet properly. Truthfully, he still wasn't accustomed to addressing people by their given names, but he was settling into it like the rest of this newness around him.

"Clifton!" Alice's voice was a hushed whisper behind him. "Are you done yet?"

It never felt strange when she uttered it. The warm tone she used had shattered the years of propriety and reserve he'd been trained to observe.

He was grateful for it. At eighty, it was time for him to live his best life. Clara had shown him the way. She'd flung off a somber old house she'd never liked and an unfulfilled life that had weighed her down like a yoke. After years of seeing her walk around the house like a ghost, he'd watched her bloom before his eyes. With her and Arthur, he'd traveled to distant shores, something he'd always wished to do as a young man.

But there were still other things he wanted to do, things that younger man had dreamed of. His time might be shorter now—June's death had proved that in heartbreaking fashion—but he was determined to make the most of it.

He wanted a grand love affair.

Alice was fond of saying that he needed to find his soulmate. The reserved part of him, still unused to this new abundance, told himself he'd be content with a great love. But he still hoped for someone who called to the deepest part of his heart, someone with whom he could share everything.

And he wished the same for Alice. Thankfully, he'd learned quite a bit about matchmaking from Clara and Arthur. When the time came, he intended to use that knowledge to help Alice find her true love. The man who earned her deepest affections would be the luckiest man out there, to his mind.

She brimmed with life, kindness, and curiosity. She was the granddaughter he'd never had. Arthur had summed up the difference best. A daughter was one you raised, guided, and celebrated. A granddaughter was someone you merely enjoyed. That had cinched it for Clifton.

Somehow he knew she was the perfect guide to help him realize his deepest dreams, ones he'd long ago buried for duty and service. She would say that's what friends and neighbors did, and that's why Alice was Alice. And that's why he wanted to do the same for her.

"I'm finished with the letter," he said, turning in his chair to regard her.

She was wearing a blue cotton dress with flour marking

the middle, likely a leftover from her chocolate scone making session with Aileen this morning.

"Great!" She rushed forward, her well of enthusiasm always overflowing. "You're moving forward, and you're not the only one! I talked to Sarah. She's game to join our chocolate shop venture—once everything settles down in the world—and she thinks her neighborhood would be the perfect place. I don't know why I didn't think of it before. It's in the Hudson River Valley in upstate New York—nothing like where you used to live in Manhattan with Clara. I love it there. Her neighbors are terrific. You'll adore them. Plus, it's got a swoon-worthy Main Street lined with cute shops with colorful awnings and window boxes bursting with flowers. Our place would be a terrific addition."

He could see himself walking the friendly strip in his mind already. "It sounds lovely, Alice."

"Of course, I hope those shops are still around after the pandemic is over. So many small businesses have had to close. But let's not think about that. I was trying to tell you..."

She never talked in a linear fashion, and he liked that she was so unfettered in her speech. She was always encouraging him to loosen up, but in ways that made him happier rather than uncomfortable.

Just the other day, she'd suggested he take off his black suit jacket to help him cool off on another hot Irish day. She'd even talked him into unbuttoning his top shirt button. Then she'd run inside and grabbed the flamenco guitar Beau had brought to play and told him to give her a song. By the time he was halfway through it, the remaining Merriam family had packed the dining room to hear him play. He'd given in to tapping his foot in a percussive rhythm as he strummed the strings with more wildness than ever.

Never had he felt so free.

The applause afterward might have embarrassed him, but it had delighted him too. Alice was already suggesting they have music nights at their chocolate shop, socially distanced if necessary. He found himself planning song lists. He could even smell the rich scent of dark chocolate in the air as he strummed a fast five-stroke tremolo.

"What were you trying to tell me?" he asked, knowing she'd gone somewhere else, something she often did when she was daydreaming.

"I think I have the name of our shop." She held out her arms, grinning. "Are you ready for it? It's totally epic, Clifton."

Oh, how dear she'd become to him. He didn't question her desire to include him in her vision. They had a shared love for chocolate, food service, and hosting others. The idea seemed perfect to him.

"What is it?" he asked, already smiling.

"The House of Hope & Chocolate," she announced, her well-lashed big brown eyes filled with light. "Isn't it perfect for these times?"

He couldn't think of anything more perfect.

WHAT'S NEXT?

Find out what kind of deliciousness Hargreaves and Alice get up to in **The House of Hope & Chocolate**, an uplifting page-turner about hope, the will to start over, and the power of friendship.

The first novel in the new Friends & Neighbors series...

The House of Hope & Chocolate

A Friends & Neighbors Novel

Meet Alice Bailey, a woman determined to realize her dreams and revitalize a beloved neighborhood with two things she believes most in: hope and chocolate.

Beyond yoga, check out the other books Arthur Hale would recommend to keep you and your family in feeling calm, focused, and in tip-top shape.

The Post-Covid Wellness Playbook

Medically reviewed

With Introductions by a practicing Internist, Psychiatrist, and Kung Fu Master

Reentering the world, but uncertain or anxious? Ava's got a practical step-by-step guide to navigating this new normal, based on her experience and expertise after nearly dying from a mysterious virus. Medically reviewed, Ava outlines a three-pronged approach to our main challenges: boosting our immunity; reducing our anxiety; and harnessing our mental focus.

ABOUT THE AUTHOR

Ava Miles is the international bestselling author of powerful books about love, happiness, and transformation. As a former conflict expert, Ava rebuilt warzones in places like Lebanon, Colombia, and the Congo to foster peaceful and prosperous communities. While rewarding, Ava recognized she could affect more positive change in the world by addressing the real roots of conflict and unhappiness. In becoming an author, she realized her best life: healing the world through books. Her novels have received praise and accolades from USA Today, Publisher's Weekly, and Women's World Magazine in addition to being chosen as Best Books of the Year and Top Editor's picks. However, Ava's strongest praise comes directly from her readers, who call her books life changing.

Made in the USA
Monee, IL
08 November 2020

47049830R00215